The Criminal Lawyer

A Novel

by

Thomas Benigno

Contact email for press, licensing, or speaking engagements: tombenigno@aol.com
Cover design by Nathan Wampler
Book formatted by: ebookpbook.com

Printed Version Library of Congress Control Number: 2016916129

ISBN 13: 978-1533109088

PRAISE FOR

The #1 International Bestseller

The Good Lawyer by Thomas Benigno

Kirkus reviews: Benigno's first effort is a crafty legal page-turner, just as good in the courtroom as it is outside...(he) fortifies his lead character with problems that his law degree can't fix. Readers who like their courtroom thrillers packed with lawyer-speak and zigzagging plot developments should find much to savor.

Publisher's Weekly: Benigno presents...legal skirmishing and moral ambiguity in the saga of Nick Mannino...The interesting glimpses of courtroom procedure and a cast of eccentric characters will intrigue readers...

The New York Post: "This one scared the briefs off me. Make room Grisham, legal suspense fiction has a new senior partner..." Mike Shain

ALSO BY THOMAS BENIGNO

The Good Lawyer
The Criminal Mind

Inspired by real crimes that occurred on Long Island

For my mother,
Ernesta Mary Benigno
1923-2014

"The loneliest moment in someone's life is when they are watching their whole world fall apart, and all they can do is stare blankly."
—F. Scott Fitzgerald

It was the perfect day and the perfect place...

He parked his green sun-bleached van on the shoulder alongside the dune. Standing beside the tall mound of sand speckled with beach grass, he had yet to see or hear another car pass on the road behind him.

Amid a warm and oddly soothing June wind, he turned to face north and the bay—a mirror of tranquility. The faint hum of a crossing motorboat was testament to the resolute serenity of this beautiful day.

He took a long deep breath, looked up at the sky, and smiled. A resplendent sun shone beside a lone white cloud, and as far as his eyes could see, he was alone but for the man sitting high on the dune, staring blankly at the ocean.

Arms outstretched for balance, he buried each wolverine boot in the sand as he climbed. Once on top, he surveyed the beach from one end to the other.

It was late afternoon. The crowd had thinned. Soaking up what remained of the sun, a few leather-skinned seniors lay face up on their recliners. Two teenagers threw a Frisbee. Others played volleyball. Parents gathered together blankets, towels and chairs while struggling to corral their small children into leaving.

In an hour or two, this quarter mile stretch between the dune and the ocean would be nearly desolate; but come morning, it would begin to populate, as ever, once again.

Because the beach is winsome, and seductive, and therapeutic.

There is no cause for worry and fear in the pure and uncomplicated world of sun, wind, and water.

As he pivoted and stepped back down, only the fleeting movement of a shadow marked his presence to the man who remained sitting on the dune, and seemed to pay him no mind.

Walking quickly past his van, he looked both ways before crossing the two-lane roadway aptly named Ocean Parkway. After twenty precise steps, and in the marsh up to his knees, he paused to study the small stretch of wetland where the stalks spread thin, then disappeared into the encroaching bay. Turning around again toward the ocean, he looked up and across *in an attempt to decipher the precise distance between the parkway lamps and the limits of their cones of light in the dead of night.*

This would be his last visit, his only visit, in the bold brightness of day. One last breath, one last taste and smell of the salty air, and he would be gone, never to return in the light, but more certain than he had ever been.

This area—so close, yet so secluded, was, bar none, the perfect place to leave the bodies.

Chapter 1

Tragedy, like a derailed freight train, did not discriminate on its errant path of ruin.

Desmond Lewis was a fifty-two year old black man.

We had much in common.

Born in the same month and year, July, 1954, we were each happily married for over twenty years (or at least *I* thought I was), with two children to show for it, a boy and a girl.

We were also hard-working to a fault and much too proud for our own good.

It was a hot summer night in June of 2005, when Desmond's son attended a party in his hometown of Valley Stream, Long Island. The boy was seventeen, and had been dating a girl from his high school. She was white and Italian American. It was his first serious relationship. It wasn't hers. She broke it off a week before the party. They had been the only interracial couple at their school.

On the evening that would forever change the Lewis family's life, and all those involved, Desmond's son and his former girlfriend found themselves at that same party. She had moved on. He hadn't. She was there with her new boyfriend, also white and Italian-American.

A beer keg in the living room and an unknown quantity of secluded hard liquor fueled the fires of discontent. Words were exchanged, and a fight broke out between the two boys. The new boyfriend got the worst of it. Bruised, beaten, and worse, embarrassed, he left the party.

At 3 AM, there was a pounding on the Lewis' front door. It woke the entire family.

Desmond Lewis was scheduled to be at work at 8 AM. He was a supervisor for the Long Island Power Authority and had just clocked in twenty-five years on the job, while his wife worked nearly as long as an elementary school teacher. They planned to retire after the kids graduated college. They would travel and see the world. They earned it. They deserved it. They raised two good kids, a son and a daughter who attended the Marianist-run parochial high school just fifteen minutes from their home.

The Lewis' were also keenly aware that black families like theirs were still a minority in Valley Stream, though the neighborhood was becoming more racially diverse with each passing year. A proud and God-fearing man, Desmond would drive his wife and two children to Sunday mass at the Blessed Sacrament Church nearby, every Sunday morning at 8:45 AM sharp. He was a member of the Holy Trinity Society. His wife volunteered at every church function. To all eyes and ears, their family was well-liked and respected. So when Desmond peeked out his bedroom window and into the darkness of that hot summer night, and saw four high school boys on his front lawn, he was as surprised as he was frightened. The boys, members of the same lacrosse team, were screaming and shouting racial epithets.

Desmond immediately told his wife to stay put and grabbed his deer rifle. She called the police the moment he left the room.

Less than a minute later, the new boyfriend was lying on that same front lawn, shot dead, a baseball bat by his side.

The Nassau County District Attorney's Office charged Desmond with second-degree murder. Jury selection began in 2006, a year later.

After a grueling one-month trial, wherein I lost over fifteen pounds and called twenty-five character witnesses, mostly white neighbors and co-workers, I delivered a two-hour summation to an all-white jury that ended in tears—mine and the jury's.

Five days later, after the foreman complained three times that the panel was deadlocked, and three times the judge sent the jury back to continue deliberating, a verdict was reached. Desmond stood in stoic silence while it was read aloud on another hot June night, only this one was rattled by a thunderstorm that lasted until daybreak.

I collapsed into my chair when the jury convicted him of second-degree manslaughter. As for Desmond, he just nodded to the jurors, and then consoled me with thanks and praise for the "fine defense work" I had done.

In retrospect, it is as clear to me now as it was then that I was not trying a case in the Jim Crow South, and that my client should have never left the house until the police arrived, even if he had to barricade himself inside.

When Desmond took the stand, he held up well during cross-examination by the head of the felony division of the Nassau County DA's Office. Evidence corroborated his testimony that his front door had been kicked and punched so hard, the deadbolt broke away part of the doorframe. Desmond also testified that all four boys surrounded him once he went outside, that he feared for his life, and fired his rifle only when the one boy—the new boyfriend, swung a bat at the air between them. The bullet pierced the boy's aorta and killed him instantly. Like Desmond's son, the boy was seventeen.

When I saw several jurors with tears in their eyes just before the verdict was read, I knew what was coming. They just couldn't reconcile my client leaving his home with a rifle in his hands. It also didn't help that the victim was a high school student, screaming drunk or not, and not previously known to act in a threatening or racist manner. The boy's father, like Desmond, had worked one job his whole life. The boy's mother was also a school teacher.

It didn't matter that the police took six minutes to arrive, and that in those six minutes, I argued, everyone in the house could've been beaten to death, especially his son, the attackers' prime target.

Desmond was sentenced to three years in State prison. He refused to allow me to ask for bail pending appeal, or to appeal the conviction at all. My primary ground would have been the DA's uniform exclusion of every prospective black juror on the panel, while I used up my peremptory challenges, excluding every apparent racist I suspected.

Desmond, who also believed he should never have left the house, was grief-stricken over the death of the boy. The appeal would have taken years. He wanted this tragedy behind him and his family as soon as possible. He was released from prison after serving less than twenty-four months.

I took no fee for Desmond's defense. After the conviction and sentence, I paid off the mortgage on his house so his wife and their two children could afford to live there on just her schoolteacher salary.

My client was furious with me for doing so. I told him it was my Uncle Rocco's mob money. He thought I was joking, and laughed. I told him I wasn't, and he stopped laughing.

As for me, the case was over. I had lost, and as a result, was impossible to live with. My wife Eleanor had seen it all before. It wasn't the first time I took my workload, and my cauldron of discontent, home with me.

Then came the inevitable meltdown.

While she was initially understanding in the face of my biting remarks and irascible behavior, in my mind's eye, I had failed, and although I seemed to be the only one who thought so, I was inconsolable.

Two months later, she got on a plane to Atlanta, and left me for good. That was four years ago.

I get it now. I didn't then.

Arms around my knees, I sat high on the dune, eyes locked on the ocean, the pulsating urge to swim to the horizon until I could swim no more, heightening with each visit.

Staring out over beach and shore, and the wide expanse of the Atlantic, I felt a comforting disconnect from the world around me. But as the sun slowly set, and the towering shadow of a man loomed over me, the world around me had a different plan. Lost in thought, and without so much as a slight turn of my head, the shadow came and went, leaving a trail of large and deep footprints in the sand, which I paid no mind to anyway.

As I left the confines of Jones Beach and drove north on the Meadowbrook Parkway, my Mercedes S600 reaching sixty-five miles per hour and coasting as silently as a capsule in space, I mulled over my last contact with Eleanor. When she phoned, it was usually about our kids. This time was no different.

"I spoke to John the other day," she said. "He sounded different. I think he's in love."

"I met the girl only once," I answered. "The three of us had lunch in the City. I didn't notice anything unusual about John though, if that's what you mean?"

"As if *you* would," she said with a slight chuckle. "But you're closer to him in geography than I am right now. So please, call me once you have a better idea of what's going on between them. Okay?"

"Okay, but she seems like a very nice girl, and smart too. Goes to CUNY Law. Reminded me of you back in the day."

"Really? Trust me. I wasn't that smart. You were the smart one. Now please get back to me on this."

Such was the extent of a typical conversation of ours since she left.

Driving faster along the empty parkway than I should have, a chord instantly struck inside me, in that sorest of places, where lost love incubates. Then, like a bolt of black lightning striking me to the core, it sent my mind reeling into a dark cloud of confusion.

With our telephone call came the realization that Eleanor sounded content, in control of her life, and even happy. We had not seen each other in four years, and she was doing just fine.

I pressed my foot firmly down on the accelerator until I could press no more. *Eleanor was gone, and for good.* I checked the speedometer. It read ninety-five miles per hour and rising. The S600 was just a few fatal moments from being one and the same with the concrete overpass ahead, when I jerked the steering wheel hard and swerved off the exit ramp.

Seconds later, I was on the street, my foot reflexively pumping the brake pedal, screeching lines of rubber on the asphalt.

I pulled over, dropped my head to the steering wheel, my mind and heart in a pit of irrepressible sadness, when suddenly a horn blast broke through the sealed quiet of the car's interior.

A green van in desperate need of a paint job was slowly coasting past. Through its heavily tinted windows, I could see the opaque silhouette of a large man behind the wheel.

Leaning over, his head turned, he seemed to be looking straight at me.

Chapter 2

I pulled away from the curb and shook my head hard, as the realization set in that I had nearly killed myself in a moment of self-pitying insanity.

With my foot firmly on the brake pedal and the car idling at a red light, I caught another glimpse of the green van. Still attempting to compose myself, my eyes, for some inexplicable reason, remained fixed on its weather-beaten rear doors until it passed the McDonald's up ahead and vanished from sight.

This was the same McDonald's I had worked in during high school, after my mom and stepdad made the big move from Brooklyn to Merrick, Long Island, in the fall of 1968, and bought a small house—their American dream—just a few blocks away. I was thirteen years old, and considering the long and bumpy road Mom and I took to get there, it was my dream too.

Though I was fortunately too young to remember it, my first home was a small apartment above a deli in Flushing, Queens. It was there, one winter morning when I was barely eighteen months old, that my biological father (or "sperm donor" as I liked to call him), kissed Mom goodbye, took what little savings they had for himself, and left for good. He even skipped the state to avoid child support.

Broke and alone, Mom moved back to Brooklyn.

Three tiny rooms above a dry cleaner was our home for the next five years. If not for my Uncle Rocco, my mother's brother and local mob boss, paying the rent (over Mom's objections), we would have wound up on the street. It was 1956. There weren't too many choices for a divorced woman with a child. Rocco, by the grace of God, or wrath of the devil, was all we had. He loved his sister. He loved me. To the rest of the world though, he was one exceedingly dangerous man.

When my stepfather, John Mannino, a senior zoning supervisor for the City of New York, came along, Rocco gradually faded out of our lives. He became an uncle from a distance. Watchful. Waiting. This was also Mom's wish and of no subtle doing.

Shortly after my fourth birthday, Mom and John Mannino married. Times were rough. They budgeted for everything. But we were a family. When I turned nineteen, I changed my last name to his and became known, forever after, as Nicholas Mannino. Two years later, a lifetime of tuberculosis having finally gotten the better of him, John Mannino died in his sleep. He was fifty-seven. He always wanted me to be a lawyer. He is the reason I became one.

Upon graduating Cardozo Law, The Legal Aid Society of New York City offered me the job I had been vying for: Associate Trial Attorney in their Criminal Defense Division. There was no better training ground for the young criminal defense lawyer. Thrown into the fray, I was assigned to their South Bronx office.

Though the total net worth of this poor man's lawyer rested on the wheels of a '66 Malibu, Eleanor Vernou, who became my blushing bride whom I'd never seen blush ever, was heir to over two hundred years of old Southern money, antebellum mansions, country clubs, and houses filled with servants and all manner of people, places and things that amassed fortunes had accumulated over time.

But life is full of ironies. Mine came in December of 1982, one month after Eleanor and I were married, when I inherited a tidy fortune upon my Uncle Rocco's death—ill-gotten gains from decades of criminal activity.

But did my in-laws' disapproval of this burgeoning, idealistic young Italian-American attorney wane, even slightly, as a result of my newfound wealth? Of course not.

Did I take the bequest from my mob uncle and give it all to charity just to show those aristocratic snobs what I was really made of—that getting rich was the last thing that mattered to me? Not even close.

I took the money and the real estate—all nine million dollars' worth—and I didn't look back. I was young. I was in love, and no Vernou from Atlanta or anywhere else was ever going to thumb their nose at me again. But I was naïve and foolish, because they did anyway.

As I exited the parkway and into Garden City, *Moon River*—the ringtone on my cell phone—began playing inside my car. It was my daughter Charlotte calling. In my current state, she was the last one I wanted to talk to. I let it go to voicemail.

There was no doubt that between John and Charlotte, she was my in-laws' favorite. As a result, at the budding age of nineteen, she gained access to a twenty million dollar trust fund. Eleanor and I were furious. Charlotte was delighted, and quickly thereafter, out of control.

After purchasing a one-bedroom condominium in Trump Tower for a cool two million, she transferred from Princeton and graduated from NYU's Stern School of Business by the grace of God and good graces of two professors she dated. When her photo appeared on the *Post's Page 6,* partying with other rich society brats, Grandpa Vernou tightened the reins. He insisted Charlotte take a job at a hedge fund he owned with a modest starting salary—a fine-print condition to continued draws from her trust—to which she readily complied.

Eleanor's parents had created a trust for John also. He only accessed it once—to pay for law school.

Another *Moon River* symphony and Charlotte was ringing my phone again. Though I figured it was about nothing more than another squabble with her condo board, I decided to answer.

"Dad, why don't you pick up when I call you?" I could hear what sounded like a subway train in the background.

"Charlotte, I must have asked you that very same question a thousand times."

"I'm trying to tell you something about John and all you can do is—" Her voice took on a weepy quality.

"I'm sorry. Really. What is it?"

"I'm on the Long Island Railroad. I just left Penn Station and I'm about to...the tunnel. I...lose you."

"You're breaking up. Is John alright?"

"I don't..." Charlotte was crying. "It's just that...It's bad, Dad...Dad?"

"Charlotte!"

I lost the call.

Chapter 3

I barely saw the road in front of me, no less anything, or anyone, and I had no idea where I was racing to. Home I suppose—Hillcrest Place—high on "the hill."

Located atop a four-block area, "the hill" provided its own private refuge for the richest of the rich of Garden City, and if its inhabitants could be accused of sporting a condescending air, it didn't help that their backyard acreage abutted the golf course of a restricted country club, with no women members allowed.

Though I knew Charlotte would be in the train tunnel for at least six or seven minutes, I repeatedly hit the green call button on my flip phone.

When I tried to call John, it also went right to voice mail.

I nearly skidded out of control as I cut a sharp left into my driveway. A hundred feet, and seconds later, I came to a screeching halt just past the large entrance doors of the stately colonial that I alone still called home.

After slamming the gearshift into park, I jumped out, keys in one hand, cell phone in the other, headed for the nearest landline. As I hurriedly walked around the car, I looked up, and stopped cold.

One of the front doors was open.

I remembered distinctly putting the alarm on when I left the house because I always did. I stood still-quiet, and listened. Aside from a bird or squirrel moving across a tree limb, I heard nothing.

I leaned on the car, my left hand on the fender, an ominous feeling I hadn't felt in decades coursing through me.

I grabbed an aluminum bat I kept hidden in the bushes. There wasn't a cop or criminal lawyer that didn't have a bat or a crow bar tucked away somewhere near the inside or outside entrances to their homes. I hadn't practiced criminal law for over four years, but it didn't matter. Once a cop, always a cop. It's no different for the criminal lawyer. The paranoia never leaves you.

I walked softly up the inlaid brick stairs. When I got to the porch landing, I quietly took two giant steps, and while staying out of the line of sight of anyone inside, I gently pushed the door with the end of the bat until it opened completely.

Pieces of broken glass were strewn about the center hall, along with chunks of an antique vase. A mirror that hung on the wall had been smashed to bits. There were drops of blood on the granite table beneath it.

My heart racing in overdrive, I suddenly came to a realization that I knew all too well as a young criminal lawyer, but had conveniently forgotten over time—no one and nowhere is completely safe, and the more money you have, the bigger the bull's-eye.

I moved quietly through the center hall, looking for some sign, any sign, that the intruder had gone upstairs. Then I crept toward the kitchen, the bat on my shoulder. Oddly, I could hear the in-ground pool's filter running, which meant that the sliding door leading out back had been left open. As I approached it, I peered into the yard. The sun had nearly set and was shining a bright orange. I put my hand up to block the glare, as the silhouette of a man on the far side of the pool came into view. His back was to me. His head was down.

It was John.

The instant I recognized him, my cell phone rang.

"John's here," I blurted.

"Dad, wait," Charlotte answered. "Before you do anything, let me tell you—"

"I have to go to him. I think…I think he's crying."

"Dad, you have to listen. Someone took Sofia, some maniac, and he called Sofia's sister."

Nothing Charlotte said was making any sense. "What do you mean he called Sofia's sister? Did the police do a trace? Do they know where the call came from?"

"No, Dad. He used Sofia's cell phone."

"How much money does he want?"

"He doesn't want money. He said the most horrible things. He's a crazy lunatic."

Charlotte's voice broke as my mind was consumed by a multitude of worst-case scenarios. "Charlotte...her family? And John..."

"He says he's going to kill himself if anything happens to her. He's in bad shape, Dad, really bad shape. Don't leave him alone."

An easterly wind blew through the cypress trees that marked the rear lot line of our yard. I welcomed the cool on my face as my son's pain drew closer and started to burn through me like a branding iron. Though John was just an arm's length away, he had been taken from me as if kidnapped himself. The house on "the hill," the millions of dollars—a fantasy of riches.

My mother was right. A good man has nothing to prove. Get a respectable job, pay your bills, and enjoy every day with the family you love—for a waiting evil can snatch it all away in an instant.

Mom's wisdom was hard-earned. Her childhood was the worst kind of awful, so I dismissed her words of caution as the byproduct of her perilous upbringing. But in that moment that I stood over my son, I understood what my mother meant, and was glad she wasn't alive to see this.

"John," I said gently.

He didn't answer. He had stopped crying and was sitting on a recliner, hunched over, his face in his hands.

"John," I repeated. "I'm here to help. Please. Talk to me" I knelt down next to him. His hair was a greasy mess, and his clothes were worn and wrinkled. "John, please come inside. You can rest inside. Please."

He dropped his hands and was nearly unrecognizable. Dark circles, black and red, surrounded moist and bloodshot eyes, and his face was wet, though I wasn't sure if it was from tears, perspiration, or both. I then noticed that the knuckles on his right hand were bleeding—the consequence of fist hitting mirror.

"You want me to rest," he said morosely, without looking up. "How in hell can I rest, Dad?" His voice was a deep baritone I had never heard before, a caustic finality in every syllable.

"John, Just tell me what—"

"Some lunatic has Sofia!" he wailed, as his eyes rolled shut and his head dropped down between his knees. "Oh my God, Dad!"

"John—"

"Dad, you've got to help! You've got to help her!"

I went to put my arms around him, but he shook me off. I then knelt down, grabbed his wrist, and checked his hand. There was dried blood on it, but no bits of glass that I could see.

"John, I'm going to do everything I can to find her. I promise. I'll comb every street, curb, and sewer if I have to."

He fell backward onto the recliner.

I then stood up, reached over, and caressed his head. In response, he turned toward the sunset, and shook me off again.

"John?" I bent over and wrapped my arms around him. "I'm calling a doctor."

This time he didn't shake me off. His reaction was much worse.

He completely ignored me.

Chapter 4

He was coasting along at thirty-five miles per hour when he stopped at a red light and pressed the windshield washer button. A few feeble squirts of soapy solution shot up onto the front glass, and amid high-pitched squeaks, most, but not all of it, was quickly swatted away.

The van needed new wipers, but that was the least of it.

He made a right turn and entered a strictly residential area where the streets were much quieter than the busy avenue he had been driving on. It was a pleasant middle class neighborhood, working people, a few up-and-comers.

Little did they know…

He rolled down his window halfway, took a deep breath of salty air, and then rolled the window back up again.

Approaching the end of the street that ran to the open bay, he turned into a driveway. After pressing a remote clipped to the visor, a garage door noisily cranked open.

Once inside, he hit the remote again, put the gearshift into park, and turned off the ignition. The light on the garage door opener would remain on for exactly two minutes—plenty of time to fumble for his keys and make his way around the van.

As he climbed a few short steps that led to an interior door, he slid open two deadbolts, then looked back to make sure the garage door was completely shut.

It was Saturday. It was early afternoon. With key in hand, he waited.

He would not move until the timed overhead light went off and the area inside the garage fell into complete darkness.

Then it did.

The deadbolts aside, he turned the key in the door, and shoved it open.

He was back again.

Chapter 5

The first thing I did was wipe the droplets of blood off the hall table with a sponge.

As I dumped the broken glass into the garbage, Charlotte pulled up in a car marked Garden City Car Service.

She threw some bills onto the front seat then kicked open the door with her high heel. Shimmying out of the cab, her dyed blonde hair blowing across her shoulders, she held a gym bag in one hand, and a large pocketbook in the other. She looked all business. But when she walked through that front door, she dropped them to the floor and I was the unexpected recipient of biggest hug she'd given me since she was eight years old and came home to find a tiny Maltese in our kitchen.

"Where's John?" she whispered.

"He's out back, but Charlotte I should warn you he's not—"

"Of course he's not well, Dad. How could he be?" She hurried through the house and into the backyard.

I watched from the kitchen as she approached her brother by the pool. She must have said something, because he turned his head toward her and attempted to sit up on the recliner. She then rushed forward, and threw her arms around him.

He hugged her back and cried.

I went into the hall and grabbed a telephone receiver off the table. I dialed Eleanor's cell. I could have speed-dialed her on the flip phone in my pocket, but I feared she would see my number and let it go to voicemail.

When I last saw Eleanor, she had just turned fifty, and was still as beautiful as ever. Her skin never lost its youthful glow. Just before she left for good, a line or two began to appear in the corners of her eyes. I suppose after a life with me some kink had to surface. Four years in Atlanta, and I wouldn't be surprised to see even those gone.

I got voicemail anyway. "Call me back, El. It's important."

After I hung up, I checked the ringer volume on my cell to make sure it was on high, then returned to the kitchen to stand watch.

Charlotte was lying in the same lounge chair with John. He was resting his head high on her chest. She was holding him in her arms like a small child.

I pulled my cell out of my pocket, and called Frank Cassisi. He was the only doctor I knew that made house calls.

I got the answering service. I told the voice on the other end that I had an emergency, and needed to speak to him right away. Cassisi had been my family physician since I was thirteen. The good doctor was well into his fifties back then. This was 2010, which would make him almost a hundred, which also meant that I had no idea who I was leaving a message for.

Ten minutes later I received a return call. It was the good doctor's daughter. She explained that her dad had died some years back. Was there something *she* could do?

"Are you a doctor?"

"I'm sorry. Of course I am."

"It's my son I'm calling about. He's in a bad way."

"How so?"

"He's had a terrible shock. He cut his hand, but that's not the worst of it."

After a few seconds of silence, within which I assumed she was deciding how to respond to what must have seemed like nothing more than an attack of the suburban blues, she asked, "What brought this on?"

I hesitated, while calculating the wisdom of telling her the whole truth. "My son's girlfriend was the victim of a serious crime. I hope that will do. I'd rather not say any more right now."

There were more seconds of silence.

She paused as if trying to contain herself, but I couldn't figure from what. "I'm sorry. Where is your son now?"

"In the backyard. His sister is with him."

"How old is he?

"Um…Oh my God I can't think. He'll be twenty-three in a few weeks. I'm at 18 Hillcrest Place in Garden City. Please. Can you come? I've never seen him like this."

"Mr. Mannino, I just put my little one to bed. When my oldest comes home, which should be very soon, I'll come right over. I live only a few blocks away."

I responded with something stupid like "whatever the cost."

"No worries," she answered. "I'll see you in a little bit."

My *Moon River* ringtone startled me back to inescapable reality. I pulled my flip phone from my pocket and read the screen. It was *Newsday*. I pressed the red button and killed the call.

More *Moon River*.

I killed the call again, and in seconds, the phone rang again. This time I hit the green button and was about to unload a barrage of expletives, when I heard a young female voice and instantly clammed up.

"Mr. Mannino, please don't hang up."

"Who is this?" I made no attempt to mask my annoyance.

"I'm sorry to be calling at a time like this." Her voice was sweet and had more than a trace of kindness to it.

"At a time like what?" I asked tersely.

"Mr. Repolla told me I should call you. He also told me to apologize for not calling himself. He's out of the country on his honeymoon."

Now Editor-in-Chief at *Newsday*, Long Island's only daily paper, Vinny Repolla was just a neophyte crime reporter when I met him outside night arraignments in 1982. Young, ambitious, and struggling to do our best work amid a mountain of obstacles in the South Bronx, a lasting friendship began. But as my marriage to Eleanor went south, we lost touch, and as more time passed, the more I distanced myself from not only him, but everyone.

"Mr. Mannino, are you still there?"

"Yes, I'm still here. What is your name anyway?"

"My name is Lauren Callucci. Mr. Mannino, we know about your son's girlfriend, and I'm sorry, but I must talk to you."

"What do you want, some kind of a statement? If so, you'll have to get it from me. My son's in no shape, and let's be clear, this is for Vinny. I'll be talking to him when he returns, and you'd better not be just throwing his name around."

"I'm sorry, but you've got me all wrong. It's me who needs to tell *you* something."

"What do you mean you need to tell *me* something?"

"That's right. You see, Mr. Mannino, this abduction is not the first. Women have been going missing for years, mostly prostitutes. Four were found dead outside a drainage ditch near Atlantic City just a year ago."

"My son's girlfriend is not a prostitute. She is a law student."

"I know. That's what makes this so peculiar."

"It's not peculiar at all. The man that took her has nothing to do with those prostitutes you're talking about." I was growing increasingly impatient by how illogical she was sounding.

"But you see, I believe he does." I sensed a sadness in her voice, and more than just the rudimentary sound of a reporter on the verge of breaking some bad news. There was a considerate tone that I found disarming. In retrospect, it should have scared the shit out of me. "Mr. Mannino, I have been covering these cases of missing girls…I mean missing prostitutes, for years."

"Years?"

"Yes, years, and the MO is almost always the same. A phone call is made to a number in a Craigslist ad for a *woman seeking male companionship*. It comes from one of those portable cell phones anyone can buy in a convenience store for cash. The police suspect he is in a car when he meets her. After the young woman gets in, she is never seen or heard from again."

"Do you know about the call to Sofia's sister?"

"I do. I spoke to the sister."

"None of this is making any sense to me." I answered abruptly. "Sofia goes to CUNY Law School. She is too smart to get into a car with a stranger.

I'm sorry, but I don't think we're getting anywhere, and I have to get off the phone. A doctor is coming for my son." I instantly regretted saying that. "Please don't print that. My son is also a law student."

"Mr. Mannino, I'm not printing anything about this call. Mr. Repolla told me to call you. This is not for any news story."

"By the way, what do you mean Vinny is on his honeymoon? There was a wedding?"

"They eloped. He told me to tell you that he is going to contact you as soon as he lands. Right now, he's on a plane headed to New York."

"Whatever... I've got to go."

"No. Please. I need another minute. Listen, I don't know why your son's girlfriend was kidnapped. Maybe she was mistaken for someone else. Maybe she got in the car because she thought she knew the guy. Maybe she was forced. I don't know, but that's not why I called you."

"Then why *did* you call me?"

"This guy, this man, the one doing the abductions, the one who called Sofia's sister—he's been writing to me, texting me actually."

"Do the police know?"

"Yes."

"But why you?"

"It's the articles I've been writing. No one has covered the cases of the missing girls more than I have. I've been sympathetic to the plight of the prostitutes, and critical of the police for not acting sooner and putting more resources behind catching this kidnapper who, I'm very sorry to say, is probably a serial killer too. The fact that a law student is now a victim will make headlines. *Newsday* has it on tomorrow's cover, and all the networks will lead with the story tonight."

"What does he text you?" I asked, as I imagined the barrage of publicity about to blanket Sofia's family at the worst time in their lives.

"Let's just say it's very cryptic. He's clever. He taunts in his calls to the families and then just texts things that seem to make absolutely no sense at all."

"How did he get your number?"

"He doesn't have my personal number. He contacted me on my *Newsday* cell."

I was afraid to ask, but asked anyway: "Has he contacted you since Sofia went missing?"

"Yes. That's the odd part. He texted me a combination of six numbers and letters. At first I was stumped, then I realized he was texting me a license plate number."

"Okay, did you run it?"

"Yes I did."

"And is it a stolen plate?"

"No, it's not. I got a real hit on a registered vehicle in New York State."

"That's great then. Maybe it will lead the police to this maniac, but what can I do?"

"I called Mr. Repolla. I was reluctant to call you with this, especially knowing how your son must be feeling. What I mean is…you may want to keep this information to yourself. Mr. Repolla said you two have real history, and that he trusts you, and he doesn't trust too many people. He really carried on about you."

"I'll keep this confidential. You have my word."

"You may have to. You see, Mr. Mannino, the plate number the kidnapper texted me…is yours."

Chapter 6

At first, she tried to convince herself that her dilemma was not real; she was asleep and lingering in some horrible nightmare. But when the punishment became too severe, shock would follow, and the real world would fade into the fog of semiconsciousness.

It had probably been days since she had last eaten. There was no way to be sure. She had no sense of when it was she had last seen the sun, or the clouds, or felt the warmth of day, or the cool of night. Her nights were anything but.

In the coarse confines, where fear enveloped every abysmal moment, she had only one escape. During bouts of unconsciousness, whether brought on by a natural or unnatural sleep, one deep and colorful dream sustained her...

The day was bright, and the temperature was perfect. She was standing on a pier beside her mother and little sister. All three were holding hands, waiting for the ferry to make its final return of the day. The aroma of lobster, clams, and calamari from the crab house nearby filled the air. It was a satisfying smell—the kind that precedes a great family dinner. It was the smell of her father, his warm embrace, his hugs, his kisses.

But if she stood too close to the edge of the dock, one careless step would send her freefalling into a swell of green slime—the murky sludge of an East River ceaselessly pounding the soaked brown pilings.

A ferry's horn sounded in the distance. Her dad was at the helm. His image grew larger and brighter with each rumble of the ship's engine.

Her mother's soft gentle hand held hers, while the other rested securely on her sister's shoulder. All three faced the incoming boat making its way across the blue-green river while carving behind it a perfect triangle of crystalline caps that sparkled under a bright orange sun.

Her dad was smiling under a sailor's cap set over a perfect mess of dark curly hair. His gray three-quarter coat was open and blowing back. Its buttons were the size of shiny silver dollars. She looked down, and the river's sludge was gone.

It had morphed into a sparkling blue.

Small fish were swimming along its surface, jumping and soaring in perfect elliptical arches.

As the ferry got closer, the fierce panorama of stone and glass that was the New York City skyline began to shrink in perfect proportion to the hulking ship's size. When it sputtered one last time, and its swinging connecting platform flattened onto the dock, the skyline disappeared, and all that remained was a pink horizon under a setting sun.

As her dad stepped off the boat with the proud gait of a fisherman who had just made his greatest catch ever, shoulders back, arms wide, a huge smile radiating with compassion, she was home.

And she wanted to stay forever.

But as quickly as the dream came, it left, and she awoke to a painful consciousness, and thanked God for this prequel slice of heaven.

It was time to accept the final reality. It was what she wanted, and attempted many times to hurry along.

She tried holding her breath, but all that resulted was convulsive heaves.

When her mouth was at last set free of the suffocating duct tape, she tried pleading with her captor. When that didn't work, she let loose with every insult and humiliating expletive she could think of. When she knew she had hit a sore spot, she also knew she had made a dangerous mistake, and was beaten into unconsciousness once again.

When retaping her mouth shut, her captor hadn't realized that a small cross at the end of a necklace she wore had dropped into it.

Awaking once again, knees against her chest, propped against a cold, musty concrete wall and inside the coarse confines of a burlap sack, she became aware of that same cross resting on her tongue. She immediately began to chew through the thin gold chain that held it in place. When the cross came loose, she swallowed it, hoping to choke herself to death.

Then there came a point in time when she knew...

The scuffing sound of work boots intensified as they descended the set of creaky wooden stairs. When they reached bottom, they slid abruptly on to the concrete floor. The sound it made reminded her of the last time she went ice-skating with her sister, and how the blades cut the rink's surface before she barreled into the side-rails.

The heavy footsteps along the basement floor got louder, and closer.

The last wish of her young life had come true.

She was on the pier again, her father reaching out to her.

Chapter 7

We all have our weak spot—that place so tender to the touch you're knocked to your knees by the slightest threat to its sanctity.

The call from Lauren Callucci had done just that. I was thunderstruck, and driven to a state of near complete disequilibrium. My right arm was all that prevented me from falling forward into hard ceramic tile.

Then the doorbell rang, followed by a series of cold hard knocks.

I have no first impression of Dr. Cassisi, and no recollection of answering the door, or the good doctor coming in. All I remember is seeing her crouched next to John, holding his hand, dabbing his knuckles with gauze, and gently asking him questions. I was standing a few feet behind them as if teleported from the center hall to the backyard. My brain and body disconnected, I was, at the time, what doctors would call "in shock."

Charlotte was standing to my left and patting my arm. "Dad, the doctor asked you a question."

Dr. Cassisi stood up, got closer, and came into focus. She was pretty, though I had no appreciation of it at the time. In her mid-forties, about five foot five, with shoulder-length brown hair, she had a look of grave concern on her face.

My focus dropped to John, lying flat on his back on the lounge, his head turned away from me.

"Forget my question, Mr. Mannino. Are *you* alright?" she asked.

"A lot on my mind right now. I'm sorry," I responded.

"I'm going to get John upstairs and into bed," she said. "I'll give him something strong to help him sleep. I doubt he's been doing much of that lately."

"Okay," I answered weakly. I had my doubts about him cooperating, downright worried was more like it. After the mirror incident, I feared he might act out if coaxed or prodded in the wrong way.

The good doctor knelt back down, took John's hand in hers, and stood back up again. "Please come with me, John," is all she said.

Whether it was the gentle grasp of her hand, or the softness of her voice, it moved him enough emotionally and physically to bring him to his feet, all six feet of him, although a bit wobbly at first. As they walked, her arm around his waist, he gradually steadied himself as she carefully led him through the house and up the center hall stairs. Charlotte followed.

I still can't fully explain why, but I felt the outcast as I watched them disappear into a bedroom on the second floor that John hadn't slept in for over a-year-and-a-half since starting Cardozo Law.

Left alone, my mind instantly drifted back to the text of my license plate, while my stomach felt like it was lined with fiery acid.

I grabbed a quart of milk from the refrigerator and a coffee mug from the overhead cabinet—a souvenir from a short-lived Broadway musical Eleanor and I had seen years ago. The letters spelled *Brooklyn*. The tickets had been a gift from Sallie Gurrieri.

Sallie was my Uncle Rocco's most trusted friend and second in command of his criminal enterprise. After Rocco's fatal heart attack in 1982, Sallie was elevated to capo supreme over Brooklyn, Queens, and Long Island. Not as clever and diplomatic in the delicate dealings of organized crime, he was far more ruthless than Rocco ever needed to be, especially in an age of wiretaps and the wide net of conspiracy charges that stemmed from the Federal RICO statutes enacted in 1970. Consequently, Sallie was facing a lengthy indictment in Brooklyn's Eastern District.

Back in the South Bronx of 1982, when I had absolutely no one else to turn to, desperate and fearful of losing all that I loved in the world, Uncle Rocco and Sallie were all I had.

Put simply, they saved my life.

Chapter 8

I awoke on the leather couch in the den to the sound of metal dinging off ceramic. Charlotte was in the kitchen stirring her coffee. It was noon. I had not slept this late since college. My head resting on a pillow, my body under a heavy quilt, the ever-present dinging was like an irreverent alarm clock.

"Dad, you awake?" The source of all the noise immediately became clear to me.

I sat up. My throat was bone dry, and my voice gravely. "Could you get me a glass of water?"

"How about some coffee? I just made a fresh pot."

"I'll have coffee after," I answered, as my eyes widened and the rest of the world around me came into focus. "I guess you're staying?"

"Of course, I'm staying. I'm not leaving my brother, and I'm not leaving you."

"Your brother will need you, that's for sure."

"And you?"

If I had been asked this same question just twenty-four hours earlier, Charlotte was the last person on earth I would have wanted around in a crisis. As a child, she would cry at the least provocation. As an adult, though naturally beautiful like her mother, she exhibited a petulant vanity and selfishness, albeit cloaked in charm, which everyone, but yours truly, tolerated.

"Of course I need you." I did my best to sound convincing.

Charlotte walked over and placed her palm on my forehead. "You're a little warm."

I shrugged. "How is your brother, and how is his hand?" I asked.

Charlotte took a deep breath. "No stitches needed. His knuckles were cut, that's all. The doctor cleaned them, and bandaged them. She said he could take the bandages off in a day or two. She then gave him an injection that put him right out. He's still sleeping."

Recurring thoughts of my son's well-being made me think of Lauren Callucci's call. "Charlotte. I'm not sure that this is the best place for you right now."

"What?" Her face instantly soured.

"Your brother is in some kind of deeply depressed state. He needs quiet and rest." I immediately realized that I wasn't entirely making sense. "Just listen." I was struggling to get my message across, while hiding my true fears. "Do you know who Sallie Gurrieri is?"

"You mean, 'Uncle' Sallie?" She made quotation marks with her fingers.

"Yes, and we both know he's not my uncle, but I still feel I can trust him, and a whole lot more than any security company filled with ex-cons and moonlighting cops. Besides, you just don't know how very close he was to my Uncle Rocco. We're talking about your grandmother's brother."

"Dad, I really have no idea what you're getting at, but I guess it may explain why he called."

"He called? When?"

"About two hours ago. He was very nice. I didn't tell him about John."

"He probably knows," I said more to myself, than to Charlotte. "Did he leave a number?"

"He said you have it. Why? Do you think we're in danger here?"

"No," I said, lying through my teeth, "but I'm not taking any chances."

"Oh, and I forgot to tell you," Charlotte interrupted. "Mom called. She is getting on the next flight to New York."

"I'm going outside," I blandly announced, and quickly stood up. A little shaky on my feet, it took a few seconds for me to secure my balance.

"Before you go, I have to talk to you about something." Charlotte sat down on the couch next to me. She was wearing sweatpants and a sweatshirt with *NYU* emblazoned on it.

I sat back down.

"I'm not sure where your head is at where Mom is concerned. I know it hurt you when she left for Atlanta."

"That was over four years ago. I love you, Charlotte, but please get to the point."

"I love you too, Dad, which is why…" She was struggling, which made me all the more uneasy—frightened was more like it. Not the kind of frightened I felt for my son, or of a killer about to descend on my family. It was a more selfish fear, cloaked by a loneliness that had grown all too familiar.

"It's fine, Charlotte. Really. Just spit it out."

Charlotte huffed. "Mom has been seeing someone, and I think it may be serious." She spit it out all right, and I felt that black lightning again, gone but not forgotten since my ride home from the beach.

"Really?" It was all I could say to sound indifferent.

Charlotte had been growing increasingly uncomfortable, but I was pleased to see her uneasiness wane a bit with my response. She probably expected I would throw a few chairs around, which is exactly what I wanted to do.

"He's some Wall Street guy," she added, and I thought: *Of course he is.* "He's about her age."

"Which makes him about my age."

"Yes, yes, that's true. He's nice too, really nice."

"You met him?" I instantly earmarked the nearest piece of light furniture to stay away from.

"Yes, Mom…" Charlotte hesitated and I could tell she was rethinking the wisdom of saying too much too soon. "He lives in the City. I think he is originally from Indiana or Louisiana. I'm not sure."

"Do you mean *New York City*?"

"Yes, I do."

"I met up with him and Mom in Manhattan. She's been back and forth a few times. He goes to see her in Atlanta also."

I must have taken on the look of one hapless clown because Charlotte began to look as sad as I felt.

"I am really sorry to have to tell you this Dad, but you needed to know. It's been over four years."

"Don't be sorry." I took Charlotte's hand. "You're right. I should have expected something like this." Charlotte was trying to smile a bit as a proffer of support. "I guess all that's left me to do now is get a girlfriend too, I suppose. Either that…or kill myself." I smiled.

"Dad!" she shrieked. "Not funny!"

I faked a chuckle. "I love you and your brother too much to leave you to the likes of Southern aristocracy and Mr. Wall Street. And thank you for telling me." I took her hand in mine and looked her square in the eyes. "You did the right thing."

"I'm really glad you feel this way, Dad, and I love you too very, very much."

"Thank you. Now please excuse me. I'm going out back to make a call."

"You're okay though, right?" she asked sweetly.

"Of course, I am." I was out the kitchen door and waved my cell phone in the air as an indication that I have moved on to something else, though I most certainly had not.

When I stepped out back, I had to shield my eyes. It was a cloudless sky and the pool was a glaring mirror under the post-noon sun. A hundred yards or so beyond the perimeter cypress trees, a few country clubbers were teeing off near the third hole. I couldn't tell one from the other. All were men dressed in light blue short-sleeved shirts and tan khakis.

I took out my cell phone and dialed Uncle Sallie.

Chapter 9

The password on her Blackberry had been disabled. How trusting, how convenient. Her photos—a collage of her life of late—were easily accessible. With the cell phone charged, he could now delve into her past any time he wanted. She was his now, and so were her memories: family, friends, places...

He kept scrolling.

For the cheap slut that she was, she apparently got around. Had some good-looking friends too—one especially.

Then there were these photos of one particular guy that kept popping up. He was with this one girl more often than not. There was also a photo of him with another—the especially hot one. Maybe she was a slut too. Must be.

Maybe his next appointment would be with her.

Now that would be special.

The guy who kept popping up though, seemed too clean cut to be her pimp. He was quickly getting sick of looking at his smug, content expression.

Then there was that special one again. She was standing on a busy avenue, smiling, key in hand, gesturing up at the building behind her like a game show host displaying the grand prize. She was tall and sexy as all hell, with long blonde hair, and a sleeveless blouse that looked as if it had been painted clean over her inviting breasts. Then there was that skintight skirt, and that hemline three quarters the way up her thigh.

He scrolled to the next photo. Her stance had changed, but more of the building came into view. It had a glass panel façade, and in striking gold the name of the developer's landmark was emblazoned on a huge marquee above its entrance doors.

In story high letters it starkly read: Trump Tower.

Chapter 10

Had I known about Mr. Wall Street just twenty-four hours earlier, I probably would have been one and the same with that parkway overpass. I had come that close. All I had accomplished in my life: my marriage, my children, my career, the devoted husband, the loving father, the good lawyer, every principle I stood for, all I was and would be remembered for would be summed up in one irrefutable moment when metal and flesh were one with concrete. All legacy would have been lost in the irreverent flooring of an accelerator.

I would have been remembered as the good lawyer who married rich, had two beautiful children, and then killed himself—the intractable consequence of an end that would forever alter the lives of everyone that mattered to me. A turn into blackness, and my children and Eleanor would have to fend for themselves in the waiting evil.

The call I made to Sallie Gurrieri rang several times before it turned into a recording that stated that he had yet to set up his voicemail, which didn't surprise me. The last thing a mob boss needs is a recorded message turning into evidence.

But no sooner did I end the call than my phone rang back—more *Moon River*. It was Sallie. "I need to see you. I'll call in ten minutes and tell you where." The call cut out the instant he stopped talking.

As I was walking back into the house, it occurred to me: Sallie Gurrieri was not calling because he thought I might need something from him; he was calling because it was he, who needed something from *me*.

A minute later and *Moon River* beckoned me once again. "Nick, it's Eleanor."

"I know. You're still on my caller ID."

"My plane is delayed." She sounded somewhat panicked. This was not the Eleanor I knew. I had always marveled at how calm she was during a crisis, even when the crisis was us—unless the end of our marriage was no crisis at all to her.

I was tempted to ask why her boyfriend hadn't sent a private jet to pick her up, the likes of which those wolves of Wall Street chartered all the time, but I couldn't muster up enough callous indifference. I never could, and starting at a time when our son was in a state of near emotional collapse was just not something I was capable of.

"Planes get delayed. It's okay," I answered.

"No, it's not," she snapped back.

"What I mean is…I'm here. Last night I called a doctor. She gave John something to help him sleep. Charlotte is also here and helping too. She's kind of looking after both of us."

"You wouldn't kid around with me at a time like this, would you?"

"No, of course not."

"Now, how *is* John? Charlotte was nearly hysterical when she called me. Is he…is he going to get through this?" Her voice broke as she attempted to keep her composure.

"I hope so, but right now he's in a state of shock. The truth is he is not doing well, and for some reason I don't think I can bring any comfort to him."

"John always felt very close to you. You may be wearing too much of your emotions on your sleeve right now. Outside the courtroom, and especially when it comes to your family, you don't have the best poker face, you know."

"No, I don't know, but I believe you. Let's leave it at that."

"And how are you doing?"

"I'm okay, I suppose."

"Charlotte said she told you about me and…" Eleanor spoke more frankly than I expected.

"Yeah," I responded, and no matter how hard I tried, my voice wasn't completely my own.

"This was no time to tell you," she said. "I wanted to myself, but it never seemed to be the right moment." As she spoke I could hear flight announcements in the background.

"It shouldn't have surprised me. It's been years after all. Have you seen a lawyer?" I asked flatly.

"Nick, we don't need to go there right now."

"I'm sorry."

"Don't be. I know you've been hurting. I have been hurting too. Neither of us were happy, and we both have a right to be. Everyone does."

I didn't answer.

"Neither of us were happy, Nick. Nick?"

I couldn't keep my mind from drifting…to better days—the early days. "I'm here. I suppose you're right."

Eleanor continued talking—something again about us *both having the right to be happy.* "I'll call Charlotte to pick me up when I get to New York," she added, in what seemed like a mad rush before the phone went dead.

I had been sitting on a step connecting the kitchen to the den when my cell phone rang again.

This time the screen read as expected: *Unknown Caller.*

Chapter 11

"Meet me behind the church." The voice was unmistakable. It was Sallie.

"What church?" I asked nervously.

"I don't know. It's Episcopal or something, on Cathedral Avenue. It's close by."

"It doesn't matter. I can't."

"You can't?" I expected him to be instantly annoyed, and eager to show it, but he was neither. "Nickie, what's up with you? You know I wouldn't ask if it wasn't important."

"I've got some serious problems, Sallie."

"You mean, Uncle Sallie." His tone was caustic.

"Yes, Uncle Sallie, which is why I need you to understand. I can't leave the house right now."

"Why the hell not?" This time his annoyance was clear. It was combined with frustration.

"It doesn't mean I can't meet with you," I shot back.

Sallie got stone cold serious. "For Christ's sake, Nickie, I need to talk to you, and face-to-face."

"Then come here. Come to my house."

"Are you sure? Can we talk there?"

He sounded genuinely confused and I was sure a slew of questions were running through his head that he was reluctant to ask. I quickly calculated the time we would have before Eleanor arrived. Even if she was boarding the plane just as she hung up, it would take at least an hour-and-a-half before she landed at JFK. Add the drive to Hillcrest Place, and Sallie and I would have at least two hours to talk life and death, and barter our souls to the devil if we had to.

"Please come now." I insisted. "I guarantee you that we will be alone."

"Except I'm not," he responded. "The circumstances being what they are, I have my people with me."

During the early days of Rocco's rise to power, Sallie was his chief enforcer, and capable of setting an example by the most horrific executions. After the two met in Holbrook Juvenile Detention Facility in Upstate New York, they quickly and mercilessly rose to prominence in Brooklyn's underworld. But despite the danger surrounding every moment of their lives, and knowing my mother as I did, to my shock and surprise from the time I was in diapers and just learning to walk, Rocco and Sallie would pick me up from Mom's apartment, and take me to their central meeting place—the Carroll Avenue Hunt and Fish Club. Sallie even made me a booster seat so I could sit and eat with the boys while all manner of misbegotten man discussed God knows what before I was old enough to understand any of it.

"It's okay if you have company," I answered. "Just pull all the way up the drive and around back. I'll leave the garages open. You can park in there."

A few seconds passed in silence, until Sallie replied hoarsely, "Fine."

I called out to Charlotte. As she descended the staircase, I told her that I had some people coming over and would she mind staying upstairs with her brother.

"Is it police?" she asked.

"No. Just some people I need to talk to. Business stuff."

"You're doing business today?"

"An old friend needs to see me. It's important. I didn't want to leave the house, so I told him to come here."

"But why do I have to stay upstairs? Are you ashamed of me?"

I was instantly reminded of my mother, who once asked me the very same question only a month after I started dating Eleanor.

Charlotte chuckled. "I'm only kidding. God, you should have seen your face."

"Maybe this isn't a day for joking, Charlotte."

Unfazed, she hurried upstairs. As soon as she disappeared from sight, I heard two cars coasting up the cobblestone drive.

Sallie's blue Lincoln Town Car pulled around to the back. Behind it was a black SUV. Both vehicles moved at a moderate pace, and to make for a smooth entry, I pressed two of the garage remotes I kept inside the house.

The Lincoln took the offer, but the black SUV remained outside and directly behind it.

I walked to the back of the center hall and opened a rear door. When Sallie and his driver looked up from inside the Town Car, I waved them both inside. Neither reacted. I watched as the SUV, with its engine still running, parked behind them. A stocky, middle-aged man, dressed in what looked like his best bowling shirt, exited the front passenger seat and headed toward the pool area.

I backed into the center hall as Sallie and his driver walked up the short set of stairs that led from the garages into the house. Sallie was smiling weakly as he entered, and continued to do so as we kissed each other on the cheek. His driver, a large man in his sixties wearing a suit jacket and button down shirt, ignored me.

"Dominic," Sallie said to the driver. "This is Nickie, Rocco Alonzo's nephew."

Dominic took a few steps back and extended a large and calloused hand. He had dyed jet-black hair and the physique of a body builder.

"Pleased to meet you," he said, as he shook my hand with his fingers only. He had a worried look. He had yet to case the first floor, and was obviously uncomfortable having to stop and say hello to me in the process.

As for Sallie, I couldn't remember the last time I had seen him. He had lost weight, and I wondered if it was the result of the stress he was under, or just another byproduct of entering his seventies. A mere five foot five, and (prior to this visit) more than a hundred pounds overweight, Sallie was always a large figure in this young boy's life.

Though the temperature outside was at least eighty-five degrees, he was wearing a gold blazer that was swimming on him. As he threw his shoulders back, the reason partially came into view. The blazer hid a shoulder-holstered pistol.

"It's been a long time, kid," Sallie said, then broke into a smile that made him look twenty years younger and more like the Uncle Sallie I remembered as a kid.

"I know," I said with a weak smile of my own.

He took my chin in his hand. "You okay, kid? You look beat to shit."

I had just turned fifty-six. He was about seventy-five. Despite his life-altering legal troubles, he looked better than I did; clean-shaven, well-groomed, and even well-rested.

I fessed up. "I had a rough twenty-four hours if you must know."

"Where can we talk?" He abruptly asked.

"How's the backyard, behind the pool? We can speak privately there."

"Lead the way," he said with the cordial air of a maître-d'.

I walked beside Sallie through the house, then along the walkway beside the pool, while Dominic remained stationed outside the kitchen slider. By the time Sallie and I comfortably sat down into cushioned upright chairs beside a cocktail table only a few feet from the diving board, I noticed that Dominic was gone.

Sallie noticed me noticing. "He's just checkin' the place out, Nickie. Don't worry about it. I told him in the car you didn't need to be frisked, that we had a long history." Sallie was smiling, but I couldn't tell if it was genuine or not.

"It's okay if he wants to, if it makes him feel more comfortable," I answered.

"I'm comfortable. That's all that matters. Now stop talkin' like that." His smile was back, and I felt affectionately scolded.

When I looked back at the house, Dominic had returned to his spot outside the kitchen, standing like a centurion: upright, attentive, and ready for any crisis that transpired in his wake. Only this time, he was holding something.

It was a black doctor's bag.

Chapter 12

"What is that?" Sallie asked, as pounding violin strings captured by the South Shore wind drifted with distinct clarity into the rear yard.

"My neighbor is a best-selling thriller writer. Almost every day before he begins writing he blasts a classical overture. He'll dial it down soon enough. He says it helps him relax."

"I got a few rich crackpots in my neighborhood too," Sallie responded.

Harlan Dugan, however, was no crackpot. A Vietnam veteran with middle class roots, and an expert in American History, Criminology, and the Forensic Sciences, he wrote his first novel in 1978. It was such a smash, it was made into a movie only one year later. A multi-million dollar publishing contract followed. Bearded and portly, Harlan was a very private person, and aside from the occasional visits of his on-again off-again girlfriend, there was absolutely no one coming or going to and from his home ever.

Except for me, that is.

After Eleanor left, I had a standing dinner invitation, and he was quite the gracious host, and one great cook.

"Oh, he's an alright guy, actually," I told Sallie, though I could tell that he hadn't heard a single word I said, which meant he was thinking, instead of listening—not necessarily the better of the two alternatives.

"You know for a time, Nickie, you were...you know, the only kid in not only your Uncle Rocco's life, but mine too." Sallie was uncharacteristically stumbling over his words. Other than Sallie's wife and daughter, I was probably the only person in the world who could say no to him and get away with it.

Sallie started to over-gesticulate with his hands. "You know your mom was alone for a while after her divorce. It was just the two of you in that little apartment on New York Avenue. Rocco and me would drop by all the time." He stretched back in his chair and glanced skyward. "Your mom could make one great tomato sauce in those days. I don't have to tell you how much I loved to eat back then. What is it now…five years since she passed?"

"Five years and four months," I answered.

"Yeah, I don't have to tell you."

"You sent the most beautiful flowers," I said.

"You know I didn't come because I know your wife…you know…she didn't want…"

"I'm sorry about that." I grabbed the top of his hand and squeezed. "You and Uncle Roc were there anyway."

He turned toward me, shifted his seated position, and sat up in his chair. "I want you to know that I loved your mom like a sister, and you like my own nephew—my own flesh and blood." Sallie's eyes started to water. "Damn, I still miss your Uncle Roc."

I glanced over at Dominic.

"What's the matter, Nickie?" Sallie asked. "Does Dominic bother you? I'll have him wait by the car."

"No. Of course not. It's just that there are some other things going on right now. That's all."

"Well…okay, then let me get to why I called." Sallie grimaced as he stood up. The heat had caused his pants to stick to his legs. He plucked them free as he watched his cuffs fall to his shoes and sat back down. "The Feds, as you probably know, really got their claws into me right now—wiretaps, surveillance cameras…"

"I'm really sorry to hear that," I responded, and meant it.

His face rounded as his expression sweetened. "Don't be, kid. It's been a long time comin'. It's just, the thing is, they got all my business and personal accounts frozen. I can't even write a fuckin' check to pay the light bill, but worse, to pay my lawyers." He looked away, then looked back. "I know I'm going away. At this point, there's nothin' I can do about it, except delay the trial comin' whenever. But right now, every day I'm out in the world, is a day they can't take away from me." He turned toward me again and got deadly serious. "That brings me to that bag Dominic is holdin'."

I turned. Dominic was staring squarely at me, and before my mind could race through its possible contents, Sallie killed the mystery.

"There's fifty thou' in that bag. I wanna leave it with you in recompense, you might say, for a courtesy I hope you'll do me."

He had me at *courtesy,* though the myriad possibilities as to what he would say next were starting to make my head ache, for I hadn't a clue what the hell he was leading up to. But I should have.

Sallie continued: "If you don't think it will be a problem, or upset anyone in your family...your wife, whatever...would it be okay, Nickie, for you to write a check to my lawyers for the fifty thousand? You see, with the Feds up my ass, these lawyers are nervous about takin' my cash." Sallie leaned closer and whispered, "Sure, they're takin' my cash, but they got to show somethin' over the table too, or the Feds will get wise."

Sallie waved to Dominic, who strode quickly over with the bag, and placed it at my feet.

"What's the name of the law firm?" I asked.

Sallie was all smiles and seemed quite relieved, not only because of a problem solved, but also because it would have hurt to hear a 'no' from me. "I love you, Nickie, and I knew I could count on you."

"Let me get my checkbook," I answered stoically.

After I passed Dominic and entered the kitchen, I expected to hear some sort of sound coming from the second floor. It wasn't like Charlotte to remain stationary and quiet for this long—attentiveness to her brother notwithstanding—but there was no talking, no running water, no footsteps of any kind. I walked around to the dining room and looked out the window.

My Mercedes was gone, which meant Charlotte had taken it to pick up Eleanor. I rushed over to the desk in the kitchen, grabbed the checkbook, and hurried back to the pool area.

After I sat back down next to Sallie, he rattled off the firm's name, "Rusoff and Conroy, P.C."

I wrote the check, and handed it to Sallie.

He stood up and hugged me. "You were always a good kid, Nickie." Two kisses followed, one on each cheek. He turned to Dominic. "Let's go, Dom."

I sat back down as Sallie began to walk away.

"Uncle Sallie, you forgot something."

He stopped and looked back at me as if straining not to appear annoyed. "What do you mean, kid?"

"The bag," I said. "You forgot the bag."

"What?" He looked completely baffled.

I walked over to him, and handed the bag back to Dominic, who took it from me without hesitation. "I have a pretty good memory too," I said, "and if not for you and Uncle Roc..." My words trailed off as I choked up saying them.

Expressionless, Sallie just stared at me, while Dominic stared down at the bag filled with fifty-thousand dollars in cash.

"If not for you and Uncle Roc, I'd have been killed in that Bronx hallway back in '82, and I wouldn't be here to help you, or anyone else for that matter. I wouldn't be here for my children."

"Nickie, no," Sallie responded. "You don't have to do this."

"It's done." I said.

"You remind me of your uncle right now. College boy, lawyer, you're still a chip off the old block, but...will this be okay with the wife?"

"It's from my personal account. Besides, we're separated."

"Yeah, I kind of heard that through the grapevine, you know, and I'm sorry." Sallie paused and looked at me inquisitively. "But there's somethin' else, Nickie. Somethin's bothering you. Tell me. What's up with you, kid?"

I walked back to the patio chair, sat back down, leaned over, and put my head in my hands. In an instant, Sallie was standing over me.

"I think some maniac may be after my family."

Chapter 13

A crust of dried blood on the mattress tickled his ear as he awoke from a deep and sound sleep, his feet dangling in the air, his boots still on.

Sleep was often the best part after...

One eye was dried shut—the byproduct of being pressed against the freshly stained mattress. It needed the help of his thumb and index finger. The other opened naturally. Squinting, he turned, and stared straight ahead at the end table lamp that burned a bleak yellow under antique stained glass in an otherwise darkened room with nothing else in it but the mattress and box spring he was lying on.

As he regained more of his senses, he heard that faint moaning again. He had fallen asleep to its irreverent yet pleasing rhythm earlier, but had no idea how long ago that was. All he knew was that it sounded different— more muffled, not as pronounced.

But it still had that calming regularity—like the ocean at night—like the waves crashing gently against the shore.

Chapter 14

Sallie sat back down and I told him everything: the gruesome phone call from Sofia's cell, John's fall into depression, the cryptic text to Lauren Callucci.

"This is some crazy shit, and your son—" Sallie muttered.

"It gets worse," I added with some reluctance. "That text to the reporter…was *my* license plate number."

"But why?" Sallie asked. "Why you? Why *your* plate number?"

"What I'd really like to know is…how did he get it to begin with?"

"Regardless," Sallie said, shaking his head. "You're not safe here. You should probably stay somewhere else for a while."

"I'm not going anywhere. John is not well, and I won't be driven from my home by some piece of shit with a cell phone."

"The cops probably don't have a clue who the fuck he is. Damn! This whole thing is crazy. I can't believe this is happenin' to you. You walk the straight and narrow every day of your fuckin' life." He slapped his hands down hard on his knees then threw them in the air. "This is why life is so fucked up."

"The girl is a law student too, a good kid. Her family owns a house in Whitestone."

Sallie looked at me inquisitively. "How do you know?"

"What I know, John told me."

"Don't take offense, Nickie. My kid lies to me all the time. I never know when she's tellin' the truth, and she's twenty-eight and married."

I looked intensely at Sallie. "John has never lied to me."

Sallie winced. "Not that you know of."

I thought again. "No. I believe what he told me."

"Let me ask you this: It's clear he loves this girl, right?"

I nodded.

Sallie continued. "So you don't think he is capable of lyin' to protect her, so you wouldn't think bad about her?"

"I'll know more when John's feeling better and I can talk to him."

Sallie leaned over. "What can I do?" he asked. "Tell me."

I just looked at him.

"Listen, Nickie,' he said. "I own a security business—licensed, no uniforms, very private, but very legitimate, no worries. There will two armed guards here by nightfall. You're afraid for your family. You should be. Let me help."

I could not and would not refuse Sallie's offer, but if Eleanor found out whose company it was, she would send the security away in an instant.

So be it. I had no intention of telling her anyway. Besides, she hadn't stepped foot in the house for over four years. The call as to how to protect 18 Hillcrest was no longer hers.

Chapter 15

I was lying on the leather sectional in the den, dozing in and out of a restless sleep when I heard several knocks. Disoriented, I got up and opened the front door to a pleasant yet anxious feminine greeting.

"Mr. Mannino, I hope it's okay that I didn't call first."

"Dr. Cassisi?"

"Guess I looked worse than I thought last night. I rushed over—"

"No no, I am so sorry. Of course, I'm still half asleep. By all means, come in." After she stepped into the center hall, I shook her right hand with both of mine. "I can't thank you enough for coming by last night, and now today. This is very decent of you, downright kind. Really. Thank you so much."

"And how are *you* feeling?" she asked.

"Still not all that clearheaded as you can see."

"That's to be expected." She widened her already large brown eyes.

"John is upstairs," I said. "Please go right up. He's probably still sleeping though, and I'm sorry again that I didn't recognize you at first."

She took a few steps, turned, and smiled. "That's really alright. Let's hope that John will." She then proceeded to climb the stairs as I stood like a lame fool next to the open front door until she disappeared from sight.

Then the doorbell rang, and I jumped.

It was Eleanor. She was standing on the porch while a yellow taxi backed out the driveway.

I yanked open the door. "Forget your key?" I asked.

She ignored the quip, and gave me a quick obligatory hug and peck on the cheek while dragging a small suitcase by its handle. She was wearing fitted jeans and a V-neck blouse, and all I could think of was how great she looked.

Although it had been four years since I last saw her, she looked twenty years younger and just as beautiful as when she first walked through that same doorway back in January of 1983, after a rather charming and matronly real estate agent was more than happy to show me this pricey home on the hill. I nicknamed the agent, "Miss Marple," because once she found out I was a lawyer, she never stopped asking me questions, and especially enjoyed telling me one whopper of a serial killer story. I told her then that I wasn't sure if she was trying to sell me a home, or scare me away from one.

Though it took Eleanor less than two minutes to float through its five bedrooms, six baths, large living room, dining room, and sunken den on two meticulously landscaped acres that included an in-ground swimming pool, she proclaimed, rather convincingly, that she loved it. But I should have known that what she was really hoping for was that we would eventually pick up and move out of New York, and the sooner the better. Over time, I was convinced this was her secret dream.

It wasn't mine.

"Where's John?' she asked.

"He's in his room. Dr. Cassisi is with him."

She needed a moment to absorb the doctor in residence notification. "Oh," she said warily. "Should I go up?"

"Sure, if you want to, but the doctor gave him something strong last night to make him sleep, so he's probably still out of it."

Eleanor abandoned her suitcase by the door and started toward the stairs.

Halfway up, she turned. "It's great that you got a doctor here. I just can't believe there's still one who makes house calls, especially in New York."

"I guess there's still a lot you don't know about New York."

She glared back at me. "I know enough."

"She lives a few blocks away," I added. "She's my old doctor's daughter."

"You don't have to explain." Eleanor was nearing the top of the stairs. The back of her head was facing me. "All that matters is that she's here."

As she turned down the second floor hallway, it occurred to me: *Where the hell was Charlotte?*

The last time I spoke to her, Sallie was on his way to the house, while she agreed to remain upstairs. But now my car—the one whose license plate number was in the hands of a maniac—was gone, and so was she.

I immediately called her cell and after a few rings got voicemail. I tried to stay calm. Eleanor was upstairs with John and the doctor, and there couldn't have been a worse time to spill my guts about the text sent to Lauren. It would surely send Eleanor reeling, and she'd probably be furious as hell with me for not divulging it sooner.

Lost in thought, I found myself standing in the kitchen, staring out at the pool, and seeking a sobering comfort in the sight and sound of the jet-powered crests rhythmically flowing across the surface. In a few hours the filter would time off, only to time on again come noon the following day.

And as an ominous foreboding began growing inside me like infectious quicksand, I couldn't help but think to myself: *These were the only occurrences in the next twenty-four hours I could count on with any degree of certainty.*

Chapter 16

I guess I wasn't moving fast enough, because the doorbell rang, then rang again before I discovered what looked like two plain-clothes detectives standing on the front porch and glaring back at me.

The taller one handed me a business card. "Packett Security," he said. "Mr. Gurrieri sent us."

"Fine," I answered. "I'll get my checkbook."

"Mr. Mannino, we've been paid already, a month in advance, for two men around the clock," said the taller and older of the two.

"Rip up the check. I don't want my...anyone else paying. I will write you a new one right now. You can go cash it. I'll call the bank myself." I looked over at the grandfather clock in the far corner of the center hall. It read 5:20 PM, but worse, it was Sunday. I thought again. "Well, you can cash it in the morning."

Both men stared back at me with deadpan expressions. The older one spoke first. He was well-groomed, about forty-five years old, with dark eyes and hair, and wearing a tailored blazer that fit him like a glove. "Mr. Gurrieri sent over a messenger and paid us in cash. We are under strict orders not to take any money from you. If you don't want us here though, we can't force our protection services upon you."

"I want you to stay," I said abruptly, and there it was. I wouldn't accept Sallie's money, but he was getting it to me anyway—two security guards, twenty-four hours a day, for one month straight. Cash is cash. I'm sure they had no objection to being paid that way, even if the money was delivered in a black doctor's bag.

"Well, that's that, gentlemen," I conceded graciously. "Please let me know if you need to come inside for any reason."

"Certainly," the older man said, his tone softening. "Know that we will be screening anyone who comes on to the property, and I suppose I don't have to tell you that we are armed and with more weapons secured away in our vehicle, which I hope you don't mind is parked behind your garages."

"I don't mind at all. What kind of car is it?"

"A Chevy Caprice. Sorry if it looks out of place here."

"Not at all." I answered. "I've got that one covered."

A perplexed look left his face as quickly as it came. "I'll need your cell number, and your home number, and your wife's cell too."

"My wife and I are separated. You can have my daughter's cell instead." *But damn it to hell, where is she?*

"How old is your daughter," the younger one asked.

"Um…she'll be twenty-eight in June. Her name is Charlotte."

The older one quickly cut in. "If you don't mind, we'll leave you alone for now. One of us will be out front, the other out back. I'm Paul. This is Vic. Vic is on the job as a police officer in Queens. I'm retired Secret Service. Another man will be coming to take my place in an hour or so." He handed me two more business cards. "Please put our numbers in all your phones."

"Will do." I looked down at the cards. "You want chairs?" I asked.

"We don't sit," Paul responded.

"Okay," I answered. "Well, thank you."

The two men stepped away, and I shut the door, but not before I heard Eleanor's voice. It had a distinct tremor to it, and I couldn't decide if the message in the tone was the result of fear, anger, concern, or a mix of all three.

"Who was that?" she asked.

"Security," I said. "Two men, 24/7, for the next month or so."

Eleanor was standing at the bottom of the stairs staring blankly at me. "What for?" Four years in Atlanta and her slight Southern drawl had returned. I had forgotten how much I enjoyed hearing it.

Since I wasn't even remotely prepared to tell her about the text of the license plate, and hadn't even begun to think through the pluses and minus of her knowing about it, I just stood there. This pissed her off even more.

"Can you call Charlotte please and find out where she is?" I asked, while trying to hide my true level of nervousness and concern.

"Why?" She asked incredulously. "What are you worried about? You know she can't sit still."

"She's got my car. I may need it."

"I know you're not telling me something," Eleanor said pointedly. "Damn it, Nick. What is it with you, and where would you be going now, and why do we need security 24/7?"

Chapter 17

The voice in his head was screaming at him again, grating on his nerves like a high-pitched train whistle. It would pass quickly, but leave behind a throbbing in his eyes that would last for hours. It was the worst kind of migraine, pounding like a recurrent electric shock in his brain. No pill or ancient antidote would ease the pain.

Biting down on something hard and metallic once helped, but no more—the voice, and the torment that accompanied it, would only dissipate when the sinister urges in the darkest corners of his mind were satisfied...at least for now...or so he thought.

Chapter 18

My cell phone rang.

It was Lauren Callucci. "They found four bags full of bones in the marsh by Field 6."

I turned to Eleanor. "I have to take this outside."

She gave me that look of exasperation I first saw early in our relationship—when she pleaded for me to quit Bronx Legal Aid, and I refused.

As I walked down the driveway and toward the street, my cell phone pressed against my ear, it pained me to concentrate. I felt as if I was about to hyperventilate as my worry and fear for Charlotte's safety heightened, while Lauren elaborated...

"A retired man in his early seventies, who often brought his German shepherd to Jones Beach for a walk along the shoulder of Ocean Parkway, decided to unleash him. When the dog ran into the marsh, the owner called out to him, and when the shepherd didn't return, the old man followed. About a dozen feet from where the marsh dropped into the bay, he found the dog sniffing away at what appeared to be an old, dirty burlap bag. When the old man grabbed the top of the bag and opened it, he saw a human skull."

I was listening so intently, I hadn't realized that I had turned a corner and was standing in the middle of Tenth Street. I heard a gentle car horn. It was my neighbor, Harlan. I weakly waved back. Consumed by every word Lauren spoke, I just kept walking aimlessly. Upon my return, I realized that I hadn't even noticed the new security guard that replaced Paul in front of the house.

Lauren continued. After the police arrived, they combed the area, and found three more bags. All four contained a skeletal mix of skull and bones except one, which also had deteriorating flesh in it. Before I could ask, she told me that all the police could determine, without forensic testing and before toxicology reports came back, was that the bones and flesh belonged to women.

"My God," I uttered.

"There's a bit more, but I would like to tell you in person. Can we meet at the diner on Franklin Avenue, the one by Lord and Taylor?"

"Sure," I said, then I realized I hadn't shaved or showered in two days. "I'll see you in thirty minutes, assuming I get my car back. My daughter took it, and I have no idea where she is."

"I'm sure she's fine," she answered, and then came to a greater realization. "Oh, you're worried because it's the car with the plate number on it."

"Hell, yes."

"But wait a minute. It's a Mercedes with a navigator tracking system. Just call the tracking company, and ask them where the car is."

"I can't believe I didn't think of that."

"I'm currently at *Newsday* in Melville. Call me if you're going to be late. It will take me at least thirty minutes to get to Garden City."

Halfway up my driveway, I saw Paul's security replacement standing by the edge of the lawn. A young kid in his twenties, with a shoulder-holstered pistol in partial view, he handed me a copy of *Newsday* off my front lawn, and sure enough, the news of Sofia's kidnapping had made headlines: LAW STUDENT ABDUCTED.

I shook my head as I imagined the scene outside the Perez home in Whitestone, Queens, their suffering exacerbated by the hoards of reporters vying for a comment or reaction to Sofia's disappearance. I then went to worst-case scenario again, imagined a similar scene outside 18 Hillcrest, and broke into a panic sweat.

I entered the house with the paper tucked firmly under my arm and heard Eleanor talking in the kitchen.

She was talking to Charlotte, and from the content of the conversation, I quickly surmised my dear daughter's mysterious flight was to none other than the nearest Starbucks.

Relief poured over me.

I took a moment to catch my breath while making a mental note to grill Charlotte for leaving the house without so much as a word. Surprisingly, my thoughts quickly shifted in priority with my last deep breath, and all I wanted to do was shave and shower, and get over to the diner to meet Lauren.

After fifteen minutes flat—a personal record—I was ready to go, but I couldn't leave without saying something to the ladies in the kitchen.

"I have to meet someone in town," I called out.

"In town?" Eleanor asked curiously.

"On Franklin Avenue, at my office."

"On a Sunday?" Eleanor asked warily.

"See you in a little bit," I said matter-of-factly, then broke away and took off out the door, but not before I heard Eleanor say to Charlotte: "Your father has not changed one bit."

As I walked into the Garden City Coffee Shop, it reminded me of the Fun City Diner in the Bronx where, in the early 1980s, I had lunched with my Legal Aid cronies between court sessions. Pristine by comparison, it had the same narrow dimension and centrally located kitchen. I looked around, having no idea what Lauren Callucci looked like or was wearing. I forgot to ask.

But Lauren was easy to spot. She was at a table in the rear, her head buried in what I recognized, even from a distance, as a police report. As I approached, she looked up, stood, and introduced herself while extending her hand.

She thanked me for meeting her on such short notice. Her gratitude and respect appeared genuine. Almost as tall as me, at five foot nine, she reminded me of a younger Julia Roberts with her permed hair and wide smile, though this was no affable *Pretty Woman*. Dressed down in an over-sized T-shirt and knock around jeans and sneakers, she was all business.

"I'm glad you were able to find me. I forgot to tell you what I look like."

"You were reading a police report, so you weren't too hard to spot."

Lauren smiled with a coquettish tilt of her head. "We're great then," she said, as her face relaxed completely and lit up like one would expect from a young woman her age—her entire adult life in front of her with all its unrealized dreams.

But as quick as that flicker of youth and beauty came, it went.

"How old are you, Lauren, if you don't mind my asking?"

"I'm twenty-eight, and why would I mind?"

"My daughter is twenty-eight, and I couldn't imagine her doing what you're doing."

Lauren sighed. "I assume you found her."

As she spoke, I noticed that unlike most young women her age, she wasn't wearing one item of accessorized clothing or jewelry—no clip in her hair, no ring or wristband, and no tattoo I could see.

"She was in my kitchen when I got home," I said. "She had gone to Starbucks." There was a tone of apology in my response.

Lauren's expression turned somber, and I became concerned that by asking her age I had gotten too familiar, too fast—that I had personally encroached in some way. Turns out, I had. Something I said had struck a nerve.

"Mr. Mannino, Mr. Repolla told me a lot about you, and I'm sure you're under a lot of stress, but I must tell you, I don't like being compared to someone else."

I quickly took a welcome cue from the approaching waitress, and asked Lauren if she wanted anything.

"Just coffee."

I turned to the waitress. "Two coffees, and two pieces of apple pie."

"No pie for me," Lauren interrupted.

"Two pieces of pie," I said emphatically to the waitress.

Lauren looked annoyed. The waitress sped away.

"I haven't eaten all day," I lamely added. "Now what is it you wanted to tell me?"

Lauren huffed, then took the police reports (upon closer look, there was more than one) and slid them into a small gym bag that was on the floor next to her chair.

"There was something else found in one of the burlap bags, the one that had more in it than just bones." Her demeanor had softened.

"You mean the one that had some flesh in it too?"

"Yes, that's right." I waited while Lauren seemed to be searching for what to say next. "Are you a religious man, Mr. Mannino?"

"No, but my mother was, and let's cut the formalities. My name is Nick."

"I don't think the killer knew that he had left it in the bag," she said.

The waitress set two cups of coffee and two pieces of pie on the table. My eyes fixed on Lauren. I said "thank you" without looking up.

Lauren continued. "Inside that victim's mouth was a chain—a thin gold necklace, and alongside it, a gold crucifix. Did your son's girlfriend wear a crucifix?"

I didn't need to think twice. "My mother wore one every day of her life for as long as I can remember. And Sofia wore one just like it."

Chapter 19

"How did you get your hands on those police reports anyway?" I asked.

"Does it matter?"

"The bodies were found yesterday. Today you're in a diner combing over the police reports on the case. It's been a few years since my last criminal trial, but I sure as hell haven't forgotten what they look like."

"Mr. Repolla—"

"Vinny, to me."

Lauren took a breath. "He told me you were a pretty smart guy, but I didn't expect you to be so blunt, considering."

"I'm just committed to finding out who did this to a wonderful young woman my son is in love with."

"What about those other girls? They don't matter?"

I leaned over and pushed the coffee and pie aside. "I represented hundreds of prostitutes as a young Legal Aid Attorney. For most of them, it's just temporary—a quick way to make a buck or finance their drug habit until they either wise up, or wind up dead. You are pleading to one seasoned bleeding heart, Lauren. I feel for all victims, no matter who they are."

Lauren sat back in her chair. "It's just that you drive up in your Mercedes. You live on the hill. What am I supposed to think?"

"That the rich are selfish and arrogant, and only care about their money and making more of it. That's not me."

"I understand if you're only interested because of your son, and the text I got."

"But what about you?" I asked. "Why are you so interested? Isn't this just another story? You sure seem to be a hell of a lot more committed than that. You told me that girls have been going missing for years. Why is this case so special, and why call me to meet you here? The police could have told me about the crucifix."

Lauren hadn't budged. The rear section of the diner had emptied out. We were the only two remaining—sitting at a table against the wall, two cups full of coffee, two plates of uneaten pie.

"And how did you get those police reports so fast? What is it you're not telling me?" I asked.

She picked up her head and rolled it slowly on her shoulders as if countering a tightness that had crept into her neck and back. She glanced up at me, then down at the table. "My sister has been missing for over eighteen months, since the day before her twenty-third birthday. She loved her crystal meth. She loved her pills. She left home at nineteen to work at a restaurant in Manhattan. My mom believed her. I knew better. The night before she went missing, she got a call from a guy who saw her ad on Craigslist. The ad was offering female companionship. He sounded okay, or so she told her roommate. He said he wanted her for the night, which meant a thousand cash. She was living in Harlem at the time. Like many girls who place these ads, she had no pimp, which meant no driver, and no protection nearby. Her roommate, also a prostitute, told her not to go. She was supposed to meet him four blocks away. Her cell phone records listed another call coming from the same unlisted phone to hers shortly after she left her apartment. The call lasted ten seconds. The police eventually identified the cell phone and traced it to an electronics store on Lexington and 68th Street. It was a ninety-minute throwaway bought with cash. My sister was never seen or heard from again."

"And the police reports?"

"My boyfriend is a Nassau County detective."

"I'm sorry about your sister," I said, in a tone more appropriate to asking forgiveness than expressing sympathy. "But the fact that your sister is missing doesn't mean the worst has happened. She could have just taken off. Hadn't she done that before—disappeared for months at a time without a word?"

"Yes, she has," Lauren answered contritely.

The waitress, without asking, slipped the check onto the table. I picked it up while Lauren seemed deep in thought, eyes barely open, but fixed squarely on me.

"So you see…she might turn up at any time."

"Mr. Mannino…"

"Call me Nick, please."

"My sister is never going to come home."

"Now, how do you know that?"

"I know that because I got a call from her cell phone the day after she went missing, just like Sofia's sister did, and you know what he said?"

"Lauren, you don't have to…"

"He said, 'I want you to know, bitch, that as we speak, I'm watching your slut of a sister dying the slow death she deserves.'"

I reached for Lauren's hand, but she pulled it away.

"He also said things I won't repeat," she added reluctantly. "He called two more times with more of the same. The police traced the calls to Times Square, and later checked the video cameras there, but it was useless. Half the people in Midtown have their cell phones out. And that wasn't the last of it, nor the worst. If I had any hope that my sister was still alive, it was gone with his next call, when he told me that he 'was watching my sister's body rot.' The police traced that one back to a cell tower along the Southern State Parkway, just twenty minutes away in Massapequa, Long Island."

Lauren then hung her head and wept, whereupon the waitress hurried over to console her. She must have heard every word Lauren and I said. Short and stocky, with dyed dirty blonde hair, she gave Lauren a warm maternal hug.

It became clear to me then why the killer was texting. He liked it personal. Torturing and killing his victims wasn't enough. He had to know and feel their families suffering too.

After the waitress and I walked Lauren to her car, though she needed no help from either of us, Lauren asked if I would meet her again. Only this time our surroundings would be much less conducive to the voluntary kindness of strangers.

Chapter 20

Dr. Cassisi had already left by the time I returned home. Her business card was on the center hall table, the one missing the mirrored glass via John's tirade the day before. It was only a matter of time before Eleanor would be asking about it.

After I picked up the good doctor's card, I noticed that she had written her cell number on the back. I put the card in my pants pocket, then turned into the dining room. As I did, I heard Eleanor and Charlotte talking in the kitchen, but it wasn't the casual talk of mother and daughter, so I slowed my footsteps to hide my anxiety and listen before being noticed. Peeking around the archway, I could barely contain myself. They were sitting with John, and talking to him.

As I walked in, feeling like an interloper, I asked, "Anyone hungry? Shall I order something?"

Charlotte spoke first. "Just a salad for me."

"Anything," answered Eleanor.

"Not hungry," John muttered.

I called the pizzeria on Seventh Street and ordered enough for six people, which included the security guards.

When the food arrived, all four of us took seats at the kitchen table. John was quiet and somber, but still helped himself to some pasta and half a slice of pizza. He didn't offer up any conversation; and I do believe that Charlotte, Eleanor and I were so delighted to have him with us, we left well enough alone and didn't say a word.

It had been over four years since all four of us sat around this same table. Over time, I tried to pretend that the cause and effect of this family meeting was born not only from the abhorrent act of a monster, but from the will and desire of four people who loved one another, and always will.

And as I sat there, I felt a fool's invincibility, the kind that comes with every dreamer's strained quest for love. For no matter what had happened or will happen to Sofia, no matter what will become of Eleanor and me, no matter what will become of Charlotte and John in the months and years ahead, for a time in that kitchen we were family again, and I never felt more certain that nothing and no one could ever change that.

Then Eleanor's cell phone rang, and she stepped outside.

Mr. Wall Street at least had the good taste to wait until evening to call, see how she was doing, see how John was, and see how things were going with yours truly.

I engaged in small talk with Charlotte, which worked well for me. She was seated in my sight line to Eleanor. Without my asking, Charlotte explained to me where exactly she went that afternoon. She told me she stepped out to have coffee with a girlfriend since my "Goombahs," as she put it, had arrived.

As she spoke, I kept glancing outside. Eleanor had her back to me with her cell phone pressed against her ear. The faint whisper of a smile disappeared on her face the moment she slid open the patio door, and a look of contentment changed to one of concentration and reserved anxiety.

Contentment? Life with me was filled with anything but. There were some *good* years, more like good times. We traveled, went to Broadway shows, had dinner with friends, made love. Then that case would come along—that cause célèbre—and I would get lost—leave home and family, and be entirely unapologetic for it.

You'd think I was an astronaut, selected from thousands of qualified candidates who'd trained their entire life for that special mission that would save mankind. But that wasn't nearly the case. I trained my entire life all right, but to save one special defendant at a time in the belief that the world, in some small but significant way, would also be a better place for it. It was the reason I became a lawyer—the reason I became a criminal lawyer. I just never figured that by losing myself in my work, I would lose my family too.

The ultimate hypocrisy is that after my South Bronx catastrophe of 1982, I swore I would forever leave the practice of criminal defense behind me. Worse, I promised Eleanor I would. The irreconcilable problem for me was this: I failed to realize that denying myself the career I aspired to since grammar school—my ultimate dream of soldiering a client's good cause—being the one with that special talent and ability to prevent a good man or woman from losing that which is most sacred—his or her freedom—was something I was just incapable of turning my back on. And during those cases and trials I was, bar none, constantly on edge, irritable, inconsolable after a bad day in court, and probably the last person on earth anyone would want to be with, no less live with.

When Eleanor sat back down at the kitchen table, she glanced up at me, then down again. I pretended not to notice. Certain that she didn't want anyone inquiring about the boyfriend's call, I didn't, and had no intention of doing so. When I asked if anyone wanted ice cream, I could see the relief on her face.

"I'll have some," she said pleasantly.

"Not me," said Charlotte. "I'm going to bed. Maybe I'll watch a movie in my room first. John, you up for it?"

"I don't think so," John answered blankly.

I prepared a dish of vanilla, then blended a chocolate malted large enough for two, and to my pleasant surprise, John drank half a glass full, and then took a little more from the blender's container.

Eleanor remained for a few minutes, spooning teaspoons of vanilla from her dish, with Charlotte sporadically joining in. Even John helped himself to some of it as well, whereupon his mom reached over, stroked his hair, and gave him a sweet kiss on the cheek.

In the several minutes of ice cream bliss, that I secretly wished would have lasted forever, all four of us just sat there, silently spooning and drinking, none of us feeling the need to do or say anything.

And I imagined for a moment that John had merely lost his pet terrier instead of the great love of his life.

Not wishing to have him catch me looking, I tilted my head down but averted my eyes up, as I carefully watched him take his last sip of malted, while still holding the glass firmly in his hand.

And I was heartbroken, once again.

Several tears were running down his face.

Chapter 21

The Nassau County Medical Examiner is centrally located on the campus of The Nassau University Medical Center in East Meadow, Long Island. Staffed by a team of board-certified forensic pathologists, it is where DNA, toxicological, and all kinds of forensic testing are conducted on those who died suddenly, or in the course of unnatural or suspicious circumstances inside the county lines. Once a body, or the remains of one, becomes subject to criminal investigation, the sanctity of what was once a vessel of life becomes nothing short of a lab specimen, to be probed and cut to bits if need be, in an attempt to get to the God-awful truth that led to his or her ultimate demise. Bones and flesh found in burlap bags in the marshland of Jones Beach fit the bill perfectly.

Lauren was waiting for me when I arrived. She was leaning against a railing that ran up a short flight of stairs outside the building's front doors. Since our goodbye in the diner parking lot, it appeared that she had cleaned up a little, but just a little. Though still in jeans, she had applied some makeup, eyeliner, and a new T-shirt and sweater.

"It's August. What's with the sweater?" I asked.

"It's cold in there," she answered. "Haven't you ever been here before?"

"Here? No. Fact is, I've never been to any Medical Examiner's Office, nor have I ever witnessed an autopsy. That's probably because they often occur before arrest."

Lauren shook her head in disbelief. "Anyway, you ready?"

"I suppose so."

"I don't quite know what to expect or how much they will let us see," Lauren said. "My boyfriend got us in by claiming that you might be able to ID Sofia."

"Jesus Christ, Lauren!"

"I know."

"Let's just hope I keep my breakfast down."

We were standing on the landing outside the building's front doors. Inside, a security guard in full regalia was waiting for us to enter. As we started walking in, I gently gripped Lauren's arm. "Wait, I'm sorry. I'm being inconsiderate. You think—"

"That one of those bags might be my sister?" she asked.

"I'm sorry, but… yes."

She looked toward the building, then back at me. "We'll find out soon enough. My sister's dental records should be arriving in a day or two."

She gestured toward the entrance, and I followed her inside.

After Lauren told the seated guard that we had an appointment with the Medical Examiner, he made a call from a phone on his desk.

A few minutes later, a short, portly man in his late sixties with gray crew cut hair, introduced himself as Dr. Mesa. "Why do I think there's more to this than a near impossible ID from a boyfriend's father?" the doctor asked.

"I don't know, Doctor." I answered. "Why *do* you think there's more to this?"

"Mr. Mannino, have you ever seen the remains of a dead body, even just a week after it's been lying outdoors?"

"No sir, I have not."

"I didn't think so. Unless there are some unusual characteristics, or an item of jewelry, perhaps, that could distinguish the victim, a viewing is not worth losing your lunch over."

"We don't care," Lauren interjected. "Can we please just get on with it, Doctor?"

We followed Dr. Mesa down a long hallway through two sets of double doors that he opened automatically once he slid his ID through what looked like a credit card scanner. Down another long hallway and another swipe, and we were inside the Autopsy Room where the temperature was no higher than fifty degrees. Although the cold didn't bother me, Lauren appeared to be shivering, and she was the one wearing the sweater.

Four burlap bags were sitting crumpled on separate metal tables. But for the bags, and the bones that lay in front of them, the place was spotless. It then occurred to me. Lauren was not shivering from the cold.

"We estimate that these bodies were in the bags anywhere from one week…to two years. The remains on the far table, with some flesh still on it, have probably been outside in the elements for only a week." The doctor spoke plainly and candidly. This wasn't his first foray into flesh and bone.

"Is that the one they found with the jewelry?" I asked.

"Yes it is, and if you can ID it, it would be of great help to us in identifying the remains."

"This piece of jewelry I'm thinking about was distinctive," I answered. "My mother wore something just like it."

"I don't know how squeamish you are," said the doctor. "Dead flesh, or what's left of it, tends to look like rotten baloney; that is, after we wash away the maggots."

As I moved closer, I could see that the tables were stainless steel and their tops were filled with drain holes. Against the wall and behind each table was a connecting sink with an illuminated X-ray board overhead. Each examination area had its own large floor drain, a tureen hanging over it, and a handheld shower hose.

I walked slowly toward the far table, and the closer I got, the greater the stench of rotting flesh. Lauren remained standing on the far side of the room next to the doctor.

"Yes, the crucifix and the chain were found in the burlap bag near the far wall," the doctor confirmed, as I got within a few feet of the table.

And the closer I came, the less I could bear to look, so I didn't.

I had no desire or need to see Sofia, or anyone else for that matter in such a state, and I did not want the nightmares.

"We determined thus far," Dr. Mesa added loudly, "that all the remains are of females under the age of thirty, and all died from strangulation."

"How do you know it was strangulation?" I asked.

"Either the larynx, windpipe or hyoid bone is fractured," answered the doctor. "In these cases, all had hyoid breaks. That's the U-shaped bone in the neck. Only strangulations that are the most violent cause breaks in the hyoid."

I looked back at the doctor. Lauren was still standing next to him, her shoulders hunched, gritting her teeth. She also had tears in her eyes. I turned back around and noticed something gold and shiny on the counter behind the remains. I stepped closer.

"Don't touch anything, please!" shouted the doctor.

"I won't," I responded as I thought to myself, *is he kidding.* Then the chain caught my eye. It was broken, but not pulled apart. The links were not stretched or extended. They were bent and crimped, as if someone was trying to break them apart. And the crucifix that lay next to it wasn't a crucifix at all. There was no Christ affixed, and no INRI encryption. It was just a gold cross, plain and simple, and not what I saw Sofia wearing that day I met her and John for lunch.

I gritted my teeth and looked at what was left of the human being before me. If the outline of bones and flesh (especially around the shoulders and chest) was any indication of size, the remains on the table were of a young woman much larger than I remembered Sofia to be. When John introduced me, the first thing Sofia did was shake my hand. It reminded me of Eleanor's, petite and soft. She then followed up with a kiss to my cheek and a cute shrug of her shoulders.

And as I remained standing in that cold room, gazing down at the empty sockets where a young woman's eyes used to be, and at the shards of dead flesh that were once the soft skin of someone's daughter or sister, all I could feel was complete and utter sorrow. And the more I looked, the more the victim on that table distinguished herself. The head was long, not round like Sofia's, because this wasn't Sofia.

I took a moment as if about to say a prayer, but didn't. I merely whispered, "I'm sorry," then walked back over to Lauren and the doctor. "I can tell that you never went to catechism class, Lauren. That's a cross, not a crucifix with Jesus on it, and for a slew of other reasons, that is not Sofia."

"Are you sure?" asked the doctor.

"I'm positive," I replied. "What do you estimate the height of that young woman to be?"

"Although I could be off a few inches," the doctor answered, "I figure her for about five foot five."

"The Sofia I met was barely five feet. It's not her," I repeated.

"Did *you* want to take a closer look at any of the remains?" The doctor asked Lauren.

Lauren shook her head in an emphatic 'no,' then turned toward me, shivering, her arms folded tightly against her chest, and asked, "If Sofia is not here, then where the hell is she?"

Chapter 22

Alicia Morrison was always tall for her age, which explained why she eas-
ily made the volleyball and basketball teams at her middle school. She was
agile too. A natural athlete, she was overjoyed when both her parents at-
tended her games.

Her mother, a beautician and partner with Alicia's aunt in a beauty par-
lor in Astoria, Queens, where the family lived, was half-African American;
her dad, one hundred percent Irish American. Tall and strong, when he
wrapped his arms around her mother's diminutive stature, it always ap-
peared to be an overt gesture of affection. A ferryboat captain, and recov-
ering alcoholic, he took his ferry five days a week from the port in Long
Island City, Queens, over to Manhattan, and back again. When Alicia was
fifteen, her dad's ferry went aground, killing twelve people waiting by the
rail to debark. He swore he did nothing wrong, that the steering mecha-
nism blew. The incident made the cover of every daily paper, and the Port
Authority suspended him without pay pending an investigation.

A year later, still out of work, and back to drinking daily, he paid
the fare one afternoon and boarded a ferry from the very dock in Long
Island City that was the site of the crash. Midway between Queens and
Manhattan, he jumped off the bow of the boat, hit his head on the hull, and
drowned. Alicia's mother received a five thousand dollar death benefit from
his union, and never saw another penny. This was the second death this
family had to suffer through in Alicia's young life. When she was ten years
old, her four-year old sister died of leukemia.

A few months after her dad's suicide, Alicia dropped out of high school,
and took a job cutting hair in her mother's shop. Then a friend told her that
there were greater opportunities in Manhattan, and she started working in

a small hair salon in the Village. Her roommate was another beautician her age who eventually quit cutting hair because she was making five times as much giving massages in a discreet second-floor location in the busy hub of Union Square, her increased pay the byproduct of tips garnered from giving many of the male clientele a happy ending. When an opening for another masseuse came, she recommended Alicia.

Her pretty face, blue eyes, light caramel skin and long-legged curvy figure made Alicia irresistible to the male clientele. As a result, she quickly graduated from fifty-dollar hand jobs to one hundred dollar blowjobs. At the same time, her mother was struggling unsuccessfully to keep her beauty parlor afloat. Eventually, six months behind in her bills, her mother had to let the business go. The chairs and equipment were auctioned off by the landlord as partial payment for back rent. Evicted from her apartment also, Alicia's mother had no choice but to move into Section 8 Subsidized Housing with her new boyfriend, who collected Social Security Disability due to an alleged scoliosis of his spine. With the minimum wage her mother earned as a cashier in a local supermarket, the two barely made ends meet.

When Alicia was arrested for propositioning an undercover police officer behind the closed curtain of her massage room, she spent the night in jail and was released the next morning after paying a small fine. The owner of the massage parlor, however, was forced to fire her, but that wasn't the worst of it. She had developed a coke problem that she had been feeding with her tip money. Within months, she was meeting men almost every night via Internet ads and Craigslist postings.

When she left her apartment on one hot, humid night in August to meet an anonymous caller who offered her one thousand dollars for an entire night, her roommate warned her not to go. The call was untraceable. It came from a store-bought cell phone with prepaid minutes. He also sounded creepy, but many clients did. To Alicia, his creepiness was merely the result of his nervousness. She had gone on this type of call before. Since she never had a pimp, and refused to pay for any type of security or protection, she had to be extra careful. But this night was different. At the stroke of midnight, she would turn twenty-two. What could possibly go wrong on her birthday? A cool thousand would suit her just fine. She would celebrate by splurging on clothes and cocaine in the morning.

At 11:30 PM, she left her apartment to meet her "one thousand dollar date," and never returned.

As always, she was wearing her deceased little sister's gold chain around her neck, and the cross that dangled from it.

Chapter 23

Upon arriving home, I noticed a new security guard out front. As I got out of the car, he greeted me with a copy of *Newsday* under his arm.

"Mr. Mannino, I'm Craig." I shook his hand, and he handed me the paper.

"Where's Paul?" I asked, "I haven't seen him since you guys first arrived."

"Mr. Tarantino doesn't really work security. He's a private investigator and was probably here because it seemed like an emergency at the time." Craig was in his early thirties, over six feet tall, and an obvious weightlifter with a wide protruding chest under a buttoned-down shirt.

"You got a pen?" I asked.

"Yes I do," he quickly responded.

I wrote down my cell number on one of his business cards, and asked him to give it to Paul. "Please have him call me. I have some new business for him."

Alone in the garage, I looked down at the copy of *Newsday*. Its headline read: BEACH MURDERS, and under it, an aerial color photo of the marsh with four red arrows pointing to the spots where the four burlap bags were found. Three were an equal distance apart, except for the first bag, which was twice as far from the rest. All four, however, were found in the marsh, the same distance from the highway.

Examining the photo, and the precise and deliberate placement of the bags, I could draw but one conclusion: all had been dropped there at the same time.

I fumbled for the house key and opened the door to the center hall. When I stepped into the den, I saw Eleanor in the backyard. She was reading a book with a wide floppy hat on her head to protect her light skin from the sun.

I stuffed the newspaper under the sofa, and went outside.

She was wearing a short frilly skirt and a tight sleeveless pullover. Flip-flops were on the ground next to her bare feet. For a woman who didn't want a speck of her porcelain skin touched by the sunlight, it was a mystery to me why she always chose to sit in its direct path.

With her legs outstretched, her frilly skirt blowing in the breeze off the golf course treated me to a full view of the curvature of her body, especially three-quarters of the way up her thigh. A cartoon artist couldn't have drawn a figure more alluring to me. I bent over the pool, and splashed my face with water.

"A little hot are we?" she asked, matter-of-factly.

A glass of ice water was sitting in the shade under a tiny table next to her. I bent down and picked it up.

"Do you mind?" I asked, as I rose the glass in the air as if to make a toast.

She glanced up at me. "Knock yourself out."

I was hoping the ice water running down my throat and into my stomach would ground me a little.

Eleanor looked up at me and squinted as the sunlight blanketed her face. "The house looks good, and I always liked it back here. The chairs, the tables, the pool, the trees—for more years than I can remember, they were like friends to me—my only friends." She lowered her head and appeared to be looking down at her book again.

"When I get them alone, I'll let them know how much you missed them."

"You do that," she answered.

I was about to say that they missed her too, but she would have read more into it, and correctly so.

"Will you be staying long?" I asked, with apparent sincerity.

She looked up from her book again. "Do you mind sleeping in the guest room, because I don't?" Her tone was direct and wily at the same time.

I had insisted that she sleep in the master bedroom simply because I couldn't bear the thought of her sleeping anywhere else. "I'm glad you're here El, even if I have to sleep in a motel. Besides, you always had a better rapport with John and Charlotte, and right now, John couldn't need you more."

This time Eleanor not only looked up, but turned in her chair toward me. "You haven't changed a bit, you know that? You're glad I'm here for John. Is that the best you can do?"

"You remember Vinny Repolla?" I asked, in a manner meant to add to the conversation, not change it.

"Of course I do." She paused and stared at me accusingly. "What is it Nick? What is it *now* that you're not telling me?"

I sat down in the chair next to her. "A reporter who works for him got me into the Medical Examiner's Autopsy Room earlier today."

"A reporter got you in?"

"Her boyfriend is a Nassau County detective. The pretext was that I might be able to identify Sofia."

Eleanor winced. "I don't know if I have the stomach for this right now."

She put her book aside, leaned forward and hung her head, then thought again "Are you saying they found Sofia's body, or not?"

"No, and I suppose you haven't read today's paper."

"No, I haven't."

"Then you don't know that these four sets of bones were found in burlap bags near Field 6."

"Jones Beach, Field 6?"

"Yes."

She shook her head. "My God, Nick. You just can't let the police handle this, can you?"

"No, I can't, not when my son is involved, and not when…Well, there's more. All of the remains are women, and all four had been strangled."

"And what made you or your reporter friend think that Sofia might be in one of those bags?"

"Lauren, the reporter who got me inside the Autopsy Room, told me that a crucifix was found inside on one of the bags. Tragically, I remembered from our lunch that Sofia also wore a crucifix because my mother wore one just like it. My visit to the Autopsy Room was to see if the same crucifix was in one of the bags. But it wasn't. Fact is, there wasn't a crucifix at all in the bag. It was just a gold cross."

Eleanor stood up and swept her flip-flops aside with her foot. "Wait a minute," she said. "What's the connection to the man who called Sofia's sister and those bags found at the beach? I know it's been a long time since I was a prosecutor, but thinking something is proof doesn't make it so. For all you know those bodies or bags of bones, some of which may have been lying there for months or years, have absolutely nothing to do with the psycho who abducted Sofia."

"Maybe not, but when the DNA and toxicology reports come back, we'll hopefully know who these women are. We'll also know if they match the ID of the prostitutes who have gone missing in the past few years."

"But Sofia is not a prostitute."

"I know that, or at least I know it from what John has said."

"Nick, don't be ridiculous. Our son would not be going out with a prostitute."

"I don't believe it either, but I'll know for certain soon enough. I plan on paying a visit to her family in Queens."

"And what's this reporter's interest in all this, and why did she contact *you*?"

"Eighteen months ago her sister went missing. She also got a call from her sister's cell phone. The voice on the other end was a man's. He said he had her sister, and then said all the horrible things he was going to do before he killed her."

Eleanor turned away. "My God, Nick."

"It gets better, or should I say, worse. Lauren's sister was a prostitute in Manhattan at the time. Lauren told this to me in confidence."

"Jesus, this is all so awful."

Eleanor was a tough and intelligent woman, and I was not surprised in the least when she started grilling me. A graduate of Brown University and

NYU School of Law, she began her legal career in as an Assistant District Attorney in Manhattan in the summer of '79 and held the position until she resigned in the fall of '82. Working closely with victims, witnesses, cops, and detectives, she had a keen understanding of when evidence added up, and when it didn't. Her points were valid.

Regardless, I chose not to tell her about the texting of my license plate number. I knew it was disrespectful and inconsiderate, but I had no gauge on her reaction to it.

With security outside the house 24/7, she knew I wasn't telling her everything because I *never* told her everything. She was smart. She would be careful, and she was one hundred percent correct about the lack of a direct evidentiary link between the burlap bags and Sofia's disappearance.

Any doubt, however, that the remains of the bones found in those bags were victims of the same kidnapper and killer were put to rest later that same evening when Lauren called me.

The killer had contacted her again and from the same cell phone, only this time, he texted only four numbers—three of them spaced evenly apart from left to right, and the fourth twice as far from the other three.

The text read: 6 6 6 6, and it was the exact line configuration of the burlap bags found in the marsh outside Field 6.

Chapter 24

I awoke to a call from Paul Tarantino. We agreed to meet the following morning at his office on Franklin Avenue, just a few blocks away. As for the day at hand, I had other plans.

I needed to know more about Sofia. I needed to pay a visit to Whitestone, Queens. But the closer I got to the Perez's two-story brick Tudor at the corner of 11th Avenue and 157th Street, the less concerned about Sofia I became.

Sculpted bushes and beds of multicolored azaleas bordered a set of heart-shaped inlaid stone stairs that cut deep into a lush green lawn. A Cadillac and Mini Cooper were parked in the driveway facing the cherry mahogany doors of a two-car garage. From the outside, I estimated the home's value at over a million dollars.

After parking the S600 at the curb, I walked up to the front door and rang the bell. A minute later, tumblers began turning on a series of locks, and the door was abruptly pulled open. A small woman, who appeared to be in her early sixties, was standing before me. She was thin, with unkempt grey and brown hair wrapped in a sloppy ponytail behind her head. Bleary-eyed, disheveled, and wearing a robe, she spoke before I got a chance to.

"I'm sorry," she said, with a Hispanic accent. "We can't tell you more than we already did. Please, talk to Detective Ruiz." She apparently took me for police or another reporter.

"Mrs. Perez, I'm John's father."

She immediately swung open the door, and with arms outstretched shrieked, "Ay Dios Mio!"

When I reached for one of her hands, she pulled me into the vestibule and wrapped her arms around me. With her head buried in my chest, she cried hysterically.

Overcome by her grief, and the emotional toll of the last forty-eight hours, I hugged her back, and wept along with her, while in the distance I could hear a trail of footsteps descending a flight of stairs.

A short, stocky, but well-built man came rushing forward. He was red-faced, and to all manner of sight and sound in a state of complete distress. "Sofia! Sofia! No!" In seconds, he was upon us, my upper arm in the vice grip of his strong left hand. Though a blazing fire of grief and rage, when he saw that I was crying too, he loosened his grip, then began screaming at his wife: "Que, Maria? Que?"

Maria Perez put up a hand to quiet her husband.

"Es el papa de John," she said, her voice choking on every syllable.

In an instant, I was in a bear hug so tight that I had to struggle to catch my breath.

A young girl in her early twenties, wearing jeans and a T-shirt, appeared. It was Sofia's sister, also named Maria. She must have heard us, because she was crying also, and fortunately, for everyone concerned, was carrying a box of tissues.

"Why did this happen? Why?" asked Mr. Perez, his red face creased with age lines, nothing short of a caricature of sorrow.

I grimaced sympathetically.

Mrs. Perez then took us both by the hand and gently pulled us into the living room, whereupon she gestured to a large leather recliner, and asked me to sit down. She introduced her husband as Manuel, as the two huddled together on the sofa, a long and narrow coffee table between us.

At first, Manuel seemed to want to say something, but couldn't form the words.

Mrs. Perez spoke first. "Your son—what a fine young man. I love him like the son I never had—so good to my Sofia, so respectful to us." She spoke with such passion and affection I grew teary-eyed once again.

"We all love him," Manuel added. "We are so sorry we have not met you before this; your wife too, though we know you are apart."

"Forgive me," I interrupted. "I didn't tell my wife that I was coming to see you, or she would have come too."

"How is John?" Mrs. Perez tactfully interrupted.

"Better. He is under a good doctor's care. I'm sorry to say that I had no idea how much he loves your daughter."

Mrs. Perez looked at her husband, and started to tear up again.

"The last thing I want to do is upset you further," I said gently, "but I want you to know that tomorrow I'm hiring what I believe to be a very good private investigator to help find who did this—to help find your daughter."

Manuel gestured to his wife. "Maria, get the checkbook."

Mrs. Perez started to get up. "That's not necessary," I said. She sat back down. "I'll take care of it. Please. I'm doing this for my son as much as I'm doing it for Sofia. I will not take your money."

"Mister—" Manuel interjected.

"Please...Call me Nick."

"Nick, I know you and your wife are wealthy."

"I wasn't always," I answered. "I inherited money when I was twenty-eight and my uncle died."

Manuel waved his hand. "You don't have to say. I know who your uncle was."

"That was a long time ago," I said quietly.

Manuel dropped his head and closed his eyes. "I love my daughter, so I did my homework you might say." He then lifted his head up and looked squarely at me. "I didn't have to dig too deep."

"Then you know that's not me."

"We do," said Mrs. Perez emphatically.

"I'm glad to hear that. Now if you don't mind, please tell me more about Sofia, her schedule, especially the day or two before she went missing. I would ask my son, but right now, I don't trust his recollection, and I'm not sure how much he is willing to talk. His mother has a better way with him."

As I expected, Mrs. Perez knew much more than her husband, and thereafter, did most of the talking. She easily summed up the details of John and Sofia's relationship, and as I listened, it saddened me deeply that I was hearing it all for the very first time—the short and romantic story of two young law students who fell in love—a story I thought I had heard once before. But I was wrong.

This one was different.

It began eight months earlier, when John, taking a break from afternoon classes, walked into a Starbucks in Union Square.

On line in front of him was a petite and beautiful young woman. She was reading a book called *Actual Innocence* while waiting to place her order. One of its authors was Barry Scheck, a professor at Cardozo Law, who had also made quite the name for himself as one of the defense attorneys of O. J. Simpson in 1995. Scheck was also one of John's professors, but that's not what John found most interesting.

"It was my Sofia," Mrs. Perez said proudly.

After each got their coffees, John took a seat across from her. When Sofia plopped her books onto the table, John easily recognized them as law school textbooks. He admitted later that before that moment, he just sat there shamelessly staring, awestruck by his instantaneous attraction to this beautiful and obviously intelligent young woman, drinking her coffee, head down in her cell phone, the pink rose petals on its designer cover complementing how lovely she looked.

When Sofia was almost done with her coffee, John knew he had to say something or possibly lose her forever to the City of New York, home to over a half-dozen law schools.

But it was Sofia who spoke first. It was obvious that John was interested, an interest she also later admitted was mutual. She told him that the coffee he bought, and was completely ignoring, "was getting cold." He immediately joined her at her table.

Two hours later, they left Starbucks and went to dinner. One month later, Sofia moved into John's apartment on Greenwich Street in the West Village.

Her parents were not pleased.

Mr. and Mrs. Perez had met John only three times. On each occasion,

John had dinner at their home and could not have been the more respectable suitor. He kissed Mrs. Perez at both hello and goodbye, stood up when she entered the room, and seemed genuinely interested in the life that the Perez family had carved out for themselves in Whitestone, Queens.

The Perezes took an instant liking to him also, but moving in with their daughter was something else entirely. It was their daughter's first serious relationship, and they feared for her emotional well-being. Manuel especially, was not happy with this sudden turn of events in his young daughter's life. Upon hearing the news, he immediately called John over to the house "for a talk." And no sooner did John walk in the door than Manuel pointedly asked him what his intentions were. John didn't hesitate. He looked him squarely in the eyes and answered, "My intention is to spend the rest of my life with her, if she'll have me."

Manuel took pause, but his expression did not waver. He told John that he was not at all happy with his daughter and John moving in together. They only knew each other a month, and whether it is 2009 or not, they "are not married and it is not right." All the while, Sofia was with her mother in the kitchen, emotionally unhinged, and listening.

John called out to her.

Without saying word, she entered the living room and sat down. John didn't waste a second. He told her that he would not disrespect her father, and that as much as he wanted her with him always, the last thing he wanted was to upset her parents.

Manuel, who at one time had six supermarkets and five hundred employees, and ruled his business with a warm heart but iron hand, was speechless.

Sofia then kissed John and said to her parents, "Now you know why I love him so much."

Manuel made Sofia promise to visit every weekend.

Mrs. Perez and Maria helped her pack, and every Sunday, accompanied by John, Sofia kept her promise, and it wasn't long before the Perez family grew an even deeper affection for him—Manuel especially.

Aside from a foray into international futbol, Manuel Perez and I, pervading tragedies notwithstanding, would have gotten along famously as well. He was an avid boxing fan, loved Frank Sinatra, Italian food, and of course, World Cup Soccer.

No doubt that John loved Italian food too (he was raised on it), and heard enough Sinatra growing up (to the chagrin of his mother) to last ten lifetimes. The real surprise, however, was the hours he would spend watching professional boxing with Manuel, while I couldn't get him to sit for more than five minutes and watch a fight with me, even when Mike Tyson was on the card. Had the tragedy of Sofia's disappearance not been looming over me, I would've been consumed by the disappointment of this simple realization: my son seemed happier with Sofia and her family than he ever was with Eleanor and me.

On the morning Sofia went missing, she drove to a local service station in Whitestone. The owner was Peruvian, like her father, and would give her a good deal on a new set of rear brakes. Manuel followed her in his Cadillac, then drove her to CUNY Law afterward. It was August. Sofia was taking summer classes and looking to graduate early. Later that same day, the gas station's owner called her and said he would need more time to get the brakes from the supply house. That evening, Sofia met John for dinner in the Village, and then went back to school to study. She would take a cab back to John's apartment when she was done. According to a classmate, she left the law library at around 10 PM. At 3 AM, her sister, Maria, awoke from a dead sleep by the ring of her cell phone. The caller ID read Sofia. Maria couldn't answer the phone fast enough. When the terrifying call ended, Maria let out a scream, and her parents ran into her room, but by the time they got there, Maria was already on the phone with John. And the nightmare of Sofia's disappearance began.

Once John hung up, he checked his phone to see if Sofia had called. She hadn't. Since he had been battling a bad cold, it was the first time since Sofia moved in that he went to bed without her. When he dialed her number and the call went right to voicemail, he couldn't hit the numbers 911 fast enough.

The police officer on intake said there was nothing he could do. Law student or not, she was only missing a few hours. He also suggested that the call could be a prank, or that Sofia might be at a friend's house, decided to sleep over, but did not want to wake John to tell him.

John believed none of it. He called back Sofia's sister, Maria.

She was crying hysterically, and he could hear in the background that her parents were also. John then got dressed, went to the ATM on the corner, took out a few hundred dollars, and went searching for Sofia. His first stop was the CUNY Law School Library, where a guard on the lobster shift offered to play back the security tapes.

At 10:02 PM exactly, Sofia was spotted on an interior video camera leaving the building. The outside cameras weren't as clear. The nighttime infrared lenses turned everything black and white, and although cars, taxis and other vehicles could be seen coming and going, Sofia was nowhere in sight. It was almost 4:30 AM when John called several of Sofia's girlfriends to ask if they had seen or heard from her, but none had.

Probably because Sofia was a law student, the local police in Queens agreed to get involved after she went missing for only twelve hours, or so John thought. The real reason was that one of the detectives knew Manuel Perez from his supermarket days. Manuel and his employees were always kind to the detective's mother, who had suffered from Alzheimer's several years before her death. The first thing the police did, however, was call John in for questioning, initially at the detective squad in Flushing, Queens, then in downtown Manhattan.

With little sleep, unshaven, disheveled, and battling a cold, John went through a vigorous round of Q & A. He was told that it was routine, that he was not a suspect, and was free to leave at any time. But he answered every question at each grueling interrogation, nonetheless. And when the police were eventually satisfied that John was nothing more than a loving boyfriend who wanted more than anything to find Sofia, they let him go. But it wasn't until two detectives went to John's building and questioned his neighbors about the young couple's relationship, that they finally ruled John out as a suspect.

When I stood up, apologized, and said that I had to leave, all three took on a look of disappointment, but saw me off as warmly as they greeted me.

Manuel Perez was a proud Hispanic man whose every word spoken was an unabashed battle with heartbreak. I would never forget the helplessness in his swollen, bloodshot eyes. When I turned to step down and out the front door, he grabbed me by the arm, but could not form the words.

"Manuel," I said. "I will find Sofia. I promise you."

"I know," he muttered quietly. "I also know that you and your wife have raised a saint in that son of yours." I turned once again to walk away, but he wouldn't let go. "I know he loves my Sofia. I know it not just by the way he treats her, but by the way he treats my wife, my daughter, and me. We all mattered to him, and he made us feel that we mattered to him as much as Sofia. That is how much he loves her, and I love him for that."

I had no words for Manuel. He touched me so deeply and on so many levels, all I could do was utter a weak thank you, and hug him in return.

He then surprised me in an altogether different way with his perceptiveness. He called out to his daughter, "Maria, now go with Mr. Mannino to his car, and tell him anything else he needs to know."

As I walked down the outside stairs leading to the sidewalk, the young Maria followed, but I could still hear Manuel Perez's words: *We all mattered to him…as much as Sofia. That is how much he loves her.* And I asked myself: *In the past twenty-eight years, had I tried, even once, to get in the good graces of Eleanor's family?*

I asked the younger Maria to walk with me.

Maybe it was the new surroundings, or maybe it was just the company of this sweet young girl. All I knew is that I felt pulled away for a time, walking along a street in New York City that had the suburban feel of Long Island with its custom landscaping, bicycles on the lawn, and curbside basketball hoops.

As we approached the far corner it was Maria who spoke first.

"How is John?" she asked tentatively.

"He's distraught," I answered.

"He was in pretty bad shape when he came to see us too," she responded. "You think he would mind if I went to see him?"

"I think he would really appreciate that." I thought about it some more. "Yes, that would be wonderful, Maria."

We were halfway up the block, and I still hadn't asked her about the call. My plan was to get to the corner, then turn around. Not knowing Maria's reaction to my blunt and disturbing questions, I didn't want to be directly in front of her house when I asked them.

"Maria, you heard me mention that I'm going to see a private investigator tomorrow. I plan to tell him to do whatever is necessary to find out what happened to your sister, and bring her back to us."

Maria began to cry.

We stopped under a newly planted maple tree. I couldn't chance her breaking down completely before I could get the information I came for. I asked her right then to tell me everything that the caller had said.

"I don't know if I can repeat it," she said, while choking through tears.

"Please try, Maria. There may be something he told you that will help us find your sister—something, anything."

I felt guilty as all hell as she retold the variety of sexual acts the caller said he would suffer upon Sofia before killing her. It was nothing short of a script from a snuff film.

Tears were streaming down Maria's face, and I told her again that I was sorry, but had to know. Then I asked the cruelest question of all. "Did he say how he was going to kill her?"

With amazing courage, she struggled to relay the manner in which some demonic monster planned to end the beautiful life of the older sister she loved dearly. "He said he was going to strangle her, and watch the life leave her eyes as he did."

Maria finally wiped what remained of the tears on her face, and I felt like a cold and cruel benefactor of pain as I continued to ask my grossly disturbing questions.

"Was there anything else, anything at all that he said, peculiar, horrible or not?"

"Yeah," she replied with a burst of coherence and attitude. "There was this one thing, and I didn't even mention it to the police or this reporter that came to see us."

"A reporter? Was it a young woman by the name of Lauren?"

"That's right. She was very nice. She seemed to really care about what happened to Sofia. That's why I talked to her."

"You're very perceptive," I said. "She does care." We walked further and I waited, hoping Maria would tell me without having to ask again, what it was she failed to mention to the police, but I could wait no longer. "What was it Maria?"

"Well," she thought for a few seconds. "He called Sofia a half-breed, said something like he knows she's a half-breed."

"Isn't Sofia one-hundred percent Hispanic?"

"Yes," she answered. "That's why I didn't understand it. So I said, what are you talking about? And he says that I must be a half-breed too."

"Did he have an accent?"

"He just sounded like some white guy from New York in his late thirties or early forties, something like that."

Maria and I had walked the length of the block again and were standing across the street from her house, looking at each other for conversation that didn't come. Once again, she broke our moment of silence.

"Mr. Mannino?"

"Nick, please."

"Do you think I could go see John tomorrow?"

"Absolutely." After upsetting her with my questions, I would have said yes to anything she asked.

"Sofia told me that you have a beautiful house."

"Sofia was at my house?"

"Once, yes. You were working. John forgot his key, so they just went for a swim then hung out outside. I think they took car service home."

"Damn." I looked away. "Why didn't John call me?"

Maria shrugged. "I don't know. Maybe they wanted to be alone. I didn't spill the beans on them, did I?"

"No, of course not," I said affectionately. "I'm just sorry I didn't get to see Sofia. I met her only once for lunch."

We crossed the street together and drifted toward the driver's side door of the S600.

"Bye," Maria said casually as she began to walk away.

"Bye," I answered, "and thank you." I watched her climb the steps leading to her front door then called out, "I'm going to find her. I promise you."

Maria turned and looked at me sadly.

I could tell she wasn't the least bit convinced.

With the clock ticking mercilessly on Sofia's life, neither was I.

Chapter 25

Hearing the Perezes talk about my son, seeing and feeling their pain—inside me and literally pressed up against my chest—sent my head and heart churning in a mix of compassion and rage. And then there was that challenge again, poking at me, breathing life into this sorry-ass excuse for a husband, father, and lawyer. 2010 or 1982. The main player was still the same, only this time, he was not just "the good lawyer" in search for that elusive innocent man. The characters in August of 2010 were boldly drawn. The line in the sand unmistakable. The victims, not just near to my heart, but inside it, and wallowing in the nothingness of my own despair was not an option. I was racing in real time, and not toward an end, but toward a beginning.

Conscious of the needle rising on the speedometer as I sped along the parkway, I chose wisely to slow it down. I couldn't wait another day or even another minute to speak to Paul Tarantino. I called him and moved our appointment to 2 PM that same afternoon.

"It's not a good time for me, Mr. Mannino, but I'll meet you anyway."

"I have a check written to cash with me for ten thousand dollars," I blurted. "It's a retainer for your services."

"Mr. Mannino, if I can help you, I will. Otherwise I won't take a nickel."

"Don't be such a choir boy. There's at least a few mortgage payments in this for you."

"I don't have a mortgage."

"Well then, give it to your wife and kids. I don't care what you do with it. Now can you help me find my son's girlfriend, or not?"

I was taking giant steps in getting to know Paul, but I was beginning to suspect that he didn't just like being a gun for hire, which is probably why he kept me waiting on an answer.

"I can help you," he said plainly.

When I entered Paul's offices, I wasn't sure if he had just moved in, or moving out. Boxes of files were piled high around the perimeter of each room I passed. Paul's private office was in the corner. In a room adjoining his, an attractive black woman about thirty years old was sitting behind a desktop computer. She seemed deep in thought, her eyes fixed on the screen in front of her. She ignored my entrance.

Paul was sitting in the middle of a U-shaped workstation that suited more a secretary or paralegal. Behind him were two computers. *Power Saving Mode* floated across the center of their screens, indicating a recent shut off. A third computer monitor was facing him. We shook hands as I sat down in a client chair in front of his desk.

"You moving?" I asked.

"No," he answered matter-of-factly. "I've been here for two years."

"Not much of an interior decorator, I see."

"I impress my clients with my results, not my furniture."

"Unlike some lawyers I know," I responded.

"Unlike some lawyers I know too," he chimed in with a smile that erased itself from his face as quickly as it came. "Now tell me, Mr. Mannino, what is it that I can do for you?"

"I'm sorry, Paul, but I need to know something first. Does Sallie Gurrieri have anything to do with this agency?"

"Why?" he asked, with deadpan seriousness.

"He is like an uncle to me, but I don't want any favors. I want results, which I am prepared to pay for."

"No, he doesn't own this agency. I do, and you won't get any favors from me that you haven't paid for. I can assure you of that."

I leaned forward. "Find my son's girlfriend, alive or...dead, and there is a fifty thousand, no, a hundred thousand dollar bonus in it for you, and I'll put that in writing."

"That's not necessary."

"The writing, or the bonus?"

"The writing," he said. "I'll take you on your word regarding the bonus."

"My word is all you need."

"I know. I checked you out, Mr. Mannino," Paul said with a trace of arrogance in his voice.

"Good then, and you can call me Nick," I answered. "And what did you find?"

"More than you can probably remember."

"Oh, I don't know about that. I have a pretty good memory. Wish I didn't, half the time."

Paul looked at me and smiled again, only this time it didn't leave his face as quickly as before. "I found out that you're just about the last guy on earth to be born with a silver spoon in his mouth; that you're a damn good lawyer and have been since you tried your first case as a third-year law student. You also flunked the bar the first time. Since it's common knowledge that you're no dummy, I suspect one handsome young Italian-American law school graduate partied a little too much for his own good."

"How the hell do you know all this?"

Paul ignored my question. Undaunted, he continued to tell me the story of my life with amazing accuracy.

"You started at Bronx Legal Aid as a criminal defense attorney after graduation; won all your trials. After your last one in Bronx Supreme, the complainant killed herself; that was Christmas Eve, 1981. Seems she had this sudden urge after the verdict to skydive out of a courtroom window three stories high. I imagine you didn't take this too well, but scrappy young Legal Aid attorney that you were, instead of quitting afterward, you took on two major publicity cases: defense of the Spider-man rapist, and defense of a teacher's aide accused of molesting his students. To make a long story short, things didn't work out too well for your Spiderman defendant; nothing you did or didn't do. And by the time you're done with the case of your teacher's aide, dead bodies are lining the streets of the city."

"That was twenty-eight years ago. Now how the hell do you know all this? There was no Internet back then. You would have had to pile through hundreds of boxes of dead files and cold cases, most of which I'm sure don't even exist anymore."

Paul continued, unmoved by my anger and attitude. "What's interesting though, is that you probably don't know about a surface print found near the dead body of one of the bad guys back then—the real Spiderman rapist. It was on the outside doorframe of his apartment. Seems there was a real struggle there, but lo and behold, no other prints were found anywhere else: not on the floor, the doorway, the doorknob, or even the doorbell. It was as if someone had wiped the place clean, except for one, that is—the tiny print of an index finger. At first, the police also found nothing, despite having dusted the shit out of the crime scene, but then the detective on the case sent them back. That's when they found the print, a mere six inches from the floor. It appears that a certain someone was on his back holding onto that doorframe for dear life, while struggling not to be pulled into the apartment."

Tarantino paused, then stared straight at me. I can't remember for how long. It was probably just seconds, and I wondered…while he knew how close I was to Sallie Gurrieri, where in hell did he get the balls to confront me like this?

I stared back, and said nothing. He turned away first, then stood and looked out the window beside his desk. I believed he was stalling, waiting for me to react, pretending to preoccupy himself.

Knowing that the only evidence of the twenty-eight-year old murder of a serial killer was a latent fingerprint on a door molding, I wasn't the least bit rattled. There were no witnesses, no other physical evidence, and the dead man was a monster terrorizing the entire city at the time. But for Uncle Rocco and Sallie racing up the stairs to save my life, I too, would have been a goner.

But the question still remained: Why did Paul still see the need to tell me about it?

He turned toward me. "Any questions?"

"Yeah, when are we going to begin talking about finding my son's girlfriend?"

He sat back down behind his desk and leaned toward me. "Nick, I wasn't just wasting my breath telling you things you already knew."

"Please don't put words in my mouth."

"I have a pretty good idea as to what happened in that Bronx hallway in 1982," Paul responded. "That psycho was after your girlfriend, who incidentally you're still married to. Maybe you had a gun. Maybe you had a knife. My money is on the gun. Regardless, he was a monster. You were young and running out of options. The world of violence though was not yours. No surprise then that he got the better of you."

"Let me know when you want to talk about Sofia?"

"Okay, let's talk about Sofia. Let's assume I find Sofia, and let's assume I find the killer too. I can't have you doing something crazy like you did back in the Bronx, especially if you feel justified."

"Sallie told you about the text of my license plate?"

"Yes. Otherwise why would I believe you had a security emergency at your home? I don't do security work. I was doing your Uncle Sallie a favor by showing up."

"I was going to tell you about the plate anyway."

"Nick, you do something crazy, gun or no gun, and I'll be the star witness against you—the one who lead you to the killer. I could even be charged as an accessory. This is Nassau County, Long Island, 2010; not the South Bronx, 1982. The District Attorney is a woman with serious political ambitions."

"I know who the District Attorney is. I tried a case against her."

"I know all about that too," Paul answered. "And you can thank Google for that one. I also know you took the Desmond Lewis case pro bono, and that you paid off the mortgage on his house after he went to jail. Now there again is your problem. You consistently let the cause get the better of you. You're too goddamn emotional. You're a good man. That's obvious to anyone who knows you, but maybe you're just too damn good for your own good."

"Whatever that means."

Paul pointed at me with his arm extended. "You have got to promise me you won't do anything crazy. If I'm going to work with you, and for you, I need you to promise me that."

"I have no problem making a promise to you that I won't do anything crazy."

"And you may have to relocate yourself and your family until this maniac is caught. Texting that reporter your plate number wasn't an invitation to dinner. He's made calls to two of his victim's sisters that we know of, Lauren, and Sofia's sister, Maria. He enjoys passing on the suffering of his victims to their families. Since he has Sofia's cell phone, he must know about John, and that you're his father—the criminal lawyer and rich man on the hill."

"I'm all for relocating my family. As for me, I'm not going anywhere."

Paul rolled his eyes and shook his head. "Listen to me, Nick. By texting your plate number, he's letting you know that *he* knows who you are. He's making a connection, and it isn't a good one. Now we know that this guy's a maniac, so I have no choice but to assume that based on his actions, you and your family are in real danger until he is caught. Now I need you to level with me. Am I going to have to worry about you?"

"No, and am I going to have to worry about you?"

"Listen, about that fingerprint in 1982…"

"When did you speak to Detective Krebs?"

"Yesterday, and how did you know?"

"Phil Krebs was the detective in charge of the Spiderman case in '82. He's a good man too, and the only living being I can think of who would have the information about me and the defendants I represented at that time, not that I'm agreeing that anything you just said is true."

"Krebs *is* a good man," Paul said. "Says you are too. Funny thing is… that fingerprint evidence got lost somehow when the cold case files were moved from the Bronx to a control facility in Manhattan back in '85."

I smiled. "Tell Krebs I said hello."

"I will," Paul said emphatically, then smiled back.

"Now let's get to the matter of Sofia Perez, if you don't mind."

"Yes, let's."

I then proceeded to tell Paul everything I knew about Sofia: her taking up residence with John, all that her parents and sister told me, the library videotape, and even my trip to the Medical Examiner's Autopsy Room. I also told him all I knew about Lauren Callucci, her missing sister, and her detective boyfriend. I speculated, based upon my conversation with Sofia's sister, Maria, that somehow a photo of my car got into Sofia's cell phone when the two paid a visit to Hillcrest Place. I just couldn't figure the 'why' of it.

In response, Paul told me that he would be personally speaking to everyone involved, including my son. He didn't seem interested in talking to Lauren's detective boyfriend. I figured that was because he had his own contacts in the Nassau County Police Department, but I was only half-right. He just didn't trust a cop he didn't know. Coming from a man who had, by my count, four computers on at all times, I thought this was a bit old school, but the more I spoke to Paul Tarantino, the more I came to understand him—the more I realized that I had never met anyone quite like him before.

Tarantino was a rare find.

Also a lawyer, he never practiced law a day in his life. After graduating from Harvard University and Harvard Law, he joined the FBI. Two years later, he was a Secret Service Agent on the President's detail, working at the White House, and guarding George H. W. Bush. Afterward, he served as an agent under Bill Clinton. When Clinton left office, Tarantino spent one year with George Bush, Jr., then resigned from the Secret Service, but continued as an investigative consultant with Homeland Security. In 2007, he opened his own P.I. office, catering to the rich and famous, but not always. He has a fifth degree black belt in karate, and is a certified expert in jujitsu, the art of fencing, and even the art of samurai sword fighting. That he was connected to Packett Security and Sallie Gurrieri (he even had a Packett business card with his name on it) shouldn't have surprised me. He had developed real relationships at all levels of law enforcement, state and federal, and with the mob. Though he gave the appearance, in demeanor and background, to be a by-the-book investigator, nothing could be further from the truth. A fixer of sorts, he could pick any lock, jump any car, even crack a safe if he had to.

It took Paul less than two weeks to find Sofia.

And when he did, she was unrecognizable.

Chapter 26

I continued to sleep in the guest room next to the kitchen, moving more of my clothes into its tiny closet each day. The less I had to gaze down at the bed I had shared with Eleanor, the one she was now sleeping in without me, the better.

Although the evenings at 18 Hillcrest were unpredictable, fearing the answer I would get when Eleanor was absent, I didn't ask why. I tried to convince myself that I had accepted her moving on, but it still hurt too much to talk about, and I didn't want to be lied to either.

When we were all at home though, it was almost like old times. When the kids were younger—in high school and college—our conversations ran the gamut—movies, TV, books, topics the kids were studying in school. During this looming crisis in 2010, when we were all thrown together for John, for each other, and even for Sofia, our table talk took on a more selective nature. Subjects of conversation, however, excluded crime and relationships, and anything Hispanic. John was still in the throes of struggling to cope with the loss of Sofia. This was evident when her sister, Maria, came to visit.

Although John seemed happy to see her, and the two talked by the pool for hours, within minutes after she left, he went up to his room, broke a chair against the wall, and sobbed.

I called Dr. Cassisi. She had a way of calming John down with and without medication.

Eleanor went to sit with him the moment Cassisi left.

As I walked the good doctor to the front door, she made casual conversation, but I could tell there was something else—something she was trying to fit into our informal small talk.

Gina Cassisi had been nothing but caring and attentive to my son, not to mention the repeated house calls, and that she had yet to send me a bill despite my repeated requests for one. But as I looked closer at her expression and demeanor, I could tell there was more—a sadness—a stirred memory she had carefully locked away somewhere.

My mom often said that everyone has a story, and everyone has at least one dark secret. I could tell from talking to Gina Cassisi over the past few weeks, whether it was over coffee and tea (my coffee, her tea) or casually by the pool, that she had gone through a bitter divorce. But it wasn't until that day that I realized there was a greater though less discernible pain she was living with, something that may have explained her overt kindness to my son—a hidden tragedy that spurred her compassion and heightened her sensitivity to the suffering of others.

When Sofia's sister, Maria, called my cell phone two days after her visit with John, I thanked her for her coming, but told her that she needed to give John more time before she visited again. Maria was only nineteen, so it broke my heart to have to ask her, however gently, to stay away. John needed time to heal, get stronger, and move on with his own young life, with or without Sofia in it, if he had to. A brighter and serendipitous consequence of the passage of time, however, was that as each day passed, John was showing gradual signs of improvement.

Then the call came from Paul Tarantino.

He told me that he was picking me up, and not to breathe a word about it to anyone.

I met Paul a block away on the corner of Hillcrest and Tenth Street.

When I got in his car, I insisted he fess up. He calmly refused, took the streets, and headed south. When we got to the Village of Malverne, he turned on to the Southern State Parkway, and headed west.

I asked him again.

"In thirty minutes the mystery will be over," he said. "I don't want you to have any preconceived notions."

When he drove onto the Long Island Expressway also going west, I asked, "So we're going into the city?"

"Nick, you'll just have to trust me, okay?"

Five minutes later, we were in Manhattan and entering a parking lot behind Bellevue Hospital. I was biting my lip hard as we walked through the hospital's entrance doors and headed over to the circular counter of a small information center.

"Is ICU still on the 10th floor?" Paul asked.

A rotund woman in her sixties with a headset on answered him. "Yes it is. Is there a patient you want me to check on? Patients get moved all the time, you know."

"No, ma'am. I'm actually here to see a Dr. Rosenblum. He's expecting me."

"The elevators are on your left," she said in a ho-hum fashion.

I followed Paul across the sprawling lobby.

"Did you know that this is the oldest public hospital in the country?" Paul asked, as we approached the bank of elevators.

"No I didn't," I said at the height of my annoyance. "Is this why I'm here, for a tutorial on Bellevue Hospital? And who is Dr. Rosenblum, and when are you going to tell me why you're taking me to see him?"

A random elevator door opened and we stepped in. We were its only occupants. Paul hit the button marked 10. While looking up at the illuminated strip overhead that announced the floors we were passing, he spoke without taking his eyes off it. "You'll understand why I brought you here in a few minutes. At least, I hope so. Regardless, I have more than one reason for not telling you shit so far."

I shook my head. "You're making less sense the more I listen to you."

When the elevator opened, I followed Paul over to the nearest nurses station behind a pair of glass doors.

"We're here to see Dr. Rosenblum," Paul said to the first nurse he saw.

"Who's the patient?" she asked.

Paul hesitated. "No one in particular, just Dr. Rosenblum please."

The nurse casually bent over the counter. "That's him," she said as she pointed to a short, stocky man in his mid-fifties, hurrying down the hall toward us with a stethoscope dangling from his neck.

"Dr. Rosenblum?" Paul asked.

The doctor stopped in his tracks and instantly displayed a friendly smile.

"This is Nick Mannino." Paul gestured in my direction.

The doctor gave me a warm and considerate handshake. "Mr. Mannino, you seem a bit lost, and I'm sorry for that," he said.

"I'm more than a bit lost, Doctor," I responded.

"Well, we hope that ends soon. Please follow me."

I had no idea who "we" were, but when the doctor turned and walked back in the direction he came, Paul followed, and I followed Paul.

"I haven't the slightest idea what you or anyone else is talking about," I added.

Dr. Rosenblum and Paul looked at each other like two co-conspirators of sorts, which only served to heighten my anxiety.

And as Rosenblum walked, he leaned to the side, an air of determination about him as he seemed to be pushing his short legs to move faster while Paul walked behind him with the gait of an emissary—a middle man—a hired gun—who may now have to bring the sad news to the grieving widow.

As we approached the end of the hall, Rosenblum glanced back at me and bit his lip. He had a gentle yet expedient manner, which made me feel like the reluctant volunteer. "Please follow me, gentlemen," he repeated, without looking back.

We followed the doctor to a large open door. The sign above it read: BURN UNIT.

Four beds, all occupied, were set far apart and paired against opposite walls. A glass enclosure was off to the left, inside of which, three men in white doctor coats sat in front of respective computer stations.

Rosenblum then led us to a bed in the far corner of the room next to a large window where refracted sunlight shone through tinted glass. If you strained your neck, a partial view of a glistening East River was visible, while a wraparound white curtain hid the bed and the person in it.

"Mr. Mannino," he said. "Please let me know if you can identify this patient."

I stared at the wall of white before me and said nothing.

The doctor continued. "She is a young woman who has been badly injured. There are broken vertebrae in her back. Both legs had to be reset. One arm is broken, and the majority of her body is badly burned. We almost lost her twice. She is intubated with a tube down her throat connected to a ventilator to help her breathe. We tried to remove it several times, but she seized up on us. She is in an induced coma until we can safely take out the tube. We plan on doing a temporary tracheotomy so we can remove it permanently, and hopefully get her on the road to consciousness. Found with no identification, her clothes burned off her body, her hands and feet so badly torched, no prints are possible at this time, and I won't allow anyone to even attempt to take them for fear of infection at this delicate stage. She is a Jane Doe to us, unless of course, you can identify her."

"My God," I uttered, and no sooner did I call out to the heavens then Dr. Rosenblum, without any degree of hesitation, yanked open the curtain.

I instantly felt as if all the blood in my body had sunk to my ankles. I had never before seen another human being in such a tragic state, alive or dead.

I glanced at Paul. He was stone-faced.

Except for her right eye, the young woman's head was completely bandaged. There were holes in the bandages for the tubes running into her nose, and a slit where her mouth was for the intubation. She was covered by a sheet and thin blanket but for her hands and feet, which were completely wrapped in white gauze. An overhead pulley system was holding up her legs with the help of connecting chains, while a computer screen on a stand to the right of her head measured her heart rate and blood pressure.

Paul broke the awful silence. "Nick, do you have any idea who this is?"

"Go closer," said the doctor.

I took three steps and was standing next to her upper torso. She was lying in a forty-five degree angle upon two pillows.

The doctor spoke warmly and sadly. "I doubt it is who you're looking for. I'm sorry, Mr. Mannino."

"How do you know? I asked incredulously. "How can anyone tell who this poor girl is in this condition?"

"She wasn't found with any possessions whatsoever," the doctor added. "No pocketbook, nothing, except what's in the drawer, and it too was badly burned along with her."

I stepped over to a night table on wheels next to the young woman's bed, took a breath, and gently pulled open the drawer.

Inside was a crumpled and discolored neck chain. Sections of its links looked as if they had been soldered together. An attached charm of sorts was face down. It too was scorched in parts, as if someone had tried to clean it, but couldn't get all the black off. I picked it up.

It was a crucifix—a cross with the figure of Jesus on it.

"Look on the back," said the doctor. "Look under the light. It's engraved."

I turned the crucifix over. Without reading glasses, I was forced to squint.

Across the vertical stipes of the cross, in tiny letters, it read: TO MM LOVE JM, which I knew all too well to mean: To Mary Mannino-Love, John Mannino.

It was my mother's crucifix.

Chapter 27

Mom always preferred the company of children. Anytime, anywhere, if there was a child around, Mom's face would light up, and a sweet, warm smile would appear in an instant.

But this woman who loved children, had to settle for just one.

When I was ten years old, due to complications dating back to my birth (which came with the help of forceps and after thirty hours of labor), to ensure her continued health and survival, she had a hysterectomy.

The woman who loved children, could have no more.

And so it was no surprise to me that after Eleanor gave birth to Charlotte, though the delivery was without incident, Mom refused to leave her side. Fact is, Charlotte came to us two weeks before her due date, and only two hours after Eleanor entered the hospital.

I had never seen a more beautiful baby. And I had never seen my mother happier.

Two years later, when Eleanor became pregnant with John, Mom became so anxious and excited waiting for him to be born, she wound up losing the twenty-two pounds that Eleanor had gained.

Two days after she attended Charlotte's graduation from NYU's Stern School of Business, Mom collapsed in her backyard while hanging the laundry. She was eighty-three years old.

As a boy growing up in Brooklyn, there was a time in my young life when I believed she was the only person in the world who truly loved me. That may or may not have been true, but what did it matter? It was how this little boy felt, and it scared me more than I could understand. It was the first memory I had of the sinking quicksand of inescapable sadness that would come and go throughout my life.

But when I witnessed the emotional collapse of both John and Charlotte upon hearing of Mom's death, I felt, however peculiar the timing, a glorious sense of pride. This woman, who had not educated herself past the ninth grade, was deeply loved by a young woman who graduated NYU and a young man who would be following in his father's footsteps on his way to Cardozo Law.

As I looked back at Paul Tarantino and Dr. Rosenblum in that hospital room, after deciphering the initials on the crucifix, I felt my mother with me.

A year before she died, she gave Charlotte a box of jewelry; nothing expensive or fashionable, nothing any rich brat would want to wear. But Charlotte, at different times, would don the pieces anyway. What I didn't know until that day was that my mother had also given the crucifix that my stepdad gave her on their first anniversary in 1959, to my son, John. She told him that this way, when she's gone, she will always be with him.

John gave Sofia the crucifix shortly after they moved in together.

After I walked over to Dr. Rosenblum, I grabbed his right hand in mine as if to shake it, but I just held it tight. "Doctor, before I contact her family, and my son, you have to level with me. Is she going to make it?"

Rosenblum took a breath. His expression soured. He spoke sympathetically. "Her burns are severe. The coma was induced or she might have died from seizures. She needs to heal more, and like I said, have a temporary tracheotomy so we can remove the ventilator tube from her throat."

"Is she brain damaged at all?" I asked.

"We don't see any evidence of that," he said, straining to be positive.

"Why does she have all those bandages around her head then?"

"Burns," he said squarely, "and cuts and scrapes, and some stitches high on her forehead."

"But her right eye is covered."

"I'm sorry, but she's going to be blind in that eye. I'm pretty sure of that. She was face down in the street when the EMT guys got to her. I'm amazed that she is still with us." He looked over at Sofia, then back at Paul, then back at me. "It's a miracle, really."

"Face down in the street?" I repeated. I grabbed Paul by the arm. It was rock hard, but I squeezed it anyway. "What kind of an animal does this to a beautiful girl?" I could sense Dr. Rosenblum's discomfort at my burst of emotion.

"I'll leave you two to talk." Rosenblum spoke quickly. "Nice to meet you, Mr. Mannino."

Before I could look back at him, he was gone.

"Nick, listen. It's not what you think." Paul said, as he ushered me over to the waiting room nearby. "Let's sit down, and I'll explain."

Chapter 28

It was windowless, but as large and comfortable as any living room. It had a big screen TV, and a U-shaped sofa. A glass wall to the left of the door separated the waiting room from the hallway. It must have been thick glass, because once inside, not a sound could be heard coming from anywhere else.

"I want the whole truth," I demanded. "Don't leave anything out—whatever nightmarish shit happened to this girl, whatever that crazy fuck did to her, I want to know. I'll then decide what I tell my son and her family."

Paul patted my knee. Despite my temperament, he remained composed. "Nick, I'm going to tell you what I know happened to Sofia, and what I believe happened from piecing together her actions and the actions of others the night she went missing, but first I need to tell you something. The DNA results came back on the bones found in the four burlap bags."

"You're not about to tell me that the person lying in that hospital bed is not Sofia, are you?"

"Of course not. You confirmed that for me after your daughter told me that your mother gave her crucifix to John."

I started to talk when Paul put up his hand. "No," he said. "I didn't tell Charlotte a thing, and I asked her a bunch of innocuous questions so she wouldn't be the wiser. Remember, you gave me Charlotte's cell number when I first showed up at your house."

"It's just that I want to be able to cushion the blow, not only with John, but with Sofia's family too, if I can."

"I can help you with that, if you want me to." Paul's bedside manner was softening.

"Thank you," I answered, then thought again. "So you knew it was Sofia. Then why didn't you tell me during the drive over?"

"All I knew is what Dr. Rosenblum told me: that there was a crucifix. I didn't know about the engravings. Do you know how many young women are wearing crucifixes these days? I needed you to confirm it was the same one your mother gave to John."

"But wait. If the DNA results are in, are you telling me that the bodies in those bags have all been identified?"

"The dates of death range from about three weeks to eighteen months."

"Three weeks?" I muttered. "So then what the hell did happen to Sofia? Paul, I'm losing my fucking mind right now. That maniac called Sofia's sister. He texted Lauren Callucci my plate number. What the fuck is going on?"

"Nick, you hired me for a reason. If this were easy to figure out, you're a bright guy, you would've figured it out already."

"Then you must be a goddamn genius!"

"I just have access to a hell of a lot more information."

"Was Lauren's sister in one of those bags?"

"Yes, the one who's estimated date of death is the earliest—about eighteen months ago."

I dropped my head, which had suddenly become exceedingly heavy. "Without Lauren, I would not have known shit to tell you."

"This brings me to Sofia," Paul said morosely.

"Tell me," I said, incapable of keeping my mouth shut.

Paul continued. "Upon reflection, it seemed to me that the only thing that definitely connected Sofia to the killer was her cell phone."

"Before the bodies were found at the beach, that was the only thing connecting the killer to any of the missing girls," I added.

"Not true," he interjected. "All of the missing girls were prostitutes, who got a call from an unknown person answering an ad on the Internet, and more specifically, on Craigslist."

"So that computer hacker in your office checked Sofia's cell phone records, and she never got such a call. Am I right?"

"Yes." Paul's eyes widened a bit. "But please don't call her a hacker, at least not in public."

"Fine, and Sofia didn't get a call because, of course, she is not a prostitute!" I was shouting without meaning to. "But we knew that."

"Well, let's face it, Nick. No offense to your son, but we weren't positive. Even you weren't sure until you visited her parents. Unfortunately, lots of girls go to college, even law school, and believe it or not, pay for their education by selling themselves."

"You're kidding, right? Lots of girls?"

"Enough, let's leave it at that. The numbers would shock the shit out of you."

"Sofia's family has money," I said.

"I know," Paul answered. "Let's get this out of the way right now. Sofia is not now, nor has she ever been a prostitute."

"Okay then."

"Okay then," Paul repeated, while spreading his hands wide to indicate a change in the direction of conversation. "So then how does our killer get his hands on her cell phone?"

"He abducted her off the street, thinking she's a hooker." I said unconvincingly.

"No," Paul said. "That's not his MO, neither is it his MO to stalk law students outside their law schools. Besides, we know that the plan was for Sofia to take a cab after leaving the CUNY Law Library. That cab was to take her to your son's apartment on Greenwich Street, where the retail stores on the block stay open until eleven. Your son's apartment is above one of the stores."

"Paul, I know this already. Would you please tell me what happened?"

Paul continued. "We know from the law library's video camera that Sofia left at 10:02 PM, so I acted on the logical assumption that at some point thereafter, she got into a taxicab, and that like all cab drivers, hers took the quickest route. This meant the Long Island Expressway to the Brooklyn Queens Expressway, then Adams Street, and then the Brooklyn Bridge. Turns out, I was right, but it's when the cab got off the bridge on Park Place in Manhattan, that all hell broke loose.

"Sometime around 10:15 PM, a young mother was trying to put her baby to sleep by rocking her carriage along the sidewalk there. As eyewitnesses tell it, and as reflected in the police reports, somehow the mother tripped and lost control of the carriage sending it rolling into the street. Sofia's cab driver, probably going too fast, cut his wheel to avoid the carriage, but was unable to avoid jumping the sidewalk and an oil truck coming down West Broadway. There was an explosion and a massive fire. Both drivers were killed. The only reason Sofia is still alive is because she was thrown from the crash. Her bag, purse, books, and whatever else she had, went up in flames. Her cell phone, which I suspect was in her hand at the time, was the first thing to go flying, while at the same time, a prostitute with a drug problem, by the name of Alicia Morrison, was en route to meet our killer. It was her bones and flesh found in the burlap bag with the cross in it that you saw in the Autopsy Room. I also checked with Alicia's roommate, still advertising on Craigslist, and she confirmed that Alicia was en route to meet someone—a route on foot that would take her right past the scene of the accident. Unfortunately, Alicia ran her cell phone battery down on the day before what would have been her birthday, but instead of waiting to charge it, she left without it. After all, our killer had agreed to pay her a thousand for the night, so she didn't want to keep him waiting."

I interrupted. "So what are you saying: that somehow Sofia's cell phone got into the hands of this prostitute?"

"Why does that surprise you? It was a new Blackberry. A hooker with a drug habit found it. Do you think for one second she's going to return it, assuming she knows it's some accident victim's phone, and forgive me here, Nick, it looked like Sofia bought the farm anyway."

"This is crazy," I said.

"You want crazy? Nine years ago, and only five blocks away from this very accident, two hijacked jetliners were flown into the towers of the World Trade Center. If you can accept that kind of crazy, you can accept the fact that a hooker would keep a cell phone she found in the street."

Paul paused for some form of affirmation from me, but I just sat there. He continued. "Alicia Morrison then winds up in the hands of our killer, as does Sofia's phone. Like all prostitutes, Alicia worked under an alias, and did not go out to meet clients with her true ID, or any ID at all. This meant that our killer had a phone he had every reason to believe was his victim's, which contained telephone numbers, and a bunch of photos, including one of your car. Why is there a photo of your car in the phone? When I called to talk to Charlotte, I also asked to speak to John."

"You spoke to my son?"

"He's a lot tougher, and a lot stronger than you may give him credit for. I didn't tell him you hired me. I just told him that I was investigating the case. He was quite forthright if you must know. He told me that one day in July, he and Sofia went to 18 Hillcrest on a whim. He was disappointed that no one was home, and that he hadn't brought a key. He wanted to show Sofia the house where he grew up, but when they couldn't get in, they went for a swim. They didn't exactly mind having the pool to themselves. Your car was in the driveway behind the house and unlocked. So let's just say they took some alone time in the only private place they could find big enough, and let's face it, the back seat of the S600 is as large as a twin bed. Afterward, Sofia joked that they had christened your car, and took a picture of it with her cell phone. To get a laugh out of your son, she made it her wallpaper. Young women do shit like that."

"So let me get this straight," I said. "Sofia is in a coma. Alicia Morrison is killed. Lauren Callucci gets texted my plate number because the killer has Sofia's cell phone that includes a photo of it." I paused to take it all in. "Fuck me, but I still don't get the text of my plate number. What was the point of that?"

"That's the really scary part." Paul said. "Whether he's trying to frighten you, control you, or just flexing his muscles, I can't be sure. Either way, I don't like it. It's a power move with a message. You don't know who he is or where he is, but he has your plate number, the ID of your car, and as a result, sure as hell knows where he can find you."

"I suppose I'll keep my 24/7 security."

"If you want to sleep at night, I would."

"And what about the bodies? Why not just bury them? Why leave them for someone to find?"

"I don't know," said Paul. "If you ask an FBI profiler, every serial killer has some hidden desire to be caught, or in some way acknowledged."

"I guess this is just over my head," I answered.

"How many perp walks have you seen where the accused has a smile on his face? David Berkowitz, the Son of Sam killer, was grinning from ear to ear."

"Yeah, but he was nuts. Wasn't the neighbor's dog talking to him?"

"Hey," Paul responded. "These are just theories, Nick."

I stood up and smacked Paul on the shoulder in thanks. "Let's just find this creature, and when we do if he wants it personal, we'll make it personal. Instead of calling the police, I've got a quote unquote uncle of mine in Brooklyn I would just love to introduce him to."

Chapter 29

There was no record of a taxicab picking up Sofia outside the CUNY Law Library, probably because she had flagged one down and did so outside the line of sight of the school's outdoor security cameras. Busy Jackson Avenue is only a block away, and while taxi drivers in New York City are required to keep a log of their pickup and drop-off locations, not all do. Regardless, any log this driver had was burned in the crash.

Such an accident, the likes of which created a major conflagration on the corner of Park Place and West Broadway in Manhattan, would have made the evening news on a slow or even moderate news night. That night, however, was anything but. It was the night a terrorist, also an American citizen, had placed a rather rudimentary bomb in a van he parked on 45th Street in Times Square. The bomb never detonated, and the perpetrator was quickly apprehended. The incident, however, was the top news story of the day, and made headlines in every morning paper in the country. A car and truck accident, fatalities or not, didn't come close to making the cut.

Meanwhile, Sofia was near death, her identity erased with the loss of her pocketbook, phone, and charred clothing, along with third-degree burns on her hands and feet. But for the crucifix found on the ground beside her body as she lay face down on the asphalt, burned and bloodied, I don't know how I, or anyone, could have possibly identified her. An EMT worker later admitted that he decided to take the crucifix, not because he thought it was Sofia's, but because he thought she was going to die and that she should have Christ with her when she does.

As for finding Sofia, when Paul's assistant checked (i.e., hacked) Sofia's AT&T phone records and found no unidentified calls before 10 PM, it became clear that the killer never contacted Sofia at all. Since Paul figured

Sofia was much too smart to get into a strange unmarked car service, and John confirmed that he did not call one for her, nor did a car service's telephone number appear on her phone records, Paul was left with but one conclusion—Sofia hailed a cab. Paul's assistant then hacked into police department records, while Paul contacted cab companies in Queens and Manhattan about unusual occurrences that night. Then came the report of the terrible accident.

I owed Paul a one hundred thousand dollar bonus, which I was glad to pay, but first I had some delicate but necessary business to attend to.

I had to break the good news that Sofia was still alive to her family, and at the same time prepare them for the near-death condition she was in, and I wanted Paul with me when I did. Though the real monster did not put Sofia in intensive care at Bellevue Hospital, he accomplished what he set out to do nonetheless. He tortured and killed a young woman, then made an innocent family's loss all the greater by terrorizing them with a phone call, and it wasn't the first time. He did the same to Lauren Callucci's sister, and to Lauren, by calling and bragging, only to finalize his messages of terror with the cruelest of epitaphs—that he was watching her sister's body rot.

I thought I had seen enough brutality to fill a lifetime as a young Legal Aid lawyer in the South Bronx of 1982—amid the nation's highest concentration per square mile of the poor, the drug crazed, and a criminal element with more evil proclivities than any decent person could imagine.

Twenty-eight years later, and a monster was on the loose again. This time, on my Long Island and littering my beautiful beaches with the bones and flesh of dead young women—prostitutes—lost girls who will never find their way home again. Field 6, my haven, the place where I would sort through all the cobwebs of my discontent, was a haven no more. A miscreant had made his mark there.

How long before another lost girl would go missing?

As Paul and I exited his car in Whitestone, Queens, the front door to the Perez house opened, and Mrs. Perez appeared. Her arms were crisscrossed and pressed against her chest. Her hands were clutching the collar of her robe. Her face was cloaked in dread. This was a woman in her late fifties, who could have passed for seventy. The gray hair on her head sprung from its roots, and with no makeup, and a deep sadness that had crept into every age line on her face, she wore the toll of her daughter's disappearance like an irreversible malignancy.

Unfortunately, she thought Paul was police, and I some dark messenger, about to deliver the worst possible news.

As we came within a few feet of Mrs. Perez standing in the doorway, I couldn't make the introduction fast enough. "This is Paul Tarantino, the private investigator I hired."

Her morose expression wavered, but only slightly. She forced a weak smile. "Please come in. Nice to meet you, Mr. Tarantino."

They shook hands, and without saying a word, Paul was exceedingly gracious.

Mr. Perez instantly appeared and quickly walked past the living room and into the vestibule to greet us. He had a look of someone bracing for bad news. Mrs. Perez yelled for her daughter, Maria, who was only a few steps behind her father.

We entered the living room together and sat down, Paul and I in respective armchairs, the three Perezes on the sofa, all of us situated around the long coffee table that had several editions of the *Daily News* and *El Diario* on it, along with a portable telephone receiver.

"We found Sofia," I began, more dramatically than I had intended.

Mrs. Perez shouted: "Dios Mio," which I knew by that point meant *My God*!

"She is alive," I continued. "She is at Bellevue Hospital in intensive care."

Both of Mrs. Perez's hands were in tight fists pressed against her face. She immediately began heaving and crying. Her daughter, Maria, forced tissues into her mother's hands, then leaned over and held her tight, while Mr. Perez just sat there staring straight ahead at nothing. He looked like a beaten man.

"She was in a very serious car accident," I added. "Her taxi tried to avoid a baby carriage, flipped over, and hit an oil truck. There was an explosion and a fire. She is badly burned and in a coma."

"Why did I get that call then?" young Maria asked, while crying alongside her mother.

Mrs. Perez yelled back, "Maria, please. She's alive. Nothing else matters."

I spoke gently, as droplets of my own tears fell onto my hand. Until then, I was completely unaware that I too was crying. Mr. Perez handed me a tissue, and I continued. "Sofia was found with no identification whatsoever. We figure that a prostitute going to meet someone, found Sofia's phone, and had it with her when she was kidnapped and murdered, but we don't have to talk about that right now. Just know that Sofia was never abducted." I glanced at Paul, then back at the Perezes. "I spoke to her doctor at Bellevue. It's going to take some time, but Sofia is going to pull through."

Mrs. Perez wailed, "Gracias, Dios Mio," as Mr. Perez put his arm around his wife and pulled her close, while he remained in stoic but painful silence.

However true or not, I hadn't the heart to conclude with anything else. Paul nodded back at me. This family had been through hell. Some hope at this crucial moment in their lives was sorely needed. The helpless, beseeching look on Mrs. Perez's face was more than I could handle another second longer.

"Paul is going to take you to Bellevue now to see her," I said, as I nodded in his direction.

"Let's go," said Mr. Perez, with a renewed resilience as all three got up and headed toward the door, while Paul and I followed. When the Perezes got to the vestibule, all three stopped and turned. After Mrs. Perez ditched her robe for a sweater, she, along with young Maria, gave us firm quick hugs, and hoarsely whispered a thank you. Since I was the last to leave, I just pulled the front door shut and remained on the sidewalk as everyone climbed into Paul's car.

Then Maria called out to me, "Does John know?"

"No, sweetie," I answered. "I'm going to him right now. We'll see you at the hospital."

I watched as the car pulled away then suddenly came to a stop. Mr. Perez, who was sitting up front, turned to Paul and handed him something. Whatever it was, it caused Paul to return the gearshift to park, get out, and walked toward me.

"Any idea how you are going to get home?" he asked.

"Shit," I blurted reflexively.

"Here," Paul said. "Mr. Perez said you can take his caddy." Paul handed me the keys.

I shook my head in acknowledgment of my own absentmindedness, then nodded a thank you to Mr. Perez. He gently waved back.

As I headed home in the Cadillac, I went over in my mind what I was going to say to John. He would be relieved to know that Sofia had not been kidnapped, and God knows what else. I couldn't help but second-guess myself on the wisdom of telling him how grave her condition was. He nearly had two nervous breakdowns already.

John lost Sofia once. I just couldn't bear the thought of how he would react if he lost her all over again.

Chapter 30

Though the day was only half over, the lives of so many good people were forever altered by its revelations. What a shame that I hadn't gotten to know Sofia better before the accident. Maybe then I could have been a greater comfort to my son when the world, as he knew it, exploded around him.

As I drove home, my penance was clear. The only image in my mind of Sofia, and the one I could not shake no matter how hard I tried, was not of her sweet smile at a lunch on a sunny afternoon, but of an unrecognizable young woman in a coma, wrapped in casts and bandages, and holding on to dear life by the grace of God.

I wondered, after my visit to Bellevue with Paul, if the world would ever look the same to me again. But who was I kidding? The world had lost that special luster that brightened the hopes and dreams of this younger and more vulnerable man long before.

On my way home to give John the news, considering the unpredictable way my day was going, I decided that I'd better call ahead.

Eleanor picked up the phone. "John left about an hour ago, said he was going to the beach."

"What for?" I asked.

"He said he needed some closure. I told him I would go with him if he wanted me too, but he insisted on going alone. He took your car."

I could understand the closure part, but I was still worried, and a bit confused. "What was he doing before he left?" I asked.

"He was reading the paper. It's still open on the kitchen table." Eleanor paused, and I could hear her footsteps moving across the floor. "Looks like he was reading an article by your reporter friend. She wrote about the burlap bags that were found and the call she received from the killer after her sister went missing."

"What kind of closure do you think he's looking for?"

"I'm not really sure," she said. "Should I be worried?"

"I think I know where he went," I answered.

I headed for the Meadowbrook Parkway and Jones Beach.

It was a hot August day, much like the past few weeks. The shoulders of the parkway were blurs of coarse brown grass, and the closer I got to the shore and the flattened world of dirt, sand, and marsh that crept with inexorable ease into the bay and the ocean, the more I appreciated the panoramic simplicity of this natural world.

And it looked the same as it did that sunny Saturday morning forty-one years ago, when I crowded into the back seat of the Clancy's VW bug on my way to beach for the very first time.

It was at the start of my first summer in Merrick, Long Island. Mr. Clancy, our next-door neighbor, was a New York City Police Lieutenant. Mrs. Clancy was a middle school teacher. These were kind, God-fearing people who attended the Protestant Reformed Church in nearby Seaford.

I was the kid from Brooklyn, the only child of the mother and stepfather, who nine months earlier had made the great migration to Long Island, fleeing a "changing neighborhood," and as much afraid of where we were going, as where we had left.

Mr. Clancy befriended me instantly.

It was 1969. His son was in first grade, but proud Papa Clancy just couldn't wait to throw the baseball around, so nearly every day that summer, Jim Clancy and I would meet up in his backyard and throw the hardball around until our arms ached.

So when his Mrs. asked me one hot summer morning if I wanted to go to the beach with their family, though a bit embarrassed by the invitation, I accepted.

And while I drove on that same Meadowbrook Parkway on a mission to find my son to break the news to him about Sofia, I secretly wished I was back in that car with the Clancys, the only thing on my mind—anticipating my very first day at the beach.

It was a several mile stretch before I passed the Jones Beach monument and turned into the sprawling parking lot of Field 6.

I picked a spot just a few spaces from my own S600, and walked toward the dune that separated the parkway from the beach.

A yellow police tape, several hundred feet long that repeated the warning DO NOT CROSS, was draped across the marsh. John was standing near the center of the tape, the Atlantic behind him to the south, and Zach's Bay to the north.

As I walked across the parkway, I called out to him.

He didn't answer or move. Wearing a pair of his oldest jeans, his shirt-sleeves rolled up, he was staring out at the bay, a warm wind blowing his hair back.

As I approached, the coarse dry grass crackled noisily under my feet, but he still didn't budge. When I gently repeated his name, he turned toward me and casually asked, "What brings *you* here?"

"Looking for you," I said.

He turned his head back around, and looked out again over the marsh and the bay beyond. "Do you think her spirit is still here?" he asked solemnly.

"No, John, no more than the spirit of anyone, who dies and leaves us, remains where they are found."

"I suppose you're right," he said softly.

"When someone dies, their spirit stays with those they loved," I added.

John turned around to face me. "That's probably why I feel Grandma is always with me." His face then took on a troubled look that was not there before. "But why don't I feel Sofia? Is it because she didn't love me as much as I thought she did?"

"Absolutely not. You don't feel Sofia here because she did not die here. All the bodies found in the burlap bags have been identified. Sofia is not one of them. That's why I came to talk to you."

John looked at me with a gloomy seriousness as I searched for the words to express the startling news that Sofia was found, but struggling to stay alive.

The longer I took to speak, the more infuriated he appeared.

"Sofia is alive, seriously hurt, but alive." I blurted. "A private investigator I hired found her."

In an instant the lapels of my shirt were crumpled inside John's clenched fists as he pulled me forward.

"Where is she?" he shouted. "Dad, please!"

He let go in an instant, and I threw my arms around him. I believe he was crying. When I pulled away, I grabbed him by the arm, and turned him toward the parking lot.

"That's Mr. Perez's Cadillac," he said, while attempting to compose himself.

"Yes," I answered. "I just came from their house. They're probably at the hospital by now. They'll be happy to see you."

As John got into the front passenger seat of the caddy, he asked, "What about *your* car? I drove it here."

"To hell with it. I'll get it later."

As I pulled away, John reached over and put his hand on my forearm. "Are you okay, Dad? I lost my mind there for a second."

"I know." I rolled my head and then my shoulders. "A little bruised I think, but thank God I don't have a bad back. You would've put me in traction."

"I'm sorry, Dad."

"It's alright. I'm fine." I was hurting a hell of a lot more than I let on.

Five minutes later, we drove past the tollbooth, then the Bay Bridge, and we were back on the Meadowbrook Parkway. The last time I was headed in this direction, my despondency nearly sent me colliding with the first concrete overpass I saw.

As I passed under it, John was looking straight ahead, his left hand still on my arm, his right hand gripping the dashboard.

"John?"

He didn't answer me.

"John!"

"Yes."

"Where did you go?"

"Nowhere. I don't know."

"I suppose I understand."

"No," he said. He turned in his seat toward me. "When you get to know Sofia better, then you'll really understand. Dad, she's so smart, and funny, really funny, and so well-read. She can talk to anybody about anything. I'm never bored, not for one second, with her around. She's damn sexy too."

John looked forward and smiled. It was a smile I had never seen on him before. It had a sweet and beautiful serenity to it, and a hope, which seemed limitless.

"John…You need to prepare yourself."

"No, I don't, Dad. However I find her, it will only be temporary. I'll stay with her. I'll take care of her. She will get better."

"But right now—"

"Right now, nothing." He turned toward me again, and spoke sternly. "She will get better. She will be fine. I know it. I feel it."

As we entered the Midtown Tunnel, I introduced the subject once again. "Sofia's parents, and Paul Tarantino, the investigator I hired, will be there, so I have to ask you again. Are you going to be alright?"

"Of course," he answered lightly. "Why wouldn't I be?"

"Well, this is the third or fourth time in the past half hour that you've drifted into a fog on me. First, at the beach—"

"I heard someone calling. I just didn't think it was you."

"You don't know your own father's voice?"

"I thought it was this weird guy who approached me earlier."

"What weird guy?"

"A big dude, about six foot six. At first, I thought he was a cop, but when I saw what he was wearing, I figured he worked at the beach."

"What did he look like?"

"All I know is that he had a big head. I couldn't see his face because he was standing with the sun shining down right behind him."

"Did he say anything?"

"He asked me what I was doing there. I told him that I was just looking out at the bay. He then said that I should be careful not to cross the police tape, which annoyed me. I was tempted to tell him to fuck off, when he asked about your car."

"What?"

"He asked if it was mine, and I asked him right back: *Why, is there a problem?* He said it was a very nice car, then just walked away. I figured him for some bored park employee, so I didn't pay him any mind after that."

"Notice anything else about him?"

"He was really cut, big time."

"What do you mean, cut?"

"Cut, like some muscular juicehead."

"Did you see where he went?"

"I didn't pay much attention to him after that, at least not until I heard a car horn and some guy yelling obscenities. Seems a man walking and dragging a cooler alongside his kids, felt that the big guy was driving much too fast as he passed them, which didn't surprise me at all. You could smell the burnt rubber as he left the parking lot."

"Did you notice what kind of car he was driving?"

"Wasn't in a car at all." John answered casually then added, "He was in one shitty, old, beat-up green van."

Chapter 31

As we parked the car in the lot behind Bellevue, John didn't speak a word.

Upon exiting on the tenth floor, I stopped him. I do believe he thought we were at Sofia's room, because he tried to jostle passed me toward the nearest doorway, but I squared up with him. Though I knew he was anxious to see her, he was surprisingly patient with me. I reached up and took his face in my hands. "Please prepare yourself. Right now, Sofia is at the beginning of what is going to be a long recovery. Her face is covered with bandages. Her legs and arms are in casts. Her feet and hands are burned and bandaged. She is currently in an induced coma and breathing through a tube down her throat."

John's face remained expressionless, but not his eyes. I could see real pain in them.

"Dad, thank you. Really." He put his hand on my shoulder and squeezed. Before I could blink and put my hand on his, he was headed down the hall and checking each doorway for signs of Sofia.

He had already passed her room, when I caught up to him, and motioned him back. I watched as he took a few steps, looked in, and the sight of the Perezes and their daughter, Maria, came into view.

He stood frozen for a second, then hurried toward them. By the time I got to the doorway, he was hugging the crying Perez family, then leaned over Sofia and kissed her repeatedly on the only part of her that wasn't bandaged—her left cheek and eye.

Two nurses and a candy striper appeared next to me in the hall. The candy striper could not hold back her tears as the Perezes huddled next to John, arms around him, gazing down at their daughter. Then John took a seat on the edge of the bed, and whispered repeatedly in Sofia's ear, "I'm here now. I'm here now."

As I looked on and listened, I became emotionally undone. I clasped my hand over my mouth for fear I would gasp aloud. Since I didn't want John or the Perezes seeing me break, I headed down the hall.

Paul Tarantino was sitting inside the waiting room and talking on his cell phone. His attention seemed to be bouncing from the content of the call to the large TV on the wall, where stock prices were running across the bottom of the screen.

I went in and sat down next to him, while attempting to compose myself. I was half paying attention as Paul continued talking to his assistant while repeating, "Seaford and Massapequa" several times. Apparently, Jasmine the computer hacker was continuing to investigate the burlap bag murders. But what surprised me most, was not what I was hearing, but what I was seeing.

Through the glass wall of the waiting room, I watched as Eleanor, Charlotte, and a tall (admittedly handsome) middle-aged man walk quickly by, only to stop suddenly in their tracks. Eleanor seemed to tell Charlotte to go ahead, and then exchange a few words with the man standing next to her before she sped away toward Sofia's room.

As Paul continued talking, I sunk down, as if by doing so I would be less visible. It was Mr. Wall Street. He turned toward the waiting room and looked in. He seemed unsure of where to go. Wearing expensive clothes, shiny dress pants, a button-down shirt, and brown loafers, he seemed to be debating whether or not to enter the room.

Then our eyes locked, and I could tell from every facial nuance and telltale movement that he knew exactly who I was. He was the first to look away and suddenly appeared to be quite uncomfortable in his own skin. He then turned toward the direction of Sofia's room, thought again, and walked back toward the elevators.

When I turned around, Paul was just sitting and staring at me.

"You okay?" he asked.

"I'm fine."

"No, you're not, but you will be."

"Thanks," I answered, though *no thanks* was etched on my face.

"To hell with thanks," he quipped back. "I assume you still want to try and find this killer. Am I right?"

I didn't hesitate. "Before he finds me first."

Chapter 32

I caught Charlotte's attention while Eleanor was talking to the Perezes, who seemed, despite the condition their daughter was in, to be genuinely pleased to meet her. Looking on, I was reminded how kind and decent Eleanor was with strangers, though the Perezes would be strangers no more. I also flashbacked to how fair and honest she was as a young prosecutor in Manhattan; how my love for her was solidified while watching her battle before a courtroom full of New York City Blue to cut a fair deal for a father who was charged with assaulting an undercover officer in a downtown bar. I saw firsthand how his ten-year-old son locked eyes with Eleanor, and melted her heart wearing his own shade of blue—his First Holy Communion suit.

While I spoke to Charlotte, and eyed Eleanor's woeful graciousness to a family grasping on to hope with nothing more than their belief in God, and an unwillingness to accept the worst, it was hard for me to walk away, and leave her with Mr. Wall Street, wherever he may have disappeared to.

I asked Charlotte to extend my apologies to the Perezes for leaving, then watched as the woman who was once my partner in life continued to embrace Sofia's family with a natural grace and genuine humility.

And as I left the hospital with Paul, my sadness at leaving Eleanor in the company of another man was replaced with an ominous foreboding. We were on our way to Field 6 to pick up my car, and Paul was wasting no time relaying to me a clear and callous warning. "It could very well be that this isn't just a serial murderer of four prostitutes." Paul had a hunch that if and when we found this killer, we would uncover a rogue degenerate, who had been doing much more in the dark of night than kidnapping women. "Sure as all hell there are many more dead skeletons than those found at Jones

Beach," he added. "Missing girls are a constant in every big city, foreign and domestic, and finding them is a near impossibility."

As I listened, I could only come to one conclusion: he was trying to prepare me for what may be a long, dangerous, and expensive investigation.

"You were talking on that phone for quite some time," I said. "Considering how fast you found Sofia, can I assume that you already have a lead on who the killer is?"

"I don't have shit yet," Paul said. "But Jasmine is on her computer and working her ass off. There isn't a server that she can't hack, but she has got to do it without being noticed, or we're the ones who'll have to run for our lives."

When we pulled into an empty parking space in the Field 6 lot, Paul took out a page from *Newsday*—a color photo printed in an earlier edition. It was an aerial view of the marsh. Red arrows pointed to the precise location where each bag was found.

"Look," he said. "Each bag of bones was placed the same distance into the marsh from the parkway. Three of them were positioned an even distance left to right from one another. The bag the furthest west was about double the distance from the other three."

"I've got my own theory. What's yours?"

"You tell me first," he countered.

"I saw the same photo. Seems everyone else, including the police, have labeled this area some sort of burial ground. Maybe so, but these bags were placed deep into that marsh, unseen from the shoulder, and just as you pointed out, three of the bags were placed evenly apart and the same distance from the parkway. No way the killer came back on a different day and measured from the exact spot he dropped the last bag. It would have taken too long, and what would be the point of that anyway? The fourth bag in the line of bags, though double the distance from the other three—a red herring if you ask me—is still the same distance into the marsh from the parkway as all the others."

I went on to make my point. "In a call about a year and a half ago to Lauren Callucci that bounced off a cell tower in Massapequa, Long Island, the killer said that he was watching her sister's body rot. But from where? The beach? Standing in the marsh? No way. He would risk being seen. He was watching that body rot in someplace very private, very secluded—his own private horror show haven."

Paul asked me to go on.

And I did.

"I believe all four bodies were dropped in that marsh at the same time, hidden from view in a general area that the killer marked with his own footsteps. Those bodies were placed out of sight, to be found only by someone who knew where to look—who knew how many steps to take from a particular point of origin. Since there was nothing found on the ground that the killer could call a marker, he probably used something else, something innocuous like maybe a particular bush or plant, a parkway sign, an overhead lamp. Once he got his bearings, he knew where to find body number one. The rest was easy, because he made it easy, by placing the bags an even distance from the road."

"Very good, Mr. Mannino," Paul said while smiling slightly. "So what we have here is a very sick bastard, who likes to kidnap young women—prostitutes as far as we know—torture them, rape them, then kill them and keep them for a while."

"Until there's nothing left of them, but their bones," I added. "Then he's still not through. He also wants to be able to visit their remains. He wants power and control over them in life, and in death."

"Maybe he wanted them to be found."

"You mean like getting credit for their kills?"

"Could be?" Paul was looking toward the boardwalk of Field 6 where a young family was walking: a pretty mom in her early thirties, the dad in his Nike shirt and shorts, a little boy about four running ahead, while his younger sister pushed a tiny baby carriage trying to keep up.

"When I was younger I would come here to relax, clear my head, dream about my future," I said sadly. "I've done this since I was old enough to drive. Even after 1982, after I swore to my wife I would never practice criminal law again—a promise I broke less than a year after I made it, I still came. The sand, the ocean, the sky, even the occasional freighter in the distance—it was all together my therapy, my Sunday in the Park, like a visit to a wise old friend. Now that these bodies have been found, all I will ever associate with this beach and this boardwalk is the murder of young women. My oasis—my sanctuary—is gone." I turned to Paul, and brightened my tone, though the melancholy was still there. "You ever just want to pack it in, and head off somewhere?" I looked toward the horizon. "I hear the hills of Tennessee are beautiful. Maybe I'll buy a dozen acres or so there, have my own little land of tranquility, read all the books I've wanted to read but never had the time, listen to the Zac Brown Band, and who knows? Maybe even fall in love again."

Paul continued to stare out the windshield. If he heard a word I had said, he sure wasn't showing it. I wondered if I was making him feel uncomfortable.

I wasn't.

"I often wondered why the hell I stay in New York myself," he stated casually. "Then I'm reminded that it's because of my wife. It's where her family is." He turned toward me. "I figure you weren't easy to live with. Neither am I. Sometimes I find it hard to compromise because of my work, but my wife's a good woman, and when I go home, I need her there. And so here I am, in New York, in a car at the beach with of all people, a criminal defense lawyer, trying to figure out how I'm going to find a serial killer before he kills again."

We chuckled in unison. The jovial moment was short-lived, however.

Paul stuck out his right hand for me to shake, and I complied. "Somebody has got to do it, or we're all fucked," he added with the casual air of a seasoned detective.

"Yeah," I replied. "I just hope we're clever enough not to get killed in the process."

"Oh, we're clever enough," Paul responded. "That still doesn't mean we're not going to get killed."

Chapter 33

In minutes I was on the Wantagh Parkway, headed north. I took the exact route the killer would have taken after he dropped the bodies in the marsh—a drop most likely made in the dead of night. If he was returning to Massapequa or nearby Seaford, this was his route. If he was going anywhere within the three-mile radius of that Massapequa cell tower coming from the beach, this was also his route.

Since his apparent goal was to heighten the anguish in his victims' families, the calls from Times Square, a virtually undetectable location—cameras on every corner, thousands of cell phones in hand—were criminally smart moves. That call from the Massapequa area though was the one time the killer tripped up. Whether it was hubris or simply the product of an uncontrollable urge, when he made that call, he slipped up big time. It placed both the killer, and the body of Lauren's sister, somewhere within the three-mile range of that cell tower. And if he was watching her body rot, it was highly unlikely that he was in transit while doing so. He had to be in a place that was private—where no one else would be entering or leaving.

After I turned east onto the Southern State Parkway, I put all thoughts of the killer's trail behind, and instead, concentrated on where I was going, and what I was going to say when I got there.

I exited on Pinelawn Road, and headed north toward *Newsday* Headquarters in Melville. It was a three-mile drive from the parkway—three miles on a one-lane roadway in each direction, and nothing but burial ground on both sides of me—the large Christian cemetery known as Pinelawn, the Long Island National Cemetery, Saint Charles Cemetery, and a half-dozen Jewish cemeteries.

And as I looked out at the white and gray tombstones that dotted the landscape, it occurred to me, once again: had the killer buried his victims in any one of the fields, forests, and sparsely traveled woodland areas that blanketed the topography of Long Island, not only would he have eliminated any evidence of murder, but also proof of death. Those lost girls would have been nothing more than forgotten names on an endless list of missing persons, and to the world outside of their friends and families, they would have mattered for naught.

But that's not what he did.

After he killed them, he left them in a place where they would eventually be found, decomposed, but ultimately identifiable.

With or without meaning to, he made them matter.

I was on my way to see Lauren. I wanted to be the one to tell her about Sofia before some other reporter picked up the story. It was only right that she should be the one to run with it, and it wouldn't be the first time I sent her boss, Vinny Repolla, a scintillating exclusive.

But Lauren worried me, and on more than one level. When she first called to tell me about missing young women and the text of my plate number, there was a determination in her voice, combined with an undercurrent of understanding. She was the consummate professional at delivering bad news. Then came the meeting in the diner, and that chip on a shoulder bruised from a lifetime of struggling to get out of her own family's way. Lauren was a young woman poked and prodded by the love she had for a mother, father, and sister incapable of living and loving without making a train wreck of their own lives. A beautiful and intelligent young woman, Lauren lived with the emotional scars of a dysfunctional family she loved, but could not save.

Lauren wasn't just investigating and reporting on her sister's killer.

Lauren had her demons.

And I had mine.

All of hers had yet to reveal themselves to me.

All of mine had yet to reveal themselves to anyone.

There were parts of this day, a day that threw me off balance for all its peculiar providence, that I would remember, and gladly so, forever; and there were parts I'd rather forget, but couldn't possibly.

When the teenage receptionist, without hesitation, directed me past a partition wall, I spotted Lauren in a far corner, at one of several dozen L-shaped desks inside a large central office.

Even though she was not expecting me, as I approached she looked up and smiled. Her cordial demeanor was all the message I needed to determine that she had not in fact heard about the forensic reports identifying her sister as one of the bodies found at Jones Beach.

As I got within a few feet of her, I smiled, said hi, and asked if we could talk privately in one of the conference rooms that lined the perimeter of the office. She escorted me into the nearest one whose interior glass blinds were already tightly shut.

As we sat down inside a space comprised of only a round table and four cushioned chairs, I told Lauren that I had one whopper of a story for her morning paper. I decided to save the worst for last.

In a gesture of both propriety and loyalty, she immediately informed me that her Editor-in-Chief, and my very good friend, Vinny Repolla, was in today. I interrupted her, and made my intentions clear: the story that I was about to give her was for her alone to run with.

She quickly left to get a pad and pen, then returned and sat down looking more like a college student than an anxious reporter. I wasted no time telling her about Paul Tarantino, the finding of Sofia, and the lost cell phone explanation for all of it.

"That's just crazy," she responded.

"What's crazy about it?"

"The whole thing. You mean to tell me that Sofia hasn't been identified for weeks. What about dental records?"

"You need an x-ray to compare them to. No one knew who she was, and it's not like fingerprints. Maybe someday there will be a central database for dental records, but unfortunately that day has yet to come. Besides, dental records are like medical records. Every patient has a right of privacy over them. That may change with time, but it's 2010, and post 9-11, and it hasn't yet."

"Let me get this straight," she said bitingly. "The same prostitute who got a Craigslist call found Sofia's phone?"

"That's right. According to her roommate, she left her apartment without her phone because it needed to be charged."

"Wait," Lauren interrupted. "What roommate? You mean you know who the killer's victim was? That means the DNA results are back."

"Yes. I was about to get to that."

Lauren's face turned ashen. "My sister's bones are in one of those bags, aren't they? She was the one whose date of death was a year and a half ago. How long were you going to wait to tell me?"

"I'm very sorry." She stared straight ahead, and stone-faced. I pulled my chair closer, reached across, and took one of her hands in mine. "Are you going to be alright? Can I call someone?"

"My boyfriend is working. There is no one else to call." Her face became red and began to swell. "I'll be alright. At least now we know who the bodies are." Lauren looked like a sad little girl, struggling with goodbye. She turned toward me. "Since Sofia has been found alive, I guess you're out of this now."

"Not on your life." I shot back.

"Really," she said, while looking down at her hands.

"First things first, are you sure you're alright?" I asked.

"I'll be fine. After all, it's been a year-and-a-half since the killer called me. I believed him then. Now I know for sure."

"I can't tell you enough how sorry I am. You can check with the police, and they'll let you know when her remains can be released so you can give your sister a proper burial."

"There's no one who gives a damn, but me, and with my school loans I barely have enough money for cremation. I guess that will have to do."

"Is cremation something you prefer?"

"It's all I can afford," she answered. "Do you have any idea what a cemetery plot costs these days?"

"It doesn't matter." I said. "I'll take care of it. I know how much you want to catch this killer. You burn the bones, and if the police need to do another forensic test for some evidentiary reason, they won't be able to get one."

"I can't let you pay," she shot back. "I barely know you. And why are you being so generous?" There was an accusatory tone in her voice.

"Lauren, just figure me for one selfish prick, who will pay anything to catch some son of a bitch serial killer who has my license plate number. Besides, I have enough money for ten lifetimes. Do you know how I got it?"

Lauren looked at me with an unsuspecting poker face. "Your mob uncle left it to you."

"And do you know how much he left me?"

"No."

"A lot, especially after I sold off all his property. And that was 1983. Let's just say I invested wisely in companies like Walmart and Home Depot. I also still have the AT&T stock he bought for me when I was born. So multiply it all by ten."

"Fuck you," she said matter-of-factly. "You should pay for everybody's funeral." She then placed her face in her hands and started crying.

I grabbed some tissues out of a box on the table, and tried to give them to her, but she swiped them away.

"You at least have some closure now," I said.

This was the second time that day that I had used the word "closure." It was a word I don't think I ever said before. That was probably because I wasn't a true believer in it. Closure implies some finality, and since there is no finality to the deep abiding loss of someone you love, there can never be real closure.

"That's not it," she said emphatically. "It's like some people are just cursed." She was breathing heavily. "And some people are just blessed." She nodded in my direction.

"You can't possibly mean that I am one of the blessed ones?"

"Well, what would you call yourself, with all that money?"

She took her hands off her face and snatched the tissues I was holding.

"Lauren, because of my so-called good lawyering back in 1982, innocent people were murdered, and that's not the half of it. I was a young and an in-over-my-head Legal Aid attorney with two monster cases on my hands. I thought I was one of the good guys. Maybe I was, but a good result sure as hell didn't come." Lauren shrugged her shoulders. "And I live every goddamn day feeling responsible."

"You didn't purposely kill anyone," Lauren said.

"Tell that to my bleeding heart of a conscience. My uncle left me his property because yes, he loved me, and I loved him, but I sure as hell didn't become blessed because of it. I kept every penny of it—money I could have just as easily turned over to charity."

I paused long enough for Lauren to cut in with her own shocking revelation that sunk me the moment I heard it.

"My sister was raped by my father...more than once." Lauren began sobbing again.

"I'm so sorry," I said. I then gave her a paternal hug until her crying trailed off again. "And...?" I asked softly and reluctantly.

"My stepdad. Once, then I ran away. So you see, Nick, my sister and I are damaged goods. Am I right? Isn't that what you would call us?"

My mouth was agape. I spoke sternly. "The only ones damaged, are your father and stepfather."

"Well, tell that to the gynecologist," she said in a dark comedic tone. "My sister couldn't have any children because she had a botched abortion at sixteen. Her insides were all fucked up, and you know what? I'm pretty sure I can't have kids either."

I thought back on my mother's life, back to the time shortly after her own mother passed away. My mom was ten. Rocco was five. "My mother was the second youngest of thirteen children," I said to Lauren, who was sitting quietly, and continuing to struggle with her own composure. "My Uncle Rocco was the youngest. They had an older sister, named Rosa. She died in a mental institution before I was born. You consider me blessed," I said. "Well, if I'm blessed, then so are you. Whether you want to believe it or not, and whether you like it or not, we're the same."

Lauren's eyes filled with inquisition and confusion. "And how is that? You're not making any sense."

I paused for a few seconds to gather my thoughts. "You told me about your sister, and yourself. Now I'll tell you something about my family and myself—something I never told anyone."

Lauren sat with her hands folded on her lap. "My boyfriend doesn't know about me, only about my sister."

I winced with empathy. "That aunt of mine, Rosa, that I started to tell you about—" My voice trailed off in mid-sentence and almost ended in a whisper, as if some ancient ghost had suddenly put its fingers to my lips. I took a breath and continued. "She wasn't insane or mentally ill in the slightest. She was an epileptic in a time when doctors knew so little about the disease. It was in December of 1935, a mere two years after her mother passed away at the age of forty-three, that a local MD signed off on Rosa's involuntary confinement. She was only eighteen, and suffered from what appeared to be bouts of uncontrollable seizures. Other than her epilepsy, she was a normal eighteen-year-old girl, kept home by her father, and sheltered cruelly and unnaturally from the rest of the world. Supposedly, my grandfather believed that Rosa was either crazy or possessed by an evil spirit, and so I relay the lamest of excuses my other aunts gave in way of both explaining and forgiving their father for Rosa's irreversible confinement. But in truth, this wasn't the reason she was sent away. Rosa was sent away to be silenced.

"A patient in a mental facility was deemed by the law of the day to be per se incompetent, whose testimony was likewise inadmissible in a court of law."

"But silenced against whom?" Lauren asked. "Your grandfather?"

"No, though he was just as guilty. It was his sacred firstborn, his oldest son, Jimmy, that he was protecting."

"My God," Lauren uttered under her breath.

"Not that anyone got prosecuted in the 1930s for child abuse of a family member. Once Rosa was out of the picture, and possibly for her own protection, as perverse a solution as that sounds, my Uncle Jimmy then moved on to the only other sister remaining in the home, who was only nine years old at the time."

"You don't mean—"

"Yes." I didn't expect my voice to crack, but despite my mother's passing years earlier, the truth still struck me hard.

"How do you know all this?" Lauren asked gently.

"My mother told me when I was fifteen."

"Your mother told you! But why?"

"My stepdad was arguing with her at the dinner table. I was eating and keeping quiet, until he began bashing Mom's side of the family. I don't recall what I said in their defense. All I remember is that as soon as I uttered a sound, he turned on me. He was angry and blurted no more than a few words, but I got the message. Mom responded by shouting him down until she grew hoarse. He quickly apologized. His paltry excuse: I was old enough to know. I wasn't. The mental image of my mother as a sweet young girl, ravaged throughout her young life, has never left me. And although I felt intensely sorry for her, I'm ashamed to admit it, but I felt worse for myself. As for my uncle, he was given the innocuous label of 'black sheep' by the adult members of the family. I, however, had a different label for him—dead man.

"A few days after I was bludgeoned with the horrible news, my mother sat me down and attempted to explain the nightmare she lived through.

"Life outside of the sexual abuse hadn't been much better for her. Her father was a cold and lonely man after her mother's death. Though she was just a little girl, he kept her home from school and put her to work. She made wine in the basement, and shaped clay pottery in the backyard for resale at outdoor markets. There was no love and affection from anyone, only the sinister bouts of depravity suffered at the hands of her oldest brother from the time she was nine to sometime after her fourteenth birthday. His ominous warning: If she spoke about it to anyone, she would be sent away like Rosa."

"I'm getting us some water," Lauren interrupted, as she jumped out of her chair and left the room. A minute later, she came back with two bottles. I drank mine down in an instant, then continued.

"My Uncle Rocco was five years Mom's junior, much too young at the time to have a clue as to what was going on. When my grandmother passed away, Rocco was only four, and my grandfather delegated his care to my mom, his nine-year-old sister. She fed him, clothed him, lied for him, and took his punishment via my grandfather's barber strap when he misbehaved, which was more often than not.

"I fantasized about killing Jimmy Alonzo a thousand times, but the pleasure was not to be mine. It was during my last year of law school that the degenerate, on his way to the incinerator drop at the end of his sixth floor hallway, was jumped by two teenagers from the projects nearby. The police report indicated that when the teenagers discovered that he had no money on him, they punched and kicked him repeatedly, then tossed him down the stairwell. Whether they intended it or not, when Jimmy Alonzo hit the landing, he broke his neck and died. He was seventy-two years old. He never had any children. He was survived by his first and only wife.

"Shortly after his death, Mom went to visit Rosa at Pilgrim State Psychiatric Institution on Long Island. On limited supervision, Rosa had been designated a field therapy worker, free to roam the grounds during daylight hours. It was also around this time, unbeknownst to Mom, that Rosa was given her discharge papers. Upon discovering this, Mom demanded Rosa's immediate release. But it wasn't the institution that was keeping Rosa confined. It was Rosa herself, and she adamantly refused to go. She continued to live at Pilgrim State until her death in 1964."

After baring my soul to Lauren, a sense of serenity washed over me. I felt as if I had unlocked a vault of demons and set them free to self-destruct in a stronger and better world than the one that created them.

But I couldn't say the same for Lauren. Tears were streaming down her face.

Of all the people in my life I thought I would have told my mother's story to—a story that I had never told anyone—a reporter would have been the last. The only person I ever planned to bare my soul to was my wife and the mother of my children, but although it crossed my mind a thousand times, I could never bring myself to do it.

There were moments I thought I could—before Eleanor and I were married, when we lay next to each other after the passion had quelled, and before all hell broke loose in the life of this wannabe, good lawyer—when I was trying to break away from my reputation as Legal Aid's Dirty Harry—the only lawyer who would unabashedly take on the representation of rapists and child molesters.

Considering my mother's horrific childhood, it was a mystery even to me how, with a conscience that was always questioning every act, word, and tactic, I took on the defense of so many monsters.

I suppose it was one self-effacing and perversely courageous way of proving myself, to no one else, but myself. The emotional baggage of my family's past—the abandonments, my Mafia uncle and Godfather's life of crime, my mother's protracted childhood abuse, was far too heavy a burden for this nascent young lawyer to cope with.

It was my genetic defect, my metabolic disfigurement, my incurable strain of domestic virus, my great shame. Should my irreversible malady be disclosed, I would never be comfortable in my own skin again. I would be no good to myself, no good to anyone, especially someone I loved. I just couldn't risk being wrong about that. This is why I never told Eleanor, which was probably my greatest mistake.

"So… are we both fucked?" Lauren asked.

We were still sitting in that tiny conference room, blinds shut to the world, staring at each other like two crime victims in a midnight therapy session.

"I don't think so," I answered. "We're still here, aren't we? Still ready to fight the good fight."

"I don't know about that," Lauren answered. "My sister's dead, and I also feel somewhat dead inside myself. The good fight? To hell with that. I'll fight any fight I have to if it gets me that motherfucker who killed her."

"Seems to me you answered your own question."

"Which question was that?" she asked.

"Whether we're both fucked."

"So are we?"

"Despite all that's happened to us and those we love, we still have our brains, and we still have our balls."

"So why then do I feel like some lost little child most of the time?" she asked.

"Because we're all lost children."

"Speak for yourself."

"No. I am speaking for both of us. Like I said, we're both the same, and if you ask me again if we're both fucked, my answer will always *be* the same. It's the other guy who's fucked, not us."

As I waited for the elevator, I was still reeling from my meeting with Lauren. She bared her soul, and I bared mine—sacrificing up the most shameful secret about the only person in the world whose loyalty to me never wavered.

Mary Mannino packed away her own bleeding scars—irreparable wounds from a life that should have been filled with dolls, imaginary tea parties, and a puppy to love. She was still a child when she forever lost the warm embrace of her mother's love and was left to the care of a father ill-equipped to be a lone parent. He was a man who fled the poverty of Naples when he was only sixteen by crossing the ocean in the belly of a steam freighter, only to work long hours as a day laborer in the New York City sewer system. He was a man hunkered down in old-world ignorance who was limited by his fears, a man who didn't believe in insurance, schooling, and banks; a man who spent his life suspicious and fearful of that which he didn't understand.

After Mom's sudden and unexpected death, friends and extended family filled the two-day wake—a blur of hugs and kisses, and tears. It was the very first death of someone who mattered to John and Charlotte, and they were stricken by it. They loved her.

As for me, I still choke up at the mere mention of the word "mother." I see an older woman walking, hear Sinatra, or simply watch children playing, and think of her.

Though the tears, in one form or another, will never leave me, they also never serve to cloud my heart or mind—the unwavering sadness accompanied a bequeathed strength and resilience that is far richer than my remaining years.

Chapter 34

My old friend, Vinny Repolla, was all smiles as I entered his corner office, where the windows overlooked the US Military Cemetery and a panoramic view of Western Long Island. When I extended my hand, he pushed it aside and gave me a warm hug.

"So you met Lauren Callucci," he said.

"She's a good kid," I responded. "A fine young woman is more like it. I came here today to tell her about her sister. She was ID'd as one of the victims in the burlap bags found at the beach."

"How did you find that out?"

"I hired a P.I., Paul Tarantino, to help find my son's girlfriend. He got the forensic results before anyone else, and you'll be even more surprised to know that despite the cell phone call, she is not one of the serial killer's victims. Her phone was lost in a horrible car accident."

"Goddamn! Is she okay?"

"She's in a coma at Bellevue, but hanging in there. From what we can figure, the killer's last victim found Sofia's phone in the street."

"That is some story!"

"That's why I came here today, to give it to Lauren, along with the news of her sister, I'm damn sorry to say."

Vinny stood up and turned to look out the large window behind his desk. About a quarter square mile of military tombstones dotted the green landscape. "Maybe I should put somebody else on it." He said pensively.

"No way," I shot back. "No one deserves this more than she does. She's stronger than you think. She'll get it together."

"She'd better," he said with the callous determination of an Editor-in-Chief.

"Hey, come on."

"I know how rough she's had it," he answered with a considerate tone. "I know that she's been on her own since she was a teenager. She's also one of my best reporters, and no one has written more about these missing girls than she has." He turned from the window. "Her boyfriend is a Nassau County detective. He's the one who's been feeding her information on the case, though he's not one of the detectives on it."

"She told me."

Vinny sat back down. He began fiddling with his cell phone. "And this guy, Tarantino, I know about him too. He can be a wildman sometimes, you know."

"How do you mean?"

"He's really not a P.I. in the traditional sense, you might say, of a Mickey Spillane."

"Okay? Now what the hell does that mean?"

"He makes his money primarily as a fixer."

"You mean he gets rich brats, celebrities, and politicians' kids out of trouble with no one the wiser?"

"You got it, and he gets big bucks for it too."

"Well, I'll be paying him big bucks."

"Trust me," Vinny said pointedly. "If he helped you find your son's girlfriend, and whatever else you're going to have him do, it's not for the money."

"What the hell are you talking about? I've hired him, plain and simple, and his team."

"You mean that black chick who sits behind the computer—the hacker?"

"Well...yes, and whoever the hell else he has working for him, and I couldn't give two shits who they are. I hired him to find this fucking killer that's dumping dead bodies on Jones Beach—on my Long Island."

"Can't blame all crime on the South Bronx like in the old days anymore, can you? It's a fucking new world, buddy boy. You better get used to it."

"Hey wiseass, if I recall correctly, you were the cub reporter, still wet behind the ears, covering all the sordid crime there while I was just trying to make the grade as a criminal defense lawyer."

"C'mon, admit it, who knew that over twenty-five years later there would be a serial killer here on Long Island, and singling you out by texting *your* plate number?"

"It's twenty-eight years, and I do owe you a big thank you for Lauren's call. I just wish I could make some sense of the text, but I'm not taking any chances. As far as I'm concerned, he's targeting me and my family, and I'm not waiting around for the police to find him. That's what I've got Tarantino for." I thought more about Lauren. "And this detective boyfriend of hers, has he done anything to find this killer? Does he really care about her?"

Vinny pointed his finger at me. "You've got a soft spot for her, don't you?"

"Yeah, I do, but not like you think." I glanced at the photo on his desk of his new, gorgeous wife, half his age. "The girl's had it rough. We both know that. I just don't want to see her get hurt anymore. Besides, she got some horrible news today."

Vinny spun completely around in his chair. I suspected his thoughts had reached past our conversation. "As for the boyfriend, I can't say much. I only met him twice. Seems to really care about her, and you don't have anything to worry about as far as *her* physical protection is concerned."

"Now, what do you mean?"

"What I mean is…" His face lit up like a little boy's would who's withholding a secret. "I just don't know too many guys who would mess with him."

"Again, what does that mean?"

"Only that the guy is fucking tremendous, that's all."

Chapter 35

He was always conscious of the time, especially when driving.

With the sun slowly setting on the New York City skyline, and his vehicle coasting as silently as a capsule in space along the Long Island Expressway, it occurred to him: what was the rush?

He would park at an off-metered spot near 6th, walk to Times Square, and as usual, set up the meeting for around midnight. Only this time, he wouldn't just wait around. There was a sexy new dance show on Broadway. He'd buy a discount ticket for a seat in the last row, not block anyone's view, and get in the mood.

But first… a drive-by of Trump Tower. Thoughts of the cell phone photo of that hot blonde were sending him reeling again.

Approaching the tollbooth that preceded the drive beneath the East River and through the Midtown Tunnel, he cut into the 'Cash Only' lane—no need to track his whereabouts through an E-Z pass or credit card.

Traffic was moving well past the toll, and after about five minutes, the lights of the city began creeping onto the tunnel walls. He checked the dashboard clock. It was 6:30 PM. He had made good time. He always did.

And as night fell into blackness, but for the startling yet implacable marquees in and around Times Square, that passage from the Bible resurfaced in his mind in the irreverent order of his own making…

There is a time for everything

A time to be born

A time to weep

A time to mourn
A time to search
A time to keep
A time to die
And a time to kill

Chapter 36

"You were right about the bodies," Paul said, while seated beside a large bulletin board covered with photos, notes, ideas, handwritten blurbs, maps of Jones Beach and the Wantagh Parkway. The one line that especially caught my eye simply read: *THE BAGS*.

I placed two envelopes, one large and one small, on the desk between us. The large one had his bonus in it of one hundred thousand dollars cash for finding Sofia. Inside the smaller envelope was a check. It was also for another one hundred thousand, payment in advance toward fees and expenses for hunting down the serial killer of Lauren's sister, the three other prostitutes, and God knows how many others.

Paul ignored both envelopes as he spoke. This didn't surprise me. Maybe Vinny was right, and Paul didn't care about the money, or maybe he just didn't want to show that he did. But to risk his life to find a diabolical serial killer?

I had to check Paul out myself.

A quick title search disclosed that he lived in a two-million dollar house in Old Brookville on the North Shore. He told the truth when he said that he had no mortgage. I then contacted Sallie Gurrieri. I'm ashamed to admit it, but I always made a point of calling him Uncle Sallie when I needed something. Consequently, he turned out to be one great source of information on Paul Tarantino.

According to Sallie, Paul had enough filthy-rich clients with problems galore to fill several lifetimes. Tarantino did not need my money.

"Nick!" Paul blurted.

I was lost in thought, and apparently hadn't heard a single word he said. "I'm sorry, could you repeat that."

"Where'd you go?" he asked.

"Yesterday was one hell of a day. After I went back and forth to Bellevue, I ended up paying Lauren Callucci a visit."

"The reporter?"

"Yes. I didn't want her finding out about her sister from someone else."

"How'd she take it?"

"She's a strong girl. She'll be okay."

"Okay then. Now did you hear anything at all that I said?"

"Something about me being right about the bodies."

"Yes, about the bodies being dropped in the marsh at the same time. It occurred to me that the answer to that didn't lie just in the placement of the bags, or in the forensic analysis of the bodies, but in the bags themselves."

"You mean the wear and deterioration was the same for all of them?"

"Correct."

"Which means the bags were sitting there for the same period of time."

"Correct again."

"But how do you know the precise stage of deterioration for each bag?"

"The Police Lab," Paul said casually.

"You mean to tell me they just gave you whatever information you wanted?"

"We have an understanding. A *quid pro quo* you might say. Does that surprise you?"

"No, not where you're concerned, it doesn't. Now are you going to take those envelopes on your desk, or should I take them back?"

Paul picked up the larger one, and peeked inside. "I can use this cash in our investigation."

"Just put it on my bill," I answered.

"If I have to, I will." He smiled slightly back at me.

I gestured to the large bulletin board. "Some display you got there." I stood up and walked over to the photo of what appeared to be four bodies wrapped in plastic lying by a ravine abutting an area of marshland similar to the one near Field 6. "What is this?" I asked.

"I'm not sure they're related," Paul answered. "Two years ago, these bodies were found alongside a culvert behind a motel just outside Atlantic City. As you can see, all the bodies are wrapped in plastic not burlap. They were placed on the ground, close together, all the heads facing Atlantic City a few miles away."

"Are they all women?"

"Yes."

"Were they prostitutes?"

"Yes."

"And I suppose if the bodies were facing Atlantic City, they were also facing the Atlantic Ocean."

Paul took a moment. "That's right, for whatever that means."

"I assume these women were murdered?"

"Strangled," Paul said. "Just like the victims found on Jones Beach."

"But I don't want us going on a wild goose chase in New Jersey, especially when I firmly believe our killer is still here on Long Island."

"And what makes you believe that?" Paul asked, masking his tone so I couldn't tell if he thought I was right or wrong.

"The call to Lauren eighteen months ago that bounced off of the Massapequa cell tower. All the other calls came from Times Square, and with the thousands of people walking around there with cell phones, our killer might as well have been invisible. That call from Long Island though, that was his slip-up."

Paul stood up and walked over to the map of Jones Beach and the Wantagh Parkway. He stared at it as he spoke. "So you figure our killer lives somewhere within the three mile radius of that tower?"

"Lives or works, yes."

Paul went back to his desk, picked up the two envelopes, including the one with the one hundred thousand dollar check in it, and placed them in his briefcase. After he closed it, he spun the combination dials near the clasps, all the while appearing to be thinking about something else. He then sat back down, looked up at the ceiling, and asked pensively, "What about that half-breed remark he made to Sofia's sister? The real victim of his last kill, according to the medical examiner, *was* bi-racial, but I can't figure out why the killer would use the term half-breed."

"That's because you're thinking about someone who's half Native American and half Caucasian, but it's also an old Italian reference used when referring to a child born from a marriage between someone from the north of Italy and someone from the south."

"Shit. Now that you mention it, I believe I heard my grandfather say half-breed once, and he sure as hell wasn't referring to someone half Native American."

"I'm sure you're aware that Massapequa, Long Island, has a huge Italian-American population—about twenty-five percent of the families who live there."

"I'm aware."

"So then you're also aware that we may just be going after one of our own."

"That's right, `paisan'."

I looked over at Jasmine in the next office. She was fixated on her computer screen, and typing on her keyboard with such ferocity it appeared she was on a mission to destroy it. I nodded as she glanced over. She didn't nod back. I turned to Paul. "She come up with anything yet?"

"No, and she's going to be a real bitch on wheels until she does."

"What exactly is she working on now?"

"Cell phone records. The killer called the prostitutes from store-bought cell phones."

"I know, so?"

"Well, here's the thing." I saw a spark light in Paul's eye. "She's looking to crack into the cell phone records of Lauren's sister, and Sofia. There's a chance our killer might have made other calls from those same phones."

I huffed. "Now there's a long shot for you."

"Yes, I know. We all believe he is too smart for that, but we're also looking into where he bought his own cell phones, the ones he used to call the prostitutes to begin with."

"Security cameras?"

"Forget it. They get erased and taped over from every twenty-four hours to every thirty days. The locations he bought them from, however, may tell us something about where he lives or works, or provide some connection to him."

I shook my head and shrugged my shoulders. "This is going to be really tough."

Paul laughed. "No kidding."

"Why haven't the cops done what we're doing?"

"They could have, if they were as committed as we are, which they aren't. They also don't have a Jasmine, and let's face it, they've got a lot of other serious matters to deal with. Besides, even though this case got a lot of press, the victims are still hookers. I guarantee you, if Sofia, God forbid, was one of the bodies in those bags, this case would be taking on a whole new energy as far as the police are concerned. But as far as I'm concerned, let the cops move on to something else. They'll only be in my way, and if I want to know what they've got, I can find out easily enough."

"There's something I should tell you," I interjected. "I'm not sure if it means anything, but yesterday when I found John at the beach near the marsh where the bodies were discovered, he told me that a man approached him asking some bullshit questions about why John was there. John couldn't see his face clearly, because the sun was in his eyes, but he did say that he was a really big guy. Only it's what he saw the guy driving that made me think a hell of a lot more about it."

"What was that?"

"Well, the same day I found out Sofia went missing, I had come home from the beach, Field 6 to be exact. While I was speeding along the Meadowbrook Parkway, without thinking, I veered off onto Merrick Road. When I did, I saw this van pass me, ever so slowly, as if spying on me."

"Why did you pull over?"

"No reason really. I just wasn't feeling good."

"Good thing you're not using that explanation as an alibi." Paul was clever enough to know that I wasn't telling him the whole truth.

"When I asked John if he thought that the man who approached him worked at the beach, he said he didn't think so because he saw him drive off, and not in a Parks Department truck, but in a shitty old green van, which is exactly what I saw pass me on Merrick Road after I pulled over."

Paul stood up. "You've got to be joking. Well, fuck me!" He threw his arms in the air and I couldn't tell if he was serious or kidding. He then walked over to a large white pad on an easel. I could see the indentations made on the blank page from the writing on the page before it. "I suppose Lauren didn't tell you." He turned dead serious.

"Tell me what?"

"There was another text today. Jasmine retrieved it off Lauren's phone. It came from another convenience store cell phone. At first, I didn't know what the hell it meant. It was one word—*vengaren*. Since I know this guy likes to taunt with cryptic messages, I figured that it was an anagram for something, so I play around with the letters for a while, but didn't get anywhere. Then I googled the word and discovered that it wasn't even English. It's some kind of colloquial Spanish word, and to make matters even more baffling, when translated to English it means—to avenge. Now you tell me about a van your son saw leave Field 6 and that it is the same type of van that you saw drive by you after *you* left Field 6."

Paul then flipped back a large white page that he had thrown over the easel after he jotted down all possible anagrams for *vengaren*. On it were various combinations of letters scribbled in different directions, and all had lines running through them, except two. One combination was circled. One wasn't. The one that wasn't read: *never nag*. Paul then pointed to the second set of circled words just as quickly as my eyes fell upon them.

In bold black letters, he had drawn a line around the only anagram solution that made any sense to him—*Green van*.

Chapter 37

John didn't come home, but that was the least of my concerns. I knew where he was.

He never left Sofia's side.

It was close to dinnertime the following day when I arrived at Bellevue, the significance of the anagram still weighing on me. The text of my license plate, two sightings of an old green van, and the *vengaren* text, could no longer be the product of one cynical criminal lawyer's paranoia.

Then my son gets approached by a goliath.

This deranged killer was getting closer.

When I entered one of the lobby elevators, and pushed the tenth floor button harder than I meant to, a wall of fear enveloped me, and a crystal-clear image of my mother's abuse flashed like an illuminated billboard in my head, along with a vision of my own children's dead bodies floating in the marsh beside four burlap bags stuffed with bones. My stomach was empty, and I reflexively started to feel nauseous and faint like that fifteen-year-old boy I once was who first heard the horrific truth about his family, his mother, and the only world he knew.

I held onto the handrail that curled around the elevator walls, while un-beknownst to me, John was waiting outside on the 10th floor. As the doors opened, he found me on one knee struggling to catch my breath.

He thought I was having a heart attack, and screamed for a doctor.

I wasn't.

I was simply overcome with a sudden debilitating sickness of the mind that left me struggling to catch my breath.

The Perezes ran over. Then a nurse, hearing the commotion, issued a Level II Emergency.

Within minutes, a staff of interns and residents swarmed around me pushing a laptop on wheels and a cart of medication. I must have shrieked, "I'm fine," over a dozen times. "It's just that I haven't eaten," I repeated, until finally Mr. Perez believed me, and warded off all comers successfully. He then escorted me down the hall and into the secluded waiting room, but not before sending his daughter to the cafeteria with instructions to get me something to eat and fast.

As I became more convincing in my protestations that I was fine, I finally got John to leave. I told him that Sofia needed him a whole lot more than I did, which was an easy call, because I didn't need him at all. Mr. Perez, however, refused to budge.

With his daughter in a coma, he was helpless to the doctors and the nurses and hospital staff attempting, on a minute-by-minute basis, to save his sweet Sofia's life. I do believe it comforted him to be of some use to me, and the more I got to know the Perez family, the more I cared for and admired them. I also understood Mr. Perez's feelings of inadequacy. I had felt them before, and depending on the time and circumstance, on many different levels.

I threw my arm around Sofia's dad, and gave him a quick brotherly hug. "Mr. Perez—"

"Call me Manuel, or I cannot talk to you."

I smiled. "Manuel, how do you say vengeance in Spanish?"

He looked at me curiously. "I hope you are not going to do something foolish."

"Not at all," I answered. "It's just that I heard a Hispanic police officer say this word, and I was wondering what it meant."

"What was the word?" he asked.

"*Vengaren*," I said louder than I meant to.

"*Vengaren*," he repeated. "Not a word that is used much at all. I can't say I ever heard someone speak it. I may have seen it written. Vengeance is *venganza* in Spanish. Avenge is *vengar*. I believe *vengaren* may be Castilian Spanish and used depending on the mood of the speaker, but not a common word at all."

"Really?"

"Yes. I can't imagine why someone would use it while speaking Spanish today."

I can, I thought to myself. If the killer was trying to explain away his actions, while at the same time delivering a teaser as to his identity in an anagram, he found the right word to do it. Of course, this only raised more questions. Did the killer feel justified? Were the killings some act of revenge, and if so, for what? And why tip us off to the green van at all? I began to wonder how much the killer really knew about me. Did he want me to be afraid? Was he taunting me to come after him?

I would gladly comply, but the more I thought about the killer—his actions and messages, the more convinced I became—I had to get to him, before he got to me first, and worse, my family.

Chapter 38

Maria returned with a platter of cafeteria lasagna and a cup of coffee. I must have been famished because all it took was a spoonful of parmesan cheese, and the lasagna was delicious. The coffee was another story, though I devoured both in a few minutes, while Manuel looked on. Considering that Sofia had yet to show any signs of recovery, it was a credit to Manuel's strength and fortitude that he was at my side and holding up so well. Oddly, I figured my false-alarm heart attack was a welcome distraction.

I spent the next hour sitting with John and the Perez family by Sofia's bedside. A few minutes into the visit, and I noticed that Sofia's eyelids had begun to flutter. Convulsions followed. I yelled for a nurse, but there was nothing that could be done except comfort her until the jerking and tremors had passed, which is exactly what John did by stroking her hair and rubbing her shoulder.

"How often does this happen?" I asked.

"Several times a day," John answered. "The doctors believe it's because of her burns. They're slow to heal and her body is reacting to it, but I think it's a good sign. It's proof that she is alive, and the tremors are part of the overall healing."

I had no idea what John was talking about, and was fairly certain he didn't either. I figured he was speaking on faith. And why not? As I took a closer look at Sofia, I noticed my mother's crucifix around her neck. Thus far, faith was all John and the Perez family had to hold on to, but since Sofia was again wearing Mom's crucifix, even I believed her odds of recovery had gotten a whole lot better.

Before I left the hospital, I asked John to step into the waiting room so we could talk in private. When he did, he refused to sit down on the couch, and insisted on standing near the door so he could see down the hallway and outside Sofia's room. I asked him how he was doing.

"I'm fine, Dad. Don't worry about me."

"Where are you sleeping?"

"In the recliner chair in Sofia's room. I leave only to go to my apartment and clean up, then I come right back. With those burns, I want to make sure everything in her room is sanitary, including me. I also try not to kiss her too much."

Color had returned to John's face. He had also shaved, and appeared to be doing so regularly. *My boy is so damn handsome*, I thought to myself.

"I love you, you know that?" I said, my hand under his chin, and my face just inches from his.

"I know you spent a lot of money finding her, Dad. I know you did that for me."

"To hell with the money. I did it for me too. I couldn't bear to see you in such a state."

"I'm lucky to have you. So is Sofia."

"I'm luckier to have you. Any chance I can get you home any time soon?"

"A good chance," he answered with a smile. "When I can come with Sofia."

I grimaced at the harsh realization of her condition, a grimace I didn't hide from my son.

"It may just be good for you to have a little change of scenery, that's all," I added. "You could rest a bit, and then come right back."

He gave me a long tight hug, then kissed my cheek and whispered in my ear. "When I can come with Sofia, you will see me there."

During the drive home from the hospital, I kept mulling over the apparent dichotomy in personalities between the horrendous calls made by the killer and the cryptic text messages.

When I sat down with Paul the following afternoon, I expected a litany of: *What do you expect from a psychopath? He's crazy. He's evil. Live with it.*

I was only half right. Paul had much more to say. After all, the coded and taunting text messages *were* consistent with someone who, instead of burying his victims where they could never be found, leaves their bones in bags alongside a highly trafficked roadway near a popular stretch of beach.

Or perhaps the killer was much smarter than we figured, his calls and texts mere distractions in a greater and more diabolical scheme than we could have ever foreseen.

The next day I had Paul place a 24-hour guard outside Sofia's hospital room. I wasn't taking any chances.

Chapter 39

The next morning, Paul and I were supposed to meet for a follow-up, but he put me off for a day. He called my cell phone and woke me at exactly 9 AM, said Jasmine was working on cracking some computer bank of information, and he wanted a little more time to lay out an investigative strategy. When I questioned him further about Jasmine's hacking exploits, he double-talked me with words like algorithms and encryptions, until I stopped him cold.

"Just give me the facts," I pleaded.

He said he would do just that, but again, on the following day. I responded with a conciliatory, "okay." Maybe a normal twenty-four hours away from prophesying over serial killers would do me some good.

A few minutes later, my cell phone rang again. It was my next-door neighbor, Harlan. He must have finished his latest thriller, because the classical and sometimes creepy overtures emanating from his rear porch and writing room had ceased more than a week before.

"Tonight I'm cooking your favorite," he announced. "Veal Dario."

"You've got to be Dario to cook Veal Dario," I snapped back.

"I've got the fontina cheese and I've been pounding the shit out of this veal for hours. Now, you coming to dinner?"

"I suppose, but the veal better be up to par."

"Oh, don't you worry, but listen there's a catch."

"Forget it then."

"You need to bring a date. My girlfriend insists on it. Bring your ex-wife if you want. Just bring somebody, or she'll have my balls. Should I have Esther call a friend?"

"Not on your life. I'll get my own date, thank you."

"See you at seven then, and don't be late."

I hung up and called Gina Cassisi. I had not received a bill from her and used that as an icebreaking pretext.

"We're practically neighbors," she responded, and then told me that she had no intention of sending me one.

"Then join me for dinner at Harlan Dugan's."

"Wow. You know him?"

"He's my next-door neighbor."

"I had no idea. That sounds nice."

"But it's tonight. Can you get a sitter?"

"My daughter is a senior in high school. She can watch my little one for me. She's always telling me I should get out more."

"Great then, and by the way, I should warn you, this son of a gun next door is one heck of a great cook, but an even bigger treat though, is his house. He can't spend his money fast enough. It makes mine look like servants' quarters."

"Don't be silly. You have a beautiful home."

"Thank you. I bought it for—" I caught myself. I was about to say, *I bought it for my wife*. Landing on my feet, or so I thought, I quickly uttered, "I bought it for a song a long time ago."

I do believe Gina picked up on my *faux pas*, but she was too classy a lady to let on. "What time should I be there?" she asked.

"Be there? Gina, you're my date. I'll pick you up, if that's okay? How's 6:30?"

"See you then."

I hadn't had a conversation like this with a woman in over thirty years. The last time was with a twenty-four-year-old Eleanor, but she was always so quick-witted, I rarely had to finish my sentences. She finished them for me. We often laughed about it afterwards, and if we were alone, our laughter would invariably turn into lovemaking.

Gina was different though. She was far more predictable. She was the kind of woman I always felt that I was expected to be with, at least where my friends, family, and more emphatically, my mother, were concerned.

With a light olive complexion, deep brown eyes, soft brown hair, and full lips, she was nothing short of an Italian-American beauty. A doctor to boot, Mom would have been delighted had I married a girl like Gina.

In some strange way, considering all else that was transpiring in my life at the time, I was looking forward to my evening at Harlan's. No doubt, come the following day, Paul was prepared to hit the ground running, and I knew it was in his mantra to come on hard and fast, which suited me just fine. Besides, it was what high-priced fixers had to do.

Paul worked with a small but efficient crew. Its size was commensurate with the clandestine nature of his work. Since yours truly, in word and action, accompanied my money, come the following day, I was prepared to enter hell with him if I had to.

Before entering the fray though, I first had to get through an evening at Harlan Dugan's and my first date in almost twenty-eight years. Since it was just past noon, I would use the remainder of the day wisely. If I was going headlong into the pursuit of a monster, I wanted my family gone from house and hill while doing so. Since the killer knew who I was, he sure as hell knew where I lived.

John wasn't a concern. He made it clear that he wasn't coming back home without Sofia, and sadly, from the state of her immediate health, that wouldn't be any time soon. I sought comfort in the fact that he slept every night in her room, and now with a 24-hour guard to boot.

I called Charlotte and lied. I told her I was letting the security guards go and didn't want her around the house without them, and although it hurt to hear her scared and uncomfortable, it got me the result I wanted. She agreed to stay at her apartment in the Trump Tower. With Saudi princes, celebrities, and The Donald in residence, I had no reason to worry. The security there was airtight.

"But Dad, what about you?"

"Don't worry about me. I'm closing my office for a while and staying at a friend's house in the Hamptons."

"You have a friend in the Hamptons?"

"Do you have to sound so surprised? And to be more precise, I have a friend who has a house in the Hamptons. He's a booking agent in the city and he's been inviting me since June. It seemed like the right time to finally accept. I could use the break."

"Damn, Dad. I really don't know everything about you, do I?"

"No my love, you don't."

"Can I come too?" Charlotte sounded like a little girl on the phone, and I almost wished I did have a house in the Hamptons to go to.

"Well, you see, the booking agent is really a she. We've been friends, you might say, until now. You know how that goes."

"Wow. Now there's a revelation, but you know what, Dad? I'm happy for you. That's right. You go out to the Hamptons and have fun. You deserve it, and don't forget to use a condom. Wait, how old is she?"

"Jesus, Charlotte!"

"Sorry, Dad. I love you. Call me. Okay?"

"You call me too, regularly, and don't forget. Oh, and listen, I'm sure I'm just being overcautious, and there's nothing to worry about, but until this killer is found, I don't want you going anywhere alone. Okay?"

"Dad, there's cameras and security guards all over this building, and as far as going out, I never go anywhere alone.'

"Okay then, and I love you too."

When I hung up, I marveled at the elaborate extent of my lies and veiled truths, then pondered a much harder task—getting rid of Eleanor—something I thought I would never want to do, and I didn't want to do then either, but I had to. It was a task, all things considered, that should've been an easier one than it turned out to be. After all, she was only in New York for John, and he was now with Sofia. I only hoped Sofia wouldn't take a turn for the worse for her sake as well as my son's.

Eleanor arrived home shortly after 4 PM. A limousine had dropped her off at the end of the driveway. All afternoon I had been pondering what to tell her without sounding spiteful or vindictive. *Now that Sofia's been found, you can head off with your boyfriend and get the hell out of my life for good. Happy now?* It hurt me to even think about saying such a thing.

My problem: Eleanor was too damn smart for her own good. As a result, my choices were limited. Besides, I already gave Charlotte one story. I couldn't very well give a different one to Eleanor. And what if I did have a friend in the Hamptons? Living with feelings of guilt did not come easy to me, and I swore to myself that I would not feel one ounce of it when I told Eleanor the same tale I told Charlotte.

But I felt guilty anyway.

Eleanor was as intuitive as a witch; a good witch that is. Therefore, I had to be very careful with her, my talents as a trial lawyer and actor in front of a jury notwithstanding. Pleading to Eleanor was not the same as pleading to strangers. Her hold on me was not to be underestimated. What surprised me though, was the hurt in her eyes when I told her, and even more surprising, was how awful it made me feel afterward.

Eleanor was not one to sit quiet in the face of adversity or bullshit. It was one of the things I admired about her. As an Assistant District Attorney, she was intelligent, articulate, and displayed when necessary—the courage of her convictions. After we were married, I expected her, at some point, to find a way to channel those qualities toward an even greater good. I figured she would go back to work in some capacity. But she never did.

It's easy to get burnt out over time from the practice of criminal law, especially as a prosecutor. The victims, the crimes, the police, the investigators, and the inevitable politics that come with being an Assistant District Attorney is the reason why very few stay in the job over the long haul. It is a dark and disturbing world. Throw into the mix that the practice of criminal defense nearly killed your husband, chilling for a while on the hill in Garden City, Long Island, in our newly renovated home, wasn't all that hard to get accustomed to.

As for Mom, she loved Eleanor. At first, I thought she was faking it for my sake, but even after twenty plus years, her affection never wavered. And I missed the biggest clue that should have made me do everything I could to keep my beautiful wife happy and with me.

I missed the signal—a signal as bright as Montauk's lighthouse.

With inexplicable fortitude, Mom had locked away every painful scar of her sinewy bloodline into a vault somewhere—a sealed room with no key, her own knotted burlap bag of bones. But the decades of decay and toxicity Mom had gracefully shed with courage and determination and an unbroken will to survive, I was an aging, implacable witness and curator to. The advice I gave Lauren, I did not and could not take myself. I was keeper of an evil talisman I could not shake, and barely tried to, and maybe the darkest truth was…I didn't want to. I lived every day beckoning the ghosts of darkness to come out of hiding so I could slay them, as if doing so would turn back the hands of time. Maybe I was a fool to feel this way. If so, this fool was determined to slay a lot more than imaginary dragons.

As I watched Eleanor turn away and walk up the stairs, her head tilted downward, her hand on the rail as if measuring the cadence of every step, the sight of her rising away sunk me.

The fool that I was, I couldn't help but wonder why those two young lovers who met in the spring of '79 at a law school dance and fell in love, couldn't stay together to the end of their days.

Thirty minutes later, Eleanor's cell phone rang on the second floor, and a limousine pulled up the driveway. Within seconds, she descended the stairs with the small suitcase she arrived with.

Without looking around for me, or anyone, she placed the key she had in her hand on the hallway table, and left. I peeked through the blinds in the kitchen and watched the driver open the rear door for her, then take her bag and place it in the trunk. Since it was a stretch limo, he didn't attempt to turn it around. He just put it in reverse, and backed out, while Eleanor peeked out the side window and look up at the house as if doing so for the last time. Her expression was somber, but what struck me most was that last look of melancholy resolve.

Even after the terrifying odyssey that lay ahead was nearly over, and my world was reduced to nothing more than a blind reel of flickering burnt out images, I would remember that look, and its last trace of unrequited hope.

She moved on.

I had to as well.

What I didn't expect though, was that a cauldron of wise advice would come that evening, not only from the wicked and clever mind of a brilliant novelist, but from Gina's retelling of the darkest chapter in her family's past.

Both would be instrumental, for the better or worse of it, in the hunt for a diabolical killer.

Chapter 40

I left the car at home. Gina's house was only a few blocks away. It was a warm night, and the walk back to Harlan's would give us a chance to talk. One of my goals was to prepare Gina, as best I could, for our flamboyant and loquacious host.

For some reason, maybe because I was an easy friend who never judged him and conveniently lived next door, Harlan liked me. Over the years, we must have sat and chatted for a hundred plus hours. He always seemed intrigued by my life story, and except for Mom's childhood tragedy, he knew almost everything there was to know about me. He was one great listener, especially when I needed him to be; and many times, particularly over the past four years, I needed him to be.

As I approached Gina's house—a sprawling one story that was set back like all of the homes in the area—at least a hundred feet from the curb, a shiny Trans Am pulled up. A high school girl, who looked about seventeen, leaned over and gave the young driver a quick kiss before bouncing out of the car. Halfway up the walkway, I heard her call out, "Mom, your friend is here!" Gina instantly appeared at the door, smiled sweetly, and asked me to come in while she went to get a sweater.

Once inside, the house appeared much larger than it did from the street. I waited for Gina in a spacious center hall. Beyond a wall of rear windows and doors was a regulation tennis court centrally located in a huge backyard.

I chuckled to myself. Mom might have figured I'd be dating a nice Italian-American girl like Gina, but she would have never figured on the tennis court. I assumed that court was largely responsible for the shape Gina was in, which was difficult to ignore with the fitted black blouse she was wearing and skintight skirt several inches above her knees.

And I couldn't help but ask myself: *What idiot divorced this woman?*

Gina returned with a light sweater draped over her shoulders. Following her was a cute little boy. He was about four years old and wearing Spiderman pajamas. He came to a halt just past the hallway arch.

"Hi buddy," I said.

He waved back.

"A little ice cream, one book with your sister, then right to bed," Gina dictated, "and that's because it's Saturday night."

He nodded back a few times more in an exaggerated fashion, while Gina called out, "Christina, we're leaving," and the pretty girl that I had seen bouncing out of the Trans Am, came running down the stairs. She gave her mom a peck on the cheek, me a once over, and told us to have a good time.

When we reached the sidewalk, Gina asked, "Where's your car?"

"I thought we would walk. It will give us a few minutes to talk before we get to Harlan's."

"Oh, that's nice. It is a nice night, after all." She looked up, then proceeded to walk alongside me with her arm in mine, and I felt myself blush, grateful for the dusk, and glad that I had done my pushups as her right hand began affectionately squeezing my left bicep.

"Your little man is a cutie," I said.

"He's so good too," Gina gushed. "Never gives me any trouble, and sensitive. God forbid I'm upset about something; he's just crushed. He took it the hardest when his father left. The man maybe calls once a week. He lives in San Diego now with his girlfriend."

"Divorce can be rough," I added gently. "As you probably know, my wife and I have been separated for over four years now. She only came back because of John."

I could tell Gina was struggling with what to say next. "Yes, I understand," was her safest bet.

"She's got a boyfriend too," I blurted, then rolled my eyes as I asked myself why.

"That must've been hard on you. I know how I felt when Jack got serious with someone else soon after, divorce or no divorce."

"It was. I won't deny it, but I expected as much—four years and all."

"I have a confession to make," Gina said coyly, while shyly hunching her shoulders a bit. "Once, when you weren't home, I went to your house to check on John, and your wife was there. We started talking."

"Dear God save me, and you still agreed to go to dinner with me?"

Gina looked down at her shoes. "It wasn't so much what she said—we were making small talk mostly—it's what she didn't say."

"I'm lost," I confessed.

"What I'm trying to tell you is that, well…I was popping in on you. I mean, what doctor does that?"

"A very caring one," I answered.

"Right," she said sarcastically. "With makeup on, and my hair just right."

"So what you're saying is…She knew I might find you attractive."

"You know my ex was clueless too about things." She stopped and turned toward me. Raising her voice, she said, "It means I might just be looking good because I wanted to."

"Oh…I get that." We resumed walking. A smile grew on my face that no matter how hard I tried, I could not erase. "That's nice. I thought I was picking up on a cue here and there, but couldn't be sure with all that was going on."

"You're not supposed to be sure. Anyway, the point that I'm trying to make is that I sensed a jealousy there."

"From Eleanor?"

"Very good. See, there's hope for you."

"Okay, but what does that even mean anyway? She's been gone for four years. I mean…how jealous could she possibly be?"

"I understand, but it's a lot different when a possible other woman is standing in front of you."

"I suppose. Well, thank you for that."

"You're thanking me for making your wife jealous?"

She instantly became stone-cold serious, and I realized I may just have stuck one huge foot in my mouth. Regardless, I would not be deterred. I would remove it as quickly as I put it there, or at least try.

"I don't mind one bit that you made my wife jealous. What I'm thanking you for is your interest in me in the first place."

She relaxed what was becoming a vice grip on my arm.

"That was a good answer," she said with sexy authority, "but I was concerned about John. You know that too, don't you?"

"Of course, I do."

"Don't you go getting a big head on me now."

"I wouldn't dream of it."

"Good."

A welcome affection returned to my bicep.

As we continued walking, I took the time to pass on a friendly warning to Gina about Harlan and his house. Everything about both, I told her, was big: his size, his personality, the volume in his voice, the rooms, the ceiling height, his kitchen, and the lavish display of food I was certain he prepared that night for ten people, instead of just four. Also, one view of Harlan's girth, and there was no doubt about it—he loved his leftovers.

As we approached Harlan's driveway, adjacent to my own, Gina released my arm, which instantly saddened me. Like some lost teenager, I immediately reached for her hand, and my emotions got a lift, once again, when she graciously took it. When we got to the foot of Harlan's porch, just a few steps from huge double oak doors that reminded me of the grand entrance to Oz, my warnings to Gina were quite *apropos*.

Harlan was waiting for us.

"Look at this fabulous couple," he squealed. "Holding hands like two smitten teenagers."

"I'm the only one who's smitten," I shot back, "and don't use words you would never put in one of your novels."

Harlan joked back. "Which word: smitten or teenager?"

I ignored him. "This is Gina Cassisi. Doctor Cassisi to you."

Gina extended her hand. "Don't listen to him. It's Gina, and it's very nice to meet you."

Harlan shook her hand, then kissed it, and then kissed her on both cheeks as well. "You have no idea how good it makes me feel to have a doctor in the house. I plan tonight on eating myself into a coma."

"Should I go get my doctor bag?" Gina asked.

Harlan laughed. "Should I go get my doctor bag?" he repeated gleefully. "She's adorable."

We entered Harlan's center hall, which was half the size of my entire house next door. I watched as Gina, her eyes wide with amazement, looked around at the opulent surroundings as she held my hand and pressed her face into the same bicep she had been squeezing during the walk over. *Was I finally on my way to getting over Eleanor?* Not completely. Of this I was certain. But I couldn't deny that each and every act of affection by Gina made me feel better than I had in years—four years to be exact.

Gina was beautiful, sexy, and funny, but thoughts of Eleanor weren't the only passing distractions that evening that kept me grounded. When I passed Harlan's rear den (he had more than one), my eyes fell on his library of bestsellers. I had read some, but knew them all: *The Dead Factory, The Killer Inside, The Murder Project, Mayhem, Witness To A Kill.* The list is twenty-five titles long. No one has spent more time inside the head of imaginary serial killers than Harlan Dugan, and if I wanted to forget for a night the looming and almost impossible task of finding a real one, Harlan's rear den was not the place to be.

But it wasn't fair to Gina, Harlan, or Esther, his girlfriend, that I should be preoccupied with the dark and dismal. My family was gone from the hill. Tarantino was on the case. John and Sofia were under guard, and Charlotte was in the secured ivory tower called Trump. The cameras and guards The Donald had fortified his building with notwithstanding, as always though, it was Charlotte I was most worried about.

As for the evening at hand, Harlan had prepared an Italian feast, and especially for me. I was in the company of a beautiful woman, who seemed to care about me. Both deserved my gratitude and appreciation, and as the night progressed, and the drinks were poured, it became easier to relent, and let the pleasantness of the evening sweep me away from the human suffering that preoccupied my every waking hour as of late.

I would enjoy myself more than I had in a long time, or at least try to.

Esther, Harlan's girlfriend, could barely keep pace with Harlan's outpouring of dialogue on subjects that ranged from the food he prepared, to the stalled politics in Washington. In simple response, she would just laugh, and when able to, get a word or two in edgewise, and every now and then, I would glance over at Gina. She had this youthful look of fascination about her, like a little girl gazing up at a Ferris wheel, and I saw a hopefulness in her eyes that I hadn't seen in a very long time—so long, that I had nearly forgotten what it looked like. And I came to realize then, that with all that had happened before and after 1982, and even long before I was born: the lost love, the crimes beyond forgiveness, the strained loyalties, the curses of my chosen profession, that I had come dangerously close to losing that which was most precious and sacred—my heart.

And in that quintessential moment that I gazed over at Gina one last time before Harlan squealed, "dinner is served," I did believe that in some small but significant way, she had helped bring it back to me.

I was drinking my favorite drink for the nondrinker that I was—a Malibu Madras—half Malibu, half cranberry juice, with a splash of orange. Two of these and the smiles came easy. Three or four and the smiles never left me, or so it seemed to me then. Gina was smiling quite a bit herself. We also did more than our fair share of eating, though all of us (except Harlan) could have used a few extra pounds; me especially.

I had been dropping weight for months. Recent events didn't help. I normally weighed in at one hundred and sixty five pounds, but life for me hadn't been normal, nor felt normal for as long as I could remember. Earlier that day I dared to step on the scale, and when I did, the digital screen read: 145.5 pounds. At five foot nine, that was Paul Newman thin, only I wasn't aging nearly as well.

Though we all fell victim to Harlan's culinary offerings, the real glutton that night was none other than Harlan himself, with me a distant second. The ladies, Esther and Gina, exerted self-control as much as I could tell, considering all the Malibu Madrases I was downing. That we stuffed ourselves to overcapacity was an understatement, but we didn't stop there. After continuing onward with helpings of strawberry cheesecake and chocolate mousse with whipped cream, we then retired (Harlan's words, not mine) to his lavish library, walled with archival literary antiquities—classics, many of which were first editions. Our alcohol high wearing down with the passage of time and creamy cappuccinos, we slowly drifted back down to earth. Wasted in mind and body on plush leather couches, shelves of books rising on all sides like a Goliath of ancient knowledge, and a moon full and beaming blue light through a large elliptical window, there was an odd romantic air in the room.

Then Harlan spoke, a glass of Jack Daniels in hand, and cracked through the richly apathetic, yet pleasant quiet time.

"You're not going to let it go, are you?" Harlan asked me with such morose seriousness, I thought he was joking.

"Let what go?" I answered, with a polite yet uncertain half smile.

"You know," he said slyly.

"Harlan, what in God's name are you talking about?" I asked.

Harlan rose from his seat, his girth jiggling beneath a plaid button-down vest, as he sidestepped over to me and sat down, the scent of Jack Daniels emanating from him nearly asphyxiating. "I know you," he said, while sticking his finger in my chest. "I saw how committed you were on that Desmond Lewis case trying to get that killer off. That young boy never got within twenty feet of Lewis' house, but Lewis gunned him down anyway."

Harlan was treading on sensitive ground with me, which forced me to sober up faster than I cared to, so as not to embarrass either one of us in front of the ladies. "That boy was an athlete wielding an aluminum bat, and there were four of them, and you aren't a black man who knows what it's like to be called a—".

Harlan cut me off. "Don't get so high and mighty with me."

"You brought it up."

"Only to make a point. You're like one of those kamikaze pilots when you set your sites on a target."

"I was his lawyer."

"My point exactly." Harlan poured himself another Jack Daniels. When he turned away, Esther added some ginger ale. "When the jury came back with the lesser charge of manslaughter, Lewis had to do some time. He lost his job, but so his wife wouldn't lose the house, you paid off their mortgage."

"Harlan—"

He cut me off again, and looked over at Gina and Esther. "That's why I love this guy." Harlan put his hand on my shoulder then rubbed the back of my head. "Come on. Who does that? No one, that's who. That's why I know you're up to something, and I'm referring to this serial killer of ours."

I looked over at Gina. She had a concerned look on her face, and I wasn't sure if it was for me, or Harlan.

"I thought you were tired of writing crime thrillers." I said, lamely attempting to inject some conviviality back into the room.

Harlan leaned away, and looked around. "I *am* tired of writing crime thrillers, but that's my publisher's problem." He was slurring his words. "You don't think those bodies found at the beach were the first girls he killed, do you?" Harlan got up, jostled away, and sat back down next to Esther.

"You mean the Jones Beach killer?" Gina spoke reluctantly.

"Must we talk about this?" Esther asked.

Harlan turned to Gina. "Yes, my dear, we are talking about the Jones Beach killer, and Nickie boy here is determined to find him."

"You are?" Gina asked.

"He is," Harlan answered.

I looked over at Gina sitting next to me, her face inches from mine. "I hired a private investigator, that's all."

"He hired the fixer," Harlan squealed.

"Nick, what does that mean?" Gina asked.

"Nothing. Harlan likes to joke around."

"Remember," Harlan said with drunken sincerity, as he stood up, drink in one hand, pointing at me with the other. "You have to trace the crumbs back to the nest. That's how you find your killer."

Less than a minute later, Harlan passed out on the sofa, but before he closed his eyes, and to let one and all know that I wasn't the least bit offended by his question and answer session, I told him, loud enough for all to hear, that I loved him too.

When a grandfather clock in the distance struck midnight, I patted Harlan on the head, kissed Esther on the cheek, who was dozing off next to him, and Gina and I saw ourselves out.

Though it was a late August night, there was a chill in the air. Since Gina forgot her sweater at Harlan's, and we didn't want to reenter the house, I suggested that we take the S600 parked in my driveway.

"The inside of this thing is huge," she said, as I turned the key in the ignition, and put the car in reverse.

"I know. I can't wait to get rid of it. I've actually seen chauffeurs driving this model around."

"You know, you should never be ashamed that you have money," she said sweetly.

"I once said that very same thing to my wife," I answered, as I put the car in drive. "I'm not ashamed of the money I've got. I'm ashamed of how I got it."

"Well, you didn't steal it so…?"

"I inherited it from my mafia uncle back in 1982, and invested wisely."

"Okay, you inherited the money. You did nothing wrong," Gina said emphatically.

"Tell that to my conscience. It's mob money, plain and simple, and if I wasn't trying to show off to my new wife's family, I doubt I would've kept a cent."

Gina squeezed my arm as I drove off. "You did nothing wrong. We all have our skeletons."

An image flashed in my mind of the crumpled skeletons of dead girls stuffed inside burlap bags. As I turned down Gina's block, I asked, "What does that mean anyway—our skeletons?"

"Skeletons… You know, in the closet."

"I know, but what closet?"

"The closet in your mind—the place where you keep your secrets, shameful or not."

"Maybe that's what he was doing?"

"Who?" she asked.

"I'm sorry. I was thinking out loud."

"You mean that killer Harlan referred to?"

"My mind was wandering. I'm sorry."

"It's okay." Gina put her hand on mine as I pulled up to her house. "I think you're doing the right thing—not to walk away because your son's girlfriend was found. After all, this guy *will* keep on killing."

"It's funny you should say that. My wife would probably be furious with me for pursuing this."

"Well, I can understand that. She'd be afraid for you, but you're not going to be on the front line with this. You hired people to do that. Am I right?"

I didn't answer quickly enough.

"Am I, Nick?"

"Yes, of course."

"Okay then. You're just putting some money to really good use."

"Right." I tried to sound convincing.

As I parked, Gina turned to face me. That full moon that shone through Harlan's elliptical window was now casting a pretty blue light on her already pretty face.

"What did you mean before though—when you said maybe that's what he was doing?" she asked.

"Well," I took a deep breath, feeling more than a bit uncomfortable discussing the mental state of a serial killer on my first date in thirty years. "It occurs to me that maybe that's just what the killer was doing. Instead of burying the bodies, he left them near the beach where eventually they would be found. It's as if he wanted the world to know that these prostitutes were murdered, not just missing. It's as if he wanted their secrets out."

"So he wanted to display their punishment, like their own scarlet letter, like burning the witches at the stake."

"I suppose. It's hard to figure him out."

"Maybe he wants recognition for his efforts."

"After the bodies were found at the beach, his crimes got a lot of media attention; but now, a month later, and it seems as if the police and the press have moved on."

"He's going to kill again. You know that, don't you?" Gina looked down at her hands, and started to rub them nervously.

"Is everything okay?" I asked.

"It's just that…When you first called me, you were in such distress over your son. You told me about his girlfriend. It broke my heart." Gina started to tear up.

"There's something you're not telling me, and you don't have to if you don't want to."

Gina glanced at me sheepishly, then looked out the windshield. She pointed to a house across the street and down the block. "You see that huge home."

"Yes."

"It wasn't always there. Ten years ago, a builder bought the land and the old house on it."

"From the looks of what's there now, he obviously tore the old house down completely."

"He tore it down because of its history. You see, a serial killer lived there. He killed nine young girls before he was caught."

I thought for a moment. "I think I heard this story."

Gina cleared her throat. "One of his victims was my Aunt Christina."

"I am so sorry."

"This happened before I was born. It devastated my family at the time."

"Of course."

"Christina was my mother's younger sister. She was in high school, very pretty, cheerleader captain, everything to live for."

"I was definitely told this story, but it was quite some time ago."

"Who was it that told you?"

"This may surprise you. It sure as hell surprised me, but it was the broker who sold me my house."

"That is so strange."

"Not really. People hear I'm a criminal lawyer, and they feel they can tell me all kinds of things."

Gina gestured in the direction of her home. "This is where Christina and my family lived at the time. My mom was twenty-two and engaged to marry my dad. They had a huge wedding planned before Christina went missing. They postponed it for a year, then made it a simple party."

"I know your dad, the doctor, passed away. Is your mom still alive?"

"No. A few years back, both died of old age within months of each other. They deeded this house to me after they purchased a home in Merrick, which already had a separate doctor's office on the first floor. The deed predated my marriage, so I got to keep the house in the divorce."

"What about your grandparents? How did they fare after...you know."

"My grandmother was never the same. To make matters worse, one year after my mom and dad married, my grandfather started up his car in the garage with the door closed and the car windows down, and killed himself." Gina lowered her head, took out a tissue, and dabbed at her eyes.

"I'm so sorry, Gina."

"Why is there so much evil in the world?"

"I don't know," I said softly. "I just don't know."

Chapter 41

Gina and I sat in my car and continued talking for at least another hour. She asked me to repeat, as best as I could remember, the story the broker had told me, or as I often referred to it over the years: "The Miss Marple Serial Killer Story."

I was careful not to be glib and insensitive as I told Gina not only what I heard, but how I came to hear it.

Returning to New York after honeymooning two weeks in and around Paris in December of 1982, was nothing short of a cultural and comedic shock. As the plane's tires touched down at JFK Airport, Eleanor and I looked at each other, and laughed. We had no place to go. Young fools, flush with stupid money, we had made no living arrangements whatsoever.

We directed our cab driver back to whence we came—the place where we had our wedding reception and spent our first night as a married couple—The Garden City Hotel.

I wasted no time. Before Eleanor could even finish unpacking, I was out looking for a house.

As I walked along Seventh Street's inlaid brick sidewalk, I came to an office called Ryan and Todd Real Estate. Conveniently situated next to a bank, I went in and parked myself at a side chair next to the desk of a middle-aged woman in her fifties, whose nameplate read *Delores Stutz*. I quickly apologized for my appearance by explaining that I had just gotten off a plane from Paris, and then added that I had been on my honeymoon for the past two weeks.

I was amazed at how easily words I had never spoken before and never imagined I would ever speak (this kid from Flatbush) rolled off my lips. *I just got off a plane from Paris. Was on my honeymoon for two weeks.*

Miss Stutz seemed like a genuine and friendly sort as she proceeded to show me photos of various houses out of a small-ringed binder. She then apologized for reminding me (as if I should have known) that she would have to prequalify me for a mortgage before she could take me out to see any of them. I told her that really wouldn't be necessary because I was paying all cash.

Her face instantly contorted from gentle consternation to a relieved sense of joy. She actually started to giggle, but quickly caught herself.

I then visualized the Merrick home I grew up in and loved, and how it could fit, in its entirety, inside Eleanor's bedroom in Atlanta.

"How about something about five thousand square feet, traditional in design, large, but still charming enough to feel like home?" I was combing through the Vernou mansion in my mind. "Mahogany trim. A lot of wood. That's right. A lot of wood trim."

"Okay." Miss Stutz answered tentatively.

I realized then that if you took that same mansion and planted it on a mere acre-and-a-half in Garden City, it would probably sell for a cool million in 1982. Not expecting to match it, I just wanted a home Eleanor would be comfortable in, and her parents wouldn't turn their noses down on. I decided to play it safe, and shoot higher in price than I originally planned.

I told Miss Stutz that I wanted to live with my wife, and raise our family, in the richest and most desirable section of Garden City—"screw the cost." After all, I had just inherited nine million dollars worth of real estate upon my Uncle Rocco's death.

We then got in her old Lincoln Town Car, which I figured for the same age as Miss Stutz, and she drove me up to "the hill."

At first, I was a little reluctant. "The hill" sounded creepy to me. I remembered the movie that scared the crap out of me as a kid—*The House on Haunted Hill,* where ghosts came out of the walls, and floated through the air.

This was not an area of southern antebellum mansions either. I would not be copying the homes that settled along Piedmont Road in Atlanta's exclusive Buckhead section. The houses along Tenth Street and Hillcrest Place, and down Eleventh, were built in the twenties and thirties: sprawling ranches, stately colonials, one larger than the next, and some so big they defied any builder's definitions I could come up with. All were repeatedly remodeled. All were set back on huge, magnificently landscaped lawns and gardens on two-to-five acres of land. At the top of the hill was Hillcrest Place, which ran from Tenth Street past Eleventh to the edge of the golf course of The Garden City Golf Club, the third and fourth holes a mere short stroke away.

With both hands firmly on the wheel, Miss Stutz turned onto Hillcrest from Eleventh. "What do you do for a living, if you don't mind my asking?"

"I don't mind at all," I answered. "My wife and I are both lawyers."

"Oh, that's so very nice. Remind me not to get in the middle of an argument between you two." She giggled as she spoke.

I turned, chuckled myself, and rolled my eyes.

"By the way, what kind of law do you practice?" she asked.

"I can't say what private practice will bring, but I was a criminal lawyer before I left for my honeymoon."

"Even better," she responded with widened eyes.

"Even better than what?" I asked.

"Well, you see, all these houses have a history."

"Every house has a history," I interrupted. "Let me save you a little time. Forgive me here, Miss Stutz—"

"Delores please," she cut in gently.

"Delores, you don't strike me as the pretentious type, which is why I walked over to you and sat down, but if you are about to tell me which Astor or which Vanderbilt cousin lived here and there, I'll take a pass. I'm buying this house for my wife. If it was up to me, I'd stay in Merrick, and maybe splurge on a two bedroom with a nice backyard."

"Well, this house I'm about to show you has a grand backyard, and even an in-ground pool, but I can show you houses in Merrick if you like."

"That's quite alright, Delores."

"What I was about to tell you though, isn't so much a story of historic wealth as it is of murder and intrigue." Her eyes gleamed like a small child's about to tell a secret.

"You have got to be kidding me," I answered.

"Do you have the stomach for an interesting crime story?" she asked, as she was starting to sound like Agatha Christie's Miss Marple. "I bet you do," she volunteered.

"Last year, I worked as a poor man's criminal defense attorney in the South Bronx, so it's safe to say my stomach's been lined quite well already."

My Miss Marple pulled over in front of a two-story colonial, set back what seemed like a mile from the street. She threw the gearshift into park, and with the car still running, she began. But first, she had a question. "Are you upset by serial murder stories?"

"Actually, I am, but unfortunately, I've gotten used to them."

"Yes, the news can be just terrible to listen to sometimes. I don't even watch it late at night before I go to bed anymore, for fear I'll have nightmares."

Delores swiveled a bit on her seat to face me. I barely turned my head in her direction. A white security car passed and paid us no mind. I suppose he knew Miss Stutz's car, or maybe he figured that in the middle of a sunny afternoon, what is so unusual about a man and a woman sitting in an old Lincoln up on the hill?

It's these assumptions, reasonable and innocent though they are, that allow the worst of crimes to go undetected.

Every time good is mistakenly profiled, so is evil.

"You know, don't you, that the very worst type of criminals—the repeaters, are a product of their darkest urges."

"Delores, are you trying to sell me a house, or scare me away from one?"

"First of all, I can tell that you are not the type of person who I can sell anything to. You know what you want, and when I find it for you, you will buy it to be sure."

I underestimated this matronly real estate agent, for I was about to witness the soft sell in its finest form—a serial murder story being the one major distraction. I shook my head in amazement, and smiled. "Please, Delores, you have me on the edge of my seat. You're a regular Agatha Christie."

"Oh my God, thank you! That is one great compliment! I just love her novels!"

"I can tell. Now go on. Please."

And she did.

"Back in the late 1950s I was just a young girl, and believe it or not, we had a murderer on the loose around here, and targeting young women."

"Is there any other kind?" I asked. Delores' expression did not waver. She apparently didn't see the humor in my remark. That's probably because there was none. The only thing that *was* funny was that I was listening to this story to begin with, but we were past that. "I'm sorry, Delores. Go on."

She then began the story of the headline grabbing, "Impala Murders" that took place in and around the Garden City area in the year 1959. Four girls, juniors and seniors in high school, had gone missing in the same three-month period before the end of the school year, while several witnesses had seen a young man in a shiny blue Impala in the area around the time the girls were abducted. He had attempted to lure other girls into his car with a pick-up line and an offer to drive them home. "A handsome young man in a shiny new car was, after all, irresistible to a teenage girl at the time. We're talking 1959, now."

Though I was only five years old then, I nodded agreeably.

Delores continued.

"Once the news about the car got out, every man in an Impala, in and around Garden City, was subject to a stop and interrogation. As a result, the abductions stopped, but the young girls had yet to be found. Two years went by before a break came in the case. A man in his twenties was caught by the police in Short Hills, New Jersey, while trying to clobber a high school girl with the edge of a tennis racket after she got into his '61 Rambler. After they arrested the man, they searched his house. Turns out, he lived with his parents. In the garage, the police found a 1958 newly painted green Chevy Impala. The family had moved to New Jersey just a few years earlier. Know where they lived before that?"

I didn't answer. I was completely lost in her story. My stomach was in knots and my worst fear was that she would tell me that they lived in the nice house we were about to view at the end of the steep driveway. I shrugged my shoulders.

"On Eleventh, here on the hill. One of his victims lived right across the street from him." My eyes must have revealed my unease because Delores was quick to add, "I still get the willies just talking about it."

"Okay, now that I am totally bugged out, how about you show me this house already." I wasn't lying. The sun was starting to set over the trees along the golf course, and the security car had cruised by three times, and with each pass, sent a more inquisitive look our way.

"But I haven't told you the best part."

"Please Delores. My wife is going to send out a search party for me if I don't get back to the hotel soon."

"I'm so sorry Nicholas, but you've got to hear this."

"Okay, Dolores." Didn't appear that I had a choice.

"When the police searched the green Impala, they found a girl's blood-stained locket under the seat cushion. Once the suspect's father hears about this, he pulls the high priced lawyer he hired to defend his son right off the case. A little odd if you ask me. The Jersey cops found it strange too, but the father wasn't talking. The police then proceed to interrogate the young man, without a lawyer. This was before that Supreme Court case that made having an attorney mandatory, you know."

"Gideon versus Wainwright," I added, somewhat in a trance.

"Yeah, right, so get this. The kid confesses, tells the cops where he buried the bodies in New Jersey. But there's more. They confront him with the locket. He then confesses to the four Garden City murders, and also tells them where he buried the four bodies on Long Island. But when they dig them up, they find a fifth body."

Returning from a Paris honeymoon, no place to live, a serial killer story to boot, and I was feeling sick to my stomach. "Delores, you are now going to show me this house and then drive me back to my hotel, so you can tell my wife where I've been, and why I took so long."

"I am sorry again, Nicholas, but you've got to admit, that was one hell of a story. Right out of *The Twilight Zone*. Don't you think?"

"Yes Miss Mar—I mean Delores." I looked at the house we were parked in front of. "Speaking of twilight, I hope the electricity is on. It looks like no one is living there."

"No one is," she responded, then took the car out of park, hit the gas and headed up the driveway, the tires screeching behind us. "But wait till you see this place. Your wife is going to love it."

"By the way, Delores, something is bothering me about your story. You said the cops found a girl's locket in the Impala, and then the father takes the high-priced lawyer off the case. I don't get it."

Delores stopped the car by a front portico that hung over double entrance doors of solid mahogany, and turned to me, a look of sweet pleasure on her face. "Nicholas, you are very sharp. The police really had no idea whose locket it was, but the father did, and the son did too. It belonged to a girl who went missing in Garden City at least two months before the original blue Impala was purchased. That girl, and the fifth body that they found buried, was none other than the killer's sister. It was her locket they found in the car."

The girl who lived across the street from the killer was his second victim, Gina's aunt, and the house he lived in was located exactly where Gina had pointed to earlier.

Since Gina was still shaken from the conversation as I walked her to her door, I asked her if she was going to be all right. She nodded 'yes.'

"I'll call you tomorrow." I said.

She nodded in the affirmative once again. Then I kissed her on the cheek and gently on the lips. It seemed to please her. She responded with a tight hug of her own.

But I didn't call Gina the following day as I said I would.

I called her the minute I got home.

When I went upstairs and back to my bedroom, the use of which I had seceded to Eleanor, I placed my cell phone on the night table.

There, resting in the dead center of the small granite top, with a message of finality that I wasn't the slightest bit prepared to accept, no matter how wonderfully my evening went, was Eleanor's wedding ring.

Chapter 42

Joanna Calabrese spun the ring on her right hand like she always did—for good luck. It was her high school ring, the last present from her parents before she dropped out of college and went to live with the amateur rapper who subsidized his lack of income from music (which was no income at all), by selling ecstasy and methamphetamine. His girlfriend, of course, got whatever she wanted for free.

When the rapper was shot dead by another drug dealer for working the wrong corner at the wrong time, Joanna went to live with a girlfriend on Avenue B in Manhattan's Alphabet City. Within a matter of weeks, she was turning tricks to support a drug habit no longer subsidized by her drug dealer boyfriend.

It was September 2009, and her story would've been an all too familiar and sad one, except for the second chance given her by what her Italian-American parents considered divine intervention. Joanna became pregnant.

When given her due date by the clinic doctor, she calculated the father to be none other than her rapper boyfriend, now deceased. She would continue in life as a "working girl" for another two months before she faced the firing squad that was her parents' rage and consternation. Joanna returned home four months before her due date.

As she walked up the steps of her parents' high ranch, located in Marine Park, Brooklyn, all she could think of was: thank God my rapper boyfriend was white and Italian-American. Her parents would never turn away an Italian-American grandchild, no matter who the father was.

Joanna gauged her parents correctly. They cried a lot more than they cursed. They were happy to have their daughter home, baby and all.

Then in mid-April 2010, Joanna gave birth to an eight-pound, four-ounce, baby girl. She named it Diana Maria, after her mother. Come late August, she left home again, and left her baby behind as well.

On the evening of August 30th, she was walking to meet her first trick since giving birth. By 1 AM on August 31st, she was in the rear of a van, her mouth sealed with duct tape, her legs and hands tied together behind her back, her body crumpled inside a burlap sack.

She could tell by the speed of the van that it was driving on a parkway, and when the speed dropped considerably and the van stopped occasionally, she knew it had moved on to local streets and avenues. When the drive became especially quiet, she knew she was in a residential area. Minutes later, she felt the van coast up the apron of a driveway, and then heard a garage door close behind her.

She had only gotten a glimpse of the driver when she first opened the front passenger door and stepped into the SUV. On the phone, he had a sweet, trusting voice. In person and up close, something about him wasn't right. When she reached for the door handle, a quick blow to her head nearly knocked her unconscious.

Once inside the garage, she listened to every step he took. His heavy, deliberate, but calm gait sent her shivering in fear each time his boot touched the hard coarse concrete floor.

Then there were stairs. Just a few. She could hear him climb them. Then silence. He remained still. He was thinking, plotting his next move. Joanna's hands were taped so tight that she couldn't feel her fingers. If she had, she would have realized that her lucky ring was gone.

Then the darkened world inside the sack suddenly got even darker.

Don't leave me here!

As quick as one perishing thought came, another followed.

No! Leave me here!

She heard three thuds as his boots quickly stepped off the stairs.

He was walking beside the van.

He was behind it.

Behind her.

The van's rear doors flew open and slammed back on its hinges.

A large hand grabbed the top of the burlap bag and Joanna's hair along with it.

In her mind, she was pleading with her captor, but all he could hear were her muffled sobs.

After he yanked her from the van, he slammed its rear doors shut.

A puddle of her urine was all that was left behind.

Chapter 43

I awoke shortly after 8 AM. Eleanor's wedding ring was right where she had left it on the night table. It was a restless night. I remember dreaming in an agitated sleep that didn't begin until about 3 AM. Thoughts of Eleanor's departure and how cold I was to her before she left, combined with the pleasant evening I had with Gina that concluded with her own family's tragic history, was enough to send my mind into an petulant spin. All things considered, I was grateful for what little sleep I got.

Upon rising, however, the one thought that plagued me and kept swirling around in my head, was Harlan's drunken late-night instruction: *You have to trace the crumbs back to the nest. That's how you find your killer!*

I hit the speed dial on my cell phone. Harlan would be pissed that I called so early, but as I knew it would, the call went straight to voice mail.

Thirty seconds later, he rang back, his voice gravelly, his temperament one of contained irritability. "Nick, this better be good."

"Whatever did you mean last night before we left?"

"I knew you would call. I just didn't think it would be so early."

"I have to be in Tarantino's office at nine-thirty."

"And you want to know what I meant by following the killer's crumbs."

"That's right. I get the nest part, but what are the crumbs?"

"Anyone else home?" he asked.

"Just me."

"Make me three scrambled eggs and some toast. Lots of butter. I'll be right over, and don't forget the eggs."

"What?"

"I want lots of butter on them too. You can add it to the pan while they're cooking."

"Jesus, Harlan. You keep eating like this you're going to die and real soon."

"Maybe so, but not before breakfast."

Harlan may have washed his face (his beard was still wet) and combed his hair, but his pajamas remained. When I opened the door, he marched right in without so much as a "good morning" and headed for the kitchen.

"First we eat," he said.

It didn't take him more than two minutes to devour all three scrambled eggs and two large slices of toasted country white. I quickly realized that the purpose of the butter was not so much for taste, but so he didn't have to completely chew his food. All of it easily just slid down his throat.

When he was done, he looked up and said, "coffee?"

I got the largest mug I could find in the overhead cabinets. It was purchased in Epcot when the kids were little. I filled it and placed it in front of him. He immediately grabbed the sugar decanter and proceeded to put five heaping teaspoons in the mug, along with a dash of half-and-half.

Harlan looked over at me with a Cheshire grin on his face. "I don't stir because I don't like it sweet."

"Harlan, this is as far as I go. Now talk to me." He leaned back in his chair, his coffee in one hand, one thick leg under the table, the other outstretched and balanced on the heel of his slipper.

"Nickie, a man does not wake up and suddenly decide on becoming a serial killer. The dark demon inside him or her was always there. It just needed its trigger, its catalyst to become an active evil part of his or her life; whether it's being abused as a child, witnessing a horrific crime, or something or someone that causes the evil to rise up within them. Perhaps some completely demoralizing event in their lives."

"You sound like a criminal psychologist," I interrupted.

"I got my Masters in Cognitive Sciences from Stanford about thirty years ago."

"Damn Harlan, and I thought all those hot middle-aged ladies were only sleeping with you for your money."

"They are, trust me. I start talking like this, and they run screaming."

"Okay, so there was a trauma. I get it, but what does that mean and how does that help me find my killer?"

"I'm not sure it does, especially since he's a killer of prostitutes, and not the first on Long Island, you know."

"I know about Joel Rifkin. What was it—seventeen prostitutes before they caught him?"

"That's right. Killed many of them in his home in East Meadow—a home he shared with his mother. Go figure."

"And there were other prostitute killers?"

"Robert Shulman, the postal worker from Hicksville."

"Billy Joel's neighborhood."

"He killed five hookers we know of. Left one in a Sears bunting bag. That's how they tracked him. Rifkin, on the other hand, was driving with a corpse in his backseat when a cop stopped him for a missing license plate."

"They got Ted Bundy on a traffic violation too."

"Right, but in Rifkin's case, he would've gotten away with a simple ticket but for the smell."

"What about the smell?" I asked. "I figure these bodies were dropped on the beach at the same time, but the girls went missing a year-and-a-half apart. That means the killer either kept them alive, or killed them and stored their bodies somehow. He did say he was watching a body rot in a call he made to a victim's sister."

"I agree with the simultaneous dropping." Harlan was staring into his coffee cup, slouched against the table, head angled downward, like some professor effortlessly dropping precious pearls of wisdom on one eager and riveted student. "Either he buried the bodies, then unburied the bones, or he kept the bodies in a freezer or refrigerator until he was ready to dispose of them."

"That must be one big walk-in box."

"Not really," answered Harlan. "Almost all these girls were petite. Tied up like a ball, you could easily fit four in a standard six-foot refrigerator or freezer."

"Why though? Why not just bury them and forget about them? No body, no evidence of murder."

Harlan straightened a bit in his chair. "That's the million-dollar question, isn't it? Maybe he wanted dominion and control over them, even after death. The calls he made to the families probably gave him the biggest rush ever. Now he had control over the living too."

"Damn. How does one make sense of this insanity?"

"Why *are* you still in this anyway? Your son's girlfriend was found." Harlan's voice went up a few octaves. "And why is there still security outside your house?"

"I swore I would find this monster even before Sofia was discovered at Bellevue. I can't stop now. I have to see this through, if only for the sake of Lauren Callucci, the *Newsday* reporter. Her sister was one of the victims, and it was Lauren who was told by the killer that he was watching her sister's body rot."

Harlan squinted at me. "There's something you're not telling me. I'm sure of it."

You mean like the text messages, the green van, the big guy who approached John at the beach? Sorry Harlan, I haven't a clue how you'll react, and it's confidential anyway. I saw no reason to make Harlan paranoid about the killer and Hillcrest Place.

"Let's get back to last night," I said.

"Go ahead. Change the subject," Harlan had more than a tilt of annoyance in his voice.

"It's the same subject. Now, tell me, what did you mean by 'follow the crumbs back to the nest'?"

Harlan got professorial again. "If you insist...There is something you can't ignore; a pattern you might say, in most serial killings." He took another sip of coffee, but his eyes were still fixed on me. I looked away in an attempt not to appear as captivated as I actually was. Harlan continued. "The trigger or catalyst isn't far from their nest or home. The evil ideas and fantasies whirling around in a killer's conscious and subconscious mind are just waiting, begging for some overt act to trigger his urge to capture and kill."

I instantly recalled Gina's family tragedy and Miss Stutz's serial killer story, one and the same though they were. The locket found in the Chevy that belonged to the murderer's sister—his first known kill; Gina's aunt, who lived just across the street, his second.

"So the initial overt act is usually committed on a victim the killer knows or is close to," I added.

"Usually," Harlan responded. "Except when the kills are prostitutes. That's when the theory goes awry. As far as anyone knows, Rifkin and Schulman only killed prostitutes who were strangers. The same is true for the infamous Jack the Ripper, who, as you well know, was never caught."

"And why target prostitutes?" I think I knew the answer, but I wanted Harlan's take on it anyway.

"Well, if you want to kill women, could there be an easier target? The killer meets them at night, alone, in private. The victims are usually desperate for money. The streetwalker that you don't see much anymore, gets in a car with a stranger, goes to a secluded spot for what—a blow job, for twenty, forty, fifty bucks? A prostitute takes her life in her hands every night, over and over again. It's a wonder the odds don't catch up to them more often than they do."

"The killer in these cases called off Internet ads."

"From cash-bought cell phones you throw away when it times out," Harlan correctly added. "There's no ID on the call. All the hooker has is her instincts to protect her—instincts often hampered by the irresistible urge that comes with supporting a drug habit."

"So what you're saying is that the 'follow-the-crumbs-back-to-the-nest' theory may not apply at all."

"That's right. With prostitute murders it may not apply, but Rifkin, Schulman, and The Ripper had to have shown some signs that they were demented killers at some point before they laid eyes on their first hooker. We just don't know about it."

"What about this killer we're chasing? He not only captures. He calls to brag about it."

"That's what makes him different. He wants to get up close and personal. That's what scares me the most about this guy."

No shit, Harlan.

Harlan adjusted himself in his chair again and leaned forward. "It's not enough to capture, rape, and kill. He wants to show off his work. He wants to be in control—in power over more than the kill. When that need for control, power, and domination is no longer satisfied by the rape, torture and murder of his victims, what then?"

Which is why I've got Tarantino. I don't plan on finding out.

"So it's still possible that his first victim is still out there who we just don't know about," I said.

"Someone up close and personal, if you ask me," Harlan responded.

"I have been asking you, and for over twenty minutes now."

I was agitated, but Harlan was unfazed, and continued.

"I surmise that his first victim was someone who had been in his sights for some time, and on a regular basis. There's just no telling when his desire to act against that person was triggered, though. It could've been two years ago. It could've been twenty years ago. One thing I would bet my next advance on. Those prostitutes found on the marsh…were definitely not his first victims."

Chapter 44

Paul's office looked like a war room. He said this was partly Jasmine's doing. She was meticulously detail oriented, but to her credit, had a clear focus on the big picture as well.

The last time I was sitting in front of his desk, it was nearly empty. This time, it was cluttered with news clippings, scribbled notes on loose papers and legal pads, and two books—one on criminal profiling, and the other entitled *Italian American Folklore*. What struck me the most though, were the five large bulletin boards against the wall, one for each of the four victims; the fifth was a list of bullet points—case notes with subheadings.

BURLAP BAGS

- mostly for landscaping
- sandbags for barriers
- holds potatoes, coffee
- deterioration the same

BUT

- kills are 1 ½ years apart
- girls kept, not killed
- girls killed, then kept

CELL CALLS

- from Times Square
- one off Massapequa cell tower

-"watching body rot"
-girls killed, then kept
-kept where?

- "Half-breed"

-half Native American/half Caucasian
-Italian-American reference or Native Italian reference

PROSTITUTES

- from Brooklyn, Manhattan, the Bronx, and upstate New York
- but dumped on Long Island

Paul was standing behind his desk. With overgrown stubble, messy hair and sleeves rolled up on a coffee stained tailored shirt that was hanging out of his pants, he looked like he hadn't slept in days.

"We have to pick a direction, move on it, and fast. I don't read this guy as someone who's gone into hiding. I believe he's savoring any and all attention he can get, pumped up, and probably about to abduct another girl—prostitute or not, if he hasn't done so already."

I sat and listened, but continued to take in the boards, the books, and the papers on his desk, all the facts and conclusions about a killer who was probably far more dangerous than I had ever anticipated.

Paul then yanked open a desk drawer and took out two .38 caliber Smith and Wesson pistols, and two holsters—one waist, and one ankle. He also took out a certificate of some sort with my name on it.

"These are yours, and this is the permit to carry them," he said.

I looked down at the guns he placed before me. "I don't need, nor do I want, any guns. I can take care of myself. I have security at the house, as you well know."

"I thought you wanted to be a part of this." He waved his hands to display all that was on his desk and around the room.

"I do, but no guns," I answered.

"You told me that the man who approached your son was huge. What are you? Five foot ten, and a hundred and fifty pounds?"

"Five foot nine, and it's rude to ask a person over fifty their weight."

"Nick, I'm not kidding. You protect yourself at all times, or I walk. I turned down two cases this morning to work on yours."

I looked up at Paul, trying to decipher exactly how serious he was, but with that dark stubble, he couldn't look anything but.

I picked up the pistols. "All right, but if I shoot you by accident, or myself for that matter, don't be surprised."

"Put them on now," he insisted. "The pistols are loaded. Keep them away from children, and keep them holstered until you mean to shoot to kill."

He walked around his desk and strapped the ankle holster on me, then snapped the pistol into place, and dropped my pant leg over it. The belt holster was the harder one to get used to. I put that one on myself, then pulled my shirt out over my pants to conceal it. Once in place, I felt like I was carrying a 1980s cell phone.

"Let's get out of here," Paul said, "but first I want to show you something."

We walked past Jasmine, head in her computer, and into a conference room with a fifty-inch television screen hanging on the wall. Paul turned it on and clicked the remote to tune in Long Island's Channel 12 News.

A blonde female newscaster was speaking about upcoming Nassau County elections.

"Give it a minute," Paul said.

In less than that, she switched to another story. It was accompanied by videotape coverage of the relatives and friends of the four murdered prostitutes conducting a vigil and press conference beside the marsh where the bodies were found. I looked closely, but didn't see Lauren there. I wasn't the least bit surprised. These were mothers, aunts, sisters, boyfriends, and neighbors who came with varying motives in mind. One blurted that she was the mother of one of the victims. Evidently, her first stop that day was not the marsh, but the beauty parlor. With teased hair and caked on makeup, she rambled on about the lack of any "real police investigation into the crimes." She kept calling her daughter "my baby," while repeating that she "deserves her justice." A high school teenager and sister to one of the victims was also interviewed. She appeared to be genuinely grieving. I thought of Lauren, and wondered whether she would ever be able to live past her anger and pain.

"Looks like they're putting on a big show, a little too late if you ask me," Paul stated with an air of certainty and condescension. "If *my* daughter ran away, I wouldn't rest until I knew she was safe back home."

"I can't possibly put myself in their shoes, so I can't judge," I answered.

"Bullshit," he said callously. "They go on TV, they put themselves out there, they deserve to be judged. And they're not helping. The killer is probably watching, and eating this shit up."

"Let's hope for not much longer." Paul shot a smile my way that made me feel more than a little bit uneasy. For someone like myself, who liked to be in control, and got increasingly anxious the more I wasn't, I would have to live with the stark realization that I would never be in control of Paul.

For some reason though, thoughts of my limits made me think of Gina. Then again, a lot of things were. Amid my escalating fear over an unpredictable and heartless killer, she had been popping in and out of my head the entire day.

After we left Paul's office, we got into his nondescript 2009 blue Chevy Caprice, completely absent exterior accessories.

"It's my P.I. car," he said. "No one notices a middle-aged man driving a plain blue Chevy."

"How about a green van?" I asked.

Paul shrugged his shoulders. "We're going shopping for flowers," he said with a wry smile.

"In late August?"

"Yeah, maybe we'll find the secret of the Black Dahlia."

"I do believe that story is over three thousand miles away, and over fifty years old."

"You know your murder mystery history, don't you?"

"We don't look back on history enough for answers to today's problems."

"You couldn't be more right about that," Paul added. "That's why I don't go out on a job without the world of information with me."

What his Chevy lacked on the outside, it made up for on the inside. Propped on the dashboard was a directional navigator, along with a satellite radio, and chargers for an iPhone, iPad, and laptop computer. A double barrel shotgun, a twenty-two rifle, cuffs, rope, duct tape, several changes of clothes, and a huge toolbox were secured safely away in the trunk.

When Paul showed all this to me, I couldn't resist asking, "You sure you're not the killer?"

"You've got to think like one to catch one," he said glibly. "When we do catch him, we got the goods here to hold him until the police arrive."

"If he doesn't kill us first," I shot back.

"That's what you got those guns for, my friend."

We were driving down Massapequa's Broadway, which bore no resemblance whatsoever to the one in Manhattan, Nashville, or any other busy boulevard by the same name. This Broadway simply consisted of a quiet stretch of avenue that ran two lanes north and two lanes south with a mix of gas stations, retail stores, one-and-two story office buildings, and residential homes. When we came to the first nursery we saw, we stopped. It's name was Colombo Farms, and I thought back to one of the notations on the bulletin boards in Paul's office that read: "BURLAP BAGS—mostly for landscaping."

After we exited the car, we looked around for anyone vaguely resembling the tall, broadly built man John described.

Since no one fit the description, Paul and I walked into the nursery, pretending to be shopping for evergreens while eyeballing the help, who incidentally left us to fend for ourselves.

After we snooped around for ten minutes, Paul asked for the manager.

When he arrived, Paul told him that a big guy, who said he worked for a nursery in Massapequa, Long Island, was kind enough to push his wife and her car off the Brooklyn Bridge after her tire blew. Paul just happened to be in the neighborhood, and wanted to thank him personally with a case of beer he had in his trunk.

I marveled at Paul's believability as he spoke. I would easily have bought the story myself. Unfortunately, there were no takers. Paul left his cell number, should someone come to mind. The next stop: the Golden Thumb Nursery, and again there was no one who recalled a man who frequented their store in any capacity that fit the description John gave me.

Five nurseries later, and I was getting thoroughly sick of the smell of flowers and evergreens. In one, I actually bought a shrine enclosure for a statue of the Blessed Mother that I had sitting in my front garden. True to form, after I paid for it, the employee at the nursery wrapped it in burlap and handed it to me.

We left Massapequa and headed west on Merrick Road and into Seaford, where we stopped at Papa Giovanni's Garden.

As soon as we entered, a dark skinned middle-aged man who resembled Dean Martin, approached us. "Everything is discounted," he said. "It's that time of year."

I said, "thank you," and that I would be "happy just to look around," while Paul ignored him and kept walking.

Next to the register was an old Italian man with a vintage wooden cane that I was certain was not vintage when he bought it. He sent a toothless smile my way.

"*Bon giorno*," he said.

"*Bon giorno*," I answered in return. His smile widened.

"*Señore*, has any really large man worked for you in the past year or two?"

He looked at me quizzically. "*Che?*"

The Dean Martin look-alike walked over. "He doesn't speak a word of English. He used to, but he's ninety-one and forgot."

"I'm sorry. I was just making conversation. He was smiling at me."

"You're special then," he responded. "He doesn't smile at too many people."

"He is Giovanni, I take it?"

"You got it. My uncle—he started the business forty-five years ago. Likes coming in, says he's got to a keep an eye out for criminals and thieves. I don't know if he's talking about those of us who work here or the customers."

"He seems like a nice old man to me."

Dean Martin raised his eyebrows, then left to help an attractive young mother who was pushing a baby carriage.

I walked over to Paul, who was outside in the yard by a roped off area where dozens of skip laurels were tied together in bunches. There were "SOLD" signs on all of them.

"You know about skip laurels?" Paul asked.

"Just that they grow in the shade."

"That's right," Paul said bitterly. "They don't need any fucking sun. Sprout little white flowers in the spring that look like caterpillars."

"And this upsets you?"

"What kind of a fucking plant doesn't need sun to survive?" Paul was now staring off in another direction—at a forest of skip laurels sitting in their own individual bowls of dirt, stalks almost six feet high, packed tightly, their bottoms wrapped in burlap.

"I'm starting to think that we're wasting our time here at these nurseries," I said.

"What's the matter? Expect to crack the case on the first day in the field? What kind of a P.I. are you?"

"I'm not one at all, and I'm not sure I have the patience for this."

"No shit. You're a hell of a criminal lawyer though. Why then don't you employ some of that creativity of argument here and open your eyes."

"My eyes are open, and so are my ears, but all I'm seeing and hearing is *nada*."

Paul turned toward me and poked me gently in the chest. "You work with what you got, and we got burlap, and that means landscaping, unless

Long Island has a potato farm somewhere, or a coffee plantation. It may also interest you to know that there was no coffee or potato residue found in the bags."

"How do we know that this killer doesn't work for the Parks Department and got the burlap bags from a stockpile filled with sand to prevent beach erosion or flooding somewhere? Maybe he works at a supermarket and dumped the bags of potatoes and coffee before he filled them with dead prostitutes."

"I told you that there was no residue in the bags. The Parks Department is always a possibility, but that would mean he's a union man, and a union man is not a loner. A union man is a family man, who bowls with the league."

"What the hell are you talking about? Robert Schulman was a postal worker."

"Postal workers don't count. They're in their own class of crazy, like David Berkowitz. No…Burlap means landscaping. It's our best lead, and we got to go with it. Now c'mon, I'm sick of looking at these skip laurels."

As we exited the nursery, the old, Italian man stood up with the help of his cane, and started blabbering to me in Italian.

He must have said something Paul understood, because it stopped him dead in his tracks. Paul then responded in Italian to the old man, who sat back down and began rocking back and forth in his chair with a wide grin on his face. Paul leaned over, shook his hand and said, "grazie," then hurried out the door. As I turned to leave, the old man smiled at me one last time, then pointed his cane at me and nodded. He was still grinning from ear to ear.

I had to jog to catch up to Paul, who was already in the car. I opened the door and jumped in. "Where are we going?" I asked.

"The Seaford Reformed Church down the road. That old man evidently understands more English than he speaks. He told me in Italian that a guy, big like we described, buys for the church regularly and does all their plantings."

"Does he drive a green van?"

"He's not sure. The old man confessed that he's color-blind."

Chapter 45

"So you speak Italian too," I said to Paul, as he drove west on Merrick Road.

"Enough to get by. My parents were first-generation, spoke it to us growing up."

"Us? Who's us."

"My sister and me."

There were seconds of silence. "Paul, are you going to elaborate or not. You have a sister?"

"Had. She died over twenty years ago."

"Was she sick?"

"No. She was murdered by her husband."

"Holy shit, Paul! God, I'm sorry."

"I'm the one who should be sorry. I was away at college at the time. He seemed like an oddball to me, but she loved him. Came home from her honeymoon with a black eye and we knew, but she still wouldn't listen. Said it was an accident with a sliding door. Said if we didn't accept her explanation, she would never talk to us again. Time passed. She had a baby. Inasmuch as we could tell, no other physical abuse occurred, but they had money problems we didn't know about. Then when the baby was three months old, they had this huge fight. It ended with him beating her to death with a bedroom lamp. Later we found out that he was married before, and arrested for beating up his first wife too. He's now doing thirty to life."

Everyone has skeletons. Gina's words were ringing in my ears.

"I don't know what to say." I was breathless, while Paul spoke as if relaying an early morning news story with such calm in his voice that he appeared completely detached from it. He wasn't, of course.

"That's why I'm here with you, my friend, catching the bad guys," he said.

I knew all along that Paul wasn't just in this for the money. I knew there had to be more. When I left his office earlier in the day, I heard Jasmine talking on the phone. "He should be available in a week or two."

It was time to change the subject. "Do you think we should have asked the nephew to confirm what the old man told you?"

"Why? You aren't getting anything out of that guy. Did you see him jump when the hot mama with the baby carriage walked in?"

"Yeah, but—"

"But what you didn't see was him wiggle his wedding ring off his finger?"

"No, but…C'mon."

"C'mon my ass," Paul said, as we pulled into the parking lot of the Seaford Reformed Church. "That nephew wasn't volunteering shit. I know the type. He might've even dropped a dime on us if he knew who the guy was."

As we got out of Paul's Chevy, I asked, "Why aren't we telling people the truth?"

"Don't know who we can trust yet."

The church was a one-story brick building with large oak doors, a huge cross on the facade, and grounds meticulously landscaped.

I followed Paul into the inner vestibule. Pamphlets of different types were neatly stacked on a folding table beside the front doors. Inside, the church was simple contemporary; no baluster breaks between the audience and the altar, no large Roman columns or majestic dome ceilings that I had come to expect from my St. Francis of Assisi days in Brooklyn. On the left side of the altar, an upright piano and several music stands marked an area reserved for a small group of musicians and singers. Front and center were two sets of steps that led to a heightened lectern where a giant crucifix hung from a peaked cathedral ceiling directly overhead. Off to the right was a doorway that led to a small sacristy and office. It was there that we found the Reverend at his desk, head buried in a notebook. He looked up as we entered, then stood, smiled, and extended his hand graciously.

"Welcome gentlemen. Can I help you?" He was eyeing us from head to toe as he spoke.

Paul began, and to my amazement, by sort of telling the truth. "My name is Paul. This is Nick. We're private investigators looking for a missing young woman. Her father, a wealthy businessman, hired us to find her. There is a reward for information."

"Okay," the Reverend replied, as his face took on a comic playfulness. "And you think I can help you? Was this young woman part of my congregation?"

"No," Paul answered abruptly, "but maybe someone who attends services here, or works here, knows her and where she is."

"Works here?" The Reverend appeared more curious than puzzled. "Well, who is the woman? I'll tell you if I know her."

"We have no reason to believe you know her, but you may know someone who does," Paul said authoritatively.

The Reverend seemed amused. "If you have a question, Paul, I would appreciate it if you would just ask it."

"I must caution you, Reverend. I need you to be honest with me. Withholding or falsifying information in an ongoing police investigation *can* make you an accessory after the fact, which in this case would be a very serious felony."

The Reverend was unshaken. "First of all, you're not police, but I'll answer you anyway, and truthfully, of course. Second, you have to ask me a question first. Now, there is a service in one hour, and I am in the process of fine-tuning my sermon. So please, ask me what it is you want to ask me."

"I meant no offense," Paul said. "It's just that I have a duty to tell you these things."

"Okay then."

"Your landscaper?"

"Gaetano? Gerry?"

"If that's his name, yes."

"What about him?"

"Can you describe him to us please?"

The Reverend sat back down in his chair and looked up. "He's a nice man, a family man, gives us a discount. He's not a member of our church, but does so anyway. He's Catholic. I'm pretty sure of that. He often comes late at night, and sometimes early in the morning; says he has to because he's busy during the day covering his regulars."

"What does he look like?"

"Don't you know?"

"Yes, but I want to make sure we're talking about the same person."

"Well, he's huge. I think that's fair to say. He has to tilt his head down when he walks under that doorframe you just passed through."

"Does he come with a crew?"

"Never, and does a wonderful job, as you can see, but always alone. I suppose he uses his workers for his regular, higher paying customers. I'm not the only church he gives a break to by the way. I'm pretty sure about that."

"When he comes here, does he drive a work truck of some kind or a work van?" The more forthcoming the Reverend became, the more Paul lightened his tone.

The Reverend thought for a moment. "I've always seen him in a station wagon. He stuffs the plantings in the back, most of them on their sides."

"Why a station wagon?" Paul spoke as if thinking aloud.

"Don't know," the Reverend answered. "Can't fit much in it, which is why he often has to make several trips."

"Several trips? To where?"

"If it's during the day, which is rare, Papa Giovanni's. The receipts are on the bills he gives me."

"What about at night?"

"Don't know. He sometimes leaves and comes back about fifteen or twenty minutes later. He must have a yard or his own place nearby where he stores stuff."

"You say, 'he must have.' Why wouldn't he? Why would you think otherwise?"

"I don't know really. It's just that the address on his business card is a PO Box in Mineola. When I see a PO Box for a business address, I figure the person works out of their home."

"Can I see the card?"

"You can have one. I have a few." The Reverend handed Paul a business card, which Paul glanced at quickly, and then put in the breast pocket of his shirt.

"How old is Gerry?"

"About my age, forty-five I suppose."

"Anything else you can tell me about him?"

"The Reverend looked up at us from behind his desk. "You know gentlemen, I'm starting to feel a bit guilty talking to you. Gerry is a good man. I never had a problem with him. He's reliable, and as you can see, does a wonderful job here. He's also had his share of sadness, so I would appreciate it, before you go prying further into his life that you be sure of what you're doing. I hate to see you upsetting him or his wife unnecessarily."

Paul didn't hesitate. "What sadness is that?"

The Reverend huffed, and leaned back. "You see," he said. "I shouldn't have said more than I needed to." He paused, and this time leaned forward, put his pen down, and rested his arms on the desk. "Five years ago, he lost his only child, a pretty little girl, only seven years old, to cancer. He and his wife were devastated. So please gentlemen, tread lightly and carefully." He picked up his pen again and looked down at his notebook, then stood as a signal for us to leave. "Now, if you'll excuse me."

Paul extended his hand, shook the Reverend's, and thanked him. When I did the same, the Reverend looked into my eyes and repeated, "please," as I turned to leave.

Paul exited the office first, with me close behind. As soon as he passed through the doorway, he stopped. "Reverend, if you don't mind my asking, do you live nearby?"

The Reverend sat back down, and already had his head conveniently buried in his notebook. He looked up. "Yes, Paul, I do live nearby," he responded, his patience strained by Paul's continued questions.

"Own your own home?"

"Yes, Paul, my wife and I, and my two boys, live quite happily in our own home."

"Does Gerry do your landscaping there?"

The Reverend's facial expression instantly showed his displeasure. "No, he does not."

I stepped aside to let Paul pass as he re-entered the office. Paul looked around, pretending to be genuinely puzzled before locking eyes with the Reverend seated cautiously behind his desk. "Seems to me," Paul said. "If you're so happy with Gerry's work here, you would also use him at home. He'd probably discount that for you too."

"My home is personal," the Reverend answered indignantly. "I wouldn't expect a discount."

"Regardless," Paul insisted. "Why wouldn't you still give Gerry the business?"

"See, this is why I regret talking to you two in the first place." It was at that moment that I figured out what Paul was leading up to.

"You said, Reverend, that he is a good man, lost his daughter and all. What am I missing here? You know, I expect you to tell me the truth." Paul looked around the room until his eyes made its own gesture in the direction of the cross on the wall. He then added, "Man of God that you are."

"I don't like your tone, nor do I appreciate the content of your questions," said the Reverend.

Paul walked over to the door and pulled it shut, then walked back and leaned over the desk. "I don't care what you like, or what you don't like. Now if you don't want me to go ask your wife the same questions, you answer them."

The Reverend pushed his chair back while he was still in it. The wheels underneath were in need of an oiling, and squeaked like the hinges on some rickety old basement door. He looked up at Paul, first sheepishly, then defiantly. "She thinks he's, well, unusual. She met him once. It was nighttime. I was working late. She came to bring me dinner. He was around. She told me that he made her feel uncomfortable."

Paul stared down at the Reverend, like a mother superior to a student who had done wrong and wasn't nearly telling the whole truth about it.

The Reverend reluctantly continued. "She said he looked creepy. There, you have it. I have now indirectly slandered an innocent man, whose suffering I can only imagine."

"Is there anything else?" Paul asked commandingly, before he placed his business card on the center of the desk and directly on top of the notebook that the Reverend had been working in.

"No," the Reverend shot back.

Paul stepped back and paused, as if to clear the air of the animus before he left. "Thank you," he said politely.

When we got back in the car, I found myself staring at Paul. "I must tell you. You were great in there. That house question…Where did that come from?"

Paul mostly ignored me. "We still don't have that fucking green van, but I'd love to know where this guy goes for just fifteen or twenty minutes when he leaves here. Mineola is at least forty minutes away."

"I don't know," I answered. "Must be somewhere nearby I suppose."

"That somewhere nearby might just be the answer to all our questions."

Chapter 46

As we were pulling out of the parking lot, I noticed a familiar car, a yellow VW bug, and its familiar driver. It was James Clancy, my next-door neighbor while I was growing up in Merrick.

He was in his late thirties then, and my very first friend on Long Island. Now approaching eighty, he unabashedly wore his years with the ragged pride of a fading soldier since losing his wife, Carol, to cancer in 2000. I will never forget his kindness toward me during the loneliest and most tender years of my young life.

The Clancy family, which included two children, were as wholesome an American family as the sinews of my bloodline were dysfunctional. When I was in law school, and the adult world of acquired ambition was pulling me in different directions, our chats grew shorter, and the time we spent together practically disappeared.

I would not let Paul pull away without saying hello to my old friend. While I knew James Clancy was religious, I had forgotten that he had been attending the Seaford Reformed Church for decades.

When Paul cut the Chevy's tires to the curb, I jumped out and headed for the yellow bug as it pulled into the church parking lot.

As I approached Mr. Clancy's car, he looked out his window and smiled. "I know you."

"I should hope so," I responded as he got out of the tiny Volkswagen, all lumbering six feet of him, and extended his hand. He was wearing a tweed jacket, overalls and black shoes. There were vases of flowers across the rear seat cushion.

He gestured toward them. "Got a good deal. Will brighten up the altar this evening. Hey, I thought you were a good Catholic boy. What'd you do, convert?"

"Not yet, but it's great to see you. How've you been, Mr. Clancy?"

He leaned against the bug. "It's great to see you too, Nick. You look thin to me, though."

"I know. I'm not getting enough Italian lately. That must be the reason."

"Too bad Carol isn't still around. Not an Italian girl, you know, but she made a pretty good sauce."

"Yes, she did, and I would've enjoyed that, Mr. Clancy."

"So what the heck are you doing here anyway?" He smiled, and gently punched my shoulder. He looked much older than I remembered. His face was pale, and since Carol had passed, the loss and loneliness appeared to have taken its toll. "Hey, you okay, Nick?" he asked.

I had drifted. "Sure," I said weakly.

"I don't believe you. What's wrong? Something I could do? Were you looking for me here?"

"No, not at all. This was a stroke of luck that I ran into you."

"All right then."

"Mr. Clancy—"

"Jim, please."

"Jim, I'm working with that man in the car over there—" I caught myself, as I was about to fess up to my old friend. Some forty years earlier, James Clancy retired as a lieutenant from the New York City Police Department. That was ages ago. The man that stood before me was a worn down old man. I couldn't bear to burden him with the ugly truth. "If you must know, I'm trying to help a client find his daughter."

"That guy?" He pointed to the Chevy with Paul in it.

"No. He's a private investigator I'm working with."

"Oh, okay, but why come to the church?"

"We think the landscaper here might know something."

"I knew that guy was strange," he answered, while shaking his head. "You know, Nick, you never lose that cop instinct."

"Then can you help me with something, in confidence?"

"Of course, of course, Nick." He put his hand on my shoulder and squeezed. "Whatever I can do. You want me to talk to the guy?"

My heart instantly skipped a beat. "No, definitely not." I took a breath and tried to quell my appearance of alarm as I became instantly afraid for my old friend. "It's just that I think the Reverend might know more than he's telling us."

"You want me to talk to him instead?"

"Please. Yes. The guy we're looking for is big, like the lawn man, but may drive a green van sometimes."

"Okay, I'll see what I can find out for you. I know the Reverend for almost ten years now. He's a good man, but he may be the kind of guy who runs a bit scared, definitely the kind who doesn't want to get involved in something like this, if you know what I mean."

"I do. Can you see if he knows whether or not this landscaper has a place around here—a yard, a business office, a house?"

"Sure, Nick."

"I can't thank you enough." I shook his hand. "If you give me your cell phone, I'll put my number in it."

"Don't have a cell phone, but I got your number at the house."

"You probably have my house number."

"That's all I need," he responded. "If you're not there, I'll just leave a message on your machine."

I gave James Clancy a warm hug, and thanked him again. As I walked away, I looked up at the sky and made the sign of the cross. It was nothing short of divine providence that I ran into him. What I didn't know then, was that it would be the last time I would ever talk to my oldest and dearest friend.

His big heart would fail him less than a year later.

It was getting close to 6:30 PM, and Paul and I were famished.

After a hearty meal, comprised of lobster-filled ravioli and the real veal Dario (not Harlan's best effort), at Dario's Restaurant in Rockville Centre, we headed back to his office. Paul dropped me beside my car in the parking lot.

As I arrived home, I waved to the security guard stationed by the garages, then went upstairs to shower. The first thing I did was take off the ankle and belt holsters and place them, along with the pistols, inside my night table drawer. As I headed to the master bath and passed the answering machine on what had *been* Eleanor's night table, I heard the repetitive beep, signaling that there was a message. It was James Clancy.

"Nick, it's Jim. Turns out that this Gaetano, or Gerry, or whatever his name is, did have a green van one time. It was an old jalopy. The Reverend made a joke about it. Seems Gaetano got a bit embarrassed, and said it was his mother's, and he was going to junk it. The Reverend never saw it again after that. This was about two years ago by the way. Hope this helps you. Now be careful, you hear me, Nick, and God bless you, and call me once in a while."

I immediately called Paul and told him.

"See you tomorrow morning," is all he said.

I don't think I got but two hour's sleep that night.

Chapter 47

When I finally decided to get out of bed because no further sleep seemed possible, I immediately checked my cell phone. There was a missed call from Charlotte. Missed, because I had silenced the ring when I entered the church the day before.

Since it was 8 AM, I would catch her on her way to work. Trump Tower was only three blocks from her grandfather's hedge fund offices.

"You promised you would call me every day," she said.

"Sorry, sweetheart. I'm glad you called instead." *Thrilled was more like it.*

"You're alone in a big house, and I'm worried about you."

Not half as much as I'm worried about you. Charlotte must have had some of her mother's instincts, because she never worried about me before. But it was my own instincts or premonitions that worried me more. "That's sweet of you, but the house is not that big, and I've still got security outside."

"I thought you were going to the Hamptons and letting them go."

From the background noise, I could tell that she was walking outdoors. The familiar sound of Manhattan traffic was in the background.

"I'm leaving for the Hamptons in a day or two. I'll let the security guards go then." My lies multiplying, the more I talked about the Hamptons and thought about the Hamptons, the more I actually wanted to go to the Hamptons.

"And I want to hear about this girlfriend of yours." Charlotte said cutely.

I couldn't imagine John being so glib about my being with a woman other than his mother, four years of separation or not. When it came, however, to the non-partying, practical, and no-nonsense ways of the world, regardless of how many times Charlotte deviated from the sensible, she often seemed smarter than John. She led with her head, he with his heart.

"I'd be happy to expound when there's more to tell," I answered.

"Alright," she said with the playful pretense of dissatisfaction.

It was time to change the subject anyway. "I'm afraid to ask John, so tell me, how is Sofia?"

"The same," she said with sober disappointment.

"Is John eating?" I asked.

"Mrs. Perez brings him food every day. He stays with Sofia constantly. I don't think he has slept in his apartment since she went missing. I try to go to the hospital every day, if only for John. The Perezes are always there too. Dad, they sure are wonderful people—a real family."

I successfully hid the instantaneous hurt I felt after Charlotte called the Perezes "a real family," although compared to the Manninos of the past four years, I shouldn't have been surprised.

"Call me if anything changes with Sofia, okay? I love you very much, and don't forget. I don't want you out and about alone."

Charlotte responded as chipper as a teenager. "You worry too much, Dad, but I won't go out alone. I promise. And I love you, too."

I lay back down on the bed with my head buried in the pillow. As I placed the cell phone back on the night table, I wondered how long I was going to leave Eleanor's wedding ring sitting where she had left it.

I made a mental note to call Gina before the day was over.

I had been coming and going from the house, often oblivious to the security stationed outside. I usually parked in the front driveway. The guards always parked in the back. I suppose it was their job to be as inconspicuous as possible, but after acquiring yesterday's leads, and believing that we had come closer than anyone thus far to finding out who the Jones Beach killer was, I was keenly aware of my surroundings—when I felt safe, and when I didn't.

And the clues, and their dangerous implications, were beginning to add up.

The green van I had seen after I left the beach, the green van John noticed the strange large man drive out of Field 6, the creepy landscaper once seen in a green van he claimed belonged to his mother, plus the *vengaren* anagram—all added up to one major lead.

But was there any real proof or evidence thus far linking this landscaper and the green van with any crime?

Not even close.

When I arrived at Paul's office, he was already barking orders while Jasmine was taking notes at his desk. He ignored me, and abruptly headed out of the room as I entered.

He barely got through the doorway, when he shouted back, "So we know who the landscaper is. We know where he lives. So what? If we go to his house, what are we going to find?" Paul walked back to his desk, picked up a photo and slapped it on to my chest. "Here's a picture of his lovely home off Nassau County's *Land Record Viewer*."

The business card that the Reverend gave Paul read: *Gaetano's Lawn and Garden Inc., Gaetano Perduto, President.* Jasmine had hacked Nassau County's new computerized deed recording system, and got a hit on a property owned by a Gaetano Perduto on Segreto Place just off Mineola Avenue. It was a large corner contemporary ranch on an oversized lot, and it looked like any man's home—well-kept, warm, friendly, and of course, beautifully landscaped.

Paul waited for me to take a good look at the photo, then continued. "All we do by going there is tip him off. What I'd really like to do is secretly get inside and see what I can find. I've already got an investigator positioned down the block with a hidden camera and binoculars. When our man finally came out of his house and went into his garage, my investigator drove by to see what was inside." Paul paused a few seconds. "No green van."

"He wouldn't keep that shitty van at his home anyway," I said.

"I know," Paul shot back. "But find the van, and we find the kill location."

"You really think this is our man?" I asked.

Paul shook his head indecisively, then paced in front of me while examining the bulletin boards filled with his war room notes and photos. "Yeah...I feel it. I'm just not a hundred percent yet."

"I think that's for the best. The lack of certainty will keep us on our toes."

"I'm already on my toes. I also had Jasmine check the motor vehicle databases for registered vans more than ten years old with owners in Seaford, Massapequa, and Amityville—all inside the three-mile radius of that cell tower the call came from. Then I had her shrink the search down to the color green. Since the Reverend told your Mr. Clancy that our suspect's van was once his mother's, I had Jasmine shrink the search down further to female owners. In total, you know how many we got?"

"I have no idea," I answered.

"Seventy-four. You believe that? With this recession, people are holding on to their cars and vans like the world's coming to an end."

"That doesn't surprise me."

"Well it surprised the shit out of me, so we narrowed the search down further to people who also own a home, and then further, who own a home with an attached garage." Paul pointed to several aerial maps taped to the wall. "The homes in these areas were built pretty close together. The killer would not be able to bring women, tied up and gagged, into a house there from a van in the driveway or the street without the risk of being seen."

"So he probably has a garage with a connecting door to the house."

"Right," Paul said emphatically.

"But what if he's not doing this in a house at all, but a place of business, a warehouse, a large garage?"

"No," Paul responded. "He keeps the girls and their bodies too long. It's got to be in a place where no one else comes and goes—a private home that only he has access to."

"Okay," I said. "Back to Jasmine's search. Attached garages. Now what numbers are we down to?"

"Thirty-three."

"Still sounds like too many, but manageable."

"Yes, manageable, and that's if I'm right."

Paul walked around his desk and sat down. I continued standing.

"You know what's strange?" Paul asked.

"This whole goddamn case?"

"What I mean is…We must have gone to a dozen nurseries and asked hundreds of questions."

I just looked at him and nodded slightly.

Paul continued. "We asked a lot of people a lot of things."

"I was there, Paul."

"Get any sense that anyone was there before us asking the same questions. You know, like the police?"

"Now that you mention it, no."

"So what the hell do you make of that?"

"I don't know. I guess they don't have our leads to run with."

"They know about the burlap, and the cell call that bounced off the Massapequa Tower. Isn't that enough?"

"I don't know. I just don't know."

"I don't know either," Paul said. "And that's what worries me."

Jasmine walked in with a sheet of paper in her hand. She spoke matter-of-factly. "This is a list of houses with attached garages in Seaford, Amityville and Massapequa once owned solely by women, who also owned a green van whose year, regardless of the make and model, was prior to 2000." She then handed the list to Paul.

"Okay," Paul said. "Now we're down to twenty-four."

Jasmine was undaunted. "Here's another list of houses with the same pedigree: attached garage, one woman once on the deed who also owned a green van older than the year 2000, but narrowed down much further, because on this list, the women who owned both the house and the car are now dead."

Paul took the list out of Jasmine's hand. "There's just five houses here. Of course." His eyes took on a glazed look. "He couldn't be killing women in a house that his mother still lives in."

"Joel Rifkin did, and in nearby East Meadow," I said anxiously.

"But he didn't torture them, and store their bodies there," Paul responded. "No, Jasmine's right to cut the list down. This house is our killer's sole hideaway, where he can imprison, torture, kill, and do whatever the hell else he wants, and answer to no one."

"This breakdown, though clever, just seems a bit too easy," I responded. "That one of these five houses could be the kill location—"

"That's why I need to get into that Mineola home," Paul said pensively.

"He lives there with his wife. What is there to find out?"

"I don't know, but before I go breaking into five different homes and maybe get myself killed, I want to make sure that this is our man, because let's face it, we've got a promising lead that at the same time proves jack shit so far."

"So what you're telling me is that we're going gangsta', and breaking into this guy's fucking house in Mineola."

"That's about right, but *you* are not going to have anything to do with it. I have two investigators outside right now. The moment an opening appears and the house is empty, I'm going in. Until then, we're on hold."

"Okay, but do we know who owns these five other houses?"

"No one with the last name Perduto, now or ever," Jasmine answered.

"Maybe the mother remarried, and has a different last name. Mine did," I said.

"If you want me to trace five family trees, including in-laws, I'll need a lot more time, and might still come up empty," Jasmine shot back. "Also, not everyone gets married in New York, you know."

My lawyer brain started spinning, and I wasn't sure who was more anxious and impatient—me or Paul. "Maybe our killer put the deed in another name prior to 2000. These five houses could be a big waste of time," I responded.

"That's why we need to get into the Mineola house ASAP," Paul reiterated.

Jasmine, thus far, seemed oblivious to the hyperactivity coming from Paul and me, until she broke her silence, once again, with somewhat of a bombshell. "You said the Reverend told you that the landscaper's daughter died of cancer. Well, you'll be interested to know that I looked up the case at Winthrop Hospital, also in Mineola. The little girl was admitted through emergency on the evening of February 26, 2005, where she was pronounced dead by the physician on duty shortly after she arrived. The cause of death was not cancer, by the way. According to her medical records, she fell down the basement stairs in her home and broke her neck. She was twelve years old at the time, not seven like that Reverend said, and she was alone in the house when it happened—alone, that is, except for her father."

Paul and I were dumbstruck and remained standing, frozen in silence, not sure if Jasmine had finished. She hadn't. After she took a deep breath, she rolled her eyes then said casually, "There's more. One of the interns, the first to see the twelve year old, noted something in tiny scrawl on the report of her initial examination in emergency. Get this—seems the little girl's hymen appeared to have been recently broken."

"And the police reports?" Paul asked.

"They just include a statement about the fall with the cause of death a broken neck." Paul was about to say something else when Jasmine put up her hand. "Before you ask, there was no police investigation into the cause of the broken hymen or the cause of death at all, and here's what's really unusual—no autopsy."

Paul was even more determined than ever to get into the Gaetano Perduto residence. The last thing he said to me, just before we parted that day, included strict words of warning.

I was not to do anything, or say anything to anyone, without hearing from him first, and I was not to call him until he called me first. There was to be no connection or link of any kind that would implicate me in any way to the break-in of the Mineola home, whether Paul got caught doing so, or not.

Paul would be acting entirely on his own.

Chapter 48

Before Paul's excursion into the private home of a likely serial killer, I decided to take a look at Jasmine's final five. Since all the homes just happened to be in Seaford, I figured it would take me no more than thirty minutes to give each a once over.

As I drove by, I slowed to eyeball each of the houses through the Mercedes' tinted windows as best I could without attracting attention. The façade and the landscaping of each property seemed different from its photo. That was because the photos taken from Nassau County's land record website were far from current. Three of them were from the year 2000, the other two from 2006. As a result, the garage of the first house I saw was missing entirely and replaced by a small basketball court, while the garage of the second had been converted to living space. I excluded a third home because of the activity in and around it. A small bicycle along with a portable hockey net, kneepads, and skates were on the lawn. The front door was also wide open, and a vacuum cleaner could be heard running with loud music playing over it. All things considered, this was no monster's hideaway.

The last two homes, however, did fit the profile. Lacking all indication of life and activity on the outside, it was hard to believe that anyone was living on the inside. The fourth home I drove past had overgrown grass, hedges in desperate need of trimming, and an old blistered white garage door. No mail was in the mailbox, and the front windows on the first floor had been left open a few inches. If there was a green van inside or around any of the first four homes, I hadn't seen it. Regardless, I set my sights on the fifth house.

It too seemed lacking occupants and activity of any kind, but there was one distinguishing feature—the finely cut lawn and perfectly trimmed bushes and trees. I even spotted several automatic sprinkler heads in the strip of grass adjacent to the curb. There would be no reason for any neighbor to complain about the look or upkeep of this home, because from the outside, it was getting regular care and attention.

It was the last house on the left of one of the most southern stretches of road in Seaford, Long Island. Eighteen-foot high evergreens lined its side and rear lot lines, though not all were visible from the street, despite my two moderately slow drive-bys. Behind the house was a narrow canal that led into the Great South Bay. Again, there was no green van in sight, just a tarnished green garage door that matched the home's sun-bleached green shutters. Like the house, the garage door was old, but maintained well. It also had two rectangular windows, but curiously, they appeared blackened somehow.

During my third pass in front of the house, I noticed that the mailbox by the front door was stuffed with supermarket ads, and though it was late summer, the blinds were closed and the windows shut. I parked my car around the block and decided to walk by like a casual pedestrian. It was then that I spotted the small air conditioner protruding from a basement window well, and my level of anxiety heightened. In a matter of seconds, I felt as if my entire body was overheating. Walking faster than I intended, I got back into the car and turned the AC up to the max to help me cool and calm down. It did neither. What did work was the shot of Seagram' 7 I guzzled down upon arriving back home. Not much of a drinker, its effect on me was nothing short of a jolt to my system. I then called Paul's office and reported my findings to Jasmine.

I gave her the address of the house, 6 Mayberry Street, and then asked to speak to Paul. She said that he was on his way to Mineola and could no longer take any calls.

"I hope he's careful," I said.

"He's determined," was Jasmine's unsatisfying answer.

Paul was moving on calls he received from the investigators stationed near the home and armed with binoculars. No security cameras or any signs of an alarm system were spotted, and from the action around the home, it appeared that Mr. and Mrs. Perduto were going out for the evening.

When the couple eventually left together around 8 PM, Mr. Perduto was observed locking the front door, then checking the handle.

Neither investigator needed their binoculars to confirm that Gaetano Perduto was one large man. They estimated him to be about forty years old, with a pretty, middle-aged wife at his side, whose petite frame easily disappeared beside him as they walked toward the black SUV in their driveway.

No sign of a green van, and no sign of a station wagon either.

When the final shades of darkness fell at about 8:30 PM, with one investigator at one end of the block, and another in a car around the corner, Paul proceeded to sneak through the backyard of the house directly behind Perduto's. His plan: Break in through the rear kitchen door by picking the lock, then get in and get out with no one the wiser.

But things did not go as planned.

Chapter 49

It was 6 PM. I kept picking up my cell phone to call Gina, but I wanted to make sure I had sufficiently calmed down. The house on Mayberry Street was still spooking the crap out of me. I felt like an innocent bystander in a David Lynch movie, where the streets were sunny and the flowers blooming, while inside the confines of bleak cinderblock walls the criminally insane were screaming "Mommy," and satisfying their demented urges.

I was also worried about Paul. Could there be anything more dangerous than breaking into the private home of a serial killer? And what if something did happen to him—an arrest, or worse, serious injury or death? How would I live with myself? I was the one who goaded him into this hunt, and the closer it seemed we got to our target, like a wolf closing in for the kill, the more resolute Paul became. I only hoped that the determination Jasmine spoke of wouldn't cloud his better judgment and concern for his own safety and survival.

If 6 Mayberry Street was the house of horrors, if Paul was rendered out of commission in Mineola, who would be left to continue the search. And, would there be any evidence remaining once the killer got wise to our hunt for him?

I was breaking into cold sweats. Though I would tell Gina nothing, the company of one pretty doctor with one pretty smile seemed like the right antidote. Either that, or I just wanted to be with her.

I made the call that I had been thinking about, on and off, the entire day.

Gina sounded genuinely pleased to hear from me. She added that her daughter was, coincidentally, in the Hamptons with friends. If I didn't mind the company of her little guy until he went to bed at 8:30, I was invited to dine Italian with the two of them.

The little guy was adorable, and Gina was the only one capable at that moment of getting my mind off 6 Mayberry Street and the impending Mineola break-in.

I gladly accepted.

Before I left the house, I grabbed the holstered pistols and placed them in the trunk of the S600. I didn't feel comfortable leaving them in my night table drawer. Besides, Paul was on one dangerous mission, and… you never know.

I drove to Gina's, and parked in the street. When she answered the door with face glowing and eyes wide, I couldn't help but smile as she leaned toward me with a ladle in her hand and planted a sweet kiss on my cheek. She was wearing fitted slacks and a sexy white blouse with string shoulders, and all I could think of was how fabulous she looked, and how lucky I felt to be there. Thoughts of Paul and 6 Mayberry Street were instantly wiped from my mind.

"I'm making lasagna. It's Joey's favorite."

The little guy was sitting in a booster seat at a small dinette table just off the kitchen.

"So Joey is your name," I said.

The little guy nodded.

"I had a friend once named Joey, but he was an old guy. How old are you?"

"I'll be five, November 30," he said excitedly, then caught me off balance with the next question. "How old will you be?"

Gina looked over at the two of us, and smiled.

"Well," I said only slightly embarrassed. Despite a full head of dark brown hair, I knew I would have to fess up. I also knew that I had at least ten years on Gina, and was hoping to keep that under wraps for a little while longer. Gina knew about my son, my somewhat estranged wife, and in a few seconds a little bit more about me than I cared to admit. "I just turned fifty-six."

"Wow," he said, "you're old, like my mom. She's going to be forty-three in December."

"Joey!" Gina shrieked.

"Women don't like to reveal their age sometimes," I whispered to him. "But when they're as beautiful as your mom, it doesn't matter."

Gina came to the table with the tray of lasagna and placed it on a decorative pad, out of little Joey's reach. She then returned with a large serving dish of veal parmesan and sat down. Joey held up his plate, one hand on each side, and with spatula in hand, Gina placed an adult portion of lasagna on it.

"Are you going to eat all that?" I asked.

He nodded back, and gobbled up a saucy face forkful.

"Oh, he can finish that and more," Gina said. "Now all we really need to do is fatten *you* up a bit. I expect you to finish everything on your plate as well, Mister."

"I'm sure I will, though my appetite, I must confess, isn't what it used to be."

"I saw how you stuffed yourself at Harlan's."

With that, I took a bite of the lasagna, which was the closest to Mom's that I had ever tasted.

"This is delicious. Damn, Gina."

"I'm glad you like it," she responded. "But there's one thing we must also put on the table right now."

"Oh boy," I said. "Here it comes."

Gina was trying hard not to smile. "So...you're fifty-six, I hear. You realize that's much too old for me."

"Mom!" Joey squealed. "You're old too."

"Hmm." Gina pretended to be pondering my fate. "Okay Joey. Are you really sure we should keep this old and crusty guy around?"

Joey looked over at me with a lasagna smile. "I don't see any crust."

"There you go," I said to Gina. "No crust."

Gina was smiling sweetly. "Okay, but once I see even the faintest trace, you're outta here."

"I can live with that."

As a final addition, Gina whipped up two cappuccinos from her own store-bought espresso machine. She insisted that I replace my usual two Equals with Stevia. I complied, and had to admit, it was a good substitute. But what I liked most was someone caring enough about what I put in my coffee to begin with. For the past four years, I was entirely on my own. It was only Charlotte, as of late, that showed any interest in my well-being, and that was a first.

After we finished our cappuccinos, and the little guy polished off a cup of chocolate ice cream with whipped cream, his mom announced that it was time for bed.

"It's only 8:30, and it's a weekend," Joey complained.

"I'll let you watch an episode of *Seinfeld* on your computer, then right to sleep," Gina commanded.

"Okay," he said cutely.

"Now say good night to Nick."

"Good night, Nick." I got that little wave again.

Gina and Joey disappeared down the hall. When Gina returned, I couldn't help but ask, "*Seinfeld*? Does he get the jokes?"

"Probably very few."

Joey could be heard laughing in the distance.

"It's the characters," she said. "Their antics just crack him up."

"They crack me up too, but as we've already established, I'm old."

"You're not that old," she said as she leaned over and gave me a quick kiss on the lips.

I offered to help clear the table, but she responded with a firm, "No thank you."

I cleared the table anyway.

After the faint childish laughter died down, Joey went to sleep. Though the unexpected kiss on the lips would have normally made me forget my own name, this was not a normal night. I checked my phone. It was 8:50 PM. *Where exactly was Paul, and what was he doing?* If things got hairy, I knew Jasmine would call. Nevertheless, I tried unsuccessfully to relax. When Gina finished with the dishes, she walked over and sat down on the couch. After kicking off her shoes, she curled up next to me, and all thoughts of Paul and his covert mission flew out of my head in an instant. They were immediately replaced with but one—holding Gina and kissing her back.

A split second later, entwined on the couch, we were French kissing each other with such reckless abandon, you'd think we had seconds left to live and our singular purpose was to enter heaven in a lustful blaze of glory. Although we were entirely aware of what we were doing, I do believe we had forgotten where we were doing it—which explains why Gina suddenly stopped, and pulled away with such a blank stare, I had no idea what to expect next. All I can remember is that I was holding her hand, and she was leading me up a short flight of stairs and into a guest bedroom on the second floor.

"*My* bedroom is right next to Joey's." She spoke softly and began kissing me again, only this time with less abandon, but with just as much intensity.

Between breaths, I answered, "Don't want to wake him. I get that."

To which she chuckled, then kissed me some more, while pulling me onto a twin size bed. In turn, I kicked off my shoes, and in a moment of patient reconsideration, amid the irrepressible levels of lust and love, I paused to stroke the side of her face with my hand, while gently and carefully kissing her on what had become a pair of very wet and inviting lips. I knew then that I had experienced this level of authentic passion before, but it was so long ago, I had no tactile memory of it.

Gina slowed down along with me, which only served to enhance my desire for her. I pulled her fitted blouse up and off then stroked her soft tight stomach, while my other hand moved from around her waist down toward her bottom. By this time Gina had unbuckled my belt and pants, but I was not having the same luck with her slacks. She laughed at my lack of success in discovering whatever it was, button or zipper, that was the key to removing them.

When I did find the clasp, which was conveniently located in the front, my symphonic *Moon River* ring tone filled the room, and stopped us cold.

Gina looked at me with concern.

"I'm so sorry, but this must be important," I said.

It was Paul calling.

Inasmuch as I was hanging on his every word, I was even more aware of my responses. I didn't want to worry Gina, and worse, I didn't want her asking questions that I couldn't answer.

"What do you mean?" I asked into the phone. "Are you sure?"

Paul laid out a case for urgency.

"You mean there is no one else?" I asked. "I want to be there, but…"

I listened as Paul, with a fierce determination that wouldn't be quelled no matter what I said, laid out his plan for the balance of the evening, and the heightened danger in it.

I closed with, "I'm on my way."

"What is it?" Gina pleaded. "It's about that killer you spoke of at Harlan's, isn't it?"

Gina stood up and began getting dressed. I had already gotten my clothes back on while talking to Paul.

"You know that I hired a private investigator."

"Yes, so why do *you* have to go?"

"He just needs me to vouch for him, and tell the police that I hired him, should they ask."

"So you're going to the police?"

"No, I'm going to one of the victim's houses. Paul wants me to assure the family that he is there to help, and not just snooping around."

"I'm not sure I understand."

"I'm really sorry, Gina. I'll explain more later." There was no way I could tell her more than I already had. One, it would take too long, and two, it would worry her sick, though it seemed that was exactly what I was doing anyway. I bent over and kissed her on the lips. "I'll call you within the hour." An unintended lie, among a slew of real ones.

As I hurried out the front door, I glanced at the green light on her alarm pad, and yelled, "Please put your house alarm on." I then slammed the door shut harder than I meant to.

After I got into my car, I drove around the block and parked in a secluded spot under the darkness of a large tree. I went into my trunk and took out the waist and ankle holsters—the .38 caliber pistols snapped in and fully loaded. I got back in the car and drove away. Keenly aware of the omnipresent Village Police, I minded the speed limit until I left Garden City, then ran every stop sign and red light, and with hell-on-wheels fury headed for 6 Mayberry Street.

Chapter 50

My nerves were getting the better of me. I could taste the lasagna again, and feared that at any moment I was going to projectile vomit all over the dashboard.

I called Paul.

With the Mercedes Bluetooth connected, I could talk with both hands on the wheel, while I drove frantically toward Seaford.

"What the hell happened?" I asked.

I could hear Paul breathing heavily amid the faint sound of screeching tires.

"After I picked the lock on the back door, it still wouldn't open. There was a goddamn sliding deadbolt on the inside. So I pushed in the door, which took part of the frame with it. I then went straight to the master bedroom. There was a picture of the daughter on the bureau with a diamond-studded communion necklace around the frame. She was standing with an elderly woman, her grandmother, I figure." Paul took another breath, and seemed distracted. Driving like a maniac will do that.

"Okay," I said in an effort to move him along.

"I wanted to get in and get out without anyone knowing I was there. That fucking deadbolt put an end to that. Now I had to make it appear like I was some drug addict just looking to grab and run. So I started pocketing some watches on the bureau. I also grabbed a laptop and threw it toward the front door. The expensive jewelry must've been hidden away, but I left the communion necklace. Fuck me! I just couldn't take it. But I wasn't thinking. No drug addict would pass on a diamond-studded necklace. I fucked up."

"Forget it."

"I then started snooping around, and came across a strong box. It weighed about twenty pounds and was locked like Fort Knox. So fuck it, I said, and broke it open with a hammer I took from the kitchen. Once inside the box, I found a death certificate for one, Millie Perduto, dated 2006, and you won't believe the cause of her death. She choked on a steak bone and died of asphyxiation. She was eighty-one."

"And the address on the death certificate?"

"Hold on, because I still don't know if this is our man. In the rush to get in and get out, I couldn't remember the five addresses Jasmine gave me."

"I have them."

"So I kept snooping around and taking infrared photos of everything when I noticed some textbooks on the floor, and get this. One of them is a book on Spanish literature, written in Spanish."

"Holy shit! You mean we got our *vengaren*?"

"It gets better. I start thumbing through some old photo albums I found in the bedroom closet. Turns out there's plenty of pictures of our man and his lovely wife, and know what I found?"

"Just tell me." My mind was scrambled eggs as I was racing along the Meadowbrook Parkway trying not to miss the Southern State entrance.

"Turns out that his wife, Mrs. Viviana Perduto, is a Professor of Spanish at Hunter College in Midtown Manhattan, and guess what? There are photos of the two of them on the bleachers in Times Square."

"What about the van?"

"I came up empty on that one."

"Paul. What's the address on the old lady's death certificate?"

"What else? 6 Mayberry Street, Seaford, Long Island. So tell me. You saw the house?"

"Hell yes, and it has an attached garage with blacked out windows and mail in the mailbox. It's also shut tight like a drum in the sweltering heat and get this, the whole place is perfectly landscaped. Oh, and for what it's worth, the only AC I saw was in a basement window well."

"I'm almost there," Paul interrupted. I again heard tires screeching in the background.

"But what happened to your two lookouts in Mineola?"

"They took off and are probably in Poughkeepsie by now. Someone must have called the cops. One of them texted me while I was in the house that he heard police sirens, so I rushed out as fast as I could, but I left the death certificate on the floor, along with that frigin' diamond necklace on its frame. Our man will catch wise as soon as he enters the house. Christ, Nick! I'm in Seaford already and you're all I've got right now."

"And what about Jasmine?"

"I sent her to Trump Tower. I sent her to stay with Charlotte."

"Trump Tower! Stay with Charlotte! Paul, what the fuck are you talking about?"

"Once I figured we found our man, I went looking for a hiding place, a secret compartment. Every criminal has one. I pulled up the carpet corners, felt under the furniture, checked the closet for a hidden panel, but I came up empty. Then I went into his night table drawer; again nothing, except a *Better Homes and Gardens* magazine, which I found peculiar. Why is our goliath reading *Better Homes and Gardens*? So I flipped through it and found a letter size piece of plain white copy paper. Scrawled on it was the word '*BITCH*' written in red ink. And in much smaller letters, the word '*next.*' Then I turned it over. On the other side was a soiled eight by ten color photo. I'm sorry, Nick, but it was a picture of your daughter, Charlotte, in a tight white dress standing outside Trump Tower."

I slammed on the brakes. "What the fuck are you telling me, Paul?"

"He must have found her photo in Sofia's phone. I don't know Nick. Maybe he thinks she is a hooker. Either way, I'm not taking any chances."

"Dear God, I have to call her. I have to go to her."

"I called her already. Besides, Jasmine should be there any minute. She's on her motorcycle and will skirt traffic and run the Midtown toll if she has to. Once she gets there, she is not going to let Charlotte leave her apartment until she hears from me. Charlotte just thinks Jasmine has some questions for her. She'll be fine, Nick. I'm taking every precaution. Now the best thing you can do for your family, and the world, is help me right here, right now. We have got to get the goods on this fucker. I just need you to stand watch outside the house, and call the police when I tell you to."

I was slowly catching my breath. I started driving again toward Seaford. "I suppose I can do that."

"Of course, you can do that. Just stay in your car. When I get there, I'll pull over and wait for you. Let me know when you're within spitting distance."

"I should be there in about ten minutes. Are you sure my daughter will be alright?"

"I'm positive. Jasmine's got her own Glock, and she sure as hell knows how to use it. Besides, our killer is out for the night with his wife, anyway. At least we think so. Now, God damn it, hurry up! It's just you and me, Nickie boy! Once this killer knows his house was broken into, he'll know it wasn't just some random burglary. He'll be on to us, and that's why I've got to get into his mom's old house before he gets wise to us. For all I know, they went to the movies and are back home again."

I stayed on the phone with Paul until I pulled onto Mayberry.

"Where are you?" I asked.

"Just cut your lights and pull over in front of me, but not too close. I'm in the Caprice. I can see you in my rear view mirror. Get your car in position so that you can see the entire front of the house, but at the same time are as far away as possible."

I drove past Paul, and did just that.

"Nice going. With that quiet S600 of yours, I could barely hear you."

"Now what?" I asked nervously.

"If this bastard comes calling while I'm inside, you've got to contact me right away. I'll have the ringer off, and the vibrate as well, but I'll see the phone light up. When I do, I'll know it's you signaling me that someone is coming."

"I got it," I answered.

"And remember this, and you'll appreciate the danger I'm in. I'm breaking into what is probably the house of a serial killer. If he finds me there, and kills me, I guarantee you the police will find no evidence of any crimes inside, except the one I committed and got caught at." I could hear Paul taking long deep breaths. "I'm going in now. If anyone comes, ring me, then take off. If I call you, and confirm that it's the kill house, don't call the police right away. Call them only when I tell you to. I repeat, only when I tell you to."

"Okay. So I'll await your instruction, and if I see anyone about to go in, just call you."

"And then get the fuck out of here, and I mean that with extreme prejudice."

Chapter 51

I watched as Paul walked by on the opposite side of the street. It was his intention to look casual and inconspicuous. Aside from the color of his clothes, he looked anything but. He was wearing all black: black sneakers, black sweatpants, and a black sweatshirt with a black hood pulled over his head. He was also holding an infrared camera at his side. The house was dark but for a dimly lit yellow light over the front door. As soon as Paul stepped onto the driveway, he made a sharp left and walked beside the tall evergreen trees that ran the property line from the sidewalk past the garage. He disappeared as soon as he made the turn. Since I had only shut the car's lights off and not the car, I decided to coast up another fifteen feet to get a closer and more complete view of the house and garage.

Thirty seconds later, a text message appeared on my cell from Paul's blackberry. *Rear door unlocked aborting.*

My cell then lit up, signaling an actual call. It was Paul, and he was whispering hurriedly. "I'm in the backyard. There's a small patio just a few steps from the rear door. Overgrown skip laurels surround the perimeter. Fucking skip laurels, can you believe that?"

"Paul, forget it. Leave."

"I want to see if I can get a visual of the basement from the yard."

Paul left his cell phone on. I could hear him scrambling around on the lawn, and brushing by plants and bushes. He grunted and gasped while crawling around on his stomach, straining to peek in a basement window that was inside a below-ground window well.

"What the fuck." He spoke in a forced whisper. "I can't see shit. Going around to the other side. Wait...I hear something humming." More scrambling. "Holy crap. The basement air conditioner is on. I'm going around back again."

Paul must've been moving fast and low to the ground. I could hear the infrared camera knocking into his cell phone. The clang echoed loudly inside the car. I disconnected the Bluetooth and put the phone to my ear. It then occurred to me…even with the volume on low, with Paul's voice filling the car, I couldn't hear much else—like another car approaching with its lights off, or noise coming from a passerby. Thus far though, to sight and sound, it was dead quiet on Mayberry.

Paul continued reporting to me. "I put my ear to the rear basement window. I'm not sure if it's a television that's on or someone groaning." A few seconds later: "It's not a television. The sound starts and stops too often." More seconds pass. "I'm going back in."

"Paul, get the fuck out of there now. You've earned your money and bonus. Now get out. I mean it."

"I'm not doing this for the money, old sport. Just do like I asked you before." The call disconnected.

I waited in the car. My anxiety at its peak, I was biting down so hard my jaw ached. Then I realized…I had been completely preoccupied in conversation, and not looking out like I was supposed to. I grabbed my chest. My heart was pounding with such ferocity I actually believed I could hear it.

The phone lit with another text message that simply read: *COPS*.

I hit the 9/11 speed dial button on my phone. After four rings, the operator answered: "Emergency?"

"Get right over to 6 Mayberry Street, south of Merrick Road in Seaford."

"What's the problem, sir?"

"I'm not sure. Just get here fast. Please."

"Before I send a car, I need to know what the problem is, sir."

"For God's sake, I'm at the house of the Jones Beach killer! Call Nassau Homicide right away! Now please, get here fast!" After I hung up, I realized that I wasn't making much sense. How many crazy sounding calls did she get in one night? I prayed that a car was on its way. But Paul had told me nothing. All I could assume was that he found clear and convincing evidence of the murders, and maybe even the kill location.

I looked over at the front door. That dim light on the outside of the house didn't do much more than cast a yellow pall on the front steps and doorframe.

Something was different though.

I pressed my forehead and nose against the Mercedes' heavily tinted driver's side window that blacked out the interior of the car from the street. Then I noticed…the front door wasn't completely closed.

Something or someone had gone in or come out that I missed completely, and it wasn't Paul.

I texted Paul. *You okay?*

I waited…nothing.

I texted him again. *Paul answer me you okay?*

This was the first and only time that I absolutely hated my flip phone. I had to hit buttons two and three times just to text the right letter.

Again, no response from Paul.

I must've said the 'F' word a dozen times while stomping my feet on the floor of the car. I had kept the AC in the S600 off so I could hear Paul as clearly as possible, but it was one hell of a hot August night, and consequently, I was soaking wet. I wiped my sweaty palms on my pants, checked that the pistol was secure in the ankle holster, and reached for the gun at my waist. I unsnapped the .38. After I pulled it from its holster, I shoved it in my pants' pocket. Since I had lost so much weight, what were once neatly fitting dress slacks had become baggy and loose. As a result, the pistol slid inside the pocket quite easily.

I straddled the console and exited the car by the passenger side door. Crouched behind the front fender on a strip of grass between the sidewalk and the curb, I stared out at the house on the opposite side of narrow Mayberry Street. Without moving a single muscle, my courage (what little I had left it) was waning with every second that passed.

I texted Paul again. *Are you okay?*

Again, nothing.

I was feeling more cowardly by the second, but continued crouching, listening, hoping, praying that I would hear a police siren or a squad car, or any car, racing down the street.

I thought of John and Charlotte, and what they would think of a father, who remained frozen, hunkered behind his Mercedes doing nothing, while a friend, willing to sacrifice himself not only for me, but my family, was in desperate need of help.

Under no circumstances, Paul said, was I to go inside the house. This became my justification. This became my excuse. I waited…continuing to hope and pray that I would hear or see someone or something in response to my police call for help.

But there was nothing. "Fuck me," I said out loud.

I made a beeline toward the house, the pistol that was in my pants' pocket, now in my hand.

When I reached the front door, I knelt down on my knees, and crawled, as if under a trip wire, into 6 Mayberry.

Chapter 52

I barely touched the front door as I crept on my belly, the yellow light on the outside wall faintly lighting my way. A few more feet, and I would be in complete darkness. Since the pistol was in my right hand, I opened my flip phone with my left. Its screen brightened, then dimmed, as opaque images of cluttered Victorian furniture came into view, along with the dark silhouette of a sewing machine against a far wall. I jiggled the phone to maximize its brightness.

Another crawl forward, and the faint outline of an interior door appeared, but there was something not right about it. It was jutting out from its frame, and I couldn't tell if it was covered with something, or open slightly. A thin crease of light that streaked from underneath it was quickly swallowed by the pluming darkness—a darkness that seemed to have its own sullen heartbeat as I inched my way deeper into it.

With my fingers gripping the shag carpet, I slowly crept past a small living room to my right and a dining area to my left, while pointing the flip phone in all directions in a feeble attempt to cast light on whatever waiting evil lay in the blackness.

The more I moved forward, the more a kitchen with its chrome rim table and four buttoned down plastic chairs, circa 1960, came into view; and behind it, a window with its blinds tightly shut and the door leading out back that Paul texted me about. Two sliding deadbolts were on its frame; one near the top, and the other near the bottom. Both were in the open position.

My palms were aching from crawling with the pistol in one hand, and the flip phone in the other. When I got to the door with the streak of light under it, I put my ear to it and listened for the groaning Paul spoke of. I heard nothing. This door, which led to the basement, seemed thicker than it should have been. I placed the phone's screen against it. The door was covered by something—green soundboard, the kind used to muffle noise.

With the pistol in one hand, and my flip phone firmly in the other dimly lighting my way, I stood up, and as I did, my shoe slid slightly. I bent down and felt around with my fingers. An oily substance was on the floor that smelled like WD-40. I stood back up, and reached for the doors hinges. They were recently sprayed. Someone in the last hour or so wanted this door to open and close without making a sound.

I hoped it was Paul.

The door also had its own sliding deadbolts, one about a foot from the top, and the other about a foot from the bottom. Like the door leading to the backyard, both were in the open position. Someone wanted to also make sure that when it was bolted shut, nothing and no one could leave, and with the soundboard cover, be heard trying to.

Every room in this small ranch style home was undersized. The kitchen was no different. Conscious of every move and every sound I made, I gently walked a few steps past the table and chairs to a third interior door which led to the garage. And I found more deadbolts—one near the top, the other near the bottom—also in the open position. I gripped the knob, pressed my body against it, and pushed. I was hoping to get a look inside while making the least amount of noise.

The door didn't budge.

There were deadbolts on the opposite side as well, but in the closed position.

If the green van was in there, I would have to wait to find out. I felt the hinges. They were dry.

I slowly walked back across the kitchen, careful not to make a sound. Not even a creak emanated from the floorboards as I reluctantly approached that basement door again. What little courage I had left was no match for my escalating feeling of dread at the prospect of a nightmare I would never wake up from, waiting for me down in that basement.

I peeked around the right side of the door and down a short, darkened hallway. I flipped open my phone again for the best first light, and slowly crept into it.

A few feet, and the doorways of two small bedrooms and a bathroom were partly visible. I leaned toward the bathroom with phone in hand and arm extended.

A glass with a toothbrush in it was on the rim of the sink, and although there was a bathtub, there were no shower doors or curtain. Black porcelain paint covered the sink, commode, and tub, and the entire bathroom was wallpapered in red velvet. I stepped over to the other doorways, repeatedly flipping the phone closed, then opened again, as I struggled to see in the momentary splashes of best light.

A thick coat of dust topped the bureaus and night tables in each bedroom. There was also a hope chest in the larger of the two, and I could only imagine what clues to a dark and disturbing family history were contained there. I made a mental note to take it with me when I left—if I left.

There was, however, one primary piece of furniture missing.

These were bedrooms with no beds.

My waning courage notwithstanding, this dark and confusing inspection of the balance of the first floor took no more than a minute, but it was a minute lost, before I had yet to come to Paul's aid. Casing the first floor was nothing more than any able-minded, private investigator would have done, but able-minded was not how I felt.

I was scared out of my mind.

Give me the dreariest courtroom, the meanest judge, the most unscrupulous prosecutor, and a jury bent on hanging my sweet, innocent client—and my anxiety over the pending verdict would not come within light years of the mind-bending and heart-throbbing fear that was coursing through me with every breath I took inside 6 Mayberry. I had yet to hear even the whimper of a police siren, and I was growing more terrified by the second. *Paul had a family. He was a good man. He could be dying in that basement, or worse, dead already.*

I thought of John and Charlotte again, and while swallowing my fear like one jagged-edged horse pill, I slipped the cell phone into my pocket, and pulled open that basement door as slowly as I could, without making a sound. Fortunately, the WD-40 had done its job on the hinges.

I said a quick prayer to my mother for strength, and slowly stepped down, about to do in reality what I had done many times in my sleep to stop the horrifying and incessant nightmares that plagued me the first four decades of my life. I was about to enter that darkened room, venture into that windy black forest, and approach the devil ghost head on.

Only this monster was real.

As I descended onto the first rickety wooden step—a cinderblock wall to my left, an interior wall to my right that ended halfway down—I moved the pistol from my right hand to my left. It was feeling unsteady in what had become an extremely sweaty palm.

After feverishly rubbing my right hand on my pants, I took back the gun, and placed a nervous but ready right index finger on its trigger, while inching my way down on to the next step, and then the next one after that. The lower I went, the louder the hum of that window well's AC. Another step and I heard the sound of an oscillating fan sweeping back and forth in its cycle. I hoped the sound of the AC and the fan would drown out any creaking noise my weight on the steps was making.

The basement floor was the first thing to come into view. A momentary bout of vertigo made it seem like I was staring into an endless tunnel. I placed my right hand, with the pistol in it, on the basement rail, shook my head, and took a few long deep breaths to regain my equilibrium long enough for the bare concrete to come into focus. A weak light shone upon it from somewhere out of my line of sight. I stopped on the stairs just before evenly-spaced balusters to the right replaced the solid interior wall, and my shoes became visible to the basement below.

Despite a stream of cool air rising up the stairwell from the AC, and the fan robotically cranking away, I started to smell and taste an acrid staleness.

I knelt down and peeked between the balusters.

A lime green couch that could comfortably sit three, was up against the wall under that humming AC. A cage of wrought iron bars separated the AC and the window well from the basement's interior. The sides of the AC were plugged with sheet rock covered in black construction paper. A scuffed walnut coffee table was in front of the couch. Two wine glasses were on it, along with a bottle of Ruffino Chianti inside a wicker basket casing.

This was a room no larger than a dozen square feet, which had only one window—the one with the AC in it. Its walls—the original concrete cinder block foundation of the house—were painted a dark shade of green. A large refrigerator sat in the corner, the oscillating table fan on top of it. Light came from a pole lamp, also circa 1960, with three hanging lights covered in cylindrical shades. Only one of the three was on.

Thus far, I saw and heard no one. I stepped off the stairs, and onto the concrete floor.

Bits of dirt and sand parted under my shoes. Across the room, opposite the large refrigerator, was another door also covered in sheetrock. I walked quietly over to it as my right hand reflexively opened and closed around the butt and trigger of the pistol. This sheetrock was also lime green. It was soundboard too. I looked up. The ceiling was covered with it as well. This door also had two deadbolts on it, one near the top, and the other near the bottom. They were also in the open position. I reached for the door hinge that was eye level.

It had been sprayed with WD-40.

Paul was right, I thought to myself. I should not have come inside.

I slowly opened the door, the pistol in my hand leading the way.

A yellow lamp with a gold-tasseled shade rested on an end table in the far corner of a dark paneled room that was even smaller than the one I left. A twin bed was centered against the far wall. There were no sheets or blankets on it, only a mattress and box spring inside a bed frame. Bondage straps lay across the four corners of the mattress. The room stunk of semen and dried blood, but in the bleak light, I could see traces of neither.

Another closed door was straight ahead. On it were also two deadbolts in the open position. I didn't bother to check the hinges for traces of WD-40, and with adrenaline pumping wildly inside me, and my head feeling like it was about to explode, I just pulled open the door, arm outstretched, pistol in hand, prepared to shoot anything that moved.

Chapter 53

But there was only blackness, and the putrid smell of rot and decay.

I pulled my cell phone out of my pocket and flipped it open. A weak light filled the area immediately in front of me. Again, I could see nothing, only the faint image of a bulb hanging in midair. I frantically felt along the wall beside the doorframe until I came across a light switch and flicked it on. As quickly as my eyes widened, I was temporarily blinded from the glare.

I had left what I believe to be the rape room, only to enter what could only be described as a chamber of torture.

Several sets of eyebolts, chest high, had been driven into the cinder-block wall in front of me. Chains and black leather wrist cuffs dangled from them. Against another wall was a long perforated metal table over a large floor drain, which looked all too familiar. I had seen the same set up in the Medical Examiner's Autopsy Room—only this table had bondage straps at its corners.

Dried splattered blood covered nearly everything in the room.

If only these visual remnants of carnage had made me even more determined to catch the beast responsible, and save Paul and anyone else who may have fallen victim. But courageous determination wasn't what I was feeling.

This was a scene from hell I hadn't visited in even my worst nightmare.

There was no opaque discolored cloud screening my view. The light from the overhanging bulb, and the bloodstains that seemed to be everywhere, were as startling as they were abysmal.

A wall of fear rose up before me, while a scuffing sound came from somewhere behind me.

I jolted forward, and turned.

My lower abdomen became a molten cauldron of fire as every organ and muscle inside me tightened, my right hand on the pistol included. A shot rang out, and a bullet careened off the concrete floor then ricocheted into the sheetrock ceiling. The gun in my hand was gone. My legs had buckled. My entire body collapsed.

I had been stabbed, and from behind. The weapon—a thick serrated hunting knife. My torso—a furnace of pain.

Hovering over me, and wearing an Izod shirt and dress pants, was a huge square-headed man. He was looking down on me with a curious expression, as if taking a moment to study my reaction to his handiwork, while I struggled with consciousness, a seething pain, and the awareness that I had suffered what was nothing short of a fatal injury. I pressed my left hand against the gaping wound while slapping the floor around me searching for the pistol. The knife he had plunged into my lower abdomen was in his left hand. My blood was dripping from it. A similar knife was in his right. He continued looking down on me, head tilted to the side, and smiling.

A strange thumping came from somewhere inside the room, and a hatch flipped opened in the floor about several feet from where I lay, bleeding and writhing in pain.

It was Paul, and he was struggling to climb out of the ground, his face a bloody mess, one eye nearly swollen shut, his dark hair streaked with blood.

He got to his feet somehow and charged the hulking mass that stood over me with such force and speed, it sent the beast slamming into the sidewall inches from my feet. Though losing consciousness, I kept jerking my head around looking for the pistol, while battling the excruciating pain.

It was nowhere in sight.

I reached for the ankle holster, but to no avail. I couldn't move my legs, nor pick myself up. I hadn't the strength, and the pain was reaching unbearable levels the more I tried to move and failed. Eventually, I would pass out. It was only a matter of time. I was losing a lot of blood.

Paul and the monster had squared off in the center of the confined torture chamber. Battered head and all, Paul was like a seasoned cage fighter, hitting the monster with kicks and punches that would have easily disabled any other man instantly—except this one.

This huge, square-headed Goliath feigned back with each punch he caught, and bent slightly with each kick received, all the while cutting through the air wildly with the knife in his right hand. The knife that had been in his left and he used on me, had fallen to the floor when Paul drove him into the wall.

Dizzy and in pain, with desperate determination, I propped myself with the use of my arms, while favoring my left side, the side that was still in one piece. I then gripped my pants legs and pulled until I was bent far enough forward to get to the holster, and unclasp it. Once I got the pistol into my right hand, there was no time to attempt to ease back safely.

Unable to control the speed or manner of my movement downward, my torso went into a free fall and the back of my head smashed mercilessly on to the rock solid concrete floor. By the grace of God and the angels, the pistol remained firmly in my hand.

On the verge of losing consciousness, with every movement an excruciating strain, I looked over at Paul. The beast was winning.

The killer had Paul pinned up against the cinderblock wall. The serrated hunting knife that had been in the killer's right hand was on the floor by their feet. The beast's hands were around Paul's throat and squeezing while Paul continued to punch and kick with no apparent effect.

My eyes about to fail me, I aimed the pistol at the killer's back, and pulled the trigger.

The beast threw Paul to the floor, picked up the hunting knife and moved toward me. From the impact of my head hitting the concrete floor, a small puddle of blood had formed next to my right ear.

The killer stood over me—a giant blur with a shiny knife.

I emptied the pistol into the blur.

A massive weight fell upon me, and when it did, the burning in my abdomen was secondary to a fierce burning in my chest.

Then the blackness came and the pain left, and a welcome sense of peace and serenity washed over me.

Chapter 54

Life has a certain symmetry, and so it was that I came into this world via a bloody forceps delivery, I would leave it on a hard and cold basement floor, stabbed in two places, unconscious, and bleeding. But in those last few seconds, when I was rapidly losing the fight for survival, there was this scintilla of awareness—a fleeting sense of joyful realization that when the final judgment came, if the rest of my life was deemed for naught, at least my end would matter.

But my end was yet to come.

When last I saw Paul, he was struggling with two large hands wrapped around his neck and squeezing hard. When last I saw the beast, he was falling forward after several shots rang out from the pistol in my hand.

Though he suffered a concussion and was almost strangled to death, Paul still had enough life in him to walk out of 6 Mayberry of his own volition, albeit with a little help.

As for me, I was not so fortunate.

I had heard and read of how people who were in a coma and near death experience visions of a light or ethereal ghostly figures, speak to loved ones, gone but not forgotten, and even have counsel with the Saints, and sometimes even God.

For the three weeks that I lie unconscious, I experienced none of these things. I don't even remember dreaming.

Everyone who cared a lick about me came to visit. Some, like my children, Gina, and even Eleanor were there at odd intervals, every single day. Charlotte had my television turned on—not for me of course, but for everyone who came and sat in quiet vigil by my bedside. Since Paul was badly beaten, he spent two days in the hospital. His doctors wanted him to stay longer and recuperate more from the worst of his injuries; especially the severe concussion he sustained from being dropped from the basement torture room onto the dirt floor of a bunker below it, to which the media quickly ascribed the name, ***The Kill Room***.

As it turned out, minutes after the last shot was fired, the police arrived. An ambulance followed. After being seriously injured from two large and deep stab wounds, I had lost a lot blood. From the looks of me, lying in an ocean of red, my head and body battered and bleeding, the police figured me for dead.

If not for a young paramedic by the name of Raymond Jackson, who refused to give up on me, I would have been.

Though I was barely breathing, and continued blood loss was about to bring about my ultimate demise, I had a pulse. Once Raymond got me into the ambulance, he pinched an artery in my leg that temporarily quelled the blood loss and saved my life. Raymond was a young black man, twenty-two years old, born and raised in the South Bronx (more symmetry).

As for the hulking killer, he was pronounced dead at the scene. It seems that one of the bullets from my gun actually penetrated his heart.

Only I wasn't the one who put it there.

When Paul and I left 6 Mayberry, we were rushed to North Shore Hospital in Plainview, Long Island. After Paul walked out two days later, I was moved to their teaching hospital, North Shore-LI J in Manhasset (the LIJ stands for Long Island Jewish—more symmetry, i.e. my alma mater, Cardozo Law—an offspring of Yeshiva University).

Gina was an affiliated doctor there, and the kids wanted me closer to home. It was also one of the best hospitals on Long Island.

I, of course, had no idea how badly injured I was, and how close to death I came.

The first knife wound had sliced my right kidney and severed a major artery in my leg. I should have died from either one of these injuries. The second stabbing, which came a split second before the killer fell on top of me with his knife raised and in hand, went clear through my chest just under my right shoulder. The puncture wound was so deep that the tip of the knife reappeared as it exited out my back. It was the monster's large head however, slamming into mine that shut my lights out with near permanence. In addition to my other injuries, I also had a severe concussion.

Within days of entering North Shore LI J, my only functioning kidney also failed. Dialysis was keeping me alive. A kidney transplant was my only hope for continued survival.

This is when the world around me, to my ignorant bliss, got very interesting.

Kidneys, I came to learn, do not grow on kidney bean trees. More people need them than there are donors willing to part with them. Thirty-five percent of those awaiting transplants die on the waiting list, which can be up to six years long; except, of course, if there is a willing family member or friend who is both a blood and tissue match. In my case, the stars miraculously aligned, and there were three: John, Eleanor and, as fate would have it, Mr. Perez, a man on a mission, and the loudest and most persistent volunteer.

But there was more.

The day after I fell into my coma, Sofia came out of hers.

The first face she saw was her father's. The first smile she saw was John's, who later that same day flooded the room with flowers and never stopped boasting about the firm and emphatic belief he always had that Sofia would return to him. After all, she was wearing his grandmother's crucifix.

I was witness to none of this, of course.

Since Mr. Perez ultimately credited me more than he credited anyone else for his daughter's recovery, he was adamant about being a crucial part of mine. In short order though, John sat Mr. Perez down and gently explained that although he had grown to love Mr. Perez like a father, the kidney that would save John's father's life, would have to come from John, and no one else, and he could not live with himself otherwise.

Mr. Perez finally understood, and reluctantly conceded, but it wasn't John's kidney that saved me.

It was Eleanor's.

Gina was one of my attending physicians, and was at my side constantly during those first few days at North Shore-LI J. She had me placed in the stroke unit, where there were only three other patients and a team of doctors on duty twenty-four hours a day, stationed a mere fifteen feet away behind a glass wall in an office filled with computers.

As John and Charlotte would tell it, the more Eleanor showed her face, especially in the company of my children, the more uncomfortable it became for Gina. In all fairness to Gina, however, I had plunged her into more tragedy and mayhem than anyone should have been expected to deal with after a thin (but quite lovely) relationship. She had two children to care for, and we barely knew each other when I left her embrace to run off and catch a killer.

I would never be able to repay her for the care and attention she gave me in those early days when my chance of survival was bleak, but it was no surprise when in the days and weeks that followed and my condition stabilized, that she would begin to feel like the outsider.

Given the news that Eleanor would be the one to donate her kidney, Gina took the high road, and bowed out for the sake of my children, if for no other reason. She was one class act, which is a hell of a lot more than anyone could say about Eleanor's Wall Street boyfriend when Eleanor just couldn't stand by and let her son lose his kidney. Were I conscious, for the love of my son and my wife, Manuel would have been my pick; but I wasn't, and the boyfriend was furious.

On the day of the operation, Mr. Wall Street showed up at the hospital in a final attempt to persuade Eleanor not to go through with it. They argued for over twenty minutes in the hallway about a dozen or so feet from my hospital room door, while John and Charlotte watched on and listened.

When the boyfriend grabbed Eleanor's arm in the most passive way, John saw an opening and intervened. "Time to go," is all he needed to say.

The way Charlotte described it, Mr. Wall Street was more embarrassed than intimidated, and immediately left.

The dumbass, however, should most definitely have been intimidated. At Field 6, I had experienced John's strength firsthand, and was grateful to God that it was the only attribute he inherited from my mob boss uncle, Rocco Alonzo.

Chapter 55

I awoke from my coma on September 18, 2010, three weeks to the day after being given up for dead on the basement floor of 6 Mayberry Street in Seaford, Long Island.

Days before I regained consciousness and opened my eyes, I faintly and sporadically heard the goings on around me. It was Charlotte, who I especially remember. She talked to me the most, whether it was about her job, her new boyfriend (who also came to visit), or Sofia and the progress she was making. She even read me excerpts from the novel she knew meant more to me than any other, F. Scott Fitzgerald's, *The Great Gatsby*.

"The loneliest moment in someone's life is when they are watching their whole world fall apart, and all they can do is stare blankly."

I still hear this passage in my dreams.

And each time Charlotte finished a reading, just before she left my bedside, she would whisper in my ear the line from this classic novel that I always wished someone had said to me: *"Remember Dad…You're worth the whole damn bunch put together."*

I still shiver at the thought of what could have been had I not had Paul Tarantino on my side.

Prior to my consequential repose at North Shore, I have to admit that I often found the sound of Charlotte's voice somewhat annoying, probably because like Gatsby's Daisy, it always seemed *full of money*. Charlotte's constant complaining since she was old enough to form words didn't exactly charm me either. But since exhibiting a loving devotion to me in a time when I needed it the most and was incapable of responding with so much as a wink or a smile, no voice would ever again sound as endearing.

Except for maybe Eleanor's.

When I finally opened my eyes, it was Eleanor's eyes that I first saw.

Pale, gaunt, with a spotty beard across my face, I was a ghastly sight. The overhead hospital room's fluorescent lights beamed brightly above her head, clouding my vision, but after a few seconds, she was unmistakable.

"How are you, Nick?" she asked gently.

My throat was dry as sandpaper. "Just great," I said hoarsely.

"You really got your ass kicked this time," she said, while smiling down at me and carefully primping the sheets.

"Water," I uttered weakly.

She brought me a cup. I took a few sips from a plastic straw. I don't believe I swallowed any of it. She patted my chin and neck dry with a paper towel.

"Wasn't so bad," I said. My throat was sore, and it hurt like hell to talk.

"Oh, it wasn't?"

"You've kicked my ass much worse than this," I whispered.

In the week that followed, John, Charlotte, and Eleanor were at my bedside 24/7, sometimes alone, sometimes together. John did double duty between North Shore and Bellevue, and I couldn't have been happier to hear about Sofia's slow but steady recovery.

Mr. and Mrs. Perez couldn't contain their exuberance when they first saw me. They repeated, in unison, that they were saying the rosary for me every day. They also had a mass said in my honor at Our Lady of the Blessed Sacrament in Bayside, Queens, where the entire congregation prayed for my full recovery.

Lauren Callucci also came to see me, but stayed only a short while. She was polite and cordial, and regretfully, just going through the motions. She asked about my current condition and the prognosis for my continued recovery. Nothing about that night at 6 Mayberry Street. No words of relief or satisfaction over catching her sister's killer. Considering the intimate details of each other's lives that we shared, this both surprised and disappointed me. Then again, her sister was dead, and neither I, nor anyone else could bring her back, no matter what happened.

My deepest regret, though, was not being able to emotionally connect with Lauren, be a meaningful friend, and help rid her of the demons locked away inside and at the core of her continued pain and suffering. The brevity of her visit, along with her distant manner, kept that vault closed, and I was in no mental or physical shape at the time to attempt to break through.

Otherwise, I was genuinely happy to welcome every visitor who came to see me, which was only part of the reason why I was constantly breaking into tears. I was just plain grateful to be alive, and as a result, I felt love for absolutely everyone and everything around me.

The morphine drip may have been a contributing factor as well.

What really puzzled me though, was the absence of Paul Tarantino. Four days passed since I had awoken from the coma, and no Paul; and it was not as if I hadn't asked for him.

John, Charlotte, and Eleanor had been taking turns sleeping overnight on the big recliner in my room. I repeatedly insisted that it wasn't necessary. I wanted my privacy. I couldn't so much as scratch myself without someone jumping up and asking if I was alright. When it was my sweet Charlotte's second turn to stay over, I took advantage of how much she hated sleeping in her sweats, especially in the large collapsible chair. She was an easy mark. As soon as we were alone, I insisted that I was well enough to hit the nurses' call button should I need anything, and that she should go home, get a good night's sleep, and come back with breakfast for two the following morning. This wasn't entirely unselfish of me. My regular night nurse was a Korean woman in her early thirties, named Sook-Joo, which in Korean means purity. If I could have figured out a way to bottle her kindness and generosity, I would have. I also owed an immeasurable debt of gratitude for my recovery to the brilliant doctors at North Shore and attentive nurses like Sook-Joo.

And so, I delivered one loaded pitch to my caring but privileged daughter.

She caved after only a few minutes, followed by a long hug and a kiss, and requests for repeated assurances that I would be fine without her. She left a little after 11 PM.

Come midnight, as I was dozing off while watching David Letterman, my fixer-man, Paul Tarantino, strolled casually into my room.

His footsteps were unmistakable. They were as sharp and as confident as he looked in his designer blazer, brightly shined black shoes, and perfectly tailored black pants. I looked at him with consternation as he smiled down on me with both hands on the guardrail of my bed.

"So how are you doing, boss?" he asked.

"What the fuck do you care?" I shot back. "And I'm not your boss, and you know it. Now where the hell have you been?"

His smile only grew wider. "I was here every day for two weeks, and I don't mind telling you it was getting quite crowded. You were out for the count. So who was I going to talk to? Your wife, your kids, your future in-laws, your girlfriend? Besides, they asked me a million questions that I couldn't answer. I had to lie and tell them that my lawyer advised me, with all the publicity and such, not to say a word to anyone, and save it for a grand jury, if there is one. I had to lie through my teeth on a daily basis to people who loved you, and had a right to know what happened to you. It was quite awkward if you must know."

"My girlfriend? You mean Gina was here?"

"Is that all you heard? Yes, every day, Casanova. She is the reason you were moved to this hospital. She is one dynamite lady, and looked after you like your own mother would."

Paul's words gave me an emotional rush. I felt like a huge frog had jumped down my throat. I was deeply touched by the news about Gina, especially since I hadn't seen nor heard from her since I awoke from the coma, and my calls were only going to voice mail. Mentioning her in the same breath with my mother was a double whammy. It was a small wonder that I didn't start bawling right then and there.

Paul handed me some tissues. I wiped my eyes and took a few gulps of water. "We had something, you know," I said.

"I figured as much."

"And what about you?" I asked. "Are you okay? You sure look okay."

"I'm fine, more than fine, and you?"

"Other than being stabbed twice, losing my kidneys, and being in a coma for three weeks, I suppose I'm doing just great."

"I'm glad to hear it." Paul was grinning as he spoke.

"Anything else you want to say to me?" I asked snidely.

"I'm good." He stepped back and looked himself up and down.

"You dress like my wife's boyfriend," I said.

"Former boyfriend, I think," he answered.

"Is there anything you don't know?"

"No."

"Okay, wiseass, enough conversation about girlfriends and wives." I had gotten excited and paid the price. A sharp pain coursed through my chest and shoulder—an unwelcome reminder of the second stab wound, and one I would have to get used to for many months to come. I hit the morphine button as I stared blankly up at Paul, but I was not to be deterred. "Now, you listen. You're not leaving here until you tell me what the fuck—" I lowered my voice to a forced whisper—"happened that night, and I want every goddamn detail."

"Calm down, and stop hitting that morphine button. I need you to have a clear head—for a few minutes, anyway."

I coughed, and it felt like I had been stabbed again in the lower abdomen. I must've been throwing off some strange signals on the computer monitor, because Sook-Joo came running into the room. I waved her off with repeated assurances that I was fine.

"If my head wasn't clear before, it sure as hell is now," I said to Paul. "Now please...spit it out."

"I waited until I knew we would be alone before I came to see you," Paul said. "That's why I'm here now. I wasn't sure what state you would be in, physical and mental, when and if, you came out of the coma. I need to know I can still trust you."

"Look at me. I went into that house and down into the basement because I wouldn't be able to live with myself if I hadn't. If you can't trust me now, who the fuck can you trust?"

Paul grabbed a chair, pulled it close to the bed, and sat down. "I told you not to come in the house."

"Consider me sufficiently reprimanded," I answered. "But all you texted me was *COPS*, and I called the fucking cops, but they never came. You think I wanted to get carved to shit like this?"

He patted my arm. "Would you take it easy. The next time the nurse comes in she's going to throw *me* out." Paul turned his head toward the door then back at me. "You probably saved my life."

"No shit. Now tell me something I don't know, like what the fuck happened, and how the hell did you wind up in that dungeon or bunker or whatever the hell it was?"

"You mean you don't know anything?"

"No, and I'm sure as hell not going to ask anyone either. It's the last thing I want to talk about, especially with my family. They're probably scared shitless to even broach the subject with me."

"They didn't tell you about the girl?"

"The girl? What girl?"

"Are you sure you're up to hearing this now?" Paul asked.

"Paul, I'm going to bust my damn stitches. Now please, just tell me what the hell you're talking about. What girl?"

Chapter 56

Seems the killer and his wife had been leading separate lives since the death of their daughter. Gaetano and Viviana Perduto were married in name only. That night, though they left the house together, he dropped her off at a cocktail party, then went about his own business—that of rape and torture at 6 Mayberry Street, or wherever else the urge took him. Seems Viviana may have had ample reason to blame Gaetano for their daughter's death. Either way, it caused a rift between them. Whether she knew about the broken hymen, is anybody's guess. Gaetano had his way of keeping things secret from his wife.

Paul then dropped another bomb on me. "The help he probably got from his brother sealed the deal on how much Gaetano got away with things."

I nearly popped my stitches when Paul told me who the brother was.

His name was Robert Perduto—Lauren Callucci's boyfriend.

And so the theory espoused by my neighbor, Harlan Dugan, had proven true. "Tracing the crumbs back to the nest," in simple terms, meant that a serial killer usually knew his first victim. If Lauren's sister was his first victim, and as far as we knew, she most certainly was, then she knew her killer, and her killer knew her.

It was only then that I understood why Lauren acted as strangely as she did when she came to see me. At the time, I had no idea of the relationship between the killer and her boyfriend, but *she* certainly did, and instead of being more connected to her by catching the killer of her sister, we were driven farther apart.

How much the boyfriend knew though, no one will ever find out.

Less than a week after it was publicly announced that his brother was the Jones Beach Killer, Robert Perduto went to see Lauren at *Newsday*

Headquarters. He had reached out to her several times before, but she refused to see him or take his calls. When he finally showed up at her office and refused to leave, she reluctantly complied. They talked in a private conference room for less than five minutes. Robert Perduto then walked out of the building, got into his car, took out his department issued pistol, and shot himself in the temple.

And the more Paul told me, the more my head ached, and the more tense I became. When he noticed that the stitches in my shoulder were starting to bleed through the bandages, he wanted to call the nurse, but I told him not to.

"Just get me a cup of water," I said.

He responded by pulling a flask filled with Jack Daniels out of the inside pocket of his blazer and handing it to me. I didn't hesitate. I unscrewed the cap and took a long deep swig.

"The house, Paul. Get back to the house," I pleaded, as I handed him back the flask.

Paul took two long gulps, screwed the cap back on, and slipped the flask back into his blazer. He then stood up, took a long deep breath, and began...

Paul's movement, once inside 6 Mayberry, was lightning fast compared to mine. It was Paul who sprayed the WD-40 on the hinges in order to make his entrances as quiet and surreptitious as possible. Though he had no reason to believe anyone was inside, he didn't know who or what he would find. He tread quietly and as quickly as he could with his pistol drawn—his own Glock 21—preparing for the worst.

Paul was far more thorough and careful than I was as he made his way down the basement stairs and through the rooms under the house. The first thing he did upon setting foot on the concrete basement floor was to check under the stairwell. There, behind a knotty pine door, was a small, enclosed storage area. It was empty when Paul looked inside. I had been completely oblivious to it, which might explain, in part, what happened to me.

Paul then went over to the refrigerator and opened it. That's when he texted me the one-word message: *COPS.*

The shelves inside the refrigerator had been removed, which allowed for the storage of the dead body of another young woman in another burlap bag. Paul did not need to look inside. He just felt the bag and knew. He then walked over to that first door, sprayed the hinges, and opened it without making a sound. That small yellow light was on inside. The bed was as I found it. The smell of blood and urine was in the air. No one was in sight.

Paul then approached the next door, but failed to spray its hinges. When he grabbed the doorknob and pushed, he instantly heard it creak open. Once inside the doorway, he didn't search for the light switch like I had, but quickly flicked on his pen flashlight. As he did, he was struck by a feeling of dread and a hard object on the side of his neck. His gun fell to the floor, and he followed. All he remembered thereafter was being thrown into a hole. A dirt floor cushioned his fall as he hit the ground hard, and was knocked unconscious.

Gaetano Perduto was already in the house when Paul arrived, which may explain why the rear kitchen door was unlocked.

When Paul regained consciousness, his head was caked with dirt and blood, and the groaning he heard from outside the house, he heard again, only this time louder and clearer. He picked himself up and used his shirt to wipe away the sweat and grime from his eyes. He looked around. He was in a small underground bunker. A pigtail light hung from a rafter. Planks and cross joists comprised the ceiling and walls, and the floor was a mix of sand, dirt, and gravel. A sledgehammer lay beside two animal cages hardly big enough to fit an organ grinder's pet monkey. One of the cages was empty. The other contained the source of all the groaning.

A thin young woman, duct tape binding her hands, feet, and mouth, wearing only a bra and panties, and covered in bruises and dried blood, was curled up inside it. The cage was padlocked, the bars much too thick to bend. Paul had tried them both.

The only way out was a set of stairs that led to a hatch in the ceiling. As he started up, he heard a loud thud, and with it, a spray of sand and dirt fell onto his shoulders, hair, and face. When he got to the top step, he saw that the hatch was a bilco door panel made of thin heavy gauge steel. He pushed it up a few inches and peeked out.

There, on the basement floor, was yours truly—lying on my back, Gaetano Perduto standing over me.

The balance of activity that occurred thereafter I bore witness to, including the ultimate demise of Mr. Perduto. Or so I thought.

Even in my debilitated and delirious state, I firmly believed that the hulking killer Paul and I had been searching for, I had shot, causing the wall of a man to fall upon me, rendering further injury to this already seriously injured criminal lawyer. I also had every reason to assume that the multiple bullets shot from the gun in my hand had found their mark and put an end to the monster, before he put an end to Paul, me, and God knows who else.

But I was wrong, and it seems everyone else was too.

As far as how the killer wound up behind me with a knife in his hand, the hair samples the police found in the enclosed storage area under the stairwell (the one I was completely oblivious to) provided the biggest clue.

At first, forensics assumed the strands of hair came from one of the victims, but they didn't. They came from Gaetano Perduto. What was Gaetano doing under the stairwell?

He was waiting for me.

Apparently it was Gaetano who had opened the front door after he had dispensed with Paul in what was quite the successful ploy designed to lure me inside. Paul, quite liberal with the WD-40 when he entered the house and basement, also sprayed the hinges of the knotty pine door under the stairwell before he opened it. Only he found no one there. This explains why I never heard it swing open when Gaetano exited and snuck up behind me. By the time I heard one of his shoes scuff the basement floor, it was too late.

The following day, and for weeks thereafter, the press had no qualms making Paul and me the heroes of the new millennium in every story and headline about the case. If not for the security standing guard outside 18 Hillcrest, and the assistance of the Garden City Police, both the local and national press would have resorted to sleeping on my front lawn in hopes of getting an interview with Eleanor, Charlotte, or John. All three were smart enough not to comment when continuously rushed by reporters while entering and exiting the hospital to questions like: *How does it feel to live with a hero? Was he always so brave? What kind of father and husband is he?* The headlines were also as bold as they were embarrassing: ***THE CRIMINAL LAWYER GETS THE CRIMINAL, LAWYER GUNS DOWN JONES BEACH KILLER, MANNINO AND TARANTINO GET THEIR MAN***, and the more accurate and accepting, *LATEST VICTIM FOUND IN UNDERGROUND BUNKER ALIVE!*

All reports out of every media outlet credited me for gunning down Gaetano Perduto.

And all the reports were wrong.

As Paul continued, I began to suspect as much, and I sure as hell wasn't going to let him leave until he told me the whole truth and nothing but the truth, about that night.

"You shot him cleanly only once buddy," Paul said. "The second bullet grazed his ribs. Another one hit the ceiling."

"I only remember three shots before I blacked out. They still ring in my head. But the newspapers say that a fourth bullet hit the killer square in the heart."

Paul grimaced, then walked over to the hospital room door, looked outside, and closed it. When he returned, he seemed even more uneasy than before.

"The son of a bitch was getting up, slowly, but getting up," Paul said incredulously. "With only seconds to pull myself together after getting a major ass-kicking, I pried the gun from your fingers, not sure what the hell I was going to do next. I thought about shooting him in the leg. I thought about shooting him in both legs. I also wasn't entirely sure how many bullets you had left, and I didn't want to risk scrambling around on the floor searching for another gun only to have this monster get the better of me— this time, for good. Besides, there was no way I could restrain that guy until the police arrived. Punching and kicking him was like hitting a steel door."

Paul paused, then looked around the room. Seconds that felt like minutes passed, while I waited for him to say something.

"And?" I asked. "C'mon. What?"

"As he was slowly getting to his feet, I took your gun," Paul whispered. "I then aimed, and shot him clean through his fucking heart. Fortunately, for you, this time he fell beside you, not on top of you. I then carefully placed the gun back in your hand."

Chapter 57

Viviana Perduto remained a mystery for years. Formerly known as Viviana Campos, by the time I came out of my coma, she was gone. Her destination was no secret. Two and a half weeks after her husband was caught and killed in the basement of his dead mother's home, a criminal lawyer bleeding to death, a private investigator seriously wounded, and a young woman bound and gagged in an underground bunker, Viviana was seen boarding a plane with a male companion. Their destination: the southern coast of Spain.

When all manner of media blasted the news that her husband was the *Jones Beach Killer*, the police and the press descended on her Mineola home, and never left. At first, the police stood guard—three patrol cars, twenty-four hours a day, for two weeks straight.

Viviana was well-liked by her neighbors. So was Gaetano, but there was always that rare breed of lunatic who wanted to exert his own style of frontier justice, after the fact, and mostly for show, but that wasn't the real problem. It was the press.

Every network, newspaper, and online media outlet—both national and international—had a representative in waiting, ready to pounce, on a moment's notice, for a possible interview or comment, however random or innocuous.

But Viviana would have none of it.

When ultimately interrogated by the police, she claimed total ignorance of her husband's evil doings, and since the District Attorney's Office hadn't the grounds for a material witness order, no cop or detective could stop Viviana from boarding her plane to Barcelona.

As for her "I know nothing" pat responses, no one seemed to believe her, least of all Paul and me.

It would be years before we made even the slightest inroad toward discovering what Viviana really knew.

Since I was in no shape, and wouldn't be for some time to come, it was Paul who gave the police almost all we had on Mr. Perduto, along with the how and why we came to trail him to the kill house in the first place. Of course, Paul omitted all mention of the Mineola break-in. In its place, he told the police that Jasmine's legit computer skills, along with applied deductive reasoning, narrowed down the possible places where the killer could be keeping his victims. Paul also overtly lied. He told them that it was the old Italian man at Papa Giovanni's Garden who told us that Perduto had a green van. Paul knew how fond I was of Jim Clancy. This falsified lead from the Italian man who barely spoke English served to keep one of my dearest and oldest friends out of the mix entirely.

As far as the texting was concerned, Paul and I must have discussed it over a hundred times in the months following my reawakening. Neither one of us believed they came from the killer. Jasmine also agreed. This was a killer who went to great lengths to conceal his numerous crimes, and, once discovered, fought back as if avoiding a meeting in hell with the devil himself. After all, he had a neat little set up at 6 Mayberry, finely landscaped front yard and all, and he didn't seem one bit the joker or cryptic code keeper or anagram enthusiast when we met up with him.

Gaetano Perduto believed he was doing no wrong by kidnapping, raping, and murdering female prostitutes—according to the legion of profilers who were more than willing to grandstand their opinion and bask in the bright gray light of publicity. It was the consensus of these experts, who, in varying degrees, had examined the case and the killer that Gaetano Perduto believed he was doing the world a service, maybe even a Godly one.

No one, however, shed more light on the convoluted simplicity of the method and madness of this serial killer, than Joanna Calabrese, the girl whose precious young life was saved that night.

A week into my coma, a large bouquet of white and pink roses was delivered to my hospital room. They were from Joanna's parents. On it was a note of thanks for my "courage and heroism," along with a promise that I would be in their prayers always. They included a photo of Joanna's three-month old daughter, Diana Maria, smiling in a frilly white christening dress.

It took six days of hospitalization before Joanna was released, and in any condition to speak to the police.

"You got your killer," her father told the detectives. "Why make her relive everything all over again."

Joanna returned to her parents' home in Bensonhurst, Brooklyn, bruised, shaken, but surprisingly resilient and coherent considering her ordeal. It was in her parents' living room that the police eventually questioned her. A civil attorney, hired by her father, was also present.

The detectives wanted to know whether she saw any evidence of other abducted women, or heard the killer talk about other victims.

"No," she answered.

Joanna also confirmed that she first met up with the killer after he called her off a Craigslist ad. He was driving a shiny black Ford Explorer and as soon as she got in, he knocked her out cold. She awoke inside a sack in the back of a van. When he pulled her out, she believed she was inside a garage after hearing the door crank to a close.

And the more the detectives pressed on, the more her father repeated, "That's enough."

The van that she referred to, and the one that Paul and I were constantly searching for, was found inside that garage at 6 Mayberry—an old and tarnished green van.

Who sent the texts? That was still a mystery.

Most serial killers keep mementos or souvenirs of their kills—a locket, under garment, a piece of the victim's clothing. But not all.

Ted Bundy didn't.

The BTK killer took photos.

Joel Rifkin had a basement closet filled with the clothing and belongings of seventeen victims.

Gaetano Perduto kept nothing—but the bodies themselves.

And he only disposed of them to make room for more.

But he didn't get rid of them entirely. He put them in a secret and calculated place that he could visit whenever he wanted to.

I'm watching your sister's body rot.

Thanks to the marvelous advancements in automotive technology, the black Ford Explorer had a GPS, and every GPS has a memory.

The police traced that memory back to the time and place of the Joanna Calabrese pick up, and even back to Times Square in Midtown Manhattan on the day Gaetano made the call to Sofia's sister.

It was Jasmine who hacked this information initially, then, playing dumb, suggested that the police do the same.

Harlan Dugan hated hospitals, so I wasn't the least bit offended when he didn't come to visit. I knew Harlan was eccentric, a not-so-quiet artistic genius who loved life (people not so much), and had enough tragedy swirling around in his own wild imagination to fill ten lifetimes. But it was his fondness for me that made him easy to forgive, along with his more than two dozen calls, and a get well plant that was so large, the hospital had to turn it away.

But what I remember most about Harlan from this precarious time is that elaborate dinner he made for Esther, Gina and me, and how awfully right he was about the advice he gave—*follow the crumbs back to the nest.*

Little did I know at the time, that the nest included the killer, his brother, Lauren, and her sister, who all attended the wedding of a mutual friend in the fall of 2008. The sister's troubled past was no secret, nor was it a secret that Lauren was constantly trying to persuade her to leave the demeaning and dangerous ranks of prostitution. The sister wasn't hard to find on Craigslist. One can only imagine her reaction when she found out that her new client was none other than the married brother of her sister's boyfriend. She probably wasn't conscious long after he showed his face.

Paul and I, however, were not convinced that it was at the ripe old age of forty that Gaetano Perduto first decided to act upon his urges to abduct, rape, and kill. It wouldn't be until many years later, when Paul got a meeting on neutral foreign ground with Viviana Campos-Perduto that the last significant revelation would be uncovered.

But first, there would be another ghastly discovery that neither surprised Paul, nor myself, and least of all Harlan.

Chapter 58

The day after Paul came to visit, Vinny Repolla showed up with his younger wife of about fifteen years. After a minute or two of introductions, she excused herself so "you two old friends can talk." She was a gorgeous, silver screen blonde with a bright radiant smile. In turn, Vinny had lost none of his boyish good looks. I was a bit disappointed when she left. Something about her reminded me of Gina. Maybe it was her smile.

Vinny had walked in with a tall paper bag in his hand, and no sooner did his new wife leave than he revealed its contents—a large chocolate malted.

"You need to get some meat on those bones," he said cheerfully.

"Isn't it wonderful at my age to have to gain weight for a change?" I asked.

"My wife's a vegetarian, and she's trying to convert me. It's goddamn awful," he responded. "First place we're going when you get the hell out of here is Peter Luger's for two juicy steaks."

"I'm in," I said. "Now tell me. How's Lauren? She came to see me, but stayed only a few minutes. I'm worried about her."

Vinny's face filled with empathy. "She's been through hell now, at least three times in her life that I know of."

"Then you know what I know."

"I'm not sure about that," Vinny answered. "Right after the boyfriend's suicide, she put in for a month's vacation. She had the time accumulated, but if you ask me, I don't think she's ever coming back."

"She's not returning any of my calls," I said "They all go to voice mail. Maybe she'll respond to her Editor-in-Chief."

"I'd give her some time, if I were you," Vinny said.

"If you speak to her, tell her I was asking about her. The world has enough innocent victims. I want to help her if I can."

"I will." Disappointment cloaked his face. "If I ever see her again."

Later the same day, two young kids who looked like they were no more than sophomores in college came into my room. I nicknamed them Ken and Barbie, because that's exactly who they reminded me of. They announced simultaneously that they were physical therapists, and it was time for me to get out of bed and into the recliner chair.

I was still on the morphine drip and taking prednisone twice a day, so my body wouldn't reject the foreign organ inside me that was Eleanor's kidney.

"If it's too much for you," Barbie said, "we'll get you right back into bed."

"No way. My back has been aching from lying down so damn much. I want out of here, so let's do this. Just close the door. I don't want anyone hearing me scream or peeking in on my scrawny ass."

She laughed. "Oh, so you're a screamer."

"Let's not go there," I answered, while Ken guided the pole on wheels with the morphine drip hanging from it.

Though I would probably be on prednisone for the rest of my life, the morphine dosages were lessening by the day. Fortunately, so was the pain.

Barbie's double entendre made me recall that night with Gina, and my level of excitement just before I received Paul's call. I was biding my time and hoping to stave off disappointment before I would perform my own private self-examination. I did so a few days later, and although it took longer than ever before, the ship's mast rose proudly, and I was never happier to see my old friend again.

When Eleanor came to see me the following day, I announced with a silly grin, "My junk works!"

"Well, bully for you," she said, then rolled her eyes. "Are you eating?"

"Now that you mention it, would you mind getting me some soup and a sandwich from the restaurant downstairs. The hospital food is alright, but I can only take so much of it."

"I'll go now." She turned to leave.

"I didn't mean this minute. You just got here."

Eleanor stopped by the hallway door, and while still facing away from me said, "Alright, I'll stay, but you have to promise not to talk anymore about your penis."

"Go ahead. Make me laugh. It hurts when I do." I had two huge bandages wrapped around me, one below my right shoulder, and the other around my lower left side.

Eleanor returned to my bedside, and seemingly at a loss at what to do, she started primping my covers. "God forbid I'm the one who makes you laugh. I wouldn't want to do that now."

Her sarcasm wasn't lost on me. "So how are *you* doing, one kidney and all?"

"Oh, is this your way of finally saying—thank you?"

I smiled. "Well, from what I understand, I was in a coma, so you'll have to forgive me for not thanking you sooner, but if I'm correct, it was John who was hell-bent on giving me his. So I can never be sure if you gave me your kidney because you wanted to, or just because you didn't want your son to give up one of his, not to mention Mr. Perez's backup kidney waiting in the wings. Let's face it, had I been conscious, I would've had a lot of kidneys to choose from."

Eleanor huffed, and looked at me with amused condescension. "You're demented, you know that?" She moved closer to the bed, and leaned over the guardrail. "Not that this interests you, but my stitches are coming out tomorrow. Oh, and I lost five pounds. So you see, some good did come out of this."

"You look great, if you don't mind my saying."

"Just shut up," she shot back.

"Now, is that anyway to talk to a man in my condition?" I put my hand up. "That's okay, though. I can take it."

"Oh, I have no doubt about that," she answered. "If that monster didn't kill you, I'm not sure anyone can."

I reached over and grabbed her hand. She pulled away, but I held on. The strain sent a sharp pain through my shoulder that I couldn't hide. She huffed again, and conceded her hand to me. It took a while for the lightning bolt to dissipate enough for me to talk normally. Whether it was the throbbing aftermath or sudden change in sentiment, but I was in no mood to joke further. A full minute may have passed before I spoke again. When I did, I was entirely serious, and the more the pain waned, the more I felt the softness of her hand in mine. Regrettably, she seemed unfazed.

"El?" She looked down at me, expressionless. If I did know better, considering the condition I was in, I would've thought she was annoyed. Maybe she was. Either way, I wasn't letting go of her hand. "El? Only you can—"

"Only I can what?" She was definitely annoyed, and slapped the covers lightly with her free hand.

"Kill me," I said hoarsely, "since I first laid eyes on you."

"If you're going to get cheesy, I'm going downstairs to get your dinner."

I let go of her hand, and she stepped back. "I'm going," she said.

"Come on, stay a little while longer. Talk to me."

"About what?" she asked defiantly, as she walked over to an upright chair against the far wall and sat down.

"Do you have to sit way over there? I liked it better when you were hovering over me."

"This is the best I can do."

"Okay, what do *you* want to talk about?" I asked.

"I don't know, Nick. I don't know what I want to talk about. I don't know if I want to talk at all. I don't know if I have anything to say that you would find interesting. I mean…Tell me, Nick. What else is there? What the hell else do you want and expect from me? Now, you even got one of my kidneys. I have nothing else to offer you."

"Well, I can think of at least two other body parts."

"You are really pressing your luck."

I was, but what truly surprised me was that she had not stormed out of the room. I moved to safer ground. "Charlotte's been great. I'm really proud of her."

"Me too, but I always was." Eleanor was staring down at her hands flat on her lap, resisting any inclination to make eye contact with me. "She is a wonderful young woman, maturing in leaps and bounds lately. She loves you very much, as does John, but then you know that already."

"Yeah, I do know that." Eleanor was looking at everything in the room, but me. "I love them very much too." Eleanor's lack of attention was driving me nuts. I'm sure the medication didn't help. Regardless, I couldn't help myself another second longer. "I love you too, El, more than life itself. You've got to know that."

I got her attention alright, but the look on her face I could have done without. "I wish I understood that 'more-than-life-itself' part," she said bitingly. "I mean, you just risked your life for a man you met a month ago, to catch the killer of the sister of a young woman you just met a month ago. Seems to me Nick, you barter that life of yours—the one you say you love me more than—for veritable strangers, and to catch the killer of other actual strangers. So before you lay some romantic line on a woman again, I think you're going to have to do a hell of a lot better than loving her more than a life you so readily put in harm's way, and nearly lost."

I looked at her intently. I never revealed my true fears about the killer to her—his apparent threat to my family via the texts, the green van, and his approaching my son at the beach; not to mention the photo of Charlotte that Paul found in his night table. Nevertheless, I tried to understand her, and appreciate from her point of view all she said, but I was completely bewildered. This was probably because I was searching for her feelings toward me in every word, when I should have been listening to the message.

My response would not save me. "Listen El, whether you like it or not, I love you, and I need you."

She bolted out of her chair, walked defiantly toward me, then gripped the bedrail, and leaned over me. She was furious, and if I didn't know better, I thought she was about to slug me. "Maybe you should have tried needing me less, and loving me more!" she shouted. At which point she turned and bee-lined out of the room so fast she nearly knocked a female orderly on her ass.

The wide-eyed young Jamaican woman looked at me in shock and amazement. She had my lunch tray in her hands, and I do believe for a moment, she was afraid to come in.

"What did you say to your wife?" she asked, as she stood inside the doorway.

"I think it's more what I didn't say."

She still didn't move.

"Either way," I said meekly. "I will need that lunch tray."

I sat in bed for about twenty minutes, overlooking the bland display of food resting on the portable hospital table in front of me. A new healthy kidney usually creates an increased appetite in its recipients. That hadn't happened to me yet. When I finally broke through my funk and reached for the fork, Eleanor walked in with a bag marked Au Bon Pain, from the restaurant in the hospital lobby.

"I thought I would never see you again," I said contritely.

She ignored me, took the tray of hospital food away, and placed a closed container of soup and a wrapped sandwich in front of me.

I grabbed her hand. She didn't pull it away this time, but there was no tactile response either. She just closed her eyes and stood there, while I didn't waste a second pouring my heart out. "Okay, I'm a fucking idiot. I know that. But I'm done, El. I'm done trying criminal cases. I'm done catching bad guys. I'm done with the law, but please don't tell me I'm done with you? I can't be someone I'm not, but that doesn't mean I can't be someone who is better for you than I've been. Since you left the room, I've been staring at this tray of food thinking that I have got to stop fucking things up between us." I reached over and gently grabbed her wrist with my free hand. "Anything. I will do anything not to see you walk out of my life again. I know I made you unhappy, but I made you happy once. I can do it again. If there's any love for me left in you, I can do it again."

Eleanor looked down at me. Her face was a combination of sadness, strength, and resolve. "These past four years have not been happy for me either. I don't want to hurt you, Nick, but I was barely breathing living with you. I had no choice but to leave once the kids were out and on their own. I know you love me, but what I didn't know, or appreciate, was how much you were suffering before I met you. I sometimes think you go to court and wherever else, taking on one impossible task after another, risking everything—including your marriage—and even your life—just to prove something to yourself. But you can't change the past. You can't change all the awful things that have happened in your young life. Your biological father will still have abandoned you. Your uncle will still have been a notorious mobster. You still will have won your big case in 1982 and innocent people back then will still be dead, and no matter how guilty you feel, it still won't be your fault. And Nick, I am sorry, but you sure as hell can't change the awful things that happened before you were born—your sweet mother will still have been the victim of child abuse."

I nearly choked on my saliva.

Eleanor didn't hesitate. "Your mom is even stronger than you think." She took a deep breath and continued. "A week before we got married, she called me and asked me to come to her home in Merrick. She made me promise not to tell you."

As Eleanor walked over to the hospital room door and closed it, I put a hand up against my face in an attempt to hide my reaction, and the tears that came. Upon returning to the bed, she continued. "She said that she wanted me to know before I married you. She told me about your Uncle Rocco too, but I told her that I knew about him already."

"I can't believe this. I can't believe you knew and didn't say anything."

"I didn't think that you ever wanted to talk about it, but I hoped you would some day."

"I still can't figure out why you stayed with me for so long while you were so unhappy."

"There was Charlotte and John. You were, and still are, the most loving father. I wasn't always unhappy."

"Still...You could've taken the kids and run many times. It's a three hour flight to Atlanta. You could have married some waspy rich guy like you got now a long time ago, and left me and all my shit behind."

This time Eleanor grabbed *my* hand. "I didn't leave for one very good reason. You were and still are the finest man I have ever known. You're kind and brave..." Eleanor smiled, and I saw a fondness in her eyes that I hadn't seen in a very long time. "And look at you, battered and all beat up. I mean...look at you."

I remained inconsolable. "So my mom told you everything, and you still married me?"

"Nick, when are you ever going to accept the simple truth that you do not have to carry around all that horrible baggage. *You* are the one who needs to be happy, and maybe then someone special in your life can be happy too."

"I'm not liking the sound of that."

"I'm sorry, but it's true."

"You were always stronger than me."

"I don't think so." Her smile was gone. "A stronger woman would have stayed, beaten the crap out of you, but stayed."

She wasn't trying to be cute. She was serious, somber was more like it. Either way, I wasn't the least bit amused. "El...so many years...don't you think we deserve another chance?"

She was gently biting her lip. "And what about your girlfriend, the doctor?" she asked.

"From what I've been told, you scared her away with your kidney."

Eleanor fought back a smile, and I couldn't figure out why she was still standing there. I was all of a hundred and forty-five pounds. Although Charlotte kept me fairly well groomed while I was in the coma, I hadn't shaved since I woke from it. I was a kidney transplant patient, and would be for life. Prednisone would be part of my daily diet, and although the prognosis was guarded but good, I was in no shape to compete with anyone.

"And what about your Mr. Wall Street?" I asked.

"He's just pissed," she said matter-of-factly.

I formed a wry smile. "Maybe he only loved you for your kidneys."

Chapter 59

It wasn't until two years had passed that I was able to persuade Paul Tarantino to track down Viviana Campos, formally known as Viviana Perduto. With Jasmine's computer hacking skills at full throttle and having improved over time, Viviana was located living a quiet life in the hillside village of Mijas, on the southern coast of Spain.

When she left Long Island and boarded a plane for Europe, she left behind a power of attorney with a local real estate attorney, and the keys to the home in Mineola with an independent realtor. Since the home was in Viviana's name and purchased with inheritance money, it was excluded from all civil claims by the victims' families.

The same was only partially true for the house on Mayberry, which was never under the Perduto name. Gaetano's mother inherited the house before she was married, and never changed the title. It remained in *her* mother's maiden name. In turn, the two Perduto brothers inherited the house from *their* mother, but only Gaetano's half was subject to civil claims. The rightful owner of the other half was Robert Perduto, who executed his own will two days before he committed suicide, leaving everything to his "one love," Lauren Callucci.

Only Lauren declined the inheritance.

The man who accompanied Viviana to Spain was none other than her younger brother, age thirty-five, previously living in a home for special needs adults in Long Beach, Long Island. His name was Carlos, but he preferred Chuck: a sweet man, quite capable of caring for himself, who collected comic books, loved James Bond films, and never liked his brother-in-law, Gaetano.

As far as Paul was concerned, as time passed, his answer to me was always the same, "Why bother this poor woman? The police got their killer. The killer is dead. His innocent wife has suffered enough."

Only I wasn't satisfied.

When the police searched the home at 6 Mayberry, all they found was evidence that substantiated what they already knew; until that is, the DNA and forensic results came back.

The results confirmed, unequivocally, that all four prostitutes found in the burlap bags by Field 6, including Lauren's sister, were in that basement at some point in time. Samples of their blood were everywhere. But there was more—traces of blood of over a dozen other unidentified victims. As a result, the police went searching. They broke under the basement floor with the help of hydraulic jackhammers, and dug up the area underneath the bunker with handheld shovels.

They found nothing.

In the spring of 2012, the house was sold to a couple in their early thirties with no children. The price was about a hundred thousand less than any comparable home in the area. The couple knew about the crimes, but didn't care. They got a great deal, and the home was delivered spotlessly clean of all traces of crimes committed there.

Or so they thought.

Around the perimeter of the backyard, the tall skip laurels remained. Since they grow uninhibited in the shade, they were planted under the long, overhanging branches of the huge maple trees nearby. Since they straddled the property line, and hid the house of horrors from view, the neighbors on both sides begged the police not to remove them.

After every square inch of the house was searched, and the basement and bunker dug up and explored ad nauseam, the backyard was next.

The police had been dug up every square inch of it, and when they came to the skip laurels along the property line, they poked long rods underneath, searching for anyone and anything that might have been buried there.

Again, they found nothing, and left the skip laurels undisturbed.

The neighbors on both sides of 6 Mayberry, along with the entire block, welcomed the young couple with open arms filled with cakes, cookies, and a welcome wagon of assorted household items. When the couple decided to reshingle the house a different color and update further with new windows and doors, all supported the change. When the new owners decided to have the skip laurels removed, and bring the rest of the world back into view, including the canal behind the house, the neighbors bonded with them again in agreement.

The roots of skip laurels, however, can run deep and wide. The crew of landscapers hired to remove them consisted of illegal immigrants working for daily pay and looking to please their per diem employer enough to get asked back. Since the job included removing all the roots from the lawn, the workers eagerly complied.

Digging thoroughly, all remnants of root from dozens of decades-old skip laurels were excavated, and then carted away in wheelbarrows. But along with the dirt, sand, and clay found in the South Shore soil, tiny bits of bones no bigger than a finger, and no thicker than a pencil, were discovered tightly mixed in with all manner of earth and root. From what the police could determine, these were human bones smashed into little pieces, and since no teeth fragments were found, identification was impossible.

When the news of the bone bits found under the skip laurels went public, I immediately called Paul. He had decidedly put the case behind him, and told me that he was leaving on vacation with his family to the southern coast of Spain. Since I was relentless in trying to tie up loose ends, and this new discovery only heightened my resolve to, I asked Paul to pay Viviana Campos a visit. He and his family were staying in Puerto Banus, a stone's throw from the quaint mountain village of Mijas.

At first, Paul refused. While on vacation with his family, the last thing he wanted to think about was that night at 6 Mayberry, or so he said. I jokingly told him to man-up, and offered to pay for his family's entire vacation if he would take just an hour to meet up with Viviana. Two years and three-thousand, six-hundred miles away from the scene of the crime, I hoped Viviana would be more forthcoming about what she knew, and when she knew it.

Paul declined my offer to pay for his vacation, but agreed that he would try to meet up with Viviana if it did not impede, in any way, on quality time spent with his wife and children.

I wasn't surprised when Paul refused all monetary incentive. After I came out of my coma, he also refused to take any additional compensation or bonus for catching the Jones Beach Killer. I do believe this was his way of thanking me for saving his life, without actually thanking me. After all, I nearly got killed in the process.

Chuck Campos gladly welcomed Paul into the small chalet he shared with his sister Viviana, and greeted him like an old friend. For a man like Chuck, who loved James Bond, it wasn't hard to figure out why he took an instant liking to Paul. After all, Paul was the only living James Bond that *I* knew of.

Viviana wasn't home when Paul arrived. To Chuck's delight, Paul seemed quite impressed with Chuck's collection of rare comics. When Viviana returned with a bag of groceries in her arms, she was hard-pressed to ask Paul to leave. Chuck was having such a grand old time with him.

Eventually though, Viviana cut in. "What can I do for you, Mr. Tarantino?" she asked, as she folded an empty shopping bag and stored it away. She was standing behind a counter that separated a small kitchen area from a quaint living room decorated with damask drapes, antique table lamps, and warm traditional furniture.

Paul apologized for the suddenness of his visit. "I hope I'm not disturbing you."

"You're not," Viviana answered, "at least, not yet."

All three sat down in the living room, Viviana in an upright wing chair, and Paul on the sofa next to Chuck, who seemed to have a permanent smile etched on his face.

"Can I speak freely?" Paul asked, while tilting his head in Chuck's direction.

"Chuck knows about Guy," Vivian said abruptly.

"You mean Gaetano?" Paul asked

"Yes. I called him Guy, so did his brother and his friends."

"Bad man," Chuck blurted with a stern face.

Paul nodded to Chuck in agreement, then turned to Viviana. "I didn't come here to upset you. You've had your fill."

"That's behind us now," Viviana said.

"And I didn't come here to dredge things up again. Frankly, I didn't want to come at all. My client—"

"How is Mr. Mannino?" she asked.

"Good," Paul answered. "He's got a bit of limp, but he hides it fairly well, but his heart is good and his new kidney took hold really well."

"I'm glad to hear that. I was worried about him, so was Chuck."

"That's nice of you to say," Paul answered. "It's Mr. Mannino that asked me to come and see you."

Viviana wasted no time. "I told the police everything I knew about my husband's crimes, which was absolutely nothing."

"I know what you told the police, but there's one thing we're having a hard time explaining."

"Only one thing?"

"Well, one big thing—the text messages."

Viviana looked up at the ceiling, and put a finger on her chin. "I read about those—"

"Did you send those messages?" Paul asked, with a contrite directness.

Viviana laughed half-heartedly. "And what would be the point of that?"

"That's another question that I had planned to ask you." Paul had a slight but respectful smile on his face.

"Well, let me save you the time." Viviana huffed as if attempting to compose herself further and do so in a reserved and patient manner. "My husband was a degenerate killer. Yes, over time I knew he was acting strange. People could say the same thing about you, Mr. Tarantino, and Mr. Mannino as well. You're both strange also; outside the norm that is, but of course, in a good way."

"I was just an investigator for hire," Paul said matter-of-factly.

"Come on. There's a whole lot better ways to make a buck, Mr. Tarantino. You're an urban cowboy, for Christ's sake."

"He's James Bond," Chuck squealed with excitement.

"Yes, he is," Vivian said to Chuck. "Now back to your question, Mr. Tarantino."

"Please," Paul said pleadingly.

Viviana explained. "I thought my husband was having an affair, and I followed him once to 6 Mayberry. He was driving his black Explorer. When he pulled up to the house, he opened the garage with a remote, left the Explorer in the driveway, and went inside. It was then that I saw his mother's van in the garage, which surprised me. I thought he sold that old van a long time ago. I never told him that I was spying on him, or that I saw him drive there. He did keep crazy hours, and even played after-hours poker. It's where I thought he was most of the time, although I did catch him lying to me once about it, which is why I followed him that night to Mayberry Street."

"How did you know he was lying?" Paul asked.

"I ran into a buddy of his that he played with. We were on the checkout line together at the supermarket. The man lives in Queens, and was visiting his aunt who lived nearby. He asked me to give Guy a message: that the poker group would meet next month as planned since the night before was canceled. When I confronted Guy about it, he lied, and said that he played in another game in the City. I knew he was lying because attendance at these games is very strict. You can't just show up. They have to be expecting you, and know who you are."

"You say he played in the City?"

"In Manhattan. There are after-hours poker games all over the city."

"Yes, there are," Paul answered pensively.

"Yes, there are, Mr. Tarantino. You also need to understand that Guy and I had grown somewhat estranged, you might say, living together, but estranged after my daughter died. This much I told the police. He was alone with her when she fell. I never forgave him. He said that he ran to her as soon as he heard the fall then rushed her to the hospital, but I didn't care. The whole thing was too strange for me. The girl ran up and down those basement steps maybe a thousand times. I examined them thoroughly afterward. There was no loose railing, or broken step, or anything that she could have tripped on. I thought I was just being bitter at first—wanting to blame someone, but then I found out about his mother."

"His mother?"

"Yes, I always thought she died from natural causes, but then I heard the true story from his brother, the detective. He had one too many beers at a barbecue one night. The man always seemed a little bit troubled to me anyhow. Well, we happened to be alone, and he started talking. Turns out, his mother didn't die of heart failure, which is what my husband once told me. Who lies about their mother's death? As it turns out, she was found at the bottom of the basement stairs at 6 Mayberry. Apparently, she fell too, and coincidentally, Guy was the one who found her."

"Why didn't you divorce him?" Paul asked.

"This may be hard for you to understand, but I'm Spanish and a devout Catholic. Devout Catholics don't divorce. They just don't. Besides, I wasn't absolutely certain about anything."

"Not divorcing him is hard to understand, I must say." Paul was probing.

Viviana slapped her hands on her knees. "So be it, then."

She was about to get up when Paul asked, "The texts? You're refusing to divorce him didn't stop you from texting though, did it?" Viviana was stone-faced.

"But how did you get the license plate number? That's what I couldn't figure out, until…" Paul took a plastic pink rose petal out of his pocket. "The police found one just like this deep between the passenger seat and the console of your husband's SUV—his Ford Explorer."

Viviana shrugged her shoulders and showed her palms as a gesture of incredulous denial, which appeared genuine.

Paul continued. "I didn't know what it was either, until I went shopping with my youngest daughter for a new cell phone, and learned that there are all kinds of fancy designer covers for them, including one with a raised pink rose on it, and coincidentally, just like the cover that was on Sofia Perez's cell phone."

Viviana seemed to grow a bit uncomfortable as she readjusted her sitting position, but her confident look never wavered.

Paul's confidence though, was real. "Then it occurred to me how this same petal must have found its way into Gaetano's SUV. Alicia Morrison, our murdered prostitute who found Sofia's phone, like any young woman with a new cell phone, was probably still checking it out when she got into the SUV. Gaetano, true to his MO, instantly knocked her unconscious, causing the phone to fall between the seat and the console. Gaetano rapes and kills Alicia. Checks her bag. No phone. Maybe even checks the car at night, but still can't find it. He drives home, his lovely wife gets in the SUV the next day, and in broad daylight, discovers the cell phone. She then sees the license plate number of the Mercedes S600 on the wallpaper, and lo and behold, has her ticket to freedom. She copies down the number, then puts the phone right back where she found it, broken petal and all."

Viviana was smiling more broadly than before, as was Chuck, but for an altogether different reason. "I find you somewhat amusing, Mr. Tarantino, with all these questions of yours, but I like you, and Chuck likes you, so I'll answer you like this."

Paul was anxiously waiting for some coy cover-up explanation, but he didn't get one.

"I'm an educated woman, Mr. Tarantino. I too, tried to understand this manner of man who slept next to me for years, so I went ahead and did some further reading into the unpleasant, and how do you say, twisted mind of someone who would do the horrible things he did, and then write about it to a reporter. And you know what I found?"

"I think I do," Paul answered.

"I found out that Jack the Ripper wrote to the press, that the Zodiac Killer in California sent twenty letters to local newspapers, and even New York's Son of Sam wrote to a columnist for *The Daily News*. Copies of these letters are on the Internet. They are boastful, taunting, arrogant, creepy, devious, and threatening."

"But not always cryptic. The text of the license plate number and the anagram—those were real clues."

Viviana looked up at the ceiling and then down at her hands resting on her knees. "Did you also know, Mr. Tarantino, that my twisted husband never left *Newsday's* jumble undone. Every day he reworked the letters to get to the final answer. Aren't those anagrams?"

"Yes they are," Paul answered.

"And the license plate number," she cried out. "My husband was a terrorist of young women, and it surprises you that he wanted to terrorize his victim's sister, and maybe in some corner of his degenerate mind, others also. *Here are the clues. Come and get me if you dare.* A sick evil mind, is a sick evil mind. Don't try to make too much sense of it."

Paul remained undaunted. "Those texts didn't come from the victims' cell phones, or the same cell phones he used to make the calls off the Craigslist ads. Those texts came from a different throw-away cell phone, also the kind you buy in a convenience store. Why would he find the need to get a different phone to text from? He already had the cell phones from the young women he killed."

Viviana huffed again, and then answered with a controlled smile. "I can't explain why he did the things he did, no more than you can. If I knew he was doing the things he was doing to young women, I would've run back to Spain and called the police from one of those untraceable cell phones you're talking about." Viviana thought again, not entirely comfortable with her answer. "Or I would have called the police from my own phone right here."

"Were you ever afraid of him?" Paul asked.

"No," she answered firmly, but her eyes told a different story. "And I'll tell you another thing."

"What's that?"

"Don't ask me how I know, but I know. I believe his mother sexually abused him."

Viviana's not-so-little bombshell, which did not take Paul by surprise, did change the direction of the conversation.

"Really?"

"And his brother too. I'm pretty sure."

"I'm sorry, but I have to ask. How do you know this?"

"You can ask all you want, but I won't tell you. It's not hard to figure out, though."

Paul sat back on the sofa, took a few deep breaths in an attempt to buy some time and gather his thoughts. Chuck was still smiling at him. "I think that I've taken up enough of your time."

Viviana stood. "I hope I answered your questions so as to finally put this all to rest."

Paul stood up too. "Thank you. I do appreciate your courtesy." He shook Viviana's hand and Chuck's as well. As Paul headed for the door, Chuck followed.

"James Bond?" Chuck whispered, as he pulled something out of a bookcase beside the door. "Take this." It was a textbook stamped Hunter College. The binding read: *Teacher's Edition*. Paul then looked back at Viviana. She was seated in the wing chair, staring off in another direction, and crying quietly.

Chuck gave Paul a hug as they parted.

Paul walked down a steep hill and passed several Andalusian white-washed stone houses built into the mountainside. He found his rented Fiat parked at a landing, and got inside. He opened the book and flipped through it until he got to the last few pages and a glossary of words. He skipped to the V's.

It was there that he found it—the word *vengaren*, the anagram for green van, and next to it, its English translation—*revenge*.

And it was sloppily underlined.

When Paul returned to his hotel in Puerto Banus, something Viviana Campos said about the text messages was gnawing at him: *"I read about those—"*

He went to the business office behind the hotel lobby, and combed the internet for every article written on the Jones Beach Killer and his capture.

For two hours, he meticulously searched for any mention, anywhere, of the text messages.

When he finished, it was just as he figured.

There were none. Lauren Callucci never reported a word about them.

EPILOGUE

It was the first day of summer, June 21, 2014, and I do believe those in attendance at the water's edge of the Harbor View Yacht Club in Greenwich, Connecticut, had not seen a lovelier bride than Gina. She wore a strapless white wedding dress, and glowed in the sunlight of a day that was as perfect as she looked.

My two children and their significant others were sitting up front. After more than eighteen months of hospitalization and in- and out-patient therapy, Sofia had made a near complete recovery. Though the burn marks on her face were barely visible, sight in her right eye never fully returned, but if you ask her she will tell you that she only needs but one to see my wonderful son's handsome face. They are engaged to be married.

She still wears my mother's crucifix around her neck.

Charlotte looked stunning in a sky blue, low-cut dress that fit, as did all her clothes, like a glove. As John described it, she turned every head in her vicinity while accompanied by her boyfriend, who she remains quite serious about. An actor on the Broadway stage and currently playing the Tin Man in *Wicked*, I found him to be genuinely funny and charming each time we met, but what I also liked most about him was that he not only cared about my daughter, but what I thought of him as well.

After I was released from the hospital in November 2010, I was in outpatient physical therapy for over four months, getting my motor skills back, and my body, as a whole, back into shape. The scar on my lower abdomen healed quite well, but the one below my left shoulder still looks like I walked into a buzz saw. I am told it only enhances my tough guy image, an image I'm happy to leave forever behind—not wanting to be, or feeling much like a tough guy these days.

By these days, I mean June 29, 2014. I'm leaning over a small round wrought iron table, writing away on a magnificent bright summer day. A large patio umbrella is open overhead, shading me and my notebook, but not my beautiful wife, my Eleanor, lounging nearby.

Upon reading aloud this last line just written, she tilts her head at me, one eye closed to the sun, and repeats with biting sarcasm, "my Eleanor?"

She is reading *The Fault in Our Stars* by John Green, and reminds me that I had better be careful, or she'll take her kidney back. It's a running joke that still hasn't worn thin, even though my sixtieth birthday is a mere one month away. John, Sofia, Charlotte, and the Tin Man will be flying down to celebrate with us.

By down, I mean to our new home—our charming colonial in Franklin, Tennessee.

After combing the South and visiting Franklin several times, Eleanor and I fell in love with the town and its people, the much larger city of Nashville a mere twenty minutes away, and how quiet, serene, and rural most of the state is with its rolling hills, brown pastures, and green grass. Needless to say, Eleanor is happy to be out of New York, but better yet, she is happy to be out of New York with me.

That wasn't the case at first.

In the latter months of 2010, and after my ultimate release from the hospital, Eleanor announced that she would remain at 18 Hillcrest until I fully recovered.

But I knew better.

She was giving us a second chance.

After three long months in the hospital, she insisted that I take the master bedroom. One week later, she joined me and confessed to absolutely hating sleeping in the guest bedroom in her own home (I did like the sound of that), and added, that if I so much as tried to touch her, I'd have another scar to worry about. It was a king-sized bed.

Over the next six weeks, I gained back a desperately needed ten pounds and was feeling better than I had in years, both of which could be attributed to a special high-protein diet that sometimes included chocolate malteds and the occasional Ring Ding. Simply put, I was taking better care of myself than I ever had. I saw a physical therapist almost every day and was starting to look rather cut for an old man of fifty-six. Meanwhile, Eleanor and I continued to be civil to each other. We ate together, went out to dinner, and even the movies. A special, though somewhat bittersweet evening, was a night we spent with Harlan and Esther at another king's feast he prepared, especially for us.

Whether Eleanor knew more than she let on, after we got home, she handed me a sealed envelope with a note in it. It was from Gina. She had asked Eleanor to give it to me, if Eleanor didn't mind, when I was feeling better. I figured there must have been an odd bonding between the two when my lights were out and it seemed they might stay that way forever.

Eleanor, secure in her own skin, as always, left me alone to read it.

I walked outside and into the backyard. It was near midnight on a rather cold February evening. The cushions on the furniture were gone, and the pool tightly and securely covered. Eleanor followed me out, placed a scarf around my neck, then went back inside.

I ripped open the envelope.

Dear Nick,

Got your calls and voice messages. You're welcome, but no need to thank me.

In the three weeks that you temporarily left this world (which seemed like years to some of us), I got to know your family.

You should be very proud of your children.

If my daughter grows up to have half the character and smarts of your Charlotte, I would be so very proud. And John...his father's son, his heart on his sleeve always, a young man of principle and great courage. They both love you madly and deeply, but you need to know this too, so does your wife, Eleanor. She did a great job of hiding it, but couldn't from me. You are one lucky man.

While you were unconscious, I oversaw every aspect of your treatment and made sure you had the very best of care from the very best doctors. Your smart and classy wife gave me full reign.

But then there came a time when I had to step aside—when I had to go.

I did fall for you Nick, and I do believe you fell for me too, and I am grateful for that.

I now remember how it is supposed to feel.

Please take good care of yourself.

Always,

Gina

It was eve of the first day of spring, 2011, when Eleanor got sick.

Her fever soared to 105 degrees.

In the middle of the night, and somewhat delirious, she went into the bathroom and fainted. I ran after her, caught her just before her head hit something hard, and rushed her to the nearest emergency room. She regained consciousness along the way, and puked several times onto the floor of the S600.

She was later diagnosed with an attack of diverticulitis, which caused her to have severe stabbing pains in her stomach and lower abdomen. The high fever, combined with the attack, caused her vagus nerve to erupt, which explained the fainting. She spent the night in the hospital at my insistence. After John and Charlotte left around midnight, I stayed with her until she was released the following day with a prescription for antibiotics and a list of dietary instructions.

From the moment she fainted (and I do admit that it sent me into a panic) until she was released from the hospital, there was a part to all this, in hindsight, which I took great comfort in. I got to hold her in my arms once again.

Upon arriving home from the hospital, Eleanor headed straight for the den. There was a sour look on her face as she laid down on the couch and stared blankly in the direction of the backyard, while I stood nearby.

"You believe this happened to me?" she asked.

"Well, you're getting old, kid. This is what happens sometimes."

She immediately sat up and turned toward me, her eyes fiery slits of anger. "In my sickened condition and all, I will still get up and smack you." Her face instantly softened as she turned away. "I just can't believe I fainted."

"I know," I said. "I caught you."

"And what made you follow me into the bathroom? It was 3 AM."

"I don't know. When I heard you get up, you didn't sound right to me. I figured you were going to tell me to get the hell out."

She took pause, and started to cry. "I hate you, you know that?"

"Yes, I do," I responded, not really knowing what else to say, and not wishing be disagreeable in any way in her current state.

"But," she continued, while throwing her hands up in the air and crying, "you tell me you love me."

I nodded meekly in agreement. "Yes, I do tell you that."

She turned toward me again. "Are you making fun of me?"

"No!" I spoke louder than I meant to. "I'm just agreeing with you."

She turned away and began staring again at the backyard through the rear wall of windows and French doors. The trees along the outskirts of the golf course had still not regained their leaves, but the cypresses, just beyond the pool, were standing, as always, full and tall.

Eleanor was inconsolable. "I stayed here in this house, watching over you, and waiting for I don't know what, for I don't know how long, and then I go into the bathroom in the middle of the night, and damn it, I'm the one who faints, and *you* catch me." She looked in my direction again, only this time with a sad pitiful expression. "Why Nick? Why is life so screwed up? What are we doing here?"

"I don't know, El. All I know is I'm glad I was there to catch you."

She reached out to me.

I tried not to move as fast as my mind was racing toward her.

I gently sat down next to her.

She kissed me on the cheek. "Thank you," she said sadly and sweetly, as a tear rolled down her face.

"El, you don't have to thank me. I love you."

She took a long deep breath, and I could see in her eyes as they widened that something had suddenly occurred to her.

"Hey, wait a minute.' She swiped the tear away with the back of her hand. "I was going to the bathroom. What happened with that?"

"Let's just say I've got another pair of pants to send to the cleaners."

Her mouth shot open, "You mean I peed on you?"

"You make it sound sexy, but yes."

She turned away again, only this time she was looking down at the floor. "Oh, my God."

"Hey listen, it could've been worse. Now when John was born…"

I did it again. I went too far.

"What?" She asked hysterically. "What, when John was born?"

I hesitated. "Well… You know when you're pushing… You know…"

"Are you serious? You mean to tell me—?"

"And only seconds later our beautiful son arrived," I quickly added.

"I'm speechless. You never told me this." She was shaking her head in exasperation.

"I figured, you knew."

"I'm pushing a watermelon out a hole the size of a golf ball. No, I didn't know. And thanks for nothing."

The following night, we made love for the first time in five years.

I never did see Gina Cassisi again. She married a neurologist she met at North Shore Hospital. I sent my well-wishes with John and Charlotte, who insisted on attending the nuptials.

I never saw Sallie Gurrieri again either. In 2011, he was tried and convicted of so many counts of racketeering, it took twenty minutes to read the verdict. He died in jail from complications from neck and head cancer just three months into his sentence. And I said goodbye to a part of my life that should have never been a part of my life to begin with.

The criminal was finally gone from the lawyer.

But if not for Uncle Sallie, there would never have been a Paul Tarantino, and without Paul Tarantino, Lord knows how long before Sofia would have been found, and how many more young women would have been murdered, not to mention the looming threat posed to my family—especially my beautiful daughter, Charlotte.

And if not for Uncle Rocco, there would have been no Sallie Gurrieri.

Life's crazy symmetry.

Paul Tarantino has continued on his trek as fixer for the rich and famous. Occasionally, he takes on a charity case: a child lost, a female abducted. The stories do not always have a happy ending. I have financed many of them, and will continue to do so.

I do worry about Paul though, but I keep it to myself. The requisite demands of the job make him an unavoidable and inveterate risk-taker.

I only hope the odds don't ever catch up to him.

Lauren Callucci never did return to *Newsday*. Seems she used her extended vacation time wisely, though. After a meaningful and therapeutic escape out of the country—a departure that was about a whole lot more than excising herself from the geographical confines of her deep-seeded malcontent—she landed a position as foreign correspondent for CNN. One evening, she even popped up on the smart TV for a brief report on the Middle East crisis, direct from the sandy terrains of Afghanistan.

I couldn't have been more pleased to see her alive and well and flourishing in a career she loved, if not here, then somewhere else where her compassion and fortitude could be of use—another soul that has suffered far more than her fair share, yet still willing to put it all aside for a greater good.

I promised myself then that I would reconnect with her again someday, somehow.

Raymond Jackson, the paramedic who saved my life in the ambulance ride from 6 Mayberry Street, quit his job as an EMT worker, got his Masters at Queens College in Education, and became an elementary school teacher at PS 152 in the South Bronx. I went to see him one weekday in the winter of 2012, and marveled at how much the South Bronx had changed since I left it in 1982. Shopping centers had sprung up everywhere, and what once comprised square miles of burnt out buildings and skeletal structures, had been rebuilt—still housing struggling neighborhoods, but on the rise.

Hope had long since returned to the South Bronx.

I didn't call before I arrived at PS 152. I wanted to surprise Raymond—thank him in person. Regrettably, I never got to meet him. He was at the Bronx Zoo on a field trip with his students. I did get to speak with his principal though, and conveyed to her how I owed my life to this young man, a veritable stranger, who kept me alive, when everyone else gave me up for dead.

I wasn't surprised when she told me that Raymond's compassion didn't begin and end on that bleak night in 2010, and how upset he was that PS 152, a school in the poorest section of the city, did not have the parental or political lobby of other school districts, and consequently, was short of even the most basic of supplies, which included pencils and notebooks. What bothered Raymond even more though, was that come lunch and break time, his kids had nowhere to play except a vacant concrete schoolyard. This was an elementary school where the children hadn't even the most basic playground to play in.

Well, they do now, and a whole lot more.

Thank you, Raymond.

It was in the summer of 2013 that we sold the house in Garden City and moved to the somewhat neutral territory of Franklin, Tennessee, but I would have gone to the darkest recesses of the Amazon Forest had Eleanor asked me to. Consequently, we travel a lot—to New York, and wherever else we care to, sometimes planned, and at other times on a moment's notice.

Since my near total recovery (I am still absent a kidney and my walk isn't what it used to be), I've done my best to make amends for a lifetime of physical and emotional separation from my in-laws. It's hard to atone for decades of ambivalence toward them and from them, but I keep trying, and I believe they are too. Both are now in their mid-eighties. Better late than never.

As far as Eleanor is concerned, she parses out her affections sparingly, but meaningfully. As for me, I'm quite the grateful hugger. I suppose it's in the blood. Either that, or I just can't help myself. But when she wakes up every morning looking prettier than when she went to bed, I'm doggedly incorrigible. I kiss her until she surrenders, or gets so annoyed that I have to stop, or ruin her morning mood—as predictable as a roulette wheel. It takes her at least an hour to truly wake up, but that's fine with me—as long as she wakes up in my morning as well.

As for our afternoons and evenings, they are often spent in our lovely town, or in nearby Nashville, attending concerts at the Bridgestone Arena or the Ryman Auditorium, or sitting quietly huddled together in the Bluebird Café, listening to country artists, up close and personal. Sometimes we even attend Tennessee Titan football games and college baseball at Vanderbilt U.

I try each day to be honest with Eleanor, honest with myself, considerate, and let her be—not just someone in this world that I love, but someone in the world who has a meaning and purpose all her own.

Sometimes though, I can't help myself, and she catches me looking at her for no apparent reason, other than I want to. But what I really want more than anything is for her to be happy. And even better yet, for her to be happy with me.

I have a Chevy convertible now, which we often just get in and drive—Zac Brown on the stereo—coasting along the country roads that cut into those serene green hills, Eleanor's hair pinned back and blowing wildly, her porcelain skin glowing, as always, in the warm sunlight.

And in those pristine moments…in that perfect place and on those perfect days…I'd swear that she hasn't aged a bit since I first saw her at that law school dance, back in 1979.

I was a wonderful fool for a time then, and still am, and although the strains of reality seem at times to crush every wish and every hope, with one hand on the wheel, and the other somewhere on her, if the stars are aligning, as they are more often than not these days, she'll smile back at me with the same sweet sexy smile she first sent my way.

And in such an empowering moment, I do believe I could package up all the evil in the world into a giant ball, and send it soaring off into some dark forbidden place as far away as the indefinable limits of infinity will allow—one grand and glorious dream...

As for Eleanor and me...we'll keep driving along those green hills, the Zac Brown Band playing, the top down, the wind in our hair...

Just as free...

Free as we'll ever be.

Thank you for reading *The Criminal Lawyer.* I certainly hope you enjoyed it. I welcome your reviews, so please post on Amazon as you wish.
Please also feel free to connect with me on:
My Amazon author page http://amzn.to/3qTCsy5
Facebook www.facebook/thegoodlawyer
Twitter @thomasbenigno
Instagram @ThomasBenignoauthor

You can also connect with me on Goodreads, Tumblr, and Pinterest, or just shoot me an email at tombenigno@aol.com. I try to respond to all readers, even if it is to just say thank you.
Also check out my author website at BenignoBooks.com.
God bless you all. T.B.

ACKNOWLEDGMENTS

Thanks to my first draft readers: My secretary of fifteen years, Fran Manz (who passed in July of 2015; I still miss you Fran), Albert Eigen, Chris Klein, Kathy Gurrieri, Maria Tullo, and Bruce Ferber. Also thanks to Mary Logue, Mike Shain, Marly Rusoff, Michael Radulescu for their counsel, editing, and support. To one terrific copy editor, Jonathan Baker. Thanks to all my friends and family, fellow counsel, friends in my hometown village for your encouragement beyond my expectations. To my children for their love and tolerance, and to my beautiful wife for the cover photo and sacrificing much of the summer of 2014 so I could finish my precious first draft.

TO MY READERS AND FANS OF *THE GOOD LAWYER*: There would have been no second novel without your daunting support, positive reviews, emails, and pleas for a follow-up novel. Humbled by your praise, I will always be grateful to you no matter what else may transpire in my writing career. You have my heartfelt gratitude. May God bless you always. I will also continue to welcome your Amazon, Facebook, Twitter, Goodreads, Pinterest, and any and all social media connections. T.B.

Please check out my other two novels:

The Good Lawyer at: **http://amzn.to/2drvzPI, and**
The Criminal Mind at: **https://amzn.to/3kBI65L**

**Audiobooks of his novels, including this one, are available on Audible.
com.**

ABOUT THE AUTHOR

A former trial attorney with the Legal Aid Society of the City of New York (Bronx Criminal Defense Division 1979-1984), Thomas Benigno currently practices law on Long Island. Also producer of the Broadway show, *Burn the Floor*, he has credits as an actor in numerous productions on Long Island, and in an award-winning short film. He is married to the same beautiful woman since graduating law school and has three adult children. *The Criminal Lawyer* is his second novel.

If you wish to read more about the Jones Beach Murders, otherwise known as the Gilgo Beach murders, or the Long Island serial killings, I suggest the following readings:

Lost Girls by Robert Kolker; publisher, Harper Perennial

Jaclyn Gallucci's articles in *The Long Island Press* @ www.longisland-press.com

CONTINUE THE SERIES!

The Criminal Mind

"An indelible cast enhances this sharp, measured mystery."-Kirkus Reviews
   "Our verdict. Get It." Kirkus Reviews

Editor's note: Third in a series that has sold over 1 million copies, *The Criminal Mind* is Thomas Benigno's darkest and most disturbing novel to date. Frightening and heartwarming at the same time, the authors he has admired the most—John Grisham, Stephen King and even Pat Conroy—rise from the ashes of this heart pounding page turner to make this novel Benigno's best.

Excerpt © Copyright Thomas Benigno 2021 Reprinted with permission.
December 2007.
Somewhere in Upstate New York.
I hear the voices again—coming from outside the box.
   Men's voices in the cabin above me—getting louder.
   The floor is creaking everywhere.
   The ceiling hatch opens.
   Footsteps descend the stairs.
   I can smell the cigars and the liquor.
   I can hear men talking and laughing. They're getting closer.
   I shut my eyes and see my friends in the playground.
   They're on the swings. The moon is shining brightly above them.
   A drawer is pulled open next to me.

There's a grab for the keys.

I'll think of something else. I'll think of Christmas. I'll be home for Christmas.

A key misses the lock that is inches from my ear—then clicks in.

There's another lock near my ankles.

I'm slipping away again.

More laughter. More drinking.

I can hear the sound of liquor spilling.

The second lock falls off.

The lid opens.

The light is blinding.

Large blurry hands reach for me.

I'm walking in the playground.

I'm inside the box crying and screaming.

I'm on a swing pumping myself higher.

I hear the cries and screams of other children.

Fear grows inside me like a monster about to tear me apart. I'm safe again—in the playground under a full moon and a thousand twinkling stars.

It was 8:00 a.m. and the ground was still wet from the rain. The tractor's shovel bore deeper than the driver intended, and when it rose into the air, the rectangular box of gray-aged wood was lifted but otherwise undisturbed. It was a clean scoop, and when the excess dirt and rocks were shaken loose, the box remained largely unscathed. If not for a break in the clouds and the early morning sun, it might have gone unnoticed, routinely dumped in a waiting truck to be hauled away and dropped into an even larger pile of dirt, sand, and unearthed gravel.s

Diego was a Mexican American and a citizen of the United States for over fifteen years. The home he shared with his wife and five kids was in a suburb just outside Ithaca, New York. Every morning he woke up at 4:00 a.m. to start his shift at 7:00 a.m., seventy miles away outside the small town of Cartersville. This day, his foreman put him on the tractor. The last thing Diego wanted was to find a box in the dirt that resembled the coffin of a small child. Two years earlier, he had buried his son in one the same size. The boy had died of brain cancer and was three years old.

At first, Diego thought he had found a hidden crate of rifles. He was tempted to put it back, bury it deeper, and not get involved as a witness against 'the wrong people.' Then he thought again. Perhaps these were the remains of someone whose family could not afford a proper burial.

He leveled the shovel to just a few feet off the ground. Arms wide, he stepped off the tractor, gritted his teeth and gripped the sides of the box. It was lighter than he expected. He gently placed it on the ground. After hesitating for a moment, he tried to lift the cover off. But it was nailed shut. He thought about calling his foreman, who cared only about time and money and keeping on schedule, and then thought again. Although Diego feared the ramifications of what he might find, he was a religious man and would not be able to live with himself if he dumped the box without knowing.

He climbed back on to the tractor, grabbed a large screwdriver from his tool bag, stepped off, and pried open the box only to have his worst fear realized.

Inside he found the skeleton of a young child, and alongside it, a tarnished copy of the children's book, *Christmas Moon.*

Continue the series — *The Criminal Mind* at: https://amzn.to/3kBI65L

Made in United States
North Haven, CT
13 September 2022

24066999R00174